KW-481-380

CATHERINE MARSH

Mid 19th Century: When circumstances force Catherine (Cat) Marsh to leave her home and her employment in the Staffordshire Potteries and take up a position as 'between maid' in a large country house, she determines to make the most of it; to learn all she can, including how to read and write. Her plans do not, at first, include a romantic liaison with the son of the house, but Fate has other ideas.

Books by Pat Lacey
Published by The House of Ulverscroft:

ROSEMARY COTTAGE
SUMMER AT SAINT PIERRE
THE VINTAGE YEAR
THE WASHERWOMAN'S DAUGHTERS

PAT LACEY

CATHERINE MARSH

Complete and Unabridged

ULVERSCROFT
Leicester

First Large Print Edition
published 2001

The moral right of the author has been asserted

British Library CIP Data

Lacey, Pat
    Catherine Marsh—Large print ed.—
    Ulverscroft large print series: general fiction
    1. Large type books
    I. Title
    823.9'14 [F]

    ISBN 0–7089–4468–X

Published by
F. A. Thorpe (Publishing)
Anstey, Leicestershire

Set by Words & Graphics Ltd.
Anstey, Leicestershire
Printed and bound in Great Britain by
T. J. International Ltd., Padstow, Cornwall

This book is printed on acid-free paper

To Hilary

1

It was upon the day that I married that I determined finally to educate myself, for it fretted me greatly that although I knew my letters and could read a little, I could put only a cross for my name beneath my husband's flowing signature. And he, immediately seeing this, offered to teach me to write, beginning even upon the short honeymoon we took at a friend's house in Armitage.

''A',' he said, inscribing the letter upon the margin of an old news-sheet as we sat at the parlour table, 'is for 'adore', as I do you.' And then, a few seconds later after I had assured him that I, too, adored him, ''K' is for 'kiss'.' And he leaned across to press one upon my cheek.

'Even I,' I said saucily, 'know that there are other letters between 'A' and 'K'!'

'Indeed there are! 'B' for 'beautiful', 'C' for my 'Catherine' — the most beautiful of them all. 'D' for . . . ' But by now our lips had found each others and we were lost to the world; as I have said, we made only a beginning upon our honeymoon!

And not only with the joining up of my

letters was I my husband's pupil but also in the art of loving. Although we were both naturally saddened that God did not immediately bless our union with a child, we were both agreed that our trying for it came as near to heaven as we could hope for in this world.

It is his idea that, while I am awaiting the birth, I should write an account of my life until now and, sitting in the garden of our house in Lichfield, breathing in the wholesome scent of roses and mignonette I am deeply aware that the contrast between my early days and my present existence could not be greater; and that, by the same token, the tranquillity and charm of this cathedral city would not have captivated me so utterly without the grime and squalor that went before.

'It is a story which our children may wish to know of,' he said. 'Indeed, *should* know of.' And I think he is right.

★ ★ ★

Marshes have been Staffordshire potters for generations, my father says, some more diligent than others, some more fortunate, but all proud of their calling. I try to remember this in 1847 as, nine years old, I scurry along to the potbank on cold winters' mornings, Ma's cut-down cloak clasped about me, and dodging the frozen puddles as best I can; for there's no knowing what pools of stinking ordure lie beneath the ice. Men taken short on their way home from the public house are never concerned where they relieve themselves. Besides, a privy or two will usually have overflowed into the gutters, so perhaps they reason a little more won't matter; although indeed, I doubt if reasoning comes into it much!

If I'm on fire-lighting and sweeping, it's not yet six o'clock, but most days it's nearer seven, although mists are still rolling up off the canal. If it's really cold and the canal frozen over, there'll be no work and I can stay in bed, warm and snug alongside my sister, Emma. But then I won't get my Saturday shilling. And Ma has promised me an extra penny for myself.

Most mornings, a dark figure steps out of the shadows halfway down the hill and stands in front of me. If it's Thomas, I breathe easy. But if it's his brother, Sam, I take to my heels, running as fast I can over the wet cobbles, my breath tearing my throat, my heart pounding, my cloak flying out behind me, for I know full well that if he catches me before I reach the gate of the potbank, he'll twist my arms behind my back and tug my hair unmercifully.

I hate Sam as much as I love Thomas. They live with their drunken sot of a father and saint of a mother in one of the narrow alleyways, not even cobbled, that run up the hill. I've been told never to go there and I never do unless it's to see Thomas when his asthma has him by the throat.

You would hardly believe that two brothers, born of the same parents, could be so different; like bone china and common clay, their sister Rosie says. For where Tom is thin and fragile, woefully puny in his limbs but kind and caring in his nature, Sam is squat and solid but dull in his mind, a natural bully.

If Sam is common clay and Tom bone china, then Rosie is a delicate, porcelain figurine. Her skin is like alabaster, veined at her temples with milky blue, and her hair dark as a crow's wing. Her eyes are violet, like her mother's or rather, like her mother's must once have been. Nowadays, they are more often black and blue where her husband has hit her, and glazed with pain. Ever since the day she and Thomas had crept into Sunday School, quiet as mice and sat beside me, I've felt responsible for Rosie.

Mr Ezekial Watkins was reading from the Bible at the time. It was a difficult passage to read, full of strange-sounding names but Mr Watkins prided himself upon his delivery. 'Enoch, Pallu, Hezron and Carmi,' he thundered, 'Onan, Jachin, Zohar and Saul.'

'Pobs, peeps and lumpy tums,' whispered Rosie in my ear in as good an imitation as I'd ever heard. Immediately, I dissolved into helpless giggles. For 'pobs' was another name for bread and milk, 'peeps' was oatmeal mixed with water and 'lumpy tums' was what we called porridge.

Ezekial Watkins' eyes swivelled in my direction like slivers of bright blue glass boring into my soul. He said nothing then but I knew I was for it. And sure enough, when the reading was finished and catechisms were being given out for the next lesson, he started walking towards us.

"Oo's this?' Thomas asked.

'Gawd, 'isself!' hissed Rosie. And indeed, he did look like I imagined God to be. Tall, full-bearded, with whiskers almost down to his waist and dressed in solemn black. The only specks of colour were those eyes.

'Cripes!' said Tom when it became apparent he was about to speak to us.

'Silence, boy!' Ezekial thundered. 'And you, Catherine Marsh, should be ashamed of yourself, sniggering at the Lord's word.'

'If you please, Mr Watkins, I wasn't

sniggering at the . . . '

'Silence!' he roared again. 'And who are these children? They are certainly not upon our books.'

I wondered how he could be so sure but then a quick, sideways glance told me he must be right. For they were both barefoot and in rags and the warmth of the stove was causing a most powerful stench to come out of them. No children would ever be enrolled in our Sunday School in such a state, although some schools, I had heard, were not so particular.

'They're my friends,' I heard myself say. I don't know who was the most startled; Ezekial or Rosie and Thomas. Or, indeed, myself.

'Is that so?' said Ezekial, heavily sarcastic. 'And do your parents, I wonder, know of this sudden attachment?'

He'd got me in a cleft stick now, and he knew it. To say that my Pa and Ma *did* know would be to tell a lie and this, inevitably, would be punished by washing out my mouth with soap when Ezekial told them of it. And yet I was determined not to admit defeat. Rosie must have seen the dilemma I was in.

'We'se going anyway,' she said. 'C'mon, Tom!' And they scrambled to their feet.

'No, wait!' I said. 'I have a penny for them,

Mr Watkins. See!' And from my pocket I took the two precious pennies Ma had given me; one for Sunday School and the weekly copper she gave me back from my wages. I held them out to Ezekial. He did not take them but gazed down at them in the palm of my hand.

'There are two children,' he observed after a moment, 'but only one extra penny.'

'But they came in only halfway through,' I pointed out. 'A halfpenny each seems a fair exchange to me.' And I narrowed my eyes and pursed my lips as my mother did when she was driving a hard bargain with a shopkeeper.

For a moment, I thought he would hit me and actually put up an arm to shield my face. But then — miracle of miracles! — he allowed his lips to uncurl slightly at their corners. You could hardly say it was a smile but if Ezekial's face had been that of a barometer, the arrow would certainly have slid from 'Stormy' to mere 'Rainy'. But then, as if regretting such weakening, he said sternly.

'If they come again, there must be an improvement in their condition and appearance. But they may stay upon this occasion.' A concession, indeed! And even more wonderful, he gave me back one penny.

'We shanna come again,' Rosie assured me

at the end of school. 'We only come in for the warm, anyway.' Although we had been outside for only a few seconds, they were already shivering and Thomas was coughing deep in his lungs. I knew that cough; little Susannah at the end of our street had died with it, only days before.

For the first time, I regretted my Sunday coat; it had been given my father as 'truck', to make up his wages, and although I knew it to have been the property of the Master's daughter until she tired of it, I loved it dearly. It was of bright scarlet wool, frogged from neck to hem with black braid and long enough to hide the patches in my Sunday skirt. At the edge of the big pocket, where it had been worn threadbare by the fingers of the Master's daughter, Ma had cleverly stitched a piece of white cloth to resemble a handkerchief. Small boys often tried to twitch it out as they ran past deeply disappointed to find that it would not come. All in all, the coat looked so splendid, I lived in fear, for some weeks, that the Master's daughter might demand its return, but then Pa assured me that she already had an even grander one.

'Does your Pa ever have truck in his wages?' I asked Rosie now.

But she didn't know what I was talking about. ''E don't have no wages,' she said.

'You mean, he plays every day?' By that, I did not mean at leapfrog or tag but being laid off from work as many men were.

'Dinna be daft, our Rosie!' Thomas interrupted. ''E's paid in ale.' And then to me, ''E's a dipper, miss. An' I 'elps 'im. Same potbank as yersel'.'

'And do you, then get paid in ale?' My knowledge of how the men received their wages was still slight. I only knew that Hannah Wilkes, for whom I worked, had to go to the public house each Saturday night to be paid out by John Finnegan, the overseer, and this was because John Finnegan was given only bills to pay us with and had to change them with the publican. Hannah said there was no reason why he should not go to a shopkeeper for the same purpose, but John Finnegan liked his ale, so that was an end to it. But she always refused to let me go with her, saying that it was not a fit place for a little girl, and instead called at our house later, with my share; a service of which both my parents were most appreciative.

Thomas laughed. 'I'm lucky if I gets any at all, miss. Father's paid for both of us but keeps most of it 'isself and drinks it. Sometimes, 'e makes me drink my share, too, but sometimes, if landlord says 'e must, 'e'll give me a coupla shillins.'

At that moment, we noticed Ezekial Watkins bearing down on us.

''Ere comes Gawd!' said Thomas. 'C'mon, Rosie!'

'No, wait!' I said, my mind made up. If I couldn't give Rosie my coat, I could at least give her my penny. With my back to Ezekial, I held it out. Her eyes nearly fell out of her head. Almost, I think, she took it. But then she shook her head. 'Na! You keep it, miss. You'se worked for it.' And then, they were gone.

When I reached home, I asked my father about them. I did not then know their family name but he recognized them from my description.

'N'eer do wells,' he said. 'Seth Bailey'll be laid off next Hirings, or my name ain't Marsh. Master's fed up with his drunken ways.'

'If he is, then Thomas will be laid off, too,' I said.

'And the other brother,' said my father, 'the boy, Sam.' The name meant nothing to me then.

'Next question?' asked my father. For he knew me well; knew that I would not be satisfied until I had wormed out of him all that I wanted to know. It being Sunday, he had time for me, while my mother cooked our dinner. It was beef that day, I remember; a great treat.

'Tell me about dipping,' I asked, for I knew little, as yet, about the work of the potbank except in the shed where I worked.

He shook his head. ''Tis pernicious work and no mistake.'

'Tell!' I demanded, one eye on my mother. With luck, Emma would be given the task of laying the table.

'Dipping,' began Pa, taking a sip from the half-pint of ale Ma allowed him each Sunday, 'is what's done to the ware while it's still in the rough. Biscuit, they call it. There's this big tub o' liquid that every article must be dipped in. 'Tis done very quickly by the men and then they pass it to their boys who carry it to the shelves for drying.'

'What's pernicious about that?' I asked.

''Tis what's in the liquid. Soda, potash, lead — and arsenic, too, I've heard.'

The names meant nothing to me — except for arsenic which I knew was a deadly poison. But surely only if you swallowed it?

'Do they drink it, then, Pa?'

He chuckled. 'Bless you, no, lass! They'd be dead in seconds, if they did. No, 'tis the rotting of the flesh. Fingers get rubbed raw and once that starts, the lead gets in twice as fast.'

I was horrified. 'Do they drop off in the end?' I hadn't noticed anything peculiar about Thomas's hands, but then I hadn't looked. The rest of him had presented quite enough problems.

''Twould happen, I suppose. If fits didn't come first. And giddy turns. And no movement of the bowels. And limbs hanging useless. And . . . '

'Cat,' said my mother sharply, coming to take the pan of tatties off the fire, 'set the table, if you please. 'Tis a pity,' she added, glaring at my father, '*your* hands don't work as fast as your tongue, Joseph Marsh!'

Ma never let him forget that he was related to those Marshes who had done well for themselves, and who now owned their own mills and potworks. At Christmas time, we would visit.

'How d'you think they've got where they have,' Ma would say to him as we left. 'Hard work, that's how. Not sitting around on their arses all day!'

Pa certainly didn't sit on *his* arse all day but at the same time, he never put himself forward at the Hirings and let other men take the best jobs if he thought they were in greater need. He was a thrower by trade, and could earn good money when he set his mind to it but that was not always the case.

'At least,' Ma told me when I began work, 'I can rely on you to be regular, Cat.' And I had swelled with pride.

But deep down, I think Ma was as proud of Pa's 'connections' as he was himself. She liked to think the Marshes were just that little bit better than their neighbours. It was for this reason, I think, that she would try to stop Emma and me from 'speaking rough' and was proud of the fact that I could read a little. But the idea of buying a book so that I could practise the art, would have been as alien to her nature as the purchase of a diamond necklace; it simply never entered her head. As for learning to write, that was not to be considered. When would I ever need to? 'Clerking' was a man's work.

'Letters?' I suggested. 'I could write letters to people.'

'What people?' she asked scornfully. And there I was stuck for I did not know any people, other than those who lived near and Hannah Wilkes, of course, and my other workmates. Although now, there were Rosie and Thomas. I had the feeling they would open up a whole new world to me. And I was right. But it was not a world my parents approved of.

2

On the Tuesday after I had met Rosie and Thomas, I made it my business to seek out Thomas in the dipping shed. I would have done so on the Monday had not John Finnegan been 'playing' that day, having drunk to excess on the Saturday and still not recovered. I wouldn't have minded this, had it not meant our working late at the end of the week so that we could catch up. Seven till nine was a long day and sometimes I would fall asleep over my work.

My work was concerned with the decorating of the pots before they were fired. The chosen pattern had already been engraved upon a copper plate and this was warmed on our stove — the same stove that I took my turn at lighting in the early morning — before being coated with colour, usually a lovely, deep blue. The plate would then be wiped clean except for the colour that had run between the lines of the engraving. John Finnegan would then place a piece of special oiled paper over the engraving and use a roller to press both together, so that the design was transferred to the paper. It was then my job to cut out the separate parts of the pattern and hand them to Hannah Wilkes who would press them carefully on to the ware in the correct position. The ware would then be immersed in a tank of water so that the paper floated off, leaving the pattern.

Normally, I loved the work for, as Hannah said, it was a job for small, nimble fingers. But when I grew tired, my eyes would sometimes begin to close of their own accord and before I knew what had happened, I would have cut the paper in the wrong place.

I had once been cuffed hard about the head by John Finnegan for letting this happen. But only once. Hannah had leapt upon him like a mad woman. 'If ever you do that again, John Finnegan, I shall tell the Master. And that'll be the end of you next Hirings. 'Tis your own fault for playing at the beginning of the week and making Cat work late now.'

''Tis I who hire my workers, not Master!' snarled John, 'And that means you, too!'

'Threats will get you nowhere, John Finnegan. There's many a printer would give good money to get me and well you know it. And I should take the little lass with me.'

And John Finnegan, grumbling but defeated, had turned away. Hannah had winked at me, at the same time that she bathed my rapidly swelling eye with cold water. 'Us woman must stick together, eh, Cat?' And 'us women' had, although John Finnegan still continued to play most Mondays. Hannah was courting Will Hoskins, the oven-man, and I was already stitching them a kettle-holder.

On this particular Tuesday, I waited until after breakfast — I'd brought bread and a hunk of dripping and we'd made tea on the stove as we always did — and then asked, 'Please may I go to the necessary, Miss Wilkes?'

'You mean, over the road?'

The privies at our potbank left much to be desired. Admittedly, there was one for the women and one for the men but they were next door to each other and with only a wooden partition between, and that with a gap at the top. It needed only a rising-up on tip-toe, for the occupant of one to peer over at the occupant of the other. I think perhaps some of the young women did this for there would often be shouts of raucous, female laughter coming from that direction and lewd comments, which I did not fully understand, when they returned to work. But I, because of my age, was allowed to use the privy of Hannah's Aunt Mary who lived in a cottage opposite the potbank. However, on this particular Tuesday morning, I had decided to forgo the privilege and brave the communal privy, for it was near the dipping shed.

'If you please, Miss Wilkes, I don't think I'd reach Aunt Mary's in time.'

She grinned. 'Your Ma been giving you the jollop, has she? Hurry up, then, lass!'

Dutifully, I hurried; past the saggar house where a couple of men were stacking the big, clay saggars in which the ware was packed for firing. The privies were in a cul-de-sac, so they knew where I was going.

'Want me to come an' 'old yer 'and, me little maid?' asked one, eyeing me up and down. My heart began to pound and my cheeks to burn. What if he were to follow me? Would anyone hear me scream? And would they take notice if I did?

''Twouldn't be yer 'and she'd be 'oldin', you dirty old bugger!' said the other. I could see no humour in this remark, but they both laughed; the loud, silly guffaw that men sometimes give vent to. Praying that they would not follow, I hurried on. And to my relief, they turned away towards the ovens.

I went first to the privy — for, indeed, I was bursting — and thanked God there was no-one next door. But as I stooped, I heard heavy footsteps and the sound of someone going in. The next minute, a shock of black hair appeared over the wall followed by a pair of dark, wicked eyes. I was standing by then, my skirt still round my waist, my fingers fumbling with the strings of my drawers.

''Allo, me pretty!' I didn't wait to tie the strings but pulled open the door and fled, my arms tight to my sides to keep up my drawers. But terrified as I was, I still had the presence of mind to run in the direction I had decided upon.

The door of the dipping shed was open and I could see the big tubs with men and boys bending over them. Taking one arm away from my side, I bent forward and pretended to adjust my shoe, peering sideways into the shed as I did so. The blood was rushing to my head before a pair of bare feet came into view, shuffling across the open doorway. The legs above the feet were dark with the marks of old weals where they weren't purple with cold. Quickly, I straightened and found myself gazing directly at Thomas.

With horror, I saw that the lid of one of his eyes was puffed up and almost closed, a dark bruise already forming around it. Clearly, he had been crying, for the tears were still wet on his cheeks, but his head was held high. As he saw me he put up his hand to wipe his face and his lips parted in a broad grin. ''Allo, Miss? How be 'ee?'

Suddenly, I was desperately afraid — for him. Whoever had blacked his eye — and I guessed it to be his father — would surely, when faced with such stubborn cheerfulness, immediately black the other.

Fear — and anger — gave me courage. But I had little time. 'Wait for me at six. At the back of the lodge,' I hissed and ran on. But not for long. In the shock of seeing him, I had forgotten my drawers. Down they tumbled about my ankles, tangling my feet so that I tripped and pitched forward; not to the ground but into arms held wide to take me.

'On fire, are we?' asked a familiar voice and I let out a great sigh of relief. It was only George! Dear, kind, friendly George!

George Hoskins was an old man; fifty, if he was a day and some said nearer sixty. Years ago, he had slipped upon wet cobbles when carrying a laden saggar upon his head and had broken his right arm. Badly set, for since he was not paying in to a Sick Society, he could not go to the infirmary, the arm had grown wasted and useless. But in the past, he had possessed great skill at the carving of wood and had often made dolls for the Master's two little daughters. It was they who had persuaded their father not to lay him off and to install him in the gate-keeper's lodge. There was little he could do now with his damaged arm, but his left had acquired the strength of two, for which I had good cause to be grateful. Often, when it was my turn to light the fire and bank it with slack, then carry in the heavy pails of water from the yard, I would find that George had already done it all. His wife had died long since but it was his son, Will, who was courting Hannah.

Immediately, George understood the dilemma I was in, and even picked up my offending nether garment. For a moment, his brow darkened. 'Has some young whipper-snapper been interferin' wi' 'ee, my maid? If so, I'll . . .'

'No, George!' I assured him hastily. ''Twas my own fault for not tying my strings.' I didn't tell him *why* I had not tied the strings.

'That's all right, then. Now, in here with you, quick!' And he pushed me into the shed where damaged ware was stacked, while he stood guard.

'Oh, George, thank you!'

''Tis my pleasure, Missy!' His kind, beaming face gave me courage and the beginning of an idea.

'George, may I come and see you tonight before I go home?'

'Course you can, lass. We'll have a sup o' tea and I'll show you me new kitten.'

'But it won't be just me, George. I hope

that Thomas Bailey will be there, too.'

He frowned, 'Just as long as 'is Da' ain't wi' 'im!'

'Oh no, George! *He's* half the trouble.'

'More'n half I'd say. Now lass, are you sure you're daicent?'

★ ★ ★

'Thomas can't possibly go on working in the dipping shed,' I stated that evening when he and I were warming our feet before George's fire, and after we had duly admired his new kitten; it was one of George's jobs to care for the cats that kept the potbank free of rats.

Both he and Thomas looked at me pityingly. 'I canna do nowt else!' said Thomas.

'His Da' would kill him if he left,' said George.

'He'll kill him if he stays,' I said.

'Look, my lass,' said George patiently. 'There are some things in life you canna change. An' human nature's one of 'em. Seth Bailey is a drunkard an' allus will be. And to buy ale, you needs money. As long as young Tom here can earn an extra shillin' or two, he'll use him.'

'Couldn't we complain to Master?' I asked.

'You know as well as I, Missy, that Master leaves it to the men to hire their own labour

— an' pays 'em accordin'.'

'But dipping's not good for people,' I said. 'Look at Tom's hands.' For now that I'd had the opportunity to study them, I could see that his hands were red and raw, some fingers even wrapped around with pieces of old rag.

'There's not many jobs at potbank,' said George, 'as are. Not for young lads, anyway. Young missies aren't too bad.'

'There's mould-runnin',' said Thomas. 'Yer in the warm wi' mould-runnin'.' He sounded envious.

'Or else in the freezin-cold,' said George. 'That don't do 'ee much good, neither.'

I made a mental note to ask Pa about 'mould-running'. I wasn't going to give these know-alls the pleasure of explaining it to me!

'We'll just have to hope for the best,' said George. 'Meanwhile, have another piece o' furmety.' It was Hannah's furmety, I knew; the delicious mixture of fruit and spices and wheat she made sometimes as a treat for Will and George. 'And then you'd best be runnin' along, young Cat, or yer Da' and Ma'll be worryin'.'

Mention of my family reminded me of Thomas's. 'Where's Rosie?' I asked him.

''Ome, if she's 'ad a good day. Still coalin', if she ain't. Or waitin' outside fer me.'

I *did* know about coaling, for I had often

seen very small children running after the coal carts, scrambling for the pieces of coal that sometimes dropped off. Indeed, I had once seen a very large piece roll off and lie, unseen by the waifs, beneath the cabbage leaves littering the gutter. I had bent to pick it up, meaning to give it to the smallest of them, but it had been snatched from my grasp by a fierce-looking infant, considerably younger than I, who had told me in a loud voice to 'bugger orff!' And I had!

Rosie *was* waiting outside. 'I bin 'ome,' she told Thomas, once she'd gobbled up the furmety George had sent her, 'but Da's in a right mood so I come out again. 'E's sent Sam to the ale 'ouse, wi' a jug.'

Thomas chuckled. ''E'll drink 'alf o't, 'isself, if I knows Sam.'

'Who's Sam?' I asked.

'Our brother. 'Im wot saw yer in the petty this morning. 'E come back an' tole me. An' I tole 'im I'd give 'im a bloody conk if 'e done it again.'

'Did you really?' My delight at hearing this quite outshone my embarrassment.

They saw me to the end of our street. 'See yer tomorrer, mebbe,' said Thomas. 'In the 'ovel, if yer early.'

'I will be!' I said.

★ ★ ★

A hovel is the space between the outer part of a bottle-oven and the oven itself and even when the oven is not being fired, its bricks hold a certain amount of heat. It was the habit of the youngsters on early to crowd into it, once their jobs were done and if it was not yet seven o'clock.

I had always preferred to spend my time in the comparative quiet of the printers' shed but on this particular morning, I went in search of Thomas. Our bank has several ovens but I guessed the one Thomas had in mind was the one near the dipping shed. And I was right; he was immediately visible, standing at the entrance.

I would have been hard put to say why the sight of such a ragged, dirty, undernourished urchin filled me with such affection. One thing was certain — my mother would never have approved of him! Though we both worked at the same potbank and he probably received — or should have received — more wages than I, because he was older and a boy, I knew quite well that Ma would not have considered either he or Rosie to be suitable companions for me. We Marshes had no money to spare but were not as poor as the Baileys by a long way. My clothes, while often

24

faded and threadbare were always clean and neatly patched, my shoes, thanks to Pa's diligence in the back kitchen, usually waterproof, and there was always enough food for Emma and me, even though Ma and Pa sometimes went short. And, above all, there were Pa's 'connections'; tenuous, perhaps, but they were there. So there was an element of forbidden fruit about Thomas's attraction for me.

'I was lookin' out for 'ee,' he said, moving aside so that I could join him. There was the sound of other children larking about beyond the curve of the oven but we were on our own.

'My Pa's explained about mould-running,' I told him without preliminaries. 'He says 'tis better than dipping but not by much.' I knew now that the mould-runners spent all day carrying the moulds into which their masters had pressed the wet clay, to the stove room to be hardened off, then carrying them back again. The stoves were kept at a very high temperature and were constantly wreathed in steam and vapour rising from the wet clay.

'The boys have to run,' my father had explained, 'from the cold of the workshop into the heat of the stoves and back again — about five hundred times a day. More if their master is catching up. One minute, the sweat is pouring off them like a river, the next drying on their skin like beads of ice.'

'But at least their hands don't drop off,' I'd said. 'Nor their bowels . . . '

'You're right!' my father had said quickly, one eye on Ma who had just come into the room with a basin of pobs for Emma's supper. ''Tis the asthma that gets the mould-runners in the end.'

That night, I'd thought about it in bed, while I'd warmed my body against Emma's. Perhaps, I'd thought drowsily, if Thomas became a mould-runner, I could knit him a little jacket that would absorb the sweat instead of leaving it to dry on his skin. Perhaps . . . But I was asleep before I could plan further.

However, on that particular morning, Thomas did not want to talk about himself. 'Rosie thinks er'll be nine afore long,' he said.

'Doesn't she *know*?' Birthdays were always a cause for celebration in our house, even if it was only bicklets with a smidgeon of grease.

He shook his head. 'Ma can't remember exactly when, but'er *thinks* 'tis nine years ago, come Easter. Anyway,' he lowered his voice, glancing over his shoulder, ''er wants a proper job, like yours. 'Er's fed up wi' coalin'. An' stealin'.'

'*Stealing?*' I was horrified. At best, people

were put in the lock-up for stealing; at worst, sent far away across the sea.

'Not *big* stealin',' said Thomas defensively. 'Jus' a tater or two from the stalls in the market. Or a turnip. Sometimes, folk gives 'er things if she cries loud enuff.'

In future, I resolved, I would never take for granted the big, soup-pan that simmered on our hearth all winter. Ma was always throwing in a handful of fresh bones she'd bought for a penny in the Shambles. 'For the dog,' I'd heard her tell the butcher.

'But, Ma,' I'd started to protest the first time I'd heard her, 'we don't *have* a . . . '

'Wipe your nose, Cat!' she'd said quickly. 'And don't chatter so!'

'Tell your Ma she can buy a big handful of bones from the butchers for a penny,' I told Thomas.

He gave me the pitying look I was beginning to recognise. ''Er don't 'ave a penny,' he said, 'if Pa's on the drink. If it weren't for folk up at Mill 'Ouse where Ma used to clean, we'd starve more often than not. But they send us down rabbits and sometimes, a bit o' beef.'

'Doesn't your mother work now?' I asked. Even Ma took in washing before Christmas when she needed the extra.

'Not since 'er cough got bad,' said Thomas.

We could hear George beginning to ring the work bell and knew we'd have to go.

'I don't *think* I can do anything about the mould-running,' I admitted, 'but I'll have a word with Hannah about Rosie.'

★ ★ ★

Cunningly, I waited until the following Tuesday evening when, once again, we were catching up, before having a word with Hannah.

'You'd think,' I said as I stifled a yawn, 'that Mr Finnegan would take on extra help on Tuesdays.'

She looked at me. 'You're not just a pretty face, young Cat! But I doubt he would. 'Twould cost him more.'

'But we'd manage more pots,' I persisted. 'And he could lay her off Wednesdays, if he was of a mind.' Once Rosie had a foot in, I thought, anything might happen.

Hannah still looked doubtful. 'Where would he find someone just for a day? Anyway, I don't want to share *my* job — Will and I needs all the money we can get.'

'But you're so *quick*, Hannah. You wouldn't need anyone else. And I know someone who'd be willing to do just Tuesdays. She has other occupations,' I explained grandly, 'for the rest of the week.'

'Polishes up her diamonds, do she?' Hannah teased, though without malice.

I smiled to myself. Coal, according to Pa, was made of diamonds!

★ ★ ★

I said no more to Hannah about employing an extra cutter but a day or two later, I noticed her in earnest conversation with John Finnegan. As a result I was told to bring 'my friend' for inspection on the following morning.

That was far too quick. It would need longer than twelve hours to clean Rosie up to Hannah's standards. The oil we used in the workshop gave off a most pungent odour but I doubted if it would totally conceal Rosie's own distinctive perfume. And while no-one expected the boys to be other than ragged and dirty because of the nature of their work, girls were expected to reach a certain standard of cleanliness.

'Her Ma's sick at the moment,' I told Hannah. This was quite true. Not only did Mrs Bailey's cough still trouble her, she was now, according to Thomas, 'expectin' another babby'.

'Another?' I'd queried for they'd never

mentioned any other children at home. An older brother and sister had, I knew, already gone their separate ways just as our brother Henry had.

'Las' two was born dead,' Thomas had said briefly.

'How can you be born dead?' I'd asked Pa later.

'Ask your Ma!' *he'd* said. And I hadn't bothered. 'Plenty of time for all that,' was what I knew she'd say.

'But she could manage the next day,' I now told Hannah and she seemed satisfied with that.

I could hardly wait to tell Thomas the good news. Not that he was much help. ''Er won't go under t'pump,' he said after I'd suggested Rosie should have a good wash. 'Not this cold weather.'

'Tell her if she wants a proper job, she's got to. You could go with her,' I added as an afterthought.

'Not me!'

I moved on to the next problem. 'Has she any best clothes?'

'Don't talk daft!'

I thought hard. Rosie was smaller than I and my last year's drawers and bodice were still lying in the cupboard waiting for the old clothes woman to call, for Ma wouldn't take things down to the market herself and barter at the stall as other women did. But how would I ever get them out of the house without Ma noticing? However, thinking of the market had given me an idea. It was a truly terrible idea and my first instinct was to discard it immediately. But when, after a minute or two of hard thought, I could see no other way, I said to Thomas.

'There's only one thing for it. She'll have to steal them from the market!'

He was deeply shocked; not at the idea of Rosie stealing but at me for suggesting it. 'Thomas,' I said solemnly, 'there's no other way.'

The next twenty-four hours were torture as I imagined Rosie freezing to death under the pump or being arrested by the watch. And it would all be my fault.

'Pa,' I said urgently, 'do they put children in the stocks these days?'

I thought he would never stop laughing. 'Bless you, Cat, Ma's not that cross with you!' For in my preoccupation, I'd allowed one of Ma's precious blue plates to slip through my fingers and shatter on the flagstones.

Next day, I managed to catch Thomas in the yard during my dinner hour. He looked like the cat who'd swallowed the cream. 'Ma washed Rosie all over in the scullery,' he told me. 'An' I used t'water arterwards!' He did indeed look a shade cleaner although I could still see where the water hadn't quite reached.

'What about her clothes?'

'That's seen to, as well. Ma's goin' up to Mill 'Ouse to see if they got anythin'.'

My relief was enormous. The folk up at Mill House, I decided, must be God-fearing Christians even though they were 'Church' and not Methodists as we were.

'It's up to Rosie now,' I told Thomas. 'Seven o'clock sharp, tell her!'

★ ★ ★

'You're in a state this morning,' Ma said. 'You've left your milk-meat.'

'Sorry, Ma!' And I hastily gobbled up the remains of my bread and milk. Ma always made sure I had something before leaving for work.

But she was right — I was in a state. 'Seven o'clock sharp!' I'd told Thomas, completely forgetting it was Candlemas Day when the potbank would open at half-past-six instead of seven and continue so until November. Master would make George close the gates before seven and pity help anyone who was late. Not only would they be locked out for half an hour, they'd lose money. And Rosie would probably lose all chances of a job.

But I needn't have worried. They were waiting for me in the hovel; and had been, they told me, since six o'clock.

'Let's have a look at you,' I said to Rosie as Ma did to me each morning, in case my petticoat showed; not that Rosie had a petticoat. Even so, in every other respect, I had to admit, the Mill House had done her proud. She wore a long, dark-blue skirt that was considerably better than mine and a lighter-blue jacket that, while it had obviously been made for someone much smaller than Rosie, did at least meet over her narrow chest. There wasn't a rent or loose thread to be seen. But it was her hair that impressed me the most. It shone like the seat of Ezekial Watkins' Sunday trousers, rippling to her waist in a cascade of waves and curls.

'Don't 'er look wunnerful?' breathed Thomas lovingly.

'Wunnerful!' I murmured back, hardly aware of what I was saying so shocked was I by the stab of pure jealousy that had pierced me as I saw the love mirrored in his eyes. I shook my head, trying to rid myself of so uncharitable an emotion. Why should Thomas not feel love for his sister? At the same time, I knew a deep-seated sense of relief that they were, indeed, brother and sister.

'You'll need a hair ribbon,' I forced myself to say briskly. And I pulled out my own; tucking my hair down into the neck of my pinafore.

'Good luck, Rosie!' said Thomas, then turned away towards the dipping shed. And for the first time, I thought of their father.

'Does your Da' know about this?' I asked Rosie.

She shook her head. 'Ma said not to tell 'im unless we 'ad to.'

I nodded. Better that Hannah didn't know of the relationship either.

'This is Rosie!' I pushed Rosie forward as we went into the workshop.

'Hallo, Rosie!' said Hannah cheerfully. 'Sit yourself down, dear, and take off your jacket.'

From the look of horror on Rosie's face, I guessed that, beneath the jacket, she was either naked or wearing something indescribably dreadful.

'She — she feels the cold something awful, Miss Wilkes,' I babbled. 'Don't you, Rosie?'

Rosie nodded so hard, I thought she'd crick her neck. Hannah looked surprised but didn't pursue the matter. 'Now, where do you live, dear?'

The alley where the Baileys lived was the

most disreputable in the town. Why, oh why, hadn't I thought up a suitable story?

'Outside the town,' I said swiftly. 'Quite a long way out, isn't it, Rosie?'

Hannah looked at me in exasperation. 'Cat, that fire needs banking. Go and fetch more stack, if you please!'

By the time I'd got back from the coal shed, she knew it all; knew that Seth Bailey was Rosie's father and Thomas her brother; knew exactly where she lived and, most important of all, that Seth must be kept in ignorance of his daughter's earnings.

'Now, dear,' she was saying. 'I'll show you what you've got to do and then you can watch Cat for a while.' What was more, Rosie's jacket was off and she was wearing one of Hannah's old pinafores. Dear, kind Hannah! I could have hugged her.

3

And so began a period of great happiness in my life. For Rosie's fingers proved as nimble as mine and Hannah, encouraged by the thought of her wedding day, had no difficulty keeping up with the extra work. And John Finnegan, who was a sensible man when sober, soon extended her time to three, and sometimes four, days a week.

Rosie, now housed and warmed for most of the day and with the extra food her mother was now able to provide, was like a bud unfolding its petals to the sun.

It was weeks before her father discovered she was working and by then there was nothing he could do about it. For, one cold night in February, Seth Bailey, returning home from the ale house drunk as a lord, fell on the roadway in front of the fire wagon careering down the street to a warehouse blaze, and was run over. That, at least, was surmised to be what happened, for so intent were the men upon reaching the fire, it was not noticed that Seth had been hit.

Naturally, no alarm was felt by his non-appearance at home, so it was left to the watch to discover his unconscious body. By then, he was in a very bad way indeed, the wheels of the wagon having passed over both his legs. The watch carried him home, for he was well-known to them as the worst drunkard in the town.

'Ma sent for Davy Jones,' Rosie told us next day, 'an' ole Ma Quiggan. An' they come straight away. But Pa's still mortal sick'. Davy Jones had some small skill with the setting of bones and Ma Quiggan was an old woman who acted as both midwife and herbalist.

'Poor man!' said kind-hearted Hannah, but the rest of us said nothing. It was hard to feel sympathy for someone who had never shown it to others. But it was left to Thomas, who had come in to the potbank to report the accident and to discover his own fate now that he no longer had a master to work for, to put it into words.

'Sam an' me'll be out o' a job but otherwise 'twill be best for everyone if the ole bugger dies.'

But 'the ole bugger' didn't die; although he could never walk again without a shoulder to lean upon or sticks to steady himself. However, as good fortune had it, Thomas fell immediately into another job.

It was as mould-runner to Benjamin Green, his previous boy having given up because of asthma. Thomas was almost speechless with joy, for Benjamin Green had the reputation of being a kind man. Only one thing marred his happiness; Sam was also to be a mould-runner in the same shed but for another man; an evil-looking ruffian named Charlie Proctor, known to be nearly as heavy a drinker as Seth.

'But canna be 'elped,' Thomas told Rosie and me in the hovel, 'an' Ma needs the money.'

'Thomas,' I asked, 'if I knit you a little weskit, would you wear it?' For I couldn't get out of my mind the dreadful wheezing cough of little Henry Briggs, the previous mould-runner.

'Be proud to!' said Thomas chivalrously, but he would, I think, have agreed to almost anything that day, so happy was he.

'Dinna worry, Cat,' Rosie said afterwards — they both called me 'Cat' now — 'Tom be stronger than 'e looks.'

Even so, under Ma's supervision, I knitted my weskit, buying the wool out of my own money. Ma still did not know the identity of my new friends, only that I now had a workmate and that her brother was a mould-runner. Since I was always encouraged to be kind to those less fortunate than myself, she looked upon the weskit as an act of charity that I might have extended to anyone.

Only Pa knew their true identity but saw no harm in the friendship.

'He'll never wear it,' he said when the weskit was finished. 'Real nesh they'll think him if he does.'

'Nesh' meaning 'soft' was almost the worst thing you could be called at the potbank.

I showed it to Rosie first. 'D'you think he'll wear it?'

'If 'e don't, I will!' she said, admiring the evenness of the stitches and the deep V of the neck. 'Could 'ee larn me to knit, Cat?'

'Of course! And to sew, if you like.'

Thomas, to my surprise, took little persuasion to wear his weskit. I think by then he had realised that the life of a mould-runner did have its drawbacks. Because Benjamin Green was such a good worker, he was kept busier than the other lads and was continually on the trot.

'One minute, I'm fearsome 'ot,' he told Rosie and me, 'the next, perishin' cold.'

'The weskit,' I explained, 'will absorb your sweat.'

'But wot'll the other lads say?'

'There'll be no need for them to see it if you wear it under your shirt.' But even as I said it, I knew there was no way the garment he called a shirt, ragged and full of holes, would hide it.

'Wear yer jacket,' Rosie suggested, for Thomas had been given an old jacket that had belonged to Benjamin's eldest son as tuck in his wages.

'Too 'ot!' said Thomas. 'I'd roast like a leg o' pork if I was to wear a jacket in the stoves. Anyway, I'd dirty it, if I did.' For incredibly, dirty unkempt Thomas had begun to develop a pride in his appearance, just as Rosie had.

However, Thomas's problem was solved because that same week, he was given one of Benjamin's shirts in his wages and not much docked because of it. And Benjamin's shirts would have fitted an elephant. There was almost no need for Thomas to wear anything else at all!

'If you can spare it for a night,' I offered, 'I'll turn up the sleeves.' For their length threatened to sweep the moulds from the boards.

Reluctantly, he parted with it. With the pieces I had cut off, I made Rosie two small handkerchiefs, embroidering the letter 'R' in a corner.

''Ow do 'ee know 'tis an R?' she asked when I explained what it was meant to be.

'I copied it,' I told her, 'from the Bible. The story about Rachel.'

'Can 'ee write then, as well as read?'

'No,' I said sadly. 'Not yet, anyway.' I didn't

admit it to Rosie, but in fact I could read the story of Rachel only with great difficulty. But I'd heard it so often, I knew it almost by heart.

I like to think my weskit helped Thomas to combat the effects of that perpetual change from heat to cold. He had a cough anyway but it seemed to grow no worse and I comforted myself by thinking that summer and the warmer weather would soon be with us. For several weeks, life continued peacefully enough, the atmosphere in our workshop being particularly harmonious. Seth Bailey's accident had been a salutary lesson to many, John Finnegan included, so that his drinking, while still regular, was less heavy and his temper much improved thereby.

Hannah's wedding was discussed daily and a date actually arranged for September. Like all festive occasions, it would be held on a Monday for, like it or not, that was the day of the week when most men played, so that time away from work would not have to be taken by those fortunate enough to be invited. These, I am pleased to say, included Rosie and myself although we were not yet sure that we would attend the actual ceremony which would, like all Non-conformist marriages at that time, be held in the local parish church.

'Cripes!' said Rosie when we went one day

in our dinner hour to inspect it. 'I aren't goin' in there!'

And it did, indeed, look most imposing with its tall spire rising out of a square tower taller than any bottle oven.

'But my Pa says anyone can,' I assured her. ''Tis the House of God.'

'Why can't 'er get wed in chapel?' Rosie asked.

'No-one does,' I told her firmly, although not knowing why. But the answer seemed to satisfy her.

'Why can't Hannah be married in our chapel?' I asked Pa that evening.

''Twouldn't be legal,' said Pa. 'Parson's the only man can tie the knot accordin' to the law. Otherwise you be livin' in sin.' Living in sin, according to Ezekial Watkins was the worst thing that could happen to anyone and meant spending eternity in a fire as fierce as any that Hannah's William lit in the ovens. But until Pa's words, I had never known exactly what it meant.

'So everyone must be married in church?' I persisted.

Pa nodded. 'As law stands at the moment. Why, maid, be 'ee thinkin' about it, then?'

I joined in his laughter but that night I had a dream. In it Thomas and I were standing together in front of Ezekial Watkins in the

42

aisle of our chapel with Rosie screaming behind us, "T'aint legal, I tell 'ee! Livin' in sin, yer'll be!' I woke up to find Emma and me running in sweat.

Once my mind was fixed upon weddings, one thing led to another in my thoughts. 'Rosie,' I asked next morning — it was our turn to light the fires and carry in the water, both tasks being much easier now there were two of us — 'd'you know how babies are born?'

'A'course!' was all she said and I realised she thought I was merely testing her knowledge and not actually seeking it. For in Rosie's eyes, I knew everything or if I didn't could find out from Pa.

Honesty, I decided was the best policy. 'Well, I don't!' I said.

Her astonishment was so complete, we had to put down the pail of water we were carrying from the yard, while she recovered. 'Yer dinna *know*, Cat?' I shook my head. 'But yer Pa knows everythin''.

'He won't tell me. Nor Ma.'

She shook her head. 'Fancy me knowin' somethin' you dinna!' For a moment, she was silent, clearly not knowing where to begin.

'I know they begin in a woman's inside,' I prompted, for I remembered Ma's swollen belly before Emma was born and its miraculous flatness afterwards. 'But I don't know how they get in there in the first place. Nor how they get out.'

Rosie was on surer ground now. 'Well, yer've seen dogs ain't yer? When they needs a pail o'water thrown o'er 'em?'

It was my turn to be astonished. I did, indeed, know about dogs, having seen my own mother hurl the precious contents of a pail she had just carried from the pump over next door's mongrel that was a'top someone's bitch on our doorstep. But that was *dogs!*

'Rosie, you don't mean . . . ?' I couldn't believe it.

She nodded, grinning all over her face. 'A'course! Many's the time I've 'eard my Da' doin' it to Ma. Ain't you ever?' I could only shake my head. 'We all sleeps in t'same room, yer see.'

'Thomas, too?'

'A'course! 'E an' Sam's one side, I'm another an' Ma an' Da's nearest t'door.'

'And how . . . ' I began for my second question was still unanswered. But at that moment, the bell began to peal and we leaped to pick up our pail.

' . . . do they come out?' Rosie finished my question. 'Down wer yer passes yer water. That's wer!' It was as well the bell was now

44

making such a clamour that speech became impossible!

I didn't believe her, of course. Not when I thought about it while we were quiet at work. To begin with, it was impossible to imagine my Pa wanting to do any such thing to my Ma and equally impossible to imagine her letting him. 'No better than the animals!' I'd heard her say to a neighbour when Mrs Oldfield down the street was said to be expecting her ninth. So there *must* be another way of doing it. Rosie said nothing more on the subject but now and then I caught her gazing at me and I knew what she was thinking about.

A couple of weeks later, she came back from the privy — for she scorned to use Aunt Mary's and, to be honest, I don't think Aunt Mary minded — with a great grin almost cutting her face in two. 'Come wi' me, Cat!' she said. 'I wanna show yer summat.'

There was something about the sauciness of that grin, her refusal to say more, that made me suspicious. 'Tell me what it is first!' I demanded.

But she shook her head, 'Na, I canna explain. 'Tis summat 'ee mus' see wi' yer own eyes.' And taking my hand, she led me away, past the biscuit oven, the saggar house, the dipping shed and the slip house. It was when we reached the slip house and were approaching the turning house that she slowed her pace and put her finger to her lips, then went on tiptoe, motioning me to do the same. And it was then that I guessed what it was she wanted to show me.

Only two people worked in the turning house — a man and a woman. Pa had told me that their work was 'special' and to do with the trimming of fine ware upon a lathe. It was in a part of the potbank that I did not often go to but I knew that the door of the house was normally kept wide open. Now, however, it had been pulled shut although the latch must have slipped, leaving an opening of several inches. As Rosie and I stood there, hardly daring to breathe, we heard a succession of peculiar grunting noises and then the sound of breath being expelled in a long, lingering gasp that was almost a shout.

Rosie stood back and motioned me to peer in through the crack. Part of me hesitated to look but a stronger, inner compulsion forced me to do so. On her back on the floor, lay the woman, her skirts pulled up above her waist, her thin, white legs spread wide. The man, lying face down with his breeches about his knees, was on top of her.

As I gazed, riveted, the man gave a great, gusty grunt such as men sometimes utter when plunging their faces into a tankard of ale, and seemed to sink even further into the woman's body.

'The poor woman!' I murmured and would have moved forward to help her had not Rosie seized me by the hand and dragged me back the way we had come. But not before I had seen the expression upon the woman's face.

'She — she was enjoying it!' I gasped when we were safely out of earshot.

'Oh, aye! Ma don't, but most 'omen do! Some of us maids, too!' she added as an afterthought.

'Rosie! You've never . . . ?' I couldn't bring myself to finish the question.

She chuckled. 'Bless 'ee, no! Thomas'd kill me if I did!'

When my blood had ceased to race and my cheeks had cooled and I was sitting quietly once more, I thought about what I had learned. It *was* like the animals. It could be pleasurable but was not always so. And Thomas would mind greatly if Rosie were to do it. Would he, I wondered, feel a similar concern about me?

★　★　★

It was soon after my discovery of the sexual appetites of some adults, that I had my first contact with Sam. I had seen him about at the potbank, of course, but always in the company of other boys. Thomas rarely spoke of him but when he did, it was easy to see there was little love lost between them; Thomas always his mother's champion and Sam, I guessed, invariably taking his father's part in any dispute.

It was a cold, windy evening in March and Rosie and I had been sent home early; John Finnegan having caught up and Hannah wishing to inspect the cottage she and William had been promised when it fell vacant. Rosie and I were cock a'hoop at our unexpected freedom for we were paid by the day, not the hour, and would lose nothing.

'I'll walk 'ee 'ome,' Rosie offered. She liked to do this, hoping, I think, that one day she would be asked to step inside. I would dearly loved to have taken her but feared to be too precipitate in case Ma should not approve. When she has shoes, I told myself, I'll ask Ma if I may. For Rosie still went barefoot, although the length of her skirt now hid this deficiency. Hannah, I knew, was as concerned as I, for I had often noticed her glancing at Rosie when she sat on her stool with her skirt tucked around her feet. The difficulty lay in that they were so small; otherwise I was sure that a pair of Hannah's would have been passed on to her long since. Thomas's feet, it went without saying, were always bare, but then all the boys' were; for it was said they ran faster unshod.

On this particular day we stopped for a moment at the end of our street and Ma, coming from our neighbour's house, saw me and waved. Of course, I waved back, then turned to Rosie to say goodbye. For a fleeting moment, I caught the expression on her face — one of a yearning so intense my heart failed me and I would have asked her in, then and there, no matter what Ma might have said, had not Rosie whispered, 'See yer tomorrer, Cat!' and slipped away.

I was doubly sorry she had not waited, for immediately I went in, Ma asked me to go back down the hill to the grocers for a screw of tea. I ran all the way, hoping to catch her up, but she was nowhere in sight, not even at the end of her alley. The tea bought, I turned to climb back up the hill. By now, it was getting dark and most folk were indoors eating their tea. Except for Sam Bailey. He was leaning on a stanchion at the end of their alley, watching me approach with a wicked gleam in his eye.

My heart began to pound but I kept my eyes fixed firmly upon the ground. Just before I reached him, he moved out in front of me, his arms stretched wide. 'Well, if it ain't li'l Miss 'Igh and Mighty, 'ersel'!'

I made to dart past him but immediately he shifted so that he was blocking my path. I moved to the other side but he was there again, arms still outstretched, legs apart. I stood stock still and forced myself to look up at him. 'What do you want with me, Sam Bailey?'

He burst into a peal of raucous laughter. Then began to mimic what I had said, in a high, silly voice. Then changed it to a menacing growl as he shot out a hand to seize my wrist, his face so close, the foul stench of his breath abused my nostrils. 'I'll tell 'ee wot I wants, Miss Cath'rine Marsh. I wants that little screw o' paper in yer 'and. One day, mebbe, I'll want summat more. That little cunt o' yours, for a start. But just now, I'll settle for wot's in yer 'and.'

It was then that I screamed — and went on screaming until his other hand lifted to strike me. But it never reached my face. A shrieking, spitting wisp of humanity hurled itself at Sam's legs, flooring him like a log. 'Dinna ever let me catch yer within a foot o' our Cat, again, Sam Bailey!' Rosie spat at him.

Such was the force of her onslaught, I think even a lion would have slunk away. Sam, rubbing at his broken knees, went without a word. Rosie turned to me. 'Be 'ee orlright, our Cat?'

'I'm all right, Rosie, thanks to you!' And leaning forward, I planted a quick kiss upon her cheek.

As I went on up the hill, slowly now, to give myself time to stop shaking before I reached home, two thoughts were uppermost in my mind. First that I would be in mortal fear of Sam Bailey for the rest of my life; for thanks to what I had seen in the turning house, I now knew full well what he had meant by his threat. But against this chilling thought, I could weigh Rosie's acceptance of me as her friend. 'Our Cat', she had called me in the heat of the moment. And that must mean Thomas, too.

★ ★ ★

'Ma,' I said one evening a few days later, 'come Monday, I'd like to go over to Wolstanton.'

'Annie'll be pleased to see you, I'm sure.' For Wolstanton was where my cousin Annie lived and she was around my age.

'Not to see Annie, Ma. Just to walk.'

At this, she raised her eyes from the rabbit pie whose edges she was crimping with a fork.

'On your own! Whatever for?' It was unheard of for anyone — except the quality and they, never alone — to walk for pleasure unless they were courting.

Annie and I always walked when I visited, for there were beautiful woods at Wolstanton as well as the Marsh, where the wind blew fresh and clean and was deemed 'good for me'.

'Breathe deep, Cat!' Pa used to say before we set out. 'Fill your lungs with the air God gave us before the greed of man took it away.'

And for the first five minutes of our walk, I would conscientiously fill my lungs to the point of bursting and grow so red in the face with my efforts that Annie would dissolve into laughter and I with her. But even so, I always felt better for my visits, returning home with 'roses in my cheeks' as Pa put it, although they soon faded once I was back under the pall of the potbank.

Although it was like a different world, it was but a mile or two in distance from home and I was astonished to discover that Rosie and Thomas had never been there.

'Why should us want to?' Rosie asked when I suggested it.

''Tis beautiful,' I told her. 'Green trees and birds. And grass and blue sky.'

'Aye, 'tis a grand place,' George confirmed

for we were in his kitchen at the time, waiting for Thomas to finish work. 'I remember it well from me courtin' days.'

'But we ain't courtin' yet,' Rosie said, 'be us, Cat?' And she poked me in the ribs and giggled wickedly.

'Not yet,' I agreed. 'But the air will do you good, Rosie. Won't it, George?'

''Twill an' all!' said George and Thomas coming in at that moment coughing his heart out, seemed to add weight to this pronouncement.

The upshot was we decided to go on the following Monday. 'Us'll 'ave to 'elp Ma a bit first,' said Thomas, 'but 'er won't mind us goin'. And us won't tell Da'.' Since Seth Bailey had become a cripple, life, I gathered, had been a lot easier in the Bailey household. 'As long as 'e don't grab yer when yer passes, yer safe,' Rosie had told me. But she still appeared at work sometimes with a great bruise on her face.

We arranged to meet at nine o'clock, bringing with us the dinner we would normally have taken to work and I went home to convince Ma it was all right for me to go. I could have pretended that I was visiting Annie as usual but I knew that eventually she would find out and I would be punished. Lies came under the heading of 'dishonesty' in our house, and was the one thing Pa would not tolerate.

'No,' I told her now, 'not on my own but with Rosie, the girl I work with. And Thomas, her brother.'

As I spoke, I glanced anxiously at Pa — for I had deliberately waited until he was home before talking to Ma.

'If the weather holds,' said Pa obligingly, ''twill be very pleasant. Daffies should be out by now.'

Ma ignored him. 'Where do Rosie and Thomas live?' she asked me.

I took a deep breath. 'Down the bottom of the hill, Ma. Near the potbank. Their mother,' I added quickly and producing what I considered my best card, 'used to work at Mill House.'

Ma suddenly put down the rolling-pin from which she was scraping the remains of the dough and gave me a most peculiar look. Then, most unusually for her so early in the evening, she sat down on the straight-backed Windsor chair beside the fire that was traditionally hers, Pa always occupying the old rocker on the other side. 'Not Lottie Bailey, by any chance?' she asked.

'I don't know about the Lottie, Ma. But she is married to Seth Bailey.'

'That's the one.' Now she gazed across at

Pa. 'And Thomas must be round about Cat's age by now.' Pa nodded solemnly, clearly following Ma's train of thought.

'That's right, Ma!' I put in, not wanting to be left out of a conversation that seemed set to become even more interesting.

'We were carryin' round about the same time,' said Ma reminiscently.

'So you know Rosie's Ma?'

'Oh, yes! I know Rosie's Ma, all right!' There was something about the way she said this that gave it a deeper meaning than the actual words implied. I waited hopefully, but all she said after a second or two, was 'How is Lottie Bailey these days, Cat?'

'Oh, expecting again,' I said and was proud of the matter-of-fact way I delivered this information. And to my astonishment, Ma seemed to accept it, as if I were her next-door neighbour and not her nine-year-old daughter. But an even greater surprise was in store.

'Randy old bugger!' she said and immediately clapped her hand to her mouth and leaped to her feet. 'For pity's sake, I don't know what came over me to say such a thing! And in front of Cat!'

Pa laughed so hard I thought he'd fall out of the rocker, and Emma who'd been curled up in his arms, fast asleep, woke up with a start and immediately started to cry. Even so,

Pa still continued to laugh his head off. The din was terrible.

'Out with you to the back kitchen, woman,' he teased, winking at me, 'and scour out your mouth with soap!'

After that, it would have been well nigh impossible for Ma to have raised any objections to my outing with Rosie and Thomas. 'I'll make you a rabbit turnover,' she offered.

'Why not make three?' I suggested. And she did.

★ ★ ★

It was a day I was to remember for the rest of my life. From the very beginning, good fortune favoured us, for we had hardly started on our way than the carrier's cart drew up beside us.

'Runnin' away, are we?' enquired the driver facetiously as he helped us up among the boxes and barrels and crates of hens. No doubt, he was surprised at the sight of three unaccompanied children stepping out so cheerfully, for to help us on our way I was teaching the others some of the hymns we sang in Sunday School.

'Oh God, our help in ages past,' we were carolling as he drew up.

'Strewth!' said Thomas. 'Tha' was quick!'

I knew I should have reproved him for such an irreverent remark but somehow, such was the happy spirit among us, I hadn't the heart. God, I felt sure, would not have minded.

'Ah, I seen you afore,' the driver said as he hoisted me up beside him. 'Li'l Cat Marsh, ain't it? Goin' to Wolstanton to see yer relations, no doubt.'

'We may look in on them,' I said, a shade distantly, for I wasn't sure I liked him knowing so much about me. 'But on the other hand, we may not!' In fact, I had already decided that I would not take Rosie and Thomas to meet Annie. Although Ma had agreed to our outing, it did not necessarily follow that my Aunt and Uncle would do the same; even though Annie, herself, would have been delighted, for she was always telling me how fortunate I was to work for my living instead of spending my days at home as she had to, learning how to grow up into a young lady. In truth, Annie was not a great scholar and, much to my disappointment, was quite unable to teach me what she had been taught.

The carrier, although inquisitive, seemed a kind man and we conversed in a friendly fashion for the rest of the journey.

'An' where would the ladies an' gen'leman

like to be put off?' he enquired as the familiar thatched cottages of Wolstanton came in sight.

'By the church, if you please,' I said. If we were lucky and the rector was about, he might allow us to view the surrounding countryside from the base of its lofty spire. However, in this respect, Fortune was not on our side and we had to content ourselves with craning our necks upwards which wasn't the same thing at all.

However, 'I ain't a'goin' up there!' said Thomas firmly, so perhaps it was as well.

'We'll go to the Marsh, then,' I said.

'Do it belong to 'ee, then, Cat?' Rosie asked. At first I couldn't think what she meant, but then I realised that indeed my name was the same.

'No,' I said gravely, for I did not want to hurt her feelings, 'we are not related.' But indeed, the question was not as fanciful as it had first seemed. 'The first Marshes may indeed have lived on marshland,' Pa told me later, 'and that could have been how we got our name.'

Wolstanton Marsh was covered with tall rushes and tussocks of coarse grass in which it was easy to lose oneself. It was strictly forbidden for either Annie or me to deviate from the path by even a single step, for there were many stories about children who had done this, attracted perhaps by the fluffy white balls of the cotton grass, and never been seen again. Even so, I loved the impression of limitless space, the feeling of freedom, that it gave.

At first, neither Thomas nor Rosie, used to the confines of buildings and the presence of people, were comfortable there, especially after I'd explained the need to keep to the path. But then suddenly, as I tried to think of words to reassure them, a lark rose into the still air and soared, warbling sweetly, into the immensity of the sky, and others followed until we seemed to be at the heart of some heavenly chorus.

''Tis better than any ole hymn!' breathed Thomas reverently. And I realised they were probably the first wild birds he had seen or heard.

After that, they did not mind the Marsh at all and would have stayed indefinitely had not a keen breeze sprung up and I remembered that neither of them were as warmly clad as I. 'We'll have our dinner in the woods,' I said.

At first, the woods disturbed them as much as the Marsh. ''Tis ghostly!' said Rosie, peering into the white blackthorn blossom at the trees' edge.

'An' 'ee canna see wot lies be'ind t'trees!' said Thomas.

'Only more trees!' said I stoutly, thinking how happily they roamed the squalid streets of our town with evil perhaps lurking around each corner and thought nothing of it, but were scared of this natural paradise. 'And a rabbit or two,' I added as I went before them beneath branches whose buds were already bursting into tender leaf.

At that moment, as if to prove my point, a baby one suddenly shot out of the under-growth straight across Rosie's bare feet. The next moment, she was in Thomas's arms screaming like a child and he, though his own cheeks were white as milk, was crooning into her ear as Ma did to Emma after applying a hot, bread poultice to a festered knee.

''Twas only a rabbit, Rosie! Ye've seen 'em 'angin' in t'market, often enuff!'

'But *they* be dead!'

'They're much prettier alive,' I assured her, while I tried to suppress the familiar pang of envy at seeing Thomas, for any reason, hold her to him. 'If we go further into the wood,' I continued, 'and keep ever so quiet, you'll see for yourself how pretty they are.' For Annie and I often did this and had once even seen a hare loping along the edge of the trees while the harriers streamed away across the valley below.

Soon, we came to a little glade at the centre of which a great beech tree towered above a purling stream and, finger to lips, I motioned Thomas and Rosie to sit beside me under the beech and stay quite still. Sure enough, a minute or two later, a rabbit hopped out into the clearing and sat there, cleaning its whiskers and twitching its little pink nose, and I watched the expression on Rosie's face turn from fear to delight. A delight which she soon found impossible to control so that she clapped her hands in excitement. Immediately, the rabbit vanished. Rosie's face dropped. 'Will 'e cum back, Cat?'

'Not while we're here. But we'll leave him a few crumbs of our dinner when we go.'

It was then we discovered that Rosie and Thomas must have dropped their bundles when we saw the first rabbit.

'I'll go back for 'em,' Thomas volunteered, although I could tell he was scared stiff.

'Ye canna go alone,' Rosie said immediately, as if he were setting off across an uncharted sea.

'Na! I'll be oright!' Whistling defiantly, he set off.

'Ain't 'e brave?' said Rosie.

'Very brave!' I agreed solemnly. We sat in silence while we awaited his return, Rosie gripping my hand tightly, and listened to the stream rippling at our feet and the birds singing above our heads. After only a couple of minutes, Thomas was back, swaggering out of the bushes with the bundles held triumphantly above his head.

After quenching our thirst at the stream, we opened our bundles. Rosie and Thomas had their usual hunks of bread, augmented today by slices of cold tatties. 'Ma made us a turnover apiece,' I said casually, laying them down on the grass and tactfully forbearing to mention what was inside them. I wished she could have seen how quickly they were eaten and how greedily fingers were licked afterwards, although Rosie still kept back the last pieces of her crust to scatter carefully around the clearing for the rabbit.

'How about a game of hide and seek?' I suggested.

Rosie looked doubtful. 'I couldna 'ide on me own, Cat!'

'We'll hide together then!' So it was Thomas who first hid his face against the smooth trunk of the beech and counted while Rosie and I, hand-in-hand, scampered off. Under my tutelage, he'd just learned to count up to twenty but could go no further as yet. (And nor could I, until Pa had instructed me, but I wasn't telling him that!)

'Count up to twenty, twice!' I instructed as we left. 'And slowly!'

Within seconds, Rosie and I were squatting behind a briar from which, while hidden, we could still see Thomas. 'Cat,' Rosie whispered after a few moments, her position no doubt reminding her, 'I wanna go!'

'Go on, then!' For it was as good a place as any.

'Look t'other way then!'

I was doing that anyway with the necessity to keep an eye on Thomas. As I watched, he raised his head. 'Comin'!' After a quick glance around, he began to walk straight towards us. Beside me, Rosie was still tinkling hard. There was nothing for it but to rise to my feet and run for the tree, hoping to outdistance Thomas.

I didn't, of course; he'd had too much practice at mould-running, and after he'd 'caught' me, he went back in search of Rosie. I waited for his shout of discovery but to my surprise, it didn't come and I could hear him crashing around among the bushes. A moment later, Rosie shot out of the trees from completely the opposite direction and ran for the tree. She reached it with seconds to spare, breathless but triumphant. 'Tha' fooled 'ee, Tom Bailey!'

After that, there was no holding them. The

woods were their kingdom. When hide and seek palled, we wandered in search of daffies, but found them still furled in fat, green buds. But there were violets a'plenty, both mauve and white, fragile little wind-flowers and clover-leaved sorrel. Thanks to Annie, I knew the names of all of them.

When it was time to go, for I doubted we'd be so fortunate as to pick up the carrier twice in one day, it was with many a backward glance. 'But we'll come again!' I promised.

★ ★ ★

'Us'll see 'ee 'ome,' said Thomas as we reached the bottom of the hill.

'An' p'raps,' Rosie said wistfully, 'us might see yer Ma and thank 'er for them pasties.' This time, I decided, I would take the bull by the horns and ask them in.

But when we reached the end of their alley, it was to find a white-faced Sam looking out for us. ''Tis Ma,' he said. 'T'babby's comin' out afore its time and Ma Quiggan ain't 'ome!'

'C'mon!' said Thomas, beginning to run with Rosie at his heels.

Instinctively, I followed but then stopped. What good would I be? But Ma would know what to do. I started to run again but up the hill this time.

I shot into the back kitchen like a ball from a cannon. 'Rosie's Ma's having her baby! And Ma Quiggan's out!'

I've never known anyone like my Ma for dealing with an emergency. She'd grabbed her cloak, hissed at Pa to mind Emma and was on her way out while I was still getting my breath back. Over her shoulder, she called, 'Bring the rag bag, Cat! I doubt there'll be clean cloths down there!' And was off again while I seized the old pillow-case from beside the back door that held all the pieces that, one day, would 'come in useful'.

'When's the baby due?' Ma panted as we slithered over the cobbles.

'Not for some time, I think.'

''Twill be another miss then. Poor Lottie!'

Looking back, it is difficult to remember the exact sequence of events of that night. I remember the cold, damp smell of the room through which we passed and the sight of Seth Bailey, stretched out, comatose, upon a make-shift couch, an empty bottle clutched to his chest, and the way my mother, even in her haste, gathered up her skirts as she rushed past him, but then we were in the inner room and I had eyes only for the whey-faced woman on the bed, her features contorted with pain, strands of long, black hair clinging damply to her forehead.

''Tis Belle Marsh, Lottie. Come to take care o' 'ee,' said Ma, crossing to the bed and lapsing into the broad speech of that part of town.

The woman managed a twisted smile.

''Tis good o' 'ee, Belle.'

'How far had 'ee gone, Lottie?'

''Bout three months, Belle.'

And then Ma drew back the thin coverlet and I saw in the half-light — for there was only a single candle guttering on the window ledge — great gouts of what must be blood.

'Rags, Cat!' Ma said turning to me and then to Rosie and Thomas, hovering in the shadows (Sam was nowhere to be seen), 'Water! A pail of it!' She glanced toward the hearth but it was cold as charity. ''Twill have to be cold!'

For the next few minutes, I stood beside my mother, folding wads of rags as she required them, while the pile of those already saturated, grew steadily larger on the floor.

'That'll do!' said Ma at last. And rose to her feet, turning to take the water that Thomas and Rosie had brought.

'Cat — go back home and bring sheets and the spare blanket. Thomas, go with her and bring kindlin' and coal. Cat'll show 'ee where 'tis. Rosie — ask Cat's Da' to fill a basin from the soup-pot.'

66

We went; I, for one, glad to get away from the stench of the blood. For once, the smoke-laden air was like a fresh, spring breeze. In silence, we climbed the hill, explained to Pa what we wanted and returned as quickly as we could with our burdens.

When we got back, we found that Ma Quiggan had arrived at last and was helping my mother put the room to some sort of rights. 'Now,' Ma said briskly, 'back up the hill all of you, and tell Pa to fill three more basins. Then stay there. 'Ee'll sleep alongside Cat tonight, Rosie. An' Thomas can curl up on t'rug.'

And that's what happened. 'Whoever would have thought,' I said sleepily to Rosie that night as she lay beside me, 'that the day would end like this!'

But there was no reply, except for a gentle little snore from the other end of the bed. For 'top to toe,' Ma had decreed, 'what with Emma being in there as well.' And at least, I reflected, the feet beside me on the pillow were now clean for Ma had seen to that, too. It was then we'd made the wonderful discovery that Emma's second-best pair of shoes fitted Rosie exactly. They stood at the bottom of the bed now, where Rosie would see them the moment she opened her eyes. Her very own shoes, at last!

4

From that day, the quality of Rosie's life was greatly improved. Now, when we were on earlies, she would stay with me overnight and when their mother's cough was bad, both she and Thomas would share our supper although, upon these occasions, Lottie Bailey would insist upon sending some contribution to the meal.

'But where does it come from?' I asked Ma, fingering a whole bag of sugar that would last us a month at least.

'From Mill House, no doubt,' said Ma. 'What puzzles me,' she added before I could probe further, 'is how it escaped Seth Bailey's grasping hands.'

'Oh, that's easily explained,' I said airily. 'Rosie's Ma hides things up the chimney where the drunken old bugger can't reach.'

I was merely quoting Rosie's own words but I should have known better. Ma shook her head at my language. 'Oh, Cat! Sometimes I wish . . . '

'Wish what, Ma?'

'That you had other friends than Rosie and Thomas.'

'Ma!' I was deeply shocked. 'I love Rosie and Thomas.'

'I know, child. It's just that . . . '

'That what, Ma?'

She sighed, 'It's wishing for the moon, but sometimes I wish we lived somewhere else. That you could grow up like your Cousin Annie.'

'But Ma, *she* envies *me*! She longs to work as I do.'

'She won't think that when she's older and her mind turns to young men and marriage. Who will there be for you to marry, Cat?'

I looked at her in astonishment. 'I shall marry Thomas, of course!'

Ma stared at me, her astonishment equal to mine but for a vastly different reason. 'Oh, Cat, what be 'ee thinkin' of? A son o' Seth Bailey's?' I can always tell when Ma is upset about something, her speech slips back into the language of her childhood.

'But I've just told you, Ma,' I insisted with the unshakeable conviction of a ten-year-old. 'I love Thomas. And he loves me. I'm sure of it.'

I was, too, although I would never want to put to the test whether he loved Rosie more than me. They were brother and sister, after all, I often reminded myself and therefore his love for her could be no real threat. But I could see that Ma could not — or would not — accept my feelings. Suddenly, I feared that I had said too much; that she would in some way try to come between us and would not welcome Thomas into our house so willingly. Fear made me cunning.

'Don't worry, Ma,' I said lightly. 'I'm not serious. I probably won't marry anyone but look after you and Pa in your declining years.' And I gave her a great hug and, I think, pacified her for Thomas still continued to be invited to our house and the matter was not discussed again.

But it did not stop me thinking about it. One day, Thomas would rise from mould-runner to presser and earn good money. I, too, might gain promotion when Hannah married and started a family and what would there be then to stop us? Pa would talk Ma round in the end, I felt sure.

And so the waiting years, as I thought of them, passed pleasantly enough although not without their worries. Greatest among these was Pa's failing health. Like most men who had worked at the potbank since childhood and breathed in the polluted air that lay over the town like a pall, he had always coughed. But now it gradually became worse and I suddenly realised one day that my mother no longer nagged at him to put himself forward at the Hirings but instead fed him nourishing little bowls of beef tea when Emma and I were tucking into tatties and bacon bits, and insisted that he always wore, even in the house, one of the comforters she'd knitted for him.

And as his health deteriorated, so did my value appreciate. I even heard them talking one night when they thought me asleep of how soon Emma could be put to work.

'I'd always hoped . . . ' I heard Ma say on a gusty sigh, and I guessed her ambition for Emma was even greater than for me.

Sunday School became a thing of the past as I learned — under Pa's supervision from his rocking chair — to cobble shoes and to split firewood so neatly that not a sliver of wood was wasted. And when Ma started to take in washing all the year round and not just at Christmas, I learned how to bake. It seemed sometimes as if I was learning everything except that which I desired most — to read fluently and to write.

Now and then, I would catch myself gazing wistfully at a news-sheet and wishing that I need not rely upon others for my scant knowledge of what was going on in the outside world and even, on occasion, upon my own doorstep. There had been rumours of strikes in some parts of the Potteries although not in our particular potbank for our master was better than many. But even he was careful not to tell us of the formation of something called Unions in certain areas where men were banding themselves together against the owners. Even so, the rumours got through. One day, I promised myself, I would learn at first hand about these happenings.

In due course, Hannah married her Will and Rosie, Thomas and I attended the ceremony, although Thomas insisted upon remaining at the rear of the church. Afterwards, we all crowded into Hannah's Aunty Mary's little cottage and ate furmety and drank ale or tea before the happy couple, to the accompaniment of much whistling and ribald comments from the men which I did not fully understand but Rosie clearly did, went off to the cottage Will had been whitewashing for the last month.

'See you in the morning!' Hannah called to us as she went.

'Don't 'ee be late, neither!' Rosie called back with great sauciness.

'Rosie!' I remonstrated.

'Ee, don't take on so, our Cat! 'Er knows I mean no 'arm.' She tucked her arm through mine and together we wandered up the hill to our house. She was to stay the night for we were on early in the morning. There, we found Pa fast asleep in his rocker and Ma and Emma out upon some errand. There was cobbling waiting to be done and a pile of stockings to be darned but somehow, after the festivities of the day, it was impossible to settle to such humdrum tasks.

It was Rosie who took down the fly-blown mirror from the kitchen wall and carried it in to the bedroom. 'Let's look at oursels, Cat!'

There was no mirror in Rosie's house and only a tiny sliver of glass in our workshop that Hannah used to put her hat on straight. The discovery of our mirror — used mostly by Pa when he was shaving — had opened up a whole new world of self-knowledge for Rosie.

'Be that me, then?' she'd whispered when, round-eyed, she'd first looked into it.

'Yes, Rosie, that's you,' Ma had agreed gently. 'And a very pretty little girl you are, too.'

I could hardly believe my ears. Ma never said anything like that to me! But Rosie *was* pretty, there was no denying it and now, on the day of Hannah's wedding, there was a beauty about her that caught at my throat. Lately, her skin had acquired a bloom and her regularly washed hair a gloss that spoke well for Ma's provision of nourishing food.

Now, she held the glass so that she could examine her chest. 'Me tits are gettin' big!'

she observed and then, glancing at me, 'So's yers, Cat!'

She was right. The little bumps on my chest were growing plump and sometimes painful and Ma had murmured something about the bodices I must soon go into.

'We'se growin' up!' said Rosie with satisfaction. 'Us'll be gettin' wed oursels, afore us knows it!' She gave me a knowing smile. 'Do men look at 'ee now, Cat? As if they wanted more'n the time o' day?'

I felt my cheeks redden with embarrassment. The only man I'd noticed looking at me like that was her brother, Sam. Since the day Rosie had flown at him, he'd remained aloof but sometimes I would catch him looking at me when our paths crossed at the potbank with a lascivious gleam in his eye and feel again the terror that had surged through me then. But there was no way I could speak to Rosie of such things. Perhaps it was as well that Ma and Emma came back at that moment and we had to tell them all about the wedding.

★   ★   ★

Two weeks before my fourteenth birthday, something happened that was to change my whole life; to change all our lives.

74

Hannah had just declared she was pregnant and that she planned to leave work in a few months. It would only be for a short while as Aunty Mary would care for the baby during the day with Hannah going over to feed it during her dinner hour.

'I've had a word with John Finnegan,' she told me, 'and he's agreeable to you taking over while I'm away. It won't be for long but 'twill give you a taste of what's to come when I have more babbies.' That Hannah would have more babies went without saying. That she had gone so long without conceiving for the first time was a source of wonderment to both Rosie and me. For by now, I was as knowledgeable as she about the facts of life, especially since I'd started my 'monthlies'.

''Tis to do with growing up, Cat,' Ma had tried to explain on the morning I'd woken with blood all over my nightdress. 'You're a woman now and able to have babbies of your own. Not that you will, of course,' she'd added hurriedly, clearly wanting to get the whole matter settled, 'not for a long time yet.'

Some devil of wickedness had possessed me to try her further. 'But how will I start the babbies in the first place, Ma?' I'd asked, tongue in cheek.

'Dinna even think such things afore you're

wed,' she'd said sharply. 'An' don't 'ee forget that, Cat Marsh!'

'But . . . ' I'd begun but then taken pity on her and closed my mouth.

'I've started,' I'd told Rosie smugly when we met at the gate of the potbank. And she knew immediately what I meant.

'Do it 'urt, Cat? Be 'ee in pain?'

'Not so's you'd notice,' I told her importantly. And in truth, it was the wad of bulky rag between my legs that was causing me the most discomfort.

On this particular day I've mentioned, neither Rosie nor Thomas had turned up for work although neither had shown any signs of illness on the previous day. When work finished, worried that something awful had happened, I screwed up my courage and turned up their alley on my way home. At once, I saw that several children were crowding around their door and as I drew near, one of them suddenly turned and ran past me, yelling something about 'fetchin' me Da'!'

My mouth suddenly dry with fear, I forced myself to walk on and in at the door which was open. The scene that met my gaze was one that I shall never forget as long as I live.

There was no door between the two rooms and through the opening, I could see Mrs

Bailey lying, with her eyes closed, on the bed with Rosie and Thomas kneeling beside her.

In the outer room, Seth Bailey was slouched on a chair, a bottle beside him, and clearly drunk as a lord. Sam stood near him. As I came in, they both looked up.

'Ah, Miss 'Igh an' Mighty,' said Sam. 'Tha's all us needs.'

Terrified but determined, I took a couple of steps towards the inner room. At the same moment, Rosie looked up and saw me. Leaving her mother's side, she ran towards me.

'Oh, Cat! I be tha' glad to see 'ee! Ma be dyin'!'

Forgetting all else, I took her hands. 'Rosie, how do you know? Has Ma Quiggan been? Shall I fetch my Ma?'

She shook her head. 'Ma Quiggan's bin an' gone. There's nuthing no-one can do. 'Er's jus' — wore out!' The last words ended on a wail of anguish. I put my arms around her and held her close. Over her shoulder, I saw Seth Bailey slurp from the bottle in his hand.

'Er's goin',' he said and there was a dreadful note of triumph in his voice. 'An' good riddance, I say. Nuthin' ter stop us doin' wot us've allus wanted ter do. An' yer know wot tha' is, Miss 'Igh an' Mighty? I'll tell 'ee. Fuck yer precious little Rosie, 'ere.

Tha's wot us'll de, once 'ers gone.'

I stared at him in horror, my mind unable to grasp the full enormity of what he was saying and when I spoke, my voice was high and shrill. 'You can't!' I said. 'Rosie is your daughter. It's against the law to — to — ' Even then, I could not say the word. But Seth Bailey had no such scruples.

'Fuck yer daughter? But she ain't me daughter, see? Never 'as been. Never will be. Ask 'er, if yer dinna b'lieve me.' And he lifted his hand to point at the poor woman on the bed.

Rosie lifted her head from my shoulder and glared at him. 'Dinna talk nonsense, Da!'

'Rosie! Come quick! Ma . . . ' Thomas suddenly called from the inner room and immediately Rosie ran to him, pulling me with her.

The woman on the bed — I had difficulty now in thinking of her as someone I knew, so gaunt and wasted had she become — was trying to say something. She tried to clear her throat and brought on a fit of coughing. Thomas put his arm around her and raised her a little from the pillow. The coughing stopped and we all three bent nearer.

''Tis true,' she whispered. 'Rosie's not 'is child. Nor mine.' She paused and Rosie leaned forward to pick up a cup of water from the floor beside the bed and hold it to her lips. She sipped and then continued. My heart, I found, had begun to pound in my breast like a hammer. Lottie Bailey was not the only one who found difficulty in drawing breath.

'My sister — Maggie,' she croaked. 'An' Frank — Mill'Ouse. 'Twas them who . . . '

And then the coughing came again and this time the water was of no help. Her eyelids fluttered then suddenly opened wide. For one brief moment, Lottie Bailey looked as she might have done when she was a young girl — her shining eyes were the colour of the violets in Wolstanton woods, her lips were parted in a smile that spoke of long-ago pleasure, even happiness. 'Bin — all — worth while,' she whispered. And then the eyelids closed and her breath seemed to shudder and then stilled.

'Oh, Ma!' Rosie wailed in a paroxysm of grief and I felt tears rolling down my own cheeks. But Thomas was on his feet, turning to face his brother whose bulk now filled the doorway.

For a brief moment, I thought he, too, had come to mourn but the delusion did not last. He was gazing at Thomas. 'Now, 'oo's master?' He jeered. And then, to my indescribable horror, he looked at me and I saw the lust in his eyes. ''Twon't be long now, Cat Marsh. There'll be no-one ter stop me, now 'er's gone. And wi' me Da' takin' care o' Rosie.' And he took a step towards me.

Afterwards, I found it difficult to remember the sequence of the events that followed. I knew only that as Sam moved towards me, Thomas seemed to leap to the corner of the room and the next moment was brandishing an old shovel that must have stood there.

'Keep yer distance, Sam Bailey. I'm warnin' 'ee.' And he raised the shovel above his head.

Whether he would actually have brought it down upon Sam's head and possibly killed him, thereby earning at best his deportation or worse, hanging at the next assizes, I shall never know. I still wake at night sometimes and shudder at the memory of it all.

But as it was, there came a sudden commotion in the outer room and the next moment a man — a stranger to me — had Sam by the arms and Rosie had leapt at Thomas and seized the shovel. And the next, like a blessed miracle, Hannah and Will were there and Hannah, after one quick glance at the bed, had put her arms around Rosie and me and was leading us away out into the darkness of the alley. Behind us, Will escorted Thomas, a Thomas still struggling to get at Sam.

'Leave 'im be, Thomas,' I heard Will say and Thomas ceased to struggle.

Then Hannah took charge. 'You'll come home with me tonight, you two. And Cat, love, you go home quickly. Your Ma'll be wonderin'. Will, see her to her door.'

And Will did, his arm around my shoulders and told Ma, as briefly as possible, what he knew of the night's events while I sobbed out the rest in her arms; sobbed for so many things that would never be the same again.

* * *

Later, after I had dried my eyes and Ma had spooned bread and milk into my mouth as if I were still a child and Emma, protesting violently, for clearly there was drama in the air, had been sent to bed, she told me the whole sad story. Pa had gone early to bed that night and heard nothing of it.

'Lottie's twin sister, Maggie, was housemaid at Mill House. A lovely girl, just like Lottie was before she took up with Seth Bailey. Men fell for her like ninepins and Master Frank was no exception. Eighteen, he was and old enough to know better you might think but he'd led a narrow life — his Pa was a proper tyrant — and meeting Maggie must have been like an answer to prayer. Anyway, upshot was she got in the family way and all hell broke loose. Young Frank, to give him his due, wanted to stick by her but of course his Pa wouldn't hear of it. He was sent off to the other side of the world to a distant relative and is still there as far as I know. If it hadn't been for his Ma standing up to his Pa for once in her life, Maggie would have been shown the door and left to manage as best she could. But as it was, she was sent away somewhere to have the baby — and she died in labour. So Lottie took the child — she'd been carrying herself at the time but her baby had been stillborn. What with Maggie and she being twins and Rosie looking so much like her Ma, hardly anyone knew. I did because I was friendly with Lottie at the time, before Seth took to the drink. And old Mrs Osborne up at Mill House stuck to her side of the bargain she'd made with Maggie and every now and then Lottie was sent something to help her care for Rosie and that's still going on as far as I know. It stopped being money early on when Seth took it for ale. I don't know what will happen now poor Lottie's dead.'

'Rosie won't stay now,' I said with certainly. 'Not now her Ma's gone. She can't.' And I told Ma as best I could about the threats Seth

Bailey had made. 'And he meant them, Ma. I know he did. Rosie won't be safe there any more.'

For a moment, Ma was shocked into silence. 'The poor little lass. What's to become of her, then?'

'Thomas will look after her,' I said. And, for the first time, I faced the full significance of what I had learned that night. Rosie and Thomas were cousins, not brother and sister. There would be no impediment now to their eventual marriage.

I couldn't bring myself that night to tell Ma of Sam's threats and by morning I didn't need to. Ma had put me to sleep alongside her in the big bed she shared with Pa and all night, when I wasn't lying awake reliving it all, I was in the grip of nightmares, threshing about and screaming out Sam's name until, Ma told me next day, she'd feared the neighbours would hear.

'You can't go back to the potbank,' she said when I'd told her the whole story, 'that's for certain.'

'But Ma, I must. We need the money. Hannah will look after me.'

'Hannah can't look after you night and day and your Pa isn't the man he was.' In fact, Pa had slept through most of the night's disturbances and was still abed.

'And you're not going in there today, anyway,' Ma added. 'You're in no fit state.' And, in truth, I wasn't. I felt as if I'd been stamped underfoot by a heard of elephants. Ma put a hand on my forehead. 'You're fearsome hot, Cat.'

In the end, Ma went down to the potbank herself, to see Hannah and John Finnegan. Two hours later, she was back — and with a new spring in her step.

'I've been taken on in your place,' she told me, 'starting next week.' And as I continued to stare at her, unable to believe my ears, 'Forgot I used to be a transferor when I was your age, hadn't you Cat?' And, in truth, I had. 'Hannah says I'll soon get the hang of it again. She'll help me. So, by the time she leaves to have the babby, I should be able to take over.'

'But Emma,' I protested weakly, 'and Pa.'

'I'll take Emma with me. She's old enough. It isn't what I had in mind for her but, needs must. And Pa?' She glanced across at Pa, already nodding off in the rocker. 'He'll be all right 'til I get home.'

'And — me?' I hardly dared ask what was to become of me.

'Ah, yes — you!' Ma looked at me with a smile on her lips. 'I'm still not sure about you! I'll have a word with your Pa when he wakes up. You go back to bed, now.'

But there was one more thing I had to know. 'Rosie?' I croaked. 'And Thomas? What of them?'

Ma sobered instantly. 'Gone,' she said, 'sometime in the night. When Hannah and Will awoke this morning, they'd just disappeared. She's that worried but what can she do?'

Although I'd half expected it, I was devastated by her news. Never to see Rosie and Thomas again! It was unthinkable. But, like Hannah, what could I do? If only they could have written a message — left some token of love and, perhaps, regret.

It wasn't until several days later when my own future had at last been decided, that I found it; the square of cloth embroidered with the letter R that I had once sewn for Rosie and which she must have kept. She must have pushed it under our door the night they left and it had been kicked aside by whoever had next opened the door, thinking it no more than a piece of rubbish.

But it wasn't rubbish. I picked it up and held it to my cheek. It was the only way Rosie could think of, to say goodbye.

5

I first came to Ashling on a summer evening, across the fields. Overawed by the lodge-keeper's cottage at the gates and the driveway stretching into the distance, I took a narrower way pointed out to me by the carrier when he dropped me there. So I walked between hedges thick with bramble flowers and wild roses, enjoying the stretching of my limbs after sitting all day in the several carts that had brought me from one end of the country to the other.

I tried not to dwell upon the tearful farewells of the morning as my family had started me upon my way.

'We'll see 'ee soon, my Cat!' Ma had whispered, pushing into my hand the packet containing the slices of bread, the pieces of pie and furmety that were to last me through the day. 'Christmas, if not afore.'

She spoke as if Lichfield were a mere stone's throw from our house, as if I would be calling in weekly if not daily. I was not at all sure about Christmas, either. Surely that would depend upon the goodwill of my new employers. All I knew of them at the moment was that they owned a big house several miles from the cathedral city of Lichfield.

'What's a cathedral?' I had asked Pa on one of his good days.

'A big church. A very big church indeed.'

'Bigger than Wolstanton?'

'I would think so.' For even Pa had not seen one.

It was Pa's relatives at Wolstanton who had arranged my new employment. A distant cousin held the post of housekeeper in another big house and she knew of this post of between servant.

'Between what?' I'd asked.

Since the news was being relayed through my uncle at Wolstanton, no-one knew.

'Between people?' Pa suggested. 'A sort of messenger between the Master and the rest of the household? 'Twould suit you well, Cat. You're a fine runner!'

'Carrying food from the kitchen to wherever the quality eat,' was Ma's idea. 'An' if 'tis so, no picking on the way, mind!'

''Twill be a good position whatever it is,' Pa said comfortingly.

'But if you don't like it,' Ma put in, 'you're to come straight back.'

But I was determined, whatever it was like, that I wouldn't go back, much as I hated to leave the familiar presence of my family. Even when I rounded a bend in the lane and saw the size of the house in front of me and felt my heart leap in sheer terror, the thought of turning my back on it never crossed my mind.

It was made of bricks but bricks of a beautiful rosy-red and with a golden creeper that sprawled around the tall windows and the massive door that was reached by two flights of curving steps. 'In the Georgian style', I was later to hear it described but at the time I saw it only as the largest, most intimidating building I had ever seen. And how was I to find my way into it?

I put down the bag of shiny, plaited straw that Ma had bought cheaply from the market and which held all my worldly goods and tried to come to terms with its grandeur; and immediately became aware that I needed to empty my bladder. Leaving my bag where it was, I went to squat behind a bush. And it was thus, in a position of some discomfort — for, as luck would have it, I had chosen a thistle to crouch upon! — that I saw Edward for the first time.

He was taller than I, but not, I guessed, much older; perhaps two or three years. And, like the house, he was beautiful. His cap was perched at the back of his head and I saw how his fair hair rose like a plume from a high forehead. His features were in perfect proportion, a long, straight nose above a full, almost sensuous mouth and the line of his jaw cleanly cut. None of this did I fully appreciate until later; all I knew at that first sight was that he was the most handsome young man I had ever seen and that I was likely to be discovered in the most embarrassing position possible.

He had come from the same direction as myself. Under his arm he held a gun and from a belt buckled around his jacket a rabbit hung. He stood gazing down at my bag and I cursed my stupidity in leaving it there. And then he looked around him and I held my breath as his eyes — a deep blue, I noticed even in my predicament — seemed to gaze straight at me. But then he moved away in the opposite direction with his back to me and I rose quickly to my feet, adjusted my dress and came out into the open. Afterwards, I was to wonder if he had, in fact, seen me and had deliberately moved away in order to give me time to collect myself.

He turned and saw me. 'Good evening!' he said, sweeping his cap from his head. 'And you are . . . ?'

From the way he spoke, I knew that he had every right to ask the question.

'Catherine Marsh, sir.' And I bobbed a

quick curtsey. 'The new between servant.'

'Indeed,' he said gravely, although I suspected he was as ignorant as I of its meaning. 'And I am Edward Marshall and I live — over there.' He nodded in a familiar fashion towards the house. 'So it seems as if we are both going in the same direction.'

He picked up my bag and walked out on to the sweep of tree-studded grass that lay between us and the house, clearly expecting me to go with him.

'Interesting, is it not,' he said, 'that our names should be so similar? I wonder if it was your family who lost a letter or two or mine who added them on?'

'I'll ask my father, sir,' I said without thinking for that was my usual reaction when faced with something I did not know. And then, remembering all over again that I would not have that opportunity for many a long day, if ever, the treacherous tears that I had fought all day, suddenly spilled over and I had to stop and knuckle furiously at my eyes.

He seemed to know immediately what the trouble was. 'Poor Catherine! I am so sorry. Have you come a long way to be a — a between servant for us?'

'From Burslem, sir. I don't know how many miles but it has taken all day.'

'And you are tired — hungry, no doubt.

The sooner we get you home the better.'

'Home, sir?' For one foolish moment, I had thought he meant back to Burslem.

He waved a hand towards the house. 'I mean Ashling, Catherine. Your home as well as mine, from now on.'

★ ★ ★

That night, as I lay in bed, longing for the warmth of Emma's body beside me — had I really complained when she'd dug her elbow into my ribs or turned on the pillow so that my mouth was full of her hair? — I thought how the last few hours had been made bearable by the knowledge that Edward was close by.

He had led me around the side of the house, across a cobbled yard where fan-tailed pigeons rose in a dappled cloud, and paused beside an open door.

'Follow me!' he ordered and went ahead down a stone passage and into an enormous kitchen. A fire, banked down for the night, smouldered between huge ovens and above it, a row of copper pans gave back the light of the setting sun. It shone through small windows set above two deep sinks and I guessed that some form of light would always be desirable in the far corners of the room. A dresser, crammed with plates of an identical blue and white pattern ran the length of one wall and in the centre of the room stood a scrubbed wooden table about four times the size of the one at home. Long benches had been pushed beneath the table.

As Edward entered, an immensely fat woman wearing a long white apron and with a frilled white cap on her head, moved towards one of the ovens, saying, 'Your supper's keeping hot, Master Edward.'

And then, seeing me, she stopped and looked me over as if I were a beast at a fat-stock market. I quite expected her to put out a hand and feel my muscles. 'Who's this, then?'

'Catherine Marsh, Mrs Clifford, and she's come all the way from Burslem to be our between servant.'

'Has she indeed?'

'You weren't expecting her?'

'The mistress did say something about her, now I come to think of it.' Instinct told me that she'd remembered full well that I was coming and that this was her way of putting me in my place right from the start. But I didn't need reminding. I stepped forward and bobbed my curtsey but waited to be spoken to directly before opening my mouth.

'I've no doubt my mother would like to

meet her,' said Edward, 'and I'm going to the drawing room. Shall I take her with me?' He must have known the suggestion was preposterous and could not have been surprised when Mrs Clifford bridled alarmingly.

'Indeed you'll do no such thing, Master Edward! *I* will do that! Come, child!' And she moved ahead of us towards a door at the far end of the kitchen. She moved slowly and I guessed her feet were troubling her at the end of a long day — but majestically as if carrying all before her. And indeed, Mrs Clifford had more than most to carry!

Winking at me behind her back, Edward motioned me to follow and then fell into position behind me. We must have presented a comic sight as we processed across the floor and certainly, the face of the young girl who came into the room as we left it, cracked into a broad grin when she saw us.

'Take that smile off your face, Ada!' ordered Mrs Clifford and immediately the grin faded. But she was about the same age as Emma and I could not resist smiling at her as we passed.

'Hello, Ada!' said Edward cheerfully. 'I'll be back for my supper, directly.'

'That you'll not be,' said Mrs Clifford over her shoulder. 'Not tonight, Mr Edward, if you don't mind.' And I guessed that it was my presence that was causing her to forbid what sounded to be a normal happening.

We processed onward down a further stone-flagged corridor and through a stout door covered, on the far side, with green baize. Beyond lay a stretch of plum-coloured carpet into which my feet sank as if it were moss. We crossed a huge hallway from which a wide stairway spiralled upwards into the shadows and paused before a white-painted door upon which Mrs Clifford knocked lightly.

'Come!' a woman's voice commanded.

I will never forget my first interview with Mrs Marshall. Perhaps it was Edward's friendly welcome that had made me think his mother would act in a similar fashion but I could not have been more mistaken.

She wore a gown of lavender silk and sat upon a velvet sofa of a slightly darker shade. Her grey hair was sculpted into a pyramid of curls with a line of them arranged like a row of button-hooks across her forehead.

Beneath them hooded eyes of a penetrating, icy blue gazed balefully out at me. The long straight nose which sat so well upon Edward's face was like a great beak upon hers and the mouth beneath was thin-lipped and shaped like Emma's when faced with a spoonful of jollop. Inwardly, I shuddered for I knew that I would never please this woman. Outwardly, I tried to remain calm.

'Catherine Marsh, ma'am,' Mrs Clifford introduced me. 'The new between.'

'I am well aware of her name and her function within the household, thank you Mrs Clifford. Well, Catherine Marsh,' and the piercing gaze held not a jot of welcome. 'I hope you realise how fortunate you are to be here?'

'Yes, Ma'am,' I managed to whisper as I came out of my curtsey. 'And I shall try to give every satisfaction, ma'am.'

'I hope so, for I'll have you know we are in no need of more servants at Ashling Hall. Your post, Catherine Marsh, has been made for you at the request of your kinswoman. I understand there was a man from whose company it was desirable you should be removed as quickly as possible. But I'll have you know, girl,' and now the voice shrilled in my ears, 'that there will be no opportunity here for sluttish behaviour. Your parents may have turned a blind eye but I will not. Is that clear?'

'But, ma'am . . . ' astonishment at such a misrepresentation of events overcame my fear, 'it wasn't like . . . '

'Silence, girl!' And now the voice could

have belonged to a sergeant leading his troop. 'Or I shall regret my decision. Had not her vicar added his pleas to those of your relative, I would never have agreed to it in the first place. Take her away, Mrs Clifford, before I change my mind.'

And the next moment, I was being marched from the room. On the way, I passed Edward, now staring, goggle-eyed, at his mother. I think he might have spoken up for me had not his mother forestalled him.

'Edward,' she snapped, 'what are you thinking of, bringing that — that creature into my drawing room?'

For a moment, I thought it was a parting shot directed at me but then realised she meant the rabbit still swinging from his belt and now spattering drops of blood upon the carpet!

Once back in the kitchen, the tears poured down my cheeks and now I did not try to stop them. 'It's not true!' I sobbed. 'It's simply not true!' And the last word ended on a wail that seemed to go on and on as if my mouth were unable to close. The next moment, I was being clasped in Mrs Clifford's mighty arms and her hand was pressing me into the comforting warmth of her bosom.

'There, there, child! Don't 'ee take on so!

Sit 'ee down an' I'll make us a nice cup o'tea.' Even in my misery, I marvelled at the change from starchy disciplinarian into humane and homely woman. This, I felt, was the real Mrs Clifford. She sat me down in one of the two big Windsor chairs that stood either side the hearth and busied herself with the making of tea in a small brown pot. At some point, Ada appeared hopefully from a scullery that lay beyond the kitchen but was despatched immediately to her bed. The tea made, Mrs Clifford poured us both a cup and took the chair opposite mine.

'I'll cut 'ee a slice o' pie in a moment, Catherine. But first tell us your story.'

And I did, in between sips of the delicious, golden liquid that was so different from the weak brew I was used to. 'So you see, ma'am,' I ended, 'it was not at all as Mrs Marshall made out. I am not — and pray never will be — a slut. And nor was Rosie, poor though she was.'

'I believe 'ee, child.'

'But if you don't really need me, ma'am, then I will look for another post immediately.'

'You'll do no such thing,' she said vehemently. 'I've been askin' for a 'tween for months now. It's not true what she said. It's her way of lettin' you know who's Mistress here, as if there was ever any doubt.' There was no bitterness in her voice, only a grim resignation to the way things were.

My relief was huge, for much as I disliked my new employer, I guessed that I could work well with Mrs Clifford. 'So, what will my duties be, ma'am?' I dared to ask.

'Oh, a bit o' this an' a bit o' that. Don't 'ee worry now, Catherine. The mornin' will do. An' sleep in, if you want.'

'Thank you,' I smiled at her gratefully, 'but I'm used to rising early. And, if you're agreeable, ma'am, I should like to be called Cat.'

'That you shall be, child, quaint little scrap that you are. An' *I* prefer Mrs C.; that's what the others call me — at least, to my face!'

I wasn't sure that I liked being called 'a quaint little scrap' but it was better than 'slut' any day of the week.

And now, as I lay in my narrow bed under the eaves, my thoughts were of Edward. It was not that he had usurped Thomas in my heart but that he seemed set to occupy a completely separate part of it. Tom, while he had been near, was someone about whom I could dream and plan. Edward was quite beyond my reach and always would be. He stood up there on his pedestal, smiling down on me and with that, I was content.

6

I soon discovered what the work of a between servant consisted of; at least, as far as Ashling was concerned. It meant trying to fill the shadowy area between the duties of the housemaids, who looked after the people living on one side of the green baize door and the kitchen staff who lived on the other. On one side was opulence and privilege and on the other hard work and discipline. And a between was at the beck and call of both worlds. 'Dogsbody' my father would have called it.

If Rachel or Katie, the two housemaids, mislaid a brush or duster while working in the bedrooms, then I was the one sent to fetch it. And on chilly mornings, when extra fires were required, I was the one who helped Ada in the laying and lighting of them. If Mr Jolly, the butler, required his afternoon tea in his pantry, I was the one who took it to him.

And if one of the family rang the drawing-room bell and everyone else was occupied, I had to change quickly from my kitchen sacking into my white apron, and answer it. This, to my horror, occurred on my first morning.

In spite of Mrs C's suggestion, I had risen at six and had found Ada filling kettles at the pump set over one of the sinks.

'They'll be in for their tea,' she said briefly, still knuckling the sleep from her eyes.

I took up the bellows from the hearth and roused the smouldering coals into life, wondering who 'they' might be. I soon found out.

'You must be the new 'tween,' said a big, raw-boned girl with a mop of flaming red hair, coming into the kitchen. 'I'm Rachel. And this gormless length o' pump water is Katie.' And she indicated the girl hard on her heels and who was, in truth, as long and pale as Rachel was round and rosy.

'I'm Cat,' I said and, to be on the safe side, bobbed a brief curtsey before going back to help Ada at the sink.

'Don't 'ee be too willin',' Rachel advised, 'or folk'll put on 'ee.'

'Ark oo's talkin'!' said Katie. 'All the same,' she raised her eyebrows at Rachel, 'perhaps 'er could take up Jolly's tea fer us?'

And that was how it happened that my first encounter with Mr Jolly was in his bedroom, although, in fact I did not clap eyes on him until later.

As I'd been instructed, I knocked on his door on the landing below mine, holding the cup and saucer carefully in my other hand, and entered immediately. The room was in total darkness except for the glimmer of light from the candlestick I had placed on the floor outside. But it was enough to show me the bed straight ahead with a huge, shadowy mound under the covers.

'There's a table beside it,' Katie had told me. 'Put down the tea, then shake 'im, ever so gentle, 'till 'e wakes. Then leave 'im.'

I put down the tea then leaned over the pillow. On it, I could just make out the tassel of a nightcap. Placing my hand where I guessed his shoulder to be, I shook. Nothing happened. I shook harder and then harder until suddenly, the mound erupted into life. An arm shot out and caught me a glancing blow on the head and a voice shouted.

'Damn an' blast 'ee, girl, get out!'

I needed no second telling. Nearly knocking over the tea in my haste, I was out of the door and down the back stairs in a trice. As I rushed into the kitchen three pairs of eyes were lifted to mine.

'Orlright?' enquired Rachel with deceptive innocence.

'Where's yer candle?' asked Katie.

'Don't 'ee worry,' said Ada, moving

forward, 'I'll fetch it. E's the same 'ooever takes it,' she added as she passed me. It was only then they told me Mr Jolly had been a sergeant in the King's Own Staffordshire Militia and couldn't abide being woken from slumber.

'But 'is bark's worse'n 'is bite,' said Rachel comfortingly.

'An' yer get used ter dodgin'!' added Katie as I felt the lump growing on my forehead. 'Come and drink yer tea.'

★ ★ ★

It was some while later, after Mrs C. had sailed into the kitchen, once more the disciplinarian and treating me as if we had never exchanged confidences on the previous evening, and we had settled to our various tasks that a bell jangled among the row that hung above the door.

Mr Jolly was in the wine cellar, Rachel and Katie were up in the bedrooms and Ada was in the wash-house, up to her elbows in sudsy water. Fred, the young lad who doubled as footman and boot boy was out in the yard and I was shelling peas at one end of the kitchen table. At the other, Mrs C. was mixing the ingredients for a cake. She glanced up at the bells.

'Drawing room,' she said. 'But change yer apron first.'

I stared at her in horror. 'M — me, Mrs C.?'

She pretended to glance around. 'Don't see anyone else 'ere, do yer?'

'But what do I say?'

'Nothin' until yer spoken to.' And then, relenting slightly. 'Don't 'ee worry, Cat. Maybe 'tis the Master. 'E's a different kettle o' fish altogether.' I knew without her saying who the other kettle was.

I scurried down the passage and through the green baize door, then dropped into a sedate walk. 'If yer meet any o' the family on the way,' Mrs C. had told me in all seriousness, 'flatten yerself into the wall, stop breathin' an' look down at yer boots.'

And don't fart! I'd almost added, thinking how Rosie would have had no hesitation in saying it. But I mustn't think of Rosie now.

Fortunately, I met no-one. I crossed the hall to the drawing room door and raised my hand to knock, then paused as I heard the raised voices within.

'Really, my dear,' a male voice remonstrated, 'there is no need for this. Sophie and I can easily manage.'

'Yes, indeed, Mama,' agreed a younger, more vibrant voice.

'But there is no reason why either of you should manage, as you put it,' came Mrs Marshall's unmistakeable baritone. 'We employ sufficient servants to render any physical effort on your part completely unnecessary.'

What on earth was I to be told to do? Curiosity overcoming apprehension, I knocked and waited.

'Come!' boomed Mrs Marshall. Bracing myself, I opened the door and found her still sitting upon her sofa, but now clad in a dark blue day dress. In front of the open casement, stood a tall, middle-aged man wearing immaculate doe-skin trousers and cut-away jacket. Beside him stood a girl of perhaps ten years of age wearing a sprigged muslin dress over her pantaloons and who must be Edward's sister. As I came into the room, both turned from their contemplation of something halfway up the casement and instead contemplated me.

'Too short!' said Colonel Marshall but giving me a kindly smile.

'Not much taller than me,' confirmed Sophie, coming forward to stand beside me and make her point.

'Keep away!' snapped her mother as if I had cholera or the pox or at best, head lice. 'Marsh,' she continued and pointing upwards to the casement 'remove that insect!'

Hardly able to believe my ears, I followed her gaze and saw that a large, hairy spider had indeed ventured in from the garden and spun a glistening web across the folds of the velvet curtain. But short of clambering on the arm of a chair, which I would certainly have done had I been alone, there was no way I could reach it.

'I'll fetch a feather duster, ma'am,' I said and turned to go. But Sophie had other ideas.

'Marsh can stand on my shoulders!' she cried. And, hands around my waist, immediately propelled me across the room.

'Better you stand on mine, miss,' I said over my shoulder, at the same time catching sight of her mother, wide-eyed with horror and presumably struck speechless.

'Capital idea!' said her father and held his daughter steady as I knelt and she placed her neat little black pumps upon my shoulders. Holding on to her ankles, I rose carefully to my feet.

'Got it!' cried Sophie a moment later. 'Out you go, spider! No, you cannot crawl up my arm! Out!'

The violent movements of her upper body which accompanied her words proved too much for our delicately balanced structure. The next moment we were both sprawled upon the carpet in a tangle of arms and legs — and in fits of uncontrollable laughter.

'Are you all right, Marsh?' Sophie spluttered.

'Yes, thank you, miss. Are you?' I managed to reply as I spat out one of her long ringlets which had lodged in my mouth.

And then I became aware of her mother's figure looming above us. 'Sophie!' she snapped. 'You're late for your lessons. Off with you to the school room!' And to me, one single word. 'Go!'

I went. So did Sophie. Outside in the hallway with the door safely closed behind us, she squeezed my arm. 'I like you, Marsh! You're fun!' And then she danced away up the staircase.

Back in the kitchen I regaled Mrs C. with an account of my escapade.

'Oh, Cat, child, yer'll be the death o' me!' she said when I had finished, and she was still wiping the tears of laughter from her eyes. 'But take care, child, or the mistress will take against 'ee.'

'But she has already, Mrs C. She hates me, I know she does and I don't fully understand why.'

Mrs C. ceased from her spooning of cake mixture from bowl to tins and gave me a long, close look. ''Tis maybe because yer different, child. Yer speak better 'an most for a start. An' there's something about yer — the way yer carry yersel', maybe — that makes people look at yer twice. So I suppose some folk might think yer 'ad ideas above yer station.'

Into my mind came the memory of Sam Bailey calling me 'Miss 'Igh an' Mighty' and I shuddered.

Mrs C. must have noticed it. 'Not that folk 'oo know yer would think anythin' o' the sort,' she added kindly. 'Now get on with them peas or there'll be more ructions.'

Fred came in from the yard at that point with a message from Mr Loftus, the gardener and her attention was diverted, but as I shucked I tried to make sense of what she had said. It was Ma, of course, with her conviction that the Marshes were 'a cut above the rest', who was responsible for my speech and Pa, with his seemingly endless store of information and his willingness to pass it on to me, who had fed my imagination. But even he, I was beginning to realise, had not known everything. The affairs of a house such as this would have been quite beyond his comprehension. It was strange to think that I, his 'little Cat', was now in a position to learn more than he ever would. But I owed a great deal to him and to my mother and I resolved for their sakes, and in spite of the mistress's dislike of me, to make a success of my new life and to learn all that I could.

'I'll need someone to 'elp carry in them tatties,' said Fred behind me.

I shucked my last pea and looked across at Mrs C. 'I'll go, shall I?' I offered. No doubt there was a wrong way and a right way and a right way even of 'carryin' tatties' and I would learn the difference.

'Good girl!' said Mrs C. as I followed Fred out into the sunlit yard.

★ ★ ★

I did not see Edward on my first full day at Ashling but I heard his voice.

It was evening and I was in the wash-house beyond the kitchen helping Ada to sort out the piles of garments for the next day's wash, and with the door open into the passage.

He had come in from the yard, presumably with a rabbit or two for I heard him call out, 'Here you are, Mrs Clifford, a couple more for the pot. And talking of pots . . .'

'No, Master Edward, I'm that sorry but you can't eat your dinner in the kitchen no more. Your mother's forbade it.'

'My mother . . . but why, for heaven's sake?'

'That wasn't for me to ask, Master Edward, I'll have Ada bring it up to the dining room, shall I?'

'If you insist, but I'll see my mother about it directly.'

'You do that, Master Edward.'

'Oh, and Mrs Clifford, how is young Catherine? Survived her first day, has she?'

'She's doin' nicely, thank you, sir,' Mrs C. said flatly. And I sensed that I was the reason for Mrs Marshall's edict and Mrs C.'s refusal to talk about it, at least while I was within earshot.

At first, cold fury possessed me and I found myself stamping upon the pile of Mrs Marshall's petticoats and camisoles that Ada had placed beside the boiler. But then I chided myself for my lack of control. After all, would she have bothered to deny Edward his visits to the kitchen if she had not seen me as some sort of challenge or undesirable diversion? And, after all, he *had* asked after me.

7

In September of that first year, I was granted a whole day's holiday. Rachel and Katie, whose families lived in Lichfield, were allowed one a month and Ada only half a day, but since her family lived near in the village of Alrewas, she was allowed to stay overnight. I, however, had had to prove myself before any such privilege.

This had not been difficult, for a happy servant is a good one. And though many might have considered my life to be hard and cheerless, compared with my previous exist-ence, it was paradise. Not a day passed when I did not open the yard door and step outside to fill my lungs with sweet, clean, air. Sometimes, the scent of new-mown hay would fill my nostrils, sometimes the delicate perfume from the rose beds I could see through the archway, or the rich, pungent smell of sweet briar. Even the odour of horse dung from the stables that lay beyond a further archway, was somehow pleasing!

And the birds! The fantails had soon accepted me as a friend, especially when I had crusts to throw them, but often the sparrows would swoop from the roofs and seize the food from under their beaks and wagtails would venture in from the garden. Even when the rain fell, I would stand with my face upturned, knowing that it was pure and clean and untainted by smoke.

Every morning, I thanked God for it and prayed that, by some miracle, Ma and Pa and Emma would join me one day, although I knew, deep down, that it could never happen. And yet, it *had* happened to me! Out of adversity had sprung a new beginning and new friends, although I would never forget the old ones.

Thanks to Colonel Marshall, I had received news that my family was well although Pa still had his 'bad days'. It had come about like this. One of my duties was to collect the morning letters and place them upon a table in the hall. If there was no-one about, I would stand for a moment, trying to decipher the writing on the envelopes. This could be difficult because the written word bore little resemblance to the printed word with which I was familiar from Sunday School, but frightened that I would forget the little I had learned, I forced myself to try.

One morning, completely absorbed in the study of a large, fat envelope covered with seals and whose address was written in a particularly ornamental style with many loops and curlicues, I nearly jumped out of my skin when Colonel Marshall's voice came from just behind my shoulder.

'And to whom is it addressed, Marsh?'

I almost dropped the package in my alarm. 'I — I do not know, sir.' And then, emboldened by his kindly gaze, added, 'I wish that I did.'

'So — you cannot read, Marsh?'

'Not properly, sir. And not at all when the letters are joined like these.'

'And you would like to learn?'

'Oh, more than anything, sir!'

He smiled at my enthusiasm. 'I will see what I can do then.'

He took the letters from me and said no more so I bobbed and left him.

All that morning, my mind seethed with excitement. What could he have in mind? Sharing Sophie's lessons with Miss White, the governess who came each day? Surely not, and yet — how else could I learn?

In the afternoon, just after Ada and I had finished washing the midday dishes, Mr Jolly came to find me.

'Are you in trouble, Marsh?'

'Trouble, Mr Jolly?' I stared at him, perplexed. 'I don't *think* so, sir. Why do you ask?' Quickly I thought back over the happenings of the day and suddenly, my heart skipped a beat. Had news of my conversation with Colonel Marshall reached the Mistress? Was I about to be dismissed for my revolutionary desire? A between wanting to read and write? Whatever next!

'I only ask,' said Mr Jolly, 'because the Master wishes to see you in the library. Apron!' he added automatically, as I dried my hands on my sacking and prepared to depart. 'And Marsh, remember that if you do ever have worries, Mrs Clifford and I are always here to listen to 'em.'

'Thank you, Mr Jolly.'

'Off with you then!'

He was a good sort was, old Jolly, I thought as I sped away. At least, once he was up and about!

As I entered the library, Colonel Marshall turned from the window. 'Ah, Marsh, come in! I won't keep you a moment.' He was jingling the small change in his pocket and I saw that he looked strangely discomfited, almost guilty. 'I'll come straight to the point, Marsh,' he continued. But he did not; he just stood there, jingling and frowning and clearly at a loss for words. 'It's a shame,' he burst out suddenly, 'it's a crying shame!'

'Sir?'

'That you cannot read or write, Marsh.'

And now I was the one who began to look guilty. 'I have tried to learn, sir, honestly . . . '

'I'm sure that you have, Marsh. That is not at all what I mean. It is a shame that you are still not to be allowed to.'

'Not — allowed, sir?'

He took a grip on himself, then. When he spoke again, his voice was quiet and controlled. 'I had hoped, Marsh, to arrange for you to receive instruction from Sophie's governess. Sadly, I have been told that this would not be — proper.'

Poor man! I thought. How could he ever have thought otherwise? For I knew immediately that it was the Mistress who had declared it to be improper.

'Don't fret, sir,' I said gently. 'I quite understand.'

He shook his head wearily. 'I doubt if you do understand fully, Marsh. But thank you for your forbearance.' And then he straightened and said, 'But perhaps there is one way in which I can help you. At the moment, I imagine it is difficult for you to communicate with your family?'

'Impossible, sir.'

'Then I will do it for you, Marsh, if you will permit. I will write to — whom? Your vicar in Burslem, perhaps?'

'We're chapel folk, sir. Nonconformist, I think you call it.'

'So you will have a minister?'

'I suppose so, sir.' I was doubtful for neither Pa nor Ma attended regularly. And then I remembered my cousin at Wolstanton. 'I have an uncle, sir . . . ' I began.

And so it was arranged. Ten minutes later, I returned to the kitchen in a daze.

'Well?' said Mr Jolly, who was drinking tea at the table with Mrs C. and clearly awaiting my return.

I smiled at them both. What kind creatures they were! And so, I reminded myself, was Colonel Marshall. I must be careful not to diminish him in their sight.

'It was about my family,' I told them. 'The Master has offered to find out for me, how they are. He will write to my uncle at Wolstanton.'

'He's a good officer, is the Master,' said Mr Jolly, rising from the table. 'Believes in lookin' after his men!' His mind clearly at rest about me and also, perhaps, satisfied that there was nothing going on among 'his men' that he did not know about, Mr Jolly inclined his head to Mrs C. and left us.

'Get yerself a cup, Cat,' Mrs C. said, 'and sit 'ee down fer a minute.'

''Tis strange,' she continued once I was

settled, 'that someone 'oo speaks so well can't write fer 'erself.'

'But it is so,' I said miserably. 'Ma could never see any reason for my learning. I think Pa could, but it was Ma's opinion that counted in our house.'

'As 'tis in most 'ouses,' Mrs C. said with a wry grin. 'Certainly in this one.'

I said nothing but looked up at her from beneath my lashes, and waited.

She poured herself another cup of tea. ''Tis a cryin' shame,' she said and I thought how strange it was that she used the very same words as the Master. 'As Mr Jolly said, the Master's a good man. But 'tis the Mistress 'oo 'as the money that keeps this place goin'. Wot's 'ers should be 'is, by rights, but it'd take a stronger man than 'im to stand up to 'er.' And then, thinking perhaps that she had said too much, she drained her cup and stood up. I did the same.

'By the way,' she said, turning towards one of the Windsor chairs, for it was time for the obligatory, daily 'resting' of her eyes, 'you can 'ave next Tuesday off. Even the Mistress can't deny yer that!'

And so it was, on this beautiful September morning that I danced my way across the fields to Alrewas — and my first ride in a steam train!

What I should do with my day off had become the main topic of conversation in the kitchen once it was common knowledge.

'Stay in bed!' said Fred, who always did. I shuddered at the thought of such a waste.

'Polish your boots,' said Mr Jolly. 'An' wash your aprons.'

'But that won't take all day,' I pointed out.

'Me Ma'd be pleased to see yer,' Ada offered. 'Yer could 'elp wi' the new babby.'

''Er don't want to *work* on 'er day off!' Rachel said.

'*I* allus 'ave to!' Ada muttered and I gave her a smile of sympathy. I knew what she meant. At least, living away from home meant that I would have the whole day to myself.

'Yer could go to *my* Ma's,' Katie suggested. ''Tis no distance from the station.'

'She can't go to Lichfield on 'er own,' said Mrs C. firmly. 'A little lass like 'er.'

'Wot's wrong wi' Lichfield?' Katie bridled. ''Tis the best city on God's earth.'

'That's as mebbee . . . ' said Mrs C. darkly.

But my imagination had been fired. 'No distance from the station,' Katie had said, not thinking twice about it for she and Rachel always travelled home on the train from Alrewas station. But I had never been on one. And I did not think that Lichfield, after Burslem, would hold any terrors for me.

'I shall be quite safe,' I told Mrs C. and, remembering my father's words, 'I'm a good runner.'

'Yer'll be safe as 'ouses,' said Rachel. 'An' tell Bert 'Ollis at the ticket office yer under twelve an e'll let yer go 'alf-price. Bend yer knees and 'e won't know the difference? Thick as a plank is Bert!'

Bert Hollis, we all knew, was sweet on Rachel — and she on him, although she would never have admitted it.

Harvest was well over, but several women and children were bent over the golden stubble as I crossed the fields, gleaning into the folds of their aprons. They looked up as I passed and returned my wave. For I waved at everything that morning; a baby rabbit that scuttled across my path — Rosie, where are you now? — a blackbird pecking away at the scarlet berries of a rowan tree, a herd of cows that gazed at me with their soft, dark eyes — and of whom I was no longer afraid.

Now and again, I stopped to pluck a blackberry from a hedge, admiring as I did so, the crimson berries of the hawthorn and the purple clusters of sloe. But I did not linger. Cat Marsh could not risk missing her first train!

I had already visited Alrewas with its quaint, half-timbered cottages and thatched roofs but it was the new station building that I headed for.

'A return, second-class ticket to Lichfield, if you please,' I said importantly to Bert Hollis but did not mention my age. However, I guessed from the amount of coins he pushed back at me along with my ticket, that he had only charged me half-fare. Wondering if Rachel might have spoken to him about me, I thanked him politely and pocketed my money carefully. There would be market stalls in Lichfield, Rachel and Katie had told me, and there would be no need for me to spend money on food for Mrs C. had packed me more slices of bread and cheese than I could possibly eat and Mr Loftus had given me a big, rosy apple.

There would be 'pumps enough to slake the thirst of a regiment', Mr Jolly had told me. 'An' 'tis the purest water in the country, pumped straight from the springs. No fear o' the cholera in Lichfield.' And we had exchanged meaningful glances for we both knew of the terrors of that dreadful disease, he from his service abroad and I from having lived among the cesspits and foul drainage of Burslem. Two of my friends had died of it when I was small. But I had no intention of spoiling this beautiful day with such grim thoughts.

119

Bert Hollis now appeared beside me on the platform and shouted out, as if addressing a multitude although I was the only person there, that the five minutes past nine train for Lichfield from Burton was about to arrive in the station. I wondered if I should thank him for the information or just gaze purposefully down the track as he was now doing. But then the appearance of the clanking, snorting monster with steam belching from its tall chimney took the decision from me; normal speech was now quite impossible.

'All aboard!' shouted Bert, still addressing his multitude, and I moved forward towards one of the carriages.

'Not that un!' shrieked Bert. 'Tha's First Class, tha' is!' and he took my elbow and directed me towards another carriage.

'That's all right, Bert!' said, or rather shouted, a familiar voice behind us and turning, I saw, to my astonishment — but also my delight — that Edward was standing there, an enormous grin threatening to split his face in two. I had not seen him for several weeks for he had been away, staying with an old school friend.

'Miss Marsh will travel with me in First Class, Bert.'

'But 'er ticket's Second,' Bert bawled. 'An' you ain't got no ticket at all Master Edward!

Beggin' yer pardon!'

'Don't worry, Bert, I'll pay at the other end. And the difference on Miss Marsh's. Promise!' he added for Bert still looked doubtful.

And the next minute, I was being helped up into a carriage, the door had been slammed and, with a mighty explosion of steam from the engine, we were leaving Bert behind. I could not have been more excited had I been going to the moon.

The journey would take only fifteen minutes to Lichfield, Edward told me so I must make the most of it, and this I did, peering from side to side, as he pointed out places of interest.

'And just over there, behind those trees, is Ashling. You can just see the tops of the chimneys.' I gazed imagining Mrs C. and the girls busy about their tasks; lugging in coals, dusting the drawing room, serving breakfast to the family. And then, I had a vision of Mrs Marshall presiding over the coffee pot while Mr Marshall read the news sheets and Sophie wolfed down her bacon and eggs.

'Edward,' I said urgently, 'that is, *Master* Edward, does your mama know that you are here with me?'

He burst out laughing. 'How can she? I did not know myself that I was to have the pleasure until Mrs Clifford told me you were bound for Lichfield on the train. As you know, I only just arrived in time.'

Slowly, I digested this information. Surely he could not mean that he was here beside me solely because he desired my company? The possibility was too intoxicating to consider; I put it to the back of my mind for future consideration.

'This is your first visit to Lichfield, is it not, Marsh?' he continued. And then, 'Confound it, I cannot continue to address you as Marsh for the rest of the day! May I call you Catherine?'

'Cat, sir, if you please.'

'Very well, then. Cat. And no more of this 'sir' and 'Master', either. My name, as you well know, is Edward.'

'Your mama would not like it,' I felt obliged to point out.

He looked around him. 'I do not see my mama here, do you?' And when I giggled helplessly, 'There, that's settled! I will show you Lichfield. If, that is, you have no other plans for the day?'

'Only to bring Mrs C. a length of purple ribbon to trim her Sunday bonnet.'

'That we will do immediately we arrive and then the rest of the day will be ours to enjoy as we please.'

And so began the greatest magic of that truly magical day.

We started, as Edward had promised, in the market place where he insisted upon paying for Mrs C.'s ribbon. Had I been on my own, I would have lingered there but he was anxious to show me what he called, 'Dr Johnson's House'. So I stared dutifully at the fine building with pillars either side its front door and steps leading up to it.

'It's a little like Ashling,' I said, 'although much smaller, of course.'

Edward beamed his pleasure at my remark. 'You are very observant, Cat. They were indeed built at around the same time. Early 18th century.'

'Indeed!' I echoed, pursing my lips and nodding wisely, although, in truth, the date meant little to me.

'And there is Dr Johnson's statue,' he continued, pointing at the seated figure of a man high up on a plinth.

'He must have been a wonderful doctor,' I said, 'for the people of Lichfield to erect such a fine statue of him. What did he do, Edward? Save the town from an outbreak of cholera, perhaps?'

He looked down at me, clearly puzzled. And then he said, slowly, 'No, Lichfield has never suffered from cholera. No, this man

123

was a great writer and scholar, a Doctor of words, you might say.'

'Oh, I see,' I said in a small voice.

'Not,' said Edward quickly, and taking my arm as he turned me away from the statue, 'that I have read many of his works. Now, let me show you our new Corn Exchange, of which we are very proud.'

I gazed obediently at an imposing building with open archways where the ground floor would normally have been, so that people could walk and, presumably, do their business sheltered from the elements. But I was still smarting from my ignorance of this wonderful Dr Johnson.

But there was no time for such unprofitable thoughts in Edward's company. I was shown, in rapid succession, yet another statue — of a James Boswell who had written a book about the wonderful Dr Johnson — a street called Conduit Street, so-called because water was brought down it by pipes from a pool which Edward promised we should visit later, a charming little street called Quonians Lane with old, black and white cottages like those in Alrewas — 'medieval' said Edward, and I would have liked to ask him what the word meant but he was making me return to Conduit Street which had turned itself into Dam Street, and was telling me to shut my eyes. Mystified, I did as I was bidden and felt his hands on my shoulders as he turned me around.

'Now, open!' he said.

I did so and found myself gazing at the biggest church I had ever seen and knew at once that this must be the cathedral of which Pa had spoken. Immediately, tears began to cascade down my cheeks.

'Why, Cat,' said Edward, obviously greatly impressed, 'you are indeed sensitive to beauty!'

I nodded, speechless; which was perhaps as well for he might have thought the less of me if he had known that I cried, not because of the building, magnificent though it was, but because of a sudden, desperate yearning for my father to see it, too.

'I'll show it to you later,' he promised. 'But for the moment, mop your eyes for there are other, more urgent matters to be attended to.'

He smiled down at my puzzled face. 'Cat, what were you up to behind that bush the first day I met you?'

As a means of drying my tears, the question could not have been improved upon. 'So you did see me!' I cried blushing furiously.

'No, I did not! But I guessed! Now, could you not use a bush at the moment, Cat?'

I did not like to tell him that I had made use of one just before reaching Alrewas and agreed that it would not come amiss. 'Follow me!' he said. And the next moment we had turned aside and entered a little shop from which the most enticing smells wafted out to greet us. I soon saw why. Cinnamon buns jostled with pikelets upon the glass counter and rich fruit cake with cherry cake and madeira. Rows of pies, some big, some small but all richly encrusted, occupied a separate counter.

A plump little lady in a frilly white cap, a white, bibbed apron over her black skirts rustled out through a beaded curtain at the back of the shop. When she saw Edward, her fact lit up.

'Why, Master Edward, what a pleasure to see you!'

'And you, too, Nanny!' And then, turning to me, 'This is my friend, Cat Marsh, to whom I am showing the glories of Lichfield. And you, of course, are the most glorious!'

'Get on with you, sir!' And then shrewd blue eyes turned and looked me up and down and I knew that they missed nothing; certainly not the patches in my second-best skirt, the toes of my boots, well-polished but cracking across the instep, my bare hands and lack of a bonnet. I bobbed nervously and said.

'Good day to you, ma'am.'

'Good day to you, Cat.' And the blue eyes suddenly wrinkled in a smile and I knew that I must have passed whatever test she had set me. Relief flooded through me for instinctively, I knew that the relationship between Edward and this woman was stronger and more loving than that between him and his natural mother.

She turned back to him. 'An' how are Miss Sophie? An' yer mother and father?'

'Well, thank you, Nanny. Sophie will be green with envy when she knows I have visited you without her.' He turned to me. 'When it was decided that Sophie and I had finally outgrown the nursery, Nanny Humphries was given the choice of retiring to one of the estate cottages or coming to live with her sister here in Lichfield. And to our great sorrow, she chose Lichfield.'

The lady bristled indignantly. 'What would I have done stuck out there on my own at the end of a farm track with no-one to talk to but the beasts in the field? As you well know, Master Edward,' and now her voice rose shrilly, 'had I been offered a position in the house, it would have been a different matter. However,' and she shrugged, 'that's all water under the bridge, now.'

'Talking of water, Nanny,' said Edward and moving towards the beaded curtain. 'I wondered if we might . . . ?'

'You know where 'tis!' said Nanny, standing aside. She motioned me to follow him through the curtain into her tiny parlour. 'My sister is out at the shops so sit 'ee down for a moment, lass. Master Edward always 'ad difficulty with 'is bladder. Get yer teeth into this while yer wait.' And she gave me a cinnamon bun on a blue and white plate. 'Now, 'ow are things at Ashling?'

'Very well, thank you, ma'am. I'm the new between and I just happened to bump into Master Edward . . . ' But she brushed aside my explanation.

''Ow's Mrs C. an' old Jolly?'

'Well, thank you, ma'am. Mr Jolly's rheumatics trouble him from time to time . . . ' But she wasn't interested in Mr Jolly's rheumatics, either.

'An' 'ow's the Master — an' the Mistress?'

'He is very well, too, ma'am. As for the Mistress . . . I don't see her very often unless I'm sent for.' I didn't mention that I would do almost anything to avoid meeting her even to the extent of squashing myself into a linen closet or broom cupboard if I saw her coming.

Nanny nodded. ''Tis better so.' And then,

as Edward could be heard coming in through the back door, she added quickly, 'Beware of 'er, Cat. Anyone Edward takes a fancy to, she'll do 'er best to be rid of. An' *I* should know!' And then, as Edward came into the room. 'Off you go, then, Cat. Bottom o' the garden. Yer can't miss it.'

As I walked the length of her little garden, bright with stocks and sweet william, towards the honeysuckle-shrouded privy, I pondered her words. It was easy to see why she had chosen to live in Lichfield rather than in lonely isolation at Ashling. Easy, too, to understand why she had been given that choice in the first place; either would mean distancing herself from her beloved Edward.

'Anyone Edward takes a fancy to,' she had said. Was I, Cat Marsh, really someone he had 'taken a fancy to'?

8

'So you can see,' said Edward, throwing the last crumbs of Mrs C.'s bread and cheese to the sparrows that lived by Stowe Pool, 'that I am torn between going to university as my mother wishes, or following my father into the army.'

He was leaning against the trunk of a silver birch while I used that of a weeping willow; between us lay the remains of our meal, the cakes and buns pressed upon us by Nanny; before us, where the willow trailed its leaves, the water lapped gently upon the pebbles and beside us, at some fifty yards distance, an old mill stood, its wheel quiet in the noonday hush, the rush of the stream that turned it, the only sound. I felt drunk with happiness.

After leaving Nanny — 'come back this afternoon and meet my sister' — Edward had shown me the interior of the Cathedral. A service had been in progress somewhere in the building, although out of our sight, as we entered through the West door. For at least a minute we stood there and then I discovered that my hand had crept into Edward's and was being tightly held.

For it was so huge! And so ugly! I could not believe that a place that had impressed me so greatly from outside with its three great spires reaching up to heaven, could fill me with such horror from inside. With its bare, white-washed walls, it reminded me of the milking shed at Ashling's Home Farm where I was sometimes sent upon errands, except that this could have accommodated several herds and I doubted, somehow, that the atmosphere would have been conducive to a good yield! Certainly I had no wish now for my father to be there with me.

True, when I tilted back my head, as Edward instructed, and gazed upwards, the fan vaulting as he called it, was beautiful. But I could not wander around for long with my head in such an uncomfortable position.

'It's — it's — ,' I sought for the right words to please Edward, in whom familiarity must have bred at least acceptance.

'Breathtaking?' he suggested.

I nodded, and indeed the extreme coldness of the place was causing me to catch my breath and shiver uncontrollably. I longed to return to the sunshine and the tranquil beauty of the Cathedral Close. With difficulty, I resisted an impulse to tug at Edward's hand. At least, as there was a service in progress, I should not have to inspect — and

131

marvel at! — the whole building. But Edward had other ideas.

'You must see the sleeping children,' he told me.

If he had said 'you must see the lions and tigers', I could not have been more perplexed, for no child could have survived for long in an atmosphere of such chill and damp, certainly not have slept unless they were ill which, of course, they soon would have been.

My footsteps dragged as Edward led me down the right-hand side of what he called the nave and into a long, narrow passage. Fearful of what I was to be shown, I fixed my eyes on my feet.

'There!' said Edward suddenly, drawing us to a halt. Slowly, I raised my eyes and was immediately filled with wonder. For the children he had spoken of had no alternative but to sleep for they were made of marble. And they truly were asleep — in each other's arms, one child obviously younger than the other and holding a posy of flowers in her hand. Once again, tears came to my eyes for it could so easily have been Emma and me.

'What happened to them?' I whispered. 'Why are they here?'

'They died,' Edward told me, 'when they were very small. The elder because her nightdress caught fire, the younger of some incurable disease. And their mother had this memorial made in their memory. It is very beautiful, is it not?'

'Very beautiful!' And I thought how wealth — for clearly, these effigies would have cost a great deal of money — did not always bring happiness.

Coming out of the Cathedral at last, I felt what I had used to feel at the potbank at the end of a working day; relief to be out in what passed as fresh air in Burslem — and very hungry!

'Shall we eat?' I asked Edward.

'A capital idea! And I know just the place.' And he led me towards a sheet of water that he called Minster Pool and where I would have been happy to stay. But he assured me that Stowe Pool was even better and indeed he was right.

Now, with the edge taken from our appetites, and with Nanny's buns and cherry cake still to come, we sat back and talked. Encouraged by Edward's obvious interest, I told him about life at the potbank and about my family.

'You love them dearly, don't you?' he said and there was envy in his voice.

'Very dearly,' I said.

'I love Sophie, although at times,' he admitted with a wry grin, 'she drives me insane. And I greatly respect my father. But, my mother . . . ' he pulled at a tuft of grass with his fingers. 'I don't know how I feel about my mother. I *want* to love her. And heaven knows, I try, but there is always something that prevents me.' He looked at me, clearly searching for the right words. 'There is no — no . . . '

'Spark?' I suggested, not yet knowing of the word 'rapport', 'Warmth?'

He nodded. 'And yet, in her way, I know she loves me — perhaps too much. For her expectations are impossibly high — I know that I cannot possibly achieve them. For instance, I am not at all sure that I have it in me to profit from a university education.'

'I cannot imagine,' I admitted, 'how anyone who has the opportunity to study does not take advantage of it.'

'You agree with my mother, then?'

'Not if you don't want to go, of course. It's just that I would welcome the chance to go to school, let alone university.'

His gaze had been on a boatman, sculling his craft across the Pool, but now he turned his head to look at me closely. 'You mean you haven't attended school, Cat?' His voice, although full of surprise, was gentle, with no implied criticism.

'Only to Sunday School and that not for

some years. I cannot read, only sometimes the printed word. And I cannot write.'

'And yet you speak in such a correct and precise manner. I had assumed . . . '

I shook my head. 'I owe that to my mother who considered our family to be superior to others. But even she could not see the point of girls learning their letters. I doubt, anyway, that the money was there, even for a Dame School. As long as I could cook and sew and keep a clean house, she thought that would be sufficient for me to find a husband. But not any old husband, of course,' I added with a smile. 'With luck, he would be a foreman or an overseer. I think, in her secret heart, she hoped for an owner of a manufactury. For my uncle at Wolstanton is one.'

'And what now, Cat, now that you are seeking fame and fortune in Lichfield, who will you marry now?'

He was teasing, of course, but I felt my cheeks redden with embarrassment. 'I could ask you the same question,' I parried. 'Who will you marry, Edward? The daughter of some wealthy landowner?'

He groaned. 'The wealthier the better, if Mama has her way. No matter if she has teeth like a buck rabbit and a squint like an old witch.'

I smiled, smugly aware that the teeth I

showed were small and white and even. But for some reason, the thought of Edward marrying anyone was not to my liking. 'So,' I changed the subject, 'if you do not go to university, you will go into the army?'

'Oh, yes! My father would like nothing better than for me to follow in his footsteps. And I would like it, too.'

'So, will you?'

He shook his head. 'I doubt it very much. What my mother decides is usually what happens.' And for the first time since I had met him, I heard bitterness in his voice. And then he turned his head and gave me a smile of great sweetness. 'Tell you what, Cat! In order to prepare for Academia, I will take upon myself the role of tutor. I will teach you to read and write. What do you think of that?'

I stared at him, my mind racing at the prospect. But then I shook my head. 'Your mother would never allow it.'

'But my mother need never know. You will have other days off, will you not? There will be plenty of opportunities at Ashling — you can pretend sudden interest in horticulture and meet me in the greenhouse. And there is the Home Farm where I know that you are sometimes sent on errands.'

I shuddered, partly through fearful antici-pation of such clandestine meetings, but mostly through sheer terror of the consequences of discovery. But he looked so pleased with himself I hadn't the heart to discourage him. 'We'll see,' I compromised, as I would to a child.

We fell to eating again then, until we could eat no more and then to dozing against our separate trees because walking the streets of Lichfield, clean and well-paved though they were, had been tiring to feet grown used to walking earthen paths.

I awoke to find Edward's face only inches from my own, his eyes dancing. 'Come along, Sleeping Beauty! Your Prince awaits!'

Surely, he hadn't kissed me! I put my hand up to my cheek and sure enough felt a moistness, an indentation that his lips had left. For a split second, I allowed my gaze to lock with his and then I rose briskly. 'Where to now?' I asked.

He drew his watch from his waistcoat pocket. 'If we're to catch a train that will get us home before dusk, we had better go directly to Nanny's to visit her sister. She is sure to insist upon giving us tea. There is still much to show you in Lichfield but there'll be other opportunities.'

I wished that I could feel so confident.

★　★　★

Dusk was falling as we reached Alrewas and Bert Hollis long gone. Our tickets were taken by a young lad who doffed his cap respectfully to Edward and thus reminded me that we had left the comfortable anonymity of the town.

'I think we should walk back separately,' I told Edward after the locomotive and its carriages had rattled away in a shower of sparks.

For answer, he laced his fingers in mine. 'I should not dream of allowing you to walk back across the fields unattended.'

I did not argue for I knew that I would savour these last minutes together at the end of our perfect day.

At first, we did not talk much. He thanked me for the pleasure of my company and I thanked him for his. He commented upon the fading streaks of gold and amber in the western sky and I agreed with his comments. And then I saw it — a slim sickle of a moon riding high above us. I stopped dead on the narrow path, causing Edward, who was right behind me, to put his arms on my shoulders to steady himself.

'Look!' I cried. 'A new moon! We must bow and wish. But not tell each other what we wish.'

I don't know what made me think then of

Thomas and Rosie. Perhaps I was reminded of the many nights when we had finished late at the potbank and had walked together as far as the end of their lane, when I had left them to run up the hill to the welcome that I knew awaited me, and they had walked, their steps dragging, to whatever awaited them in that sordid hovel.

Please, oh please! I urged the moon as I bent low before it, let them be safe, wherever they are.

I straightened to find Edward still staring up at the sky. 'I've always been told that one should turn over one's money before wishing.'

'In that case,' I said, 'I will have another wish.' And, my hand in my pocket, I turned over what remained of my wages. And this time, of course, I wished that Edward would not go away to wherever it was he had said.

'Edward,' I asked as we resumed our walk. 'Where is this place you mentioned? This Aca — Academ . . . ?'

He looked down at me, 'Academia?' he said after a moment, and now his voice was as warm and gentle as it had been when I had confessed my ignorance of Dr Johnson. 'It's not a place really, Cat. Only in the mind. Like — like Arcady, in a way.'

But Arcady meant nothing to me either. At

least, this time he couldn't see my blushes. 'I see!' I said as I had before.

He drew me to a halt, his hands once more on my shoulders. 'Dear Cat,' he said and now his voice was very gentle indeed. 'It matters not at all that you are unaware of these things. They're not important. What *is* important is to be what you are — honest and true and loyal. And very . . . ' he paused, ' . . . lovable!' he finished. And bent and kissed me on the forehead. 'Now, we must hurry — or Mr Jolly will be out looking for you.'

★ ★ ★

Mr Jolly was not out looking for me. He was sitting with Mrs C. at the kitchen table. As I came in, full of apologies for being late, they turned their heads. And the words died on my lips. Their faces were so solemn that I knew something dreadful must have happened.

'Cat,' said Mrs C. 'the Master wants to see yer. In the library.'

'Wh — why?'

She shook her head. ''E wants ter tell 'ee 'isself, Cat.'

I had always been aware that Mrs C. modified her speech when Mr Jolly was present, as she did, of course, when speaking to the Family, and now a small, detached part of my brain registered that, upon this occasion, she had ceased to care, he had forgotten. Whatever Mr Marshall wished to tell me, must be very serious indeed. Surely, he could not have heard already that I had spent the day with his son?

'We'll be here when you come back, Cat,' said Mr Jolly, rising to his feet and taking the unprecedented step of holding open the door for me.

I ran down the passage, hardly slowing even when I was through the green baize door. When I knocked on the library door, I was breathless.

'Come in!' Colonel Marshall called out.

I went in and bobbed, then stood, head bowed, awaiting his next instruction.

'Close the door and come and sit down, Marsh,' he said in the tone of voice I'd heard him use when gentling a horse or picking up Sophie when she'd fallen on the gravel driveway. I lifted my eyes and saw that he was beckoning me to sit in a chair opposite him. And I saw, too, that his eyes were full of compassion. Trembling now and with a dreadful premonition, I obeyed him. Had I not done so, I think my legs would have given way altogether. Once again, I felt moved to

141

help him out of his predicament. But I could not do so. Until it was put into words, it had not happened.

He cleared his throat. 'I have just heard from your uncle in Wolstanton, Marsh. It is very bad news, I'm afraid. A few days ago, your father took a sudden turn for the worse and has since died. Peacefully, your uncle said and in no pain. Your mother and sister were with him. I am so sorry to have to tell you this, Marsh.'

And now the tears came; silent tears that fell unchecked on to my clasped hands. While I had been enjoying my day in Lichfield with Edward, Pa had been dead and I had not known. At least, I clutched at a crumb of comfort, I had thought of him and wished that he had been there with me. I blinked back the tears.

'When . . . ?' I began, meaning to ask when the funeral might be. But I never finished the question and it was several years before I knew the answer to it. For at that precise moment, the door crashed open behind me.

'So there you are, Marsh!' Mrs Marshall's voice was like thunder. I rose to my feet and turned to face her. Never before had I seen such venom and hatred on a woman's face. She was beside herself with fury and I knew that she had learned where Edward had been all day and with whom.

'You will leave this house this instant, and you will never . . . '

'No!' interrupted the Colonel rising to his feet and I knew then how he must have sounded on the battlefield — powerful and strong and completely in command. Certainly, it brought his wife, if not to her senses, at least to silence. He turned to me.

'Leave us now, Marsh. And have no fear. You will *not* be leaving this house, unless you go of your own free will. And Marsh,' as I turned to go, 'I am deeply sorry for your loss.'

'Thank you sir!' And I turned and left them — to what acrimonious exchange of words, I could only imagine.

★ ★ ★

Next day, I watched from an upstairs window as the carriage bore Edward away — to stay with yet another school friend. And 'the following month,' I heard the Master telling Mr Jolly, 'he will be going up to Oxford University.'

9

'Unless you go of your own free will', Colonel Marshall had told me in front of his wife; a spontaneous remark made in the heat of an impassioned moment, but it was to have an extraordinary effect upon the rest of my life.

'Should I go?' I sobbed into Mrs C.'s shoulder on the night I was told of my father's death. We were alone in the kitchen by then, Mr Jolly, after a few words of condolence and several embarrassed pats on my shoulder, having gone to his room.

'To the funeral, love? Did the Master say . . . ?'

'No!' I shook my head. 'Not the funeral. That would never be allowed. I mean, should I go altogether? Leave Ashling?'

'For pity's sake, child. Wot's put that idea into yer 'ead?' And then, looking down at me more closely, 'It's the Mistress, ain't it? She knows where yer've been today?'

If Mrs C. knew then probably everyone knew.

'When Edward came in 'ere this mornin',' she continued, 'an' asked where yer was an' I told him, 'e was off like a cannon ball.

Caught up with yer, did 'e?'

I nodded. 'We had a lovely day, Mrs C. and Nanny Humphries sends her love and says when are you going to call and see her?'

'Ah, she's a lovely lady is Nanny Humphries. An' another one the Mistress couldn't abide — just because Edward thought the world of 'er.'And then going back to my original question. 'A' course yer mustn't go, Cat. Yer like it 'ere, don't yer?'

'I love it, Mrs C. Were it not that my family is so far away, I could not be happier.'

'Well then, that's yer answer. An' I'm sure yer Ma would agree wi' me. A picture of 'ealth, yer are now, compared wi' when yer came. Proper pale an' poorly yer looked then.'

I had not thought of that aspect of my new life, although I knew that my face was fuller now and my cheeks rosy with health.

'No — I'll tell'ee what yer must do,' she continued, sitting me down at the table, and going to make the inevitable pot of tea. 'Yer must 'ave a plan. Just like I did.' She shovelled a lavish spoonful of the best Darjeeling into the small brown pot. 'I ain't allus been a cook, yer know.'

'No?' I scrubbed at my eyes with my sodden handkerchief and prepared to listen. Anything to put off going to my room and lying awake, tossing and turning and thinking of Pa.

'I was summat called a still-room maid over at a big 'ouse, Shrewsbury way. They don't 'ave 'em much now an' even then, wot it really meant was skivvyin' fer the 'ousekeeper. The Mistress 'olds the purse-strings 'ere but in that 'ouse, the 'ousekeeper was the one ter be reckoned with. If she'd 'ave told me to go an' scrub the stable-yard, I'd 'ave been on my knees out there afore yer could say knife.'

''Twas 'ard but never dull. Part of 'er duties was orderin' the stores an' part was picklin' an' preservin' an' making sweeties fer the children. So she 'ad a fair bit to do wi' the cook. An' I was allus there to 'elp. So I learned a lot. She said she could read an' write but she couldn't really. She remembered numbers up to ten an' she copied the first two letters if the bags of sugar an' tea an' flour 'ad writin' on 'em an' drew little pictures if they 'adn't. I uses 'em meself, as yer may 'ave noticed, an' it works a treat.'

I had indeed noticed and admired the speed with which she ordered from the tradesmen who presented themselves at the back door.

'An' I made it my business to get in wi' the cook,' she went on, 'an' learn 'ow to make things. An' then, when I was eighteen I put in fer an undercook at a big 'ouse Durham way. No-one were more surprised 'n me when I got it, but my references were good. So why don't 'ee do the same, young Cat? Yer've got brains — more'n I'll ever 'ave if I live to be an 'undred — an' I'll learn yer all I know, when the others ain't around to see wot I'm doin'.'

I stared at her, my mind so full of tumultuous thoughts I did not know which one to consider first. But I was aware of a mounting excitement. At the potbank, before I had discovered the true relationship between Rosie and Thomas, my future had been clear, to me, at least. But now, at Ashling, I was still finding my feet, still uncertain about what I wanted to happen, for it had never occurred to me until now that *I* might be able to cause something to happen.

I looked at Mrs C. with an even greater respect than before — and with even greater affection. 'You're so very kind,' I said humbly. 'I really don't deserve it.'

'Nonsense!' said Mrs C. stoutly. 'I shall enjoy learnin' yer, Cat. None o' the others would give a thank you but yer different. Yer've got spunk, same as me.'

I dared then, to ask her something I had long wondered about. 'Is there a Mr Clifford somewhere, Mrs C?'

'Bless 'ee, no, child! I never 'ad no time fer larkin' about! An' nor will 'ee, if yer follow in me footsteps.'

'Follow in my father's footsteps,' Edward had said and I thought then how different were the paths we each must tread. And yet, I could still feel the touch of his lips on my cheek and remember the way we had gazed into each other's eyes. And for a moment, I allowed myself to consider how different things might be, had my circumstances been the same as his. But the gap between Edward and myself was unbridgeable and would always be so and I must never forget it. I shook my head to rid it of such unprofitable thoughts and found Mrs C. gazing at me with a shrewd look in her eye.

''Ave yer dreams, if yer must, Cat. But never let 'em rule yer life. An' now — off ter bed with 'ee.' And then she added something that touched me greatly, perhaps even more than her offer of instruction.

'Mine's a big bed — more'n big enuff fer a little thing like you alongside o' me, Cat. If yer don't want ter be alone tonight . . . '

I put my arms around her and hugged as hard as I could. 'Thank you, Mrs C., more than I can say. But I'll be all right.'

And, surprisingly, I was. Worn out by the

happenings of the day, I slept almost immediately, although I dreamt — of Pa as he had been before he became ill; tall and strong, swinging me up on to his shoulders as if I were no more than a wisp of gossamer. And I awoke with my pillow wet with tears.

★ ★ ★

'Me rheumatics is real bad today,' announced Mrs C. next morning. 'I shall need yer to 'elp me, Cat.'

'Of course!' I said. Ada and I were busy cleaning the kitchen knives. Soon after I'd come down, I'd realised that Mrs C. must have told everyone about Pa's death because, although no-one actually said anything, everyone was particularly kind to me. Katie had taken up Mr Jolly's tea, Rachel had offered me a fancy from the box Bert Hollis had given her and Fred had offered to show me a badger's sett he'd found in the woods. And Ada had volunteered to rub the moistened brick dust into the knife blades, thus leaving the infinitely cleaner task of rinsing and drying to me.

'I'll finish 'em,' she now offered.

I soon realised that Mrs C.'s purpose was to give me my first lesson. After I had brought out oatmeal and flour, salt and yeast, she informed me that we were making oatcakes.

'The Master loves 'em wi' black puddin'. An' so does Mr Jolly.'

The rheumatics seemed to have attacked her arms as well as her legs because I then had to weigh out the oatmeal and flour, crumble the yeast and mix in sufficient warm water for a batter-like consistency.

'Now we'll let it stand for a while,' said Mrs C. 'while we make the cider sauce for their lunch. It's 'ot boiled bacon today. An' then we'll get on wi' bonin' the pheasants fer tonight.'

And so it went on throughout the day. 'I've never known 'er screws so bad,' said Ada at the end of it after I'd been allowed to join her at the sink. 'An' this pan's burned, Cat!'

'Sorry! The almond custard must have caught. Let me do it.'

'Well, I'm glad it was you an' not me,' said Ada, passing over the pan, 'She kept you at it an' no mistake.'

'I didn't mind,' I said.

In fact, I'd enjoyed it; it was like helping Ma again although *she* wouldn't have known what to do with half the ingredients Mrs C. had at her disposal. And in the afternoon, she'd allowed me a few minutes respite while

I did what I'd resolved to do when I awoke that morning.

It was the Master's habit to ride in the afternoons after his lunch had settled. And today we'd watched him walk across the yard with Sophie at his side. I think she was wearing a pair of Edward's old breeches for they were bunched about her tiny waist with a piece of string.

'That girl's a tomboy and no mistake,' said Mrs C. 'Good job 'er Ma can't see 'er.' For the Mistress, we knew, had already departed in the governess cart on a round of afternoon calls.

'Mrs C.' I said urgently. 'Can you spare me for a minute? I just want to thank the Master. He was very kind to me last night.'

She looked surprised but nodded her consent. 'Don't be long.'

I found them watching Ned, the stable lad, saddling up Moonbeam, the Colonel's big grey and Toffee, Sophie's bay pony. I walked up to them and bobbed.

'Yes, Marsh?' said the Colonel encouragingly.

'Hello, Marsh!' said Sophie, giving me a broad smile. And then her face became solemn. 'Dear Marsh, I was so sorry to hear about your father. Pa told me this morning.' And she threw her arms around me and gave me a great hug. At the same time, she whispered in my ear, 'And Edward, too, asked me to give you his condolences. He's gone, you know.'

And then she drew back and I said quickly, 'Thank you, miss, you're very kind.' And to her father, 'I wanted to thank you, too, sir, for your kindness last night. And for — for — everything,' I finished lamely, deeply conscious that it would not be tactful to be more specific.

'Not at all, Marsh. And I have replied to your uncle's letter, of course. No doubt we shall hear from him again very soon.'

'Thank you, sir!' And I bobbed again and turned to go.

'Goodbye, Marsh!' called Sophie, preparing to fling a leg over her pony's back and, with her face turned from her father, giving me an enormous wink.

'Goodbye, miss!' I replied, controlling my face with difficulty.

★   ★   ★

The most impressive aspect of Mrs C.'s instruction, I soon decided, was her memory.

'I don't even think about it,' she said when I commented upon the way she remembered all the ingredients and their quantities. ''Alf the time, I don't even bother to weigh or

152

measure. You'll get to be the same,' she added confidently.

But during the weeks that followed, I began to realise that, in fact, I did not *want* to produce an exquisite Apple Charlotte or Fricassée of Veal Sweetbreads or whatever the Family required for their sustenance.

I wanted — and astonished myself by so doing — to be independent and work for myself. More and more I found myself remembering the trays of buns and cakes and pies in Nanny Humphries' little shop, the look of satisfaction on the faces of those of her customers I had seen during my brief visit and the no-less satisfied expression on Nanny's face as she took their money. How splendid, I thought, to decide for myself what my customers wanted, to perhaps introduce something new if I so wished, and then judge their reactions to it; to cater, perhaps, for children — with gingerbread men, fancies and toffee apples in season. If I was ever granted another day off, I would visit the shop again.

I said nothing of this to Mrs C., of course, for it would have seemed rank ingratitude for the trouble she was taking over me; although I think she enjoyed having a reasonably apt and appreciative pupil. Anyway, what chance did I — a between maid earning the vast sum of £7 per annum out of which I must provide my working clothes — have of ever achieving such an ambition? None at all — and yet, during those months that led up to Christmas, the prospect seldom left my thoughts.

10

At the beginning of December, Edward came home for Christmas; and was immediately swept up in a round of festivities that took him far and wide across the county.

'And there will be a big dinner party here,' Sophie confided. I'd met her flying along the schoolroom corridor one morning when I was taking Miss White's morning tea up to her. 'Which, of course, I shall not be allowed to attend.'

'Never mind, miss,' I tried to console her. 'You soon will be at the rate you're growing.' For she was now nearly as tall as I.

'That's what Edward says.'

'How — how is Master Edward?' I dared to ask.

'Oh, as horrid as ever! But its wonderful to have him home. He asked after you, by the way, Marsh, when Mama was out of earshot.'

'Did he really?'

'Really! I think he has a soft spot for you, Marsh.'

'What nonsense, miss! And don't let your Mama hear you say such things!'

'I'm not a fool Marsh! And Marsh,'

pausing to look back over her shoulder as she walked on.

'Yes, miss?'

'I *shall* be at that dinner party. Not that anyone will see me for I shall be sitting on the stairs. Why don't you join me there, Marsh, and I'll point out our local celebrities to you?'

I shook my head reprovingly. 'The ideas you get, miss!'

'Think about it, Marsh!' And she danced on her way. And I continued on mine in a more sober style but with my heart dancing with her. Edward had asked after me!

★   ★   ★

I had little time to think of Edward during the days that followed; if I had thought myself busy before, I knew now that it had been a gentle routine compared with the frenzy that led up to Christmas.

It had begun, peacefully enough, in October, with the making of the Christmas puddings — six for the Family, two for the servants. Breathing in its delicious aroma, Ada and I stirred the mixture for what seemed like hours; anyone who came into the kitchen was invited to 'have a stir for luck' while we rested our arms. Occasionally, Mrs C. would appear at our elbows to 'have a taster' and after much sucking in of her lips would prescribe a drop more lemon juice or pinch more of nutmeg or twist or two of peel.

Finally, Mr Jolly was summoned to add 'a good tablespoonful of whisky'; this inevitably required several further tastings before the mixture was finally spooned into the basins and a shining sixpence inserted into each one. Then they were covered and placed in a huge steamer where they remained for the next five hours, titillating our nostrils with their rich, spicy goodness.

Mincemeat came much later with the boiling of lemons, peeling of apples and stoning of raisins. This time, Mr Jolly added a good measure of brandy before it was packed into huge stone jars. 'An' no liftin' the lid 'til Christmas or yer won't get a single pie,' threatened Mrs C.

And so it went on; the plum cakes, the brandy snaps, the crystallised fruits, the shortbread biscuits. It became difficult to find room in the larders and cold rooms.

★　★　★

A fortnight before Christmas, the snow came. I'd seen it often before, of course, but in Burslem it had turned almost immediately into a filthy grey slush. Here, it transformed

157

our work-a-day world into a fairy paradise; for it had snowed steadily through the night but stopped before dawn, so that the sun, rising in a clear blue sky, turned the yard into a carpet of silver-blue crystals. Against it, the fantails, as they ventured out from the cote for the scraps I threw them, seemed almost shabby by comparison. I had never seen anything like it.

'Isn't it wonderful?' I enthused, going back into the kitchen.

Ada, who had slept at home on the previous night and had arrived with her skirts stuffed into an old pair of her father's breeches, scowled at me.

'Yer wouldn't say that if yer'd 'ad ter struggle 'ere across the fields. Up to me knees it was, in places.' However, she soon cheered up when her boots had dried out and she'd curled her fingers around a cup of hot tea.

'Any errands for the Home Farm this morning,' I asked Mrs C. hopefully when she came down. I was terrified it might all melt away before I could get out into it.

'Not this side o' two o'clock,' she said and then, when she must have seen my face fall, added, 'Though come to think of it, if the Mistress wants trifle fer dinner tonight, I'm goin' ter need more eggs. But not 'til the breakfast dishes are washed an' put away, mind. An' the kitchen table scrubbed.'

I scrubbed and scoured until my hands were raw and ten o'clock found me on my way to the farm, the Master's Labrador, Rex, bounding ahead of me. I had found him in the stable yard trying without success to persuade the stable cat to come out to play and had given up the hopeless task to accompany me; snow, he seemed to be telling the world as he barked and leaped and made tunnels through it with his nose, was for sharing.

Our path had been well-trodden already by the men sent up with the morning milk and we made steady progress but I had to stop now and then to marvel at the way the hedges in some places were no more than a line of twigs above the drifts and to watch farm workers haul out a sheep from a snow-filled ditch where it had taken shelter. For animals and wild life, I reflected, the snow was not welcome. To his intense surprise, Rex put up a fox and we watched it slink away, Rex wondering what he should do next, its tawny fur bright against the snow. But not as bright as the breast of the robin, fluffing out his feathers on a gatepost. I wished I'd brought some crumbs with me instead of scattering them all to the fantails.

In the farmyard, the ducks were sliding

down the banks of snow around their pond in a flurry of wings and a frenzy of quacks.

Mrs Roberts, the farmer's wife, gave me a cup of tea and a slice of seed cake and filled my basket with eggs still warm from the hen house. 'There's frost in the air,' she warned, covering them with a snow-white napkin. 'Go careful!'

The tip of my nose told me she was right, as Rex and I plodded home although the sun was warm on my back. When we reached the stableyard, there came the sound of raised voices beyond and I quickened my pace. And then, as we went in under the archway, Rex bounded forward, his tail wagging furiously.

In the middle of the yard, Edward and Sophie were putting the finishing touches to an enormous snowman. It stood at least five feet tall and had a carrot for a nose, two nuggets of coal for its eyes and what looked like potato peeling for its mouth from which a cherrywood pipe stuck out at a rakish angle. An old straw hat was on its head and as I came into the yard, Edward was tying a tartan scarf around its neck and Sophie was sticking in more nuggets to make a row of shiny black buttons down its front.

At the kitchen door, stood Fred, his hands resting on the spade with which he'd been clearing a pathway around the house. At the kitchen window, I could see Mrs C.'s face under the white blob of her morning cap.

It was Sophie, turning to pat Rex and seeing me standing there, who threw the first snowball. Edward must have followed suit immediately because suddenly we were all at it; Edward and Sophie, Fred and me with Rex bounding madly between the four of us. Fortunately, I did have the sense to put down the basket of eggs against the wall before I started to scoop and throw, scoop and throw, all the time laughing so hard, my open mouth must have made an easy target.

It was Fred who had the best aim although I wasn't far behind. Edward in his big, caped ulster wasn't difficult to hit nor Sophie in her scarlet coat although she was leaping around like a jack-in-the-box.

It was just after I had aimed a particularly hard-packed snowball at Edward that it happened. He saw it coming and ducked and, to my horror, it landed fair and square upon the head of the woman who had just appeared through the garden archway, sending her bonnet flying. It was the Mistress and behind her there now appeared the Master!

Frozen with terror, I just stood there. It was Edward who moved with lightning speed to stand between his mother and me, who took her by the shoulders and turned her away, and Sophie who immediately ran to her, crying out, 'I am sorry, Mama! I had intended to hit Edward!'

It was left to Fred to pull me quickly into the shelter of the kitchen passage. There, we stood for at least a minute, leaning against the wall while we got our breath back.

'Where's them eggs, then?' asked Mrs C., turning from the table as we came in.

'I'll get 'em,' Fred said quickly. 'Cat jus' put 'em down a minute while she rested 'er arm,' he offered as an explanation as he went.

'Did she indeed?' said Mrs C. with heavy sarcasm. 'Sorry to 'ear yer gettin' so weak in yer old age, Cat! Can't lift a cup o' hot chocolate neither, I don't suppose!'

'Oh, I think I could manage that, Mrs C.,' I said quickly, for hot chocolate was a rare treat.

'Thought yer might,' she said with a wicked grin, 'after all that exercise! An' make one for Fred an' me, while yer about it.'

★　★　★

From then on, an almost sisterly bond developed between Sophie and myself. No embargo had been put upon her visits to the kitchen and, as Christmas approached, hardly a day passed when she did not come to see us.

'What's it to be today, dear Mrs Clifford? Bread and butter pudding or jam roly-poly?' Very fond of her puddings was Sophie.

'Neither if yer don't let me get on,' Mrs C. would say, pretending to lose patience and usually adding, 'An' pull up yer drawers, Miss Sophie, a'fore yer tread on 'em!'

For Sophie had recently been allowed to substitute long white knickers for her pantaloons and although their frilly white edge was supposed to show a little beneath her skirts, hers always seemed to be at 'half-mast', as Mr Jolly put it, with at least one leg halfway to her ankles.

'May I help Marsh if I do?' she'd ask, hitching away at her waist or, if we were on our own, lifting her skirts and petticoats and pulling up the offending garment directly.

'Ain't yer got no lessons?' Mrs C. asked on this particular day.

'No, Miss White has been driven home as more snow is threatened. Or hoped for,' she added, giving me a wink.

'Well, then 'elp Marsh stone them raisins for five minutes. But whistle while yer doin' it!'

'I can't whistle, Mrs C., although Edward's trying to teach me. I'll talk instead, shall I?'

''Eaven 'elp us! I'm off!' And raising her eyebrows in a way that made Sophie collapse into giggles, she crossed the passage into one of the cold rooms.

'Now, listen carefully, Marsh,' said Sophie as soon as we were alone. 'Tomorrow is the Christmas dinner party.'

'I know, miss. I'm looking after the upstairs cloakroom.'

'Couldn't be better! You'll be able to join me on the stairs!'

'But, miss . . . '

'No buts, Marsh! You'll be quite safe once they've all arrived. And they stay in the hall for ages, drinking sherry, before they go in for dinner. Plenty of time for me to show you . . . '

'Show yer wot?' asked Mrs C., coming in with a can of milk in her hand.

'How to make a cat's cradle,' said Sophie swiftly, 'I'll bring a length of twine next time I come, Marsh, and show you.'

★　★　★

'It's a cryin' shame,' Mrs C. had declared, 'to 'ide yer upstairs. With yer gentle ways, the front door's the place for you, bobbin' an' smilin' an' taking their cloaks.'

'I shall be more than happy out of sight

upstairs, Mrs C. Anyway, won't Mr Jolly be at the front door?'

'A' course! But 'e can't do everythin'. Ada's sister Polly's bein' brought in to 'elp 'im. An' last year, she dropped Mrs Greene's cloak on the floor. I don't know wot the Mistress is thinkin' of.'

But I did. On the upstairs landing, I would be safely out of Edward's sight. Since the day of the snowfight I had had only a distant glimpse of him when he'd been crossing the yard on his way to the stables with a friend who had come to stay. I do not think it was my imagination that he had glanced directly at the kitchen windows as he passed and from that I had taken a little comfort.

However, once I had had my duties explained — by Mr Jolly with a face like a poker — I guessed there was another reason for my being given them. Although Ashling had its own cesspits, there was only one watercloset in the house and that was off the Mistress's bedroom. The room to be used for the ladies to retire to, to make themselves comfortable after dinner, was a smaller bedroom but with a dressing room leading off. Within this inner sanctum, a portable watercloset would be placed. This, however, would not have the advantage of running water and one of my tasks would be to remove the pail before it became embarrassingly full. Once I had removed it, I was to replace it immediately with a clean one — several of these would be standing on the back stairs landing — and carry the used one to the same landing from where, in the fulness of time — around midnight, I estimated — I would take them all out to the yard, where they would become Ned's responsibility to empty. It was something, I supposed that I had been spared this last part of the arrangement.

Care must be taken, intoned Mr Jolly, now staring, po faced — I suppressed a giggle at the thought — over my head, that the pails were not carried out when there were ladies present or in sight. I hadn't the heart to enquire exactly how this might be done but instead had taken the precaution of marking down a broom cupboard halfway along the front landing which could be useful as a staging post.

★   ★   ★

The day of the dinner party found the kitchen in a state of near frenzy. The bill of fare had been discussed for days previously by Mrs C., Mr Jolly and the Mistress. From these meetings, held in the morning room,

Mrs C. would return muttering furiously and Ada and I would hastily plump up the cushions on her chair, make tea in her special pot or pour a restorative glass of her cowslip wine. On one occasion, we even removed her shoes and massaged her feet until she was soothed.

'I shan't stay fer another Christmas,' she'd say, much to my alarm until Ada hissed in my ear.

'Don't take no notice! She says that every year!'

Eventually, the bill of fare was agreed. First would come 'Potage Alarain' — this flummoxed Ada and me until Sophie explained that it was French and should be pronounced Potage a la Reine and that it meant Queen's Soup. Then came Turbot in Lobster Sauce followed by Fowl a la Montmorenci — this caused several ribald jokes as Montmorency happened to be the name of the stable cat. The meal would end with a vast array of trifles, jellies and custards with, as centrepiece, a reproduction of Ashling, made entirely of almond paste. This last concoction was to be constructed by Nanny Humphries who, to my great joy, was to come and stay for two days to help Mrs C.

Also being 'brought in', besides Ada's sister Polly, were two extra girls from Alrewas to help serve at table and Bert Hollis's young brother to help Mr Jolly with the wines — there would be a different one for each course.

Ada and I had been kept busy all day preparing mounds of vegetables and it was with a certain sense of relief that I donned my best dress, tied on my best apron and went to the first floor landing.

Making sure that all was ready in the cloak room, I thoroughly enjoyed myself inspecting the Castile soap imported especially from Spain, the bottles of rosewater and cologne and the huge dish of pearl powder with the puffs of cottonwool beside it. Next to it was a smaller dish of pink powder and I was wondering what this could be, when Sophie's face peeped around the door. The rest of her, clad in nightdress and dressing gown followed immediately.

'Hello, Marsh! Isn't this exciting? That's for your cheeks,' she added as she saw what I'd been looking at. 'It's called rouge and Mama doesn't really approve but she has to go with the fashion. Look!' And before I could stop her she'd put two fingers in the bowl and planted blobs of pink on my nose and cheeks then, seizing a hand mirror, she held it in front of me. I could not help but laugh; I looked like Mr Jolly sometimes did when he was 'recovering' in his pantry from the effort of serving Sunday dinner; only much worse. And then I came to my senses. Seizing Sophie by the shoulders I pointed her at the door.

'Out, this minute!' I cried as if I were talking to Emma.

But it had little effect upon Sophie. 'You, too, Marsh!' she cried. And the next moment, I was being dragged out on to the landing. At least, I thought as she dragged me to the head of the stairs, she can do no harm out here.

'Sit here!' she commanded, pulling me down beside her on the top stair. 'No-one will see us.'

And she was right. The staircase curved before it reached the landing so that anyone sitting on the top stair and protected by thick, oaken banisters, was out of sight of the hall. At the same time, there was just enough space between the banisters to allow a magnificent, birds-eye view of the people already congregating below us. And no-one could mount the staircase without my seeing them.

As yet, the hall was by no means full so that it was easy to study each individual as Sophie pointed them out to me. Several of the ladies wore crinolines, although the younger ones favoured what Sophie told me was the 'Princess' style with skirts flowing out from a bodice cut low and heart-shaped to reveal their shoulders. In sharp contrast to their bright, jewel colours, the men were, without exception, in tail coats and narrow trousers of a sober hue. It was in the style of their waistcoats that they showed their personal taste. Some were of velvet or satin and intricately embroidered, some had a row of jewelled buttons that caught the light of the candles in the cut-glass chandeliers that sparkled overhead.

'Look!' whispered Sophie, indicating a middle-aged gentleman immediately below us. 'That is Mr Richard Greene, the banker. See — he is in great cahoots with Papa.'

As befitted a man of such responsibility, Mr Greene's waistcoat was of the same dark hue as his coat, with only a single line of darker braid to distinguish it. Beside him must be the lady whose cloak Polly had dropped last year. This year, presumably, no such accident had occurred for she looked perfectly relaxed, gazing up at her host over the ivory sticks of a large fan.

'Over there,' Sophie continued, 'is his daughter Caroline, talking to Edward. His other daughter, Georgina, is quite a friend of mine, although *she* will be putting up her hair long before me!' she added enviously.

But I wasn't listening any more, my gaze

was fixed on Edward, standing a little apart from the crowd and engaged in animated conversation with a young girl clad in the very height of fashion in powder-blue velvet from whose swathes and folds, her shoulders emerged in creamy splendour. Her hair was looped back from her face and held in a chignon by some huge white flower. That was her only ornament; she needed no other.

Edward, as I would have expected looked impossibly handsome in his evening clothes; *his* waistcoat was of some stiff, white fabric that seemed to illuminate his whole face and he was clearly in the best of spirits. For the first time since I had learned of the true relationship between Thomas and Rosie, I felt the pangs of jealousy and self-pity. It wasn't fair! It simply wasn't fair that this girl who obviously had everything money could buy should have Edward too, whereas I had nothing — and no-one.

'An engagement there, would please Mama,' Sophie said and I remembered how Edward had told me that his mother wanted him to marry into money, 'even if she has teeth like a buck rabbit and a squint like an old witch'. And this girl had neither!

'Mama looks rather grand, don't you think.' Sophie observed, having turned her attention elsewhere.

I forced myself to look down on Mrs Marshall. She was very grand indeed in an enormous purple crinoline and with her hair swept up and festooned with a cobweb of purple ribbons. She was conversing with a vigorous-looking man, somewhere in his late thirties, I estimated. She, surprisingly, was hanging on his every word.

'That's Mr McClean she's talking to,' Sophie told me. 'Papa thinks a great deal of his ability. It was he who constructed the railway at Alrewas and now, Paps says, he is much concerned with diverting the waters of Lichfield to places less fortunate. Stowe Pool, they say, would be completely dried up.'

I studied Mr McClean with mixed feelings; true, the water of towns like Burslem could be much improved but the thought of Stowe Pool, where Edward and I had spent those few, idyllic hours, disappearing from sight was too sad to consider. Did progress in one direction, I wondered, necessarily mean destruction in another?

'I wonder,' said Sophie, suddenly standing up beside me, 'if I could land a gob of spit on Mama's head? My aim is excellent.'

Horrified, I leaped to my feet and dragged her back. 'Don't you dare do any such thing, miss!'

'Oh, all right, if you feel that strongly!

Anyway, there's someone coming up. Don't worry,' she added as I saw there was indeed a lady beginning to mount the staircase, 'it's only Mrs Swinfen. She's *fun*!'

Fun or not, I faced the lady who came into the cloakroom a minute or two later with considerable trepidation. Had she seen my mad flight along the landing? But she gave no indication of it.

'Good evening!' she said cheerfully as I bobbed. Her voice was thrilling; soft and warm and with a lilt that I had heard before in the Welshmen at the potbank but, while theirs had been so broad I'd had difficulty understanding it, this lady's was just enough to give it a rich, musical quality that I found most attractive.

'Good evening, ma'am!' I smiled at her. It was impossible to do otherwise for she was dark-haired and rosy-cheeked and very pretty. 'Won't you sit down?' And I gestured towards the chair I had placed in front of a toilet table bearing a large swing mirror.

'Thank you, no. It's something else I need and urgently. I nearly had to ask my husband to stop the coach while I relieved myself into the ditch!'

'In here, ma'am,' I said quickly and flinging open the door to the inner sanctum. 'It's these cold nights, ma'am,' I

173

dared to add, as she entered.

When she came out, a few minutes later, she was breathing a sigh of relief. 'That's much better!' And then, peering at me more closely, 'Are you all right, child? You have a distinct rash on your cheeks.'

Forgetting myself completely, I fled to the mirror, moving the candlestick to obtain a better reflection. The face of a painted doll stared back at me.

'Oh, ma'am!' I said, scrubbing at the spots of rouge with a puff of cottonwool. 'I'm so sorry, ma'am! It was a silly joke, ma'am!'

'Most likely perpetrated by young Sophie whom I've just passed in her usual position on the staircase! I know her of old. Well, thank you, my dear, and a happy Christmas.' And to my astonishment, she opened a little, beaded bag she carried on her wrist, extracted a shilling and placed it on the toilet table, at the same time giving me an enormous wink before she swept from the room.

I stared at the shilling. Should I rush after her and say that I could not possibly accept it? Or should I not? It would mean the purchase of the thread I needed to finish my Christmas handkerchiefs. And Rachel and Katie, I knew, were frequently left what they called 'perks' by departing guests, although

174

the practice was frowned upon by the Mistress.

By the end of the evening, I had the grand sum of three shillings and six pence in my pocket and several interesting items of Staffordshire gossip in my head; it was extraordinary how some ladies seemed to think that servants were born with defective hearing.

When the last guests departed just before midnight, six full pails were lined up on the back stairs landing and one awaiting collection in the broom cupboard. There should be just time, I decided, to collect this before the family came up to bed. But I was mistaken.

'I'm going straight up,' I heard Mrs Marshall declare as the last carriage rolled away and the next moment she was mounting the staircase.

Two moments later, I was in the broom cupboard with the pail. It was cowardly of me, I knew, but I was very tired and my back was aching. A confrontation — as I was sure there would have been for she, too, must be tired — was the last thing I wanted. And besides, I was still guilt-ridden about my 'perks', although determined to keep them.

I heard her heavy tread pass by and then came the sound of her door closing. I waited a few moments then picked up the pail and put my head out; to find Edward only a pace or two away. There was no possible means of escape.

'Cat!' He seemed delighted to see me although surely he must have wondered why on earth I was coming out of the broom cupboard at that hour of the night. 'How are you?' he continued and standing stock still as if we'd just met in the street and had all the time in the world for a good gossip.

'Very well, thank you, Master Edward.'

And then he saw the pail. 'Allow me!' And he seized it from me before I realised what he was doing.

'Careful!' I almost shrieked as he seemed to be prepared to swing it high. 'It's full of slops!'

'Ah! Then I will treat it with due reverence! And where would you like these slops put, dear Cat? Out on the midden?'

He was, I suddenly realised, more than a little drunk. 'Just as far as the back stairs,' I began, 'but I'm quite capable . . . .'

'You are more than quite capable, my dear Cat. You are enorm — enormously capable!'

'Please, Edward! Give it to me!' I was almost in tears by now, frantic that his voice would reach to his mother.

But I might have saved my breath, he was already heading for the door to the back stairs. What on earth would he make of the half-dozen buckets already out there? Insist on carrying them all out to the midden?

I ran on ahead of him and flung open the door, meaning to take the pail from him and then, if necessary, shut the door in his face. And then I saw that a miracle had happened — there wasn't a pail in sight! Dear, kind Ned must have come up and carried them all down for me.

I turned to Edward and took the pail from him. 'Thank you, Master Edward! And good night!'

'Goodnight, dear Cat! Hap — happy Christmas!' And he kissed me full on the lips.

★   ★   ★

Next morning, I sought out Ned to thank him and to give him a sixpence from my hoard.

'Cat, you needn't. Honest!'

'Please, Ned! You've no idea how relieved I was to find you'd taken them'. And then, as I turned away to go back into the house I saw him spit, with great accuracy at a passing bantam. So that was where Sophie had learned her skill!

To Ada, I gave a whole shilling because I knew she had worked harder than anyone and with no material recognition. She took it without hesitation but I knew that both she and Ned thought the better of me for remembering them, and that I could rely upon them in the future for whatever help I might need. Quite what help that would turn out to be, I had no idea then.

11

Although I longed to have Ma and Emma with me, it was in many ways the best Christmas I had ever had. I think we, on our side of the green baize door, enjoyed it even more than the Family on theirs.

On Christmas Day itself, we all worked until we dropped. There were house guests staying — a cousin of Mrs Marshall's from London with his wife and daughter, Charlotte — of about Sophie's age — and son, Jack.

'She is an utter nincompoop!' Sophie said of Charlotte when she visited the kitchen on Christmas morning. 'She does not ride unless the sun is shining, she cannot skate and she spends all day buffing her nails and telling me how wonderful it is to live in London and how she will be presented to the Queen when she is seventeen.'

'What about Master Jack?' I asked.

'Oh, he is quite a different matter. He is to go into the Cavalry and can ride like a trooper. Edward, of course, is green with envy.'

Edward, too, came to wish us a happy Christmas but did not pay me any particular attention other than to untie my apron strings as I stood at the sink peeling potatoes with Ada. But then he did exactly the same to her and, as we turned our heads in protest, produced a sprig of mistletoe from his pocket and kissed us both on our cheeks. Then he kissed Mrs C. — although he did not dare unloose *her* apron strings. I doubt if he remembered anything of our meeting on the night of the dinner party, other than the headache he must have had next day.

Edward was followed soon after by the Master who presented Ada and me with four yards of dark brown calico for our summer working dresses. Mrs C. had already been given a pound of her favourite tea when she'd paid her daily visit to the morning room.

It was the day after Christmas when the kitchen staff truly celebrated. The morning had been devoted to the riders who came to Ashling for the traditional Christmas meet and Ada and I, Rachel and Katie and even Mr Jolly were kept busy with trays of sherry and hot punch. I felt very proud of the Master and Edward in their red coats — 'pink' corrected Mr Jolly when I said as much to him — and Sophie, too, looked very handsome in her riding habit for she was riding side-saddle that day.

Once the horses had clattered away, the

hounds streaming beside them, the rest of the day was ours for the Family's dinner would be a cold meal and had already been prepared. Our dinner was almost a replica of the Family's on the previous day but without the trimmings and it was served to us by Mr Jolly and Mrs C.

'Officers always serve the men at Christmas,' declared Mr Jolly and proceeded to carve us all great slices of roast beef, while Mrs C. brought the Yorkshire Puddings from the oven. 'An' we'll drink to Her Majesty now,' he added prudently, 'in case we forget at the end.'

It was a wise precaution for the Master had been generous in his allowance of table wine and Mr Jolly, I suspect, had already broached his bottle of Christmas brandy before the meal had started. Certainly, by the time the plum pudding had been cleared away and the men were choking over their Christmas cigars and Mrs C. was pouring us all cups of coffee, Mr Jolly would have been no more capable of rising to his feet for the Loyal Toast than flying to the moon. I made a mental note to beat an even hastier retreat than usual when I took up his tea next morning.

However, he did manage 'Absent Friends' from a sitting position and we all drained our glasses and thought, no doubt, of our nearest and dearest. I thought of Ma and Emma who would be spending the day at Wolstanton in the comparative affluence of my uncle's house. But of Thomas and Rosie, I could not bear to think for long, for I had no way of telling if they were even still alive or had perished in some ditch, overcome by the rigours of winter. I thought instead of Hannah and hoped that her baby was well and of old George nodding in front of his fire with a cat on his lap.

'I can't see Mr Jolly doin' the dishes,' said Ada in my ear. 'Nor Mrs C., neither.' For she was sitting in her chair with her feet up and balancing her cup on the swell of her bosom.

'We'll 'elp,' said Ned, getting to his feet. 'Won't us, Fred?'

'S'pose,' said Fred with a marked lack of enthusiasm.

'An' then us'll play cards,' said Ned.

Mrs C. opened an eye. 'Not fer money, yer won't! Not in my kitchen!'

'Oh, come on, Mrs C.' said Ned beginning to carry the dishes to the sink. 'Where would the likes of us get money to gamble with?' But he gave me an enormous wink as he passed and I wondered if Ned, too, had a secret hoard. I'd noticed him earlier in the day, standing by an open field-gate as the hunt moved away, doffing his cap respectfully as the horsemen jostled through and some had certainly thrown him a coin.

That was the night I learned to play Patience; an accomplishment I was to find most useful over the years.

★ ★ ★

The New Year brought heavy frosts and chilblains.

'Yer'll 'ave ter stop feedin' them birds,' grumbled Mrs C. as she gave me some spirit of turpentine to rub into the itchy red swellings on my feet. 'Steppin' outside inter the yard every mornin' does yer no good.'

'I get them every year,' I assured her.

'Well, mind yer don't get 'em on yer 'ands or yer'll be in right trouble.'

For I was now spending more and more time helping her in the kitchen. When Rachel had surprised us all by announcing she was to marry Bert Hollis in a month or two, Ada, to her astonishment, had been promoted to house-maid.

''Tis yours by rights,' Mrs C. told me, 'but I didn't think yer'd want it. An' I doubt the Mistress would 'ave agreed.'

I had no doubts whatsoever. And I had no wish to do other than to continue learning my 'trade' as I now thought of it.

'I've said I need yer in the kitchen wi' me,' Mrs C. continued. 'But I 'ave got yer a reg'lar day off a month an' a raise. Eight pounds, ten shillins yer'll be gettin' now. An' Ada's sister, Polly, starts Monday as kitchen maid.'

The new arrangement suited me very well indeed, especially the extra money. And I now had another source of income. Nanny Humphries, to whom I had presented one of my embroidered handkerchiefs as a Christmas present, had been loud in her praise of it.

'I know a draper in Lichfield'd take as many as yer can make,' she said. 'Shall I ask 'im?'

'Oh, Nanny, would you really?'

'Of course! You'll mebbee get a day off in the New Year an' can bring in a few ter show 'im. Twopence a time I reckon 'e'd pay for work this fine.' For I had not only used thread, I had done what Sophie had told me many ladies were doing and used long strands of my hair; and Sophie's too, for she had thought it a great game.

For Rachel's wedding present, I embroidered a nightdress case with entwined hearts but for this I used ordinary thread. She was married in Lichfield on a bright, breezy day in March, at St Chad's Church, near Stowe Pool. We could not all be spared to go but Mrs C. went and also Mr Jolly, for it was upon his arm that Rachel walked down the aisle, her father having died when she was a baby.

'An 'andsome pair they made,' Mrs C. related when she returned, meaning Mr Jolly and not Bert and I hoped that Bert had not had his nose put out of joint on this, his special day. 'An' Rachel 'ardly showed,' Mrs C. continued, for there had been no doubt in anyone's mind as to why she was being married in such haste.

The day was particularly memorable for me because I had been entrusted with preparing the Family's luncheon in Mrs C.'s absence. She, of course, had arranged it all before she left; there had been no discussion in the morning room for me.

'It's as simple as I could get,' she told me. 'Clear, gravy soup, boiled fowl with a white sauce and an Apple Charlotte. Yer'll manage it standin' on yer 'ead!'

It was certainly well within my capabilities but that didn't stop me from expecting a summons to the drawing room for a good hour after the meal was finished. However, all that happened was a quick visit from Sophie to tell me that my Charlotte had been 'simply scrumptious'. It was left to Ada, who had been waiting at table, to tell me that the Mistress had complained that the soup was over-salted, the fowl stringy and the Charlotte too sweet.

'But she still ate the lot,' said Ada, 'An' 'ad a second go at the Charlotte!'

★ ★ ★

Soon after Rachel's wedding, on a day when daffodils were bursting their fat green buds under the beech trees that canopied Ashley's main drive and primroses were like clotted cream in the hedgerows, I visited Nanny and her sister and took with me half a dozen of my handkerchiefs.

'I've told Mr George yer comin',' Nanny greeted me. 'An' I was thinkin',' she added, 'if yer goin' into business, yer'll need ter put yer money somewhere safe so think about puttin' it in the Savins Bank, same as us.'

It was heady talk for a girl of fifteen whose worldly wealth was a few coins wrapped in an old sock and kept under the mattress.

'A penny ha'penny each,' said Mr George, the draper, when he interviewed me in the little office behind his shop.

'Two pence,' I said firmly although my heart was hammering. 'And twopence ha'penny for the ones done with human hair. They take twice as long.'

'H'mmm.' He studied me over the rims of

186

his pince-nez. 'Drive a hard bargain, don't you?'

'And subject to reconsideration at the end of six months,' I continued, mindful of Nanny's promise to watch out to see how much he actually sold them for. 'There *are* other drapers in Lichfield, Mr George,' I reminded him, 'who would be interested in my work.'

To my astonishment, he burst out laughing. 'You're a bright one and no mistake! And I'll tell you this, missy, if ever you want to work behind a counter, come and see me. All right, then, two pence and twopence ha'penny, terms to be reviewed at the end of six months.'

And so began, not only a business arrangement but also a relationship that was to stand me in good stead over the years.

★ ★ ★

I spoke to Edward just once during that year, for on fine days when I was not helping Mrs C., I was sitting out in the yard, making full use of the strong sunlight to do my embroidery, for I had no wish to risk my eyesight under a bedroom candle.

'I oughter charge yer for these,' said Polly, who had a head of luxurious red hair, as she presented me with yet another strand of it.

'Six strands a farthing, then,' I said immediately for I had already considered the possible transaction.

'Done!' she said and we shook hands solemnly.

Sophie struck a different bargain. 'A gingerbread man for every hair!' she insisted, for her hair was now braided into a thick plait and extracting just one or two hairs required time and patience.

It was while I was returning one afternoon in July from the Home Farm, where I had been sent for a pitcher of cream, that I met Edward. He was leading his horse and limping slightly.

'Did you have a fall?' I asked anxiously.

He grinned ruefully. ''Fraid so. A bird flew up from under his feet and old Satan shied like a yearling. I should have been ready for it but I wasn't, my thoughts were miles away.'

I longed to ask him what he had been thinking of but instead asked if I could help.

'You could hold Satan, if you would, while I inspect the damage.'

So I put down my pitcher in a leafy ditch and took the reins of the big black horse, not much liking the way it rolled its eye at me but determined not to show any fear.

Edward leaned against a gatepost and

pulled down one of the thick socks he wore with his breeches. His ankle was badly swollen.

'Cold compresses,' I said, 'that's what you need. And you shouldn't walk on it.'

'Easier said than done, if I'm to get home.'

'I could go and get help,' I offered.

'That would take time,' he said, 'and I'm dining this evening over at Shugborough and they dine early.'

Shugborough, I knew, was the country seat of Lord Lichfield. 'Well, then,' I said, 'you'll have to get back on to your horse somehow and walk him home. Can I help you mount?'

He looked at me thoroughly then, as if assessing my capabilities as stable lad. 'Why, Cat,' he said, 'you've grown!' But it wasn't just my stature he was considering and I felt a blush rise in my cheeks. I had made up my four yards of dark brown calico but I had been meaning, for some time, to let out the side seams. The swell of my breasts thrusting against the thin fabric was greater than modesty dictated and I had draped a fichu of white muslin around my shoulders. But this, as I'd put up my arms to hold the horse, had slipped away. And my hair, too, had loosened from its ribbon so that it tumbled upon my shoulders.

'You're turning into a beauty, Cat, did you

know that?' said Edward slowly.

'Oh, yes!' I scoffed but refusing to meet his eyes. 'Anyway,' I continued, embarrassment lending me courage, 'I can bend a knee as well as any man. But I shall have to let Satan go to do it.'

'I think we can manage, if you're sure.' And he took the reins and manoeuvred the great beast round. I knelt on one knee and cupped my hands to throw him up; fortunately it was his left ankle that was hurt.

He was back in the saddle in a trice. 'Thank you, Cat. That was very clever of you. May I now have the pleasure of your company back to the house?'

So, having collected my pitcher from the ditch and with Satan obligingly accommodating his stride to mine, we set off.

'What have you been doing with yourself, Cat, since we last walked together nearly a year ago now?'

'Oh, this and that,' I said lightly. 'Helping Mrs C. Learning to cook.'

'And very well, too, my sister tells me. Mrs C. will have to look to her laurels.'

'And you?' I asked. 'Are you enjoying — Academia?' And I smiled up at him to show that I was no longer sensitive about my lack of worldly knowledge.

He grinned back at me. 'I am — very

much. This last term, I have played a great deal of cricket, swum almost daily and represented my college at archery.'

I burst out laughing 'And do you not study at all?'

'Well, that is rather a sore point at the moment between me and my tutor. But I have promised him to mend my ways next term. Although once hunting has started — that may be a little difficult.'

'Oh, Edward!' I shook my head in mock reproof. 'Life is too easy for you.'

'You may be right, Cat. But I promise you, when the time comes I shall be a good landlord and generous to a fault.'

'But you must also know what you are doing or people will take advantage of you.'

'Oh, I shall employ a good bailiff, never fear. And by then, you will have stepped into Mrs C.'s shoes, no doubt, and I am sure you will see that not a crumb is wasted in my kitchen.'

'That,' I said, 'will depend entirely upon your wife. She will hold the purse strings.'

'Ah, yes! My wife!' He shrugged wearily. 'I've no doubt that at Shugborough this evening there will be some doting mama — in cahoots with my mama — who will be parading her daughter for that very role. I'll make you a bargain, Cat. When *you* marry, *I* will marry and not a moment before!' And he gazed down at me in triumph, clearly delighted with himself.

'You may have to wait a very long time,' I told him.

'I can believe that. For I wager you'll be very particular, indeed, Cat Marsh.'

By then we were going into the stable yard and Ned came out to take Satan and to help Edward down and I went on to the kitchen. Just *how* particular, he would never know.

12

And so the years passed pleasantly enough.
The friendship between Sophie and me
continued to grow, although her visits to the
kitchen became less and less frequent as her
time was taken up with learning the
accomplishments required of young girls of
her breeding.

A music teacher came regularly to instruct
her on the pianoforte and to try and improve
the quality of her singing. I say 'try' advisedly
for she was tone deaf and could, she proudly
maintained, 'change key six times in two bars
and not know that I have done it!'

Every week she was taken to dancing
classes in Lichfield and performed, I
gathered, with reasonable success; although
'the other girls are so dull, Cat, and the boys
smell! They do, honestly! They sweat like
horses but are not nearly such good
company!'

An impoverished clergyman's widow, who
lived nearby and gave sewing lessons to the
daughters of the gentry, was persuaded to
include Sophie among her pupils and I was
continually being brought a blood-stained

piece of petit-point or embroidered chemise to 'put right' before Sophie's next lesson.

'I do try, Cat,' she told me, 'because Mrs Selby is an old lady and needs the money.'

'Don't worry,' I told her, 'as long as she has you for a pupil she will never lack employment! Anyway, think of all the things you *can* do. You can speak French, you can turn out an excellent Abernethy biscuit' (for Mrs C. on one rainy afternoon had allowed me to instruct her) 'and you can ride better than any other girl in the county. Ned is always saying so.'

'Is he really?' She had brightened considerably at this piece of news but then sank back into despondency. 'But that's another thing. I've had to give up hunting.'

'Sophie, why?' For hunting, from which she had returned, spattered with mud but rosy-cheeked and happy, had always been one of her greatest enjoyments.

'Because it's so cruel?' And she alarmed and disconcerted me by bursting into tears and flinging her arms around my neck. 'I'm not usually in at the kill because Toffee isn't that fast but a couple of weeks ago, the fox doubled back on itself and I was. And it was dreadful, Cat. Oh, I know I was blooded, like Edward, when I was a child but I didn't actually see the fox killed. I just remember the Master telling Papa that I was 'a champion little rider' as he gave me the brush, and that pleased me very much.'

'So, haven't you hunted since?' I asked.

'No — I've said I wasn't feeling well. And Mama told Papa it was probably 'my age' — whatever that may mean — and I would soon get over it. But I won't, Cat, I know I won't.'

'Don't take on so,' I tried to soothe her. 'Why not tell your Papa exactly how you feel? He is a very kind man and I am sure he will understand.'

She tried to wipe away her tears with the back of her hand. 'You are right. I must tell him the truth. But what about Edward? He will tease me dreadfully.'

'I doubt it once he realises how deeply you feel about it. And does he not do something at Oxford called Drag Hunting where riders simply follow another horseman who drags a sack that smells of aniseed? I heard him telling Ned about it, only the other day.'

She sniffed and I took her handkerchief from her pocket and held it to her nose. 'Blow!' I instructed, as Ma had used to say to me. 'One for your Mama, one for your Papa, one for Edward . . . '

'And one for my dear friend, Cat!' she grinned through her tears. 'Oh, Cat, you're such a comfort! I do so wish you were my sister.'

'We'd probably fight like cat and dog,' I told her, so pleased at the compliment I was unaware of my play on words. But Sophie wasn't.

'Oh, *very* funny!' She chuckled and danced away, her tears forgotten.

I watched her go. For once, I felt a certain sympathy with her mother; finding a suitable partner for such a wayward, albeit delightful, character would not be easy.

★ ★ ★

In May of 1854, the whole household was plunged into mourning when the Marquess of Anglesey passed away. He was one of Mr Jolly's heroes for it was he, apparently, who had inspired Mr Jolly to join the army in the first place.

'I couldn't decide what to do with my life,' he'd confided to me once when I was cleaning some silver in his pantry. 'I'd tried carpenterin' to please my father but I knew it wasn't for me. I wanted to spread my wings, see a bit of life. An' when Old One Leg, as we called him came ridin' into the city after Waterloo, at the head of his men, with bands playin' an' colours flyin' an' the people cheerin' their heads off, I knew that was it. I joined the Militia the next day. My father never forgave me.'

It took two days to bury him. As befitted such a famous personage — his titles were endless — he was to be buried in the cathedral. And on Friday, May 5th, the Master and Edward and Mr Jolly, all in the same conveyance, drove to Lichfield where the body was to be brought to the Trent Valley Railway Station, then escorted through the streets to the George Hotel where a guard of honour of the Staffordshire Militia awaited its arrival.

'Then we all filed past to pay our last respects,' Mr Jolly told us when he came back. 'Several thousand, they said. Old One Leg would have been mighty pleased. An' next mornin', we buried him in the family vault.' He spoke as if he had been part of that family and, indeed, I think his grief could not have been greater, if he had. At his request, we continued to wear our black mourning bands on our sleeves for several days after the ceremony.

* * *

A couple of months later, another death occurred in the county. Mr Jolly, as usual, brought the news to the kitchen.

'Mr Henry Swinfen has passed away,' he announced in solemn tones. He spoke, of course, to Mrs C. but Polly and I stopped what we were doing to listen. I waited until Mrs C. had expressed her regret and then asked,

'Is that the husband of the couple who came to dinner at Christmas, Mr Jolly?'

'The same,' said Mr Jolly and then indicated to Mrs C., with a swivelling of his eyes and a slight turning of his head that she should join him in his pantry. When they had gone, Polly and I exchanged glances. That meant Mr Jolly had some news or gossip he considered unsuitable for the ears of us, lesser mortals.

'Mebbee she'll tell us when she comes back,' said Polly.

And she did. She was so obviously bursting with excitement, we just stood there and waited.

'Now,' she began, as she always did upon these occasions, 'wot I'm goin' ter tell yer is only 'earsay and mustn't be repeated. Is that understood?'

'Of course, Mrs C.!' we chorused as we always did.

'Well, then, rumour 'as it that old Mr Samuel Swinfen — that's the father of the gentleman that's just passed away — wants the estate to go to Mr 'Enry's widow, Mrs Patience Swinfen, when 'e goes. An' that won't be long, by all accounts. But they say there's a gentleman somewhere — in the army, Mr Jolly thinks — a nephew of the old man, 'oo's more entitled than Mrs Patience. So — there could be ructions — bad ructions.'

'But hasn't old Mr Samuel made a will?' I asked.

'That's wot we don't know. But one thing's fer sure. 'E'd better 'urry up if 'e ain't!'

She was right. Old Samuel Swinfen died two months later but not before he'd made a new will bequeathing his estate at Swinfen to his daughter-in-law, Patience.

It was Nanny who imparted this piece of information to me on one of my now regular visits. 'But they do say,' she told me, her voice lowered although there was no-one in the shop at the time, 'that 'e weren't in 'is right mind when 'e did it. An' 'is signature's just a scrawl. Mind you,' she added gloomily, ''twere made wi' one o' those new pens wi' nibs, so mebbe it weren't legal.' Nanny was mistrustful of progress of any description.

Legal or not, rumour had it that Patience Swinfen had taken over the running of the estate upon her father-in-law's death.

'Poachers daren't go near the place no more,' said Ned who seemed to hear about such things. 'After their guts, she is.'

'I don't blame her,' I said tartly.

'Yer wouldn't say that if yer was married to one,' Ned rejoined, 'An' dependin' on a rabbit or two for the pot.'

'I can't 'ardly see Cat married to a poacher in the first place,' said Polly and dissolved into giggles at the thought.

'I can't see Cat married to *anyone*!' said Ned. 'She'll be stichin' away at 'er 'andkerchiefs till she's bald! And you, too, Polly, if yer don't watch out!'

I laughed with them but I knew that what Ned said was true, although I had no intention of embroidering handkerchiefs for the rest of my life. They were only a means to an end, but to what end, exactly, I still wasn't sure, only that I wanted to have some sort of a shop, although not necessarily one quite like Nanny's. I knew a little more about Nanny by then; knew that she and her sister had been left money by an uncle who had 'panned for gold' somewhere in America, not only panned but found it, although he'd died in the attempt. With their inheritance, they had leased their little shop with living accommodation attached and, situated as it was in the very heart of the city, had never looked back.

But nothing like that was likely to happen to me. True, I, too, had a wealthy uncle at Wolstanton, but he was in excellent health and, in any case, had a family who would inherit. However, from hints dropped by Nanny from time to time, I knew that they might one day consider offering me employment as they grew older and, indeed, I knew that I could be of use to them. But was that what I wanted? And how would I ever bring myself to leave Ashling? At the same time, I knew that I could not stay there for ever. Mrs C. had many working years left in her, God willing, and the Mistress would never employ two adult cooks. I would have to move on.

So I determined that I would make as much use as possible of the months still left to me. A house like Ashling could teach a girl of my background so much. Why should I stop at the kitchen?

'Want any help?' I surprised Ned by asking when Mrs C. had given me a half hour off.

'Yer can give Satan a rub-down if yer like,' he told me, for he had just brought the great beast in after exercising him as he did while Edward was away.

'Show me then!' I said. So, nothing loath, Ned seized a dandy brush and comb and set to work on the already glistening flanks. Then he showed me how to lift each massive hoof and check that there were no stones lodged around the shoe.

'Now you,' he said. 'But remember yer've got ter whistle 'tween yer teeth while yer do it. The hoss don't like it if yer don't! An' remember to steer well clear of 'is back legs,' he added with a wicked grin.

I didn't need telling! I took the brush and comb, determined to conquer my fear, and whistling between my teeth as Ned did, went to work. But I soon had a problem. 'I can't reach his back,' I complained. 'Can I have a chair or a box?

At this, he burst out laughing and said it would be easier if he put me to work on Toffee. 'He needs saddlin' up for Miss Sophie's afternoon ride.'

Toffee was much more my size and I had often fed him carrots as I passed his box. Now, he nuzzled me playfully as, under Ned's direction, I thrust the bit between his teeth and buckled the many straps on his bridle. 'Want to get up?' asked Ned when we had secured the girth of his saddle. 'Go on! Just to see 'ow it feels. Miss Sophie ain't due fer a coupla minutes.'

Almost, I did. But then I saw the gleam of laughter in his eyes and guessed that he only wanted to see the flash of my bloomers as I pulled up my skirts.

'Not today, thank you,' I said primly. 'But perhaps another day, you'll show me how to harness up the governess cart.'

'Goin' callin' wi' the Mistress then, are we?' Ned taunted.

'I just want to know how,' I told him. 'You never know when it might be useful.' For at the back of my mind was the thought that when I had my own Establishment, as I now called it in my mind, then I might provide a delivery service of whatever it was I would be selling, be it cakes, crumpets or tintacks!

By the same token, whenever I was sent down to the kitchen garden, perhaps for a handful of herbs or a basket of fruit, I would look carefully at what was being done there and then ask so many questions that Mr Loftus eventually stood back from the bed he was preparing for early potatoes, and gave me a quizzical stare and asked if I wanted his job.

'I just want to *know*,' I told him, as I had Ned. For my Establishment had now acquired a sizeable plot of land where there would be room for vegetables — and livestock?

'What do you feed them on?' I asked Mrs Roberts at the Home Farm when I was next sent down for eggs and we were looking for them in the strange places that hens seem to choose for laying.

'What do they eat?' I asked her husband when I found him leaning over the rail of the pigsty.

Sometimes, I would have a good laugh at myself for the apparently limitless extent of my over-imaginative mind. But then I would think of Pa and how he had known so much about so many things but had never used his knowledge to improve his circumstances and I would vow to at least do something with all that I was now trying to cram into my brain. I was encouraged in this determination, strangely enough, by none other than Mrs Patience Swinfen.

She rode into the stable yard one afternoon to find Ned showing me how to manoeuvre Floss, a pretty little bay pony, between the shafts of the governess cart which the Mistress had ordered to be brought round in fifteen minutes. She dismounted unaided and, looping her reins over her arm, sauntered over to us.

'I'll take 'er from yer in just a minute, ma'am,' Ned assured her, wrestling with a particularly obstinate strap. He knew Mrs Swinfen well for she often rode over to see the Master about some matter concerned with the running of her estate. We all called it *her* estate although we had heard that a certain Captain Frederick Swinfen was laying claim to it as being its rightful heir.

'No hurry,' she said. And then, looking at me more closely. 'Have you changed your position from housemaid to ostler, then, my dear?'

'Why, n — no, ma'am,' I stammered uncertainly but was saved by Ned, who said cheerfully,

'Says she just wants ter know 'ow, ma'am. But I reckon she's after me job!'

Patience gave me a shrewd look. 'Knowing how never did anyone any harm, and I should know. Here, Ned, let me finish that off for you while you take Lady.'

'Right, ma'am! Thank 'ee!' And Ned led her horse away.

With expert fingers, Patience secured the straps that put Floss safely between the shafts, then rested her arms on the pony's broad back and gazed across at me.

'What's your name, my dear?'

'Marsh, ma'am. Cat Marsh.'

'And do you, as they say, have ideas above your station, Marsh? No — answer me,' for I had begun to shift uncomfortably, not sure how I should react to such direct speech from someone of her standing. 'Because you're never going to get anywhere in this life unless you have. Not knowing your place, is another way of putting it.'

'Well, yes, ma'am,' I admitted. 'I mean I know where my place is *now*, but I don't want it always to be so.'

'Good! I felt the same when I was your age. So much so, that I and my sister upped and left our home in Wales and went to London to seek our fortune.'

'Did you really, ma'am? I hadn't thought of going further than Lichfield.'

'There's a sight more going on in Lichfield than there ever was in Llanfair Caerinion!' she assured me. 'And I think your choice is very wise. Do you know what you want to do in Lichfield exactly, Cat?'

'I want a shop, I think, ma'am,' I said all in a rush. 'My own establishment.' At last I had actually put it into words — and, moreover, to this woman whom I had only met once and for a very short space of time. I was staring at her, still amazed at my daring, when Mrs Marshall, impatient presumably of the delay, appeared under the garden archway.

'Why, Patience!' she began and then, seeing me, said sharply. 'What are you doing there, Marsh? Is there nothing to be done in the kitchen?'

'A great deal, I expect, eh Marsh?' said Mrs Swinfen sweetly but dropping the eyelid furthest away from the Mistress. 'Good luck, Cat!' she said under her breath. 'I hope I shall see you again.'

I bobbed swiftly, murmured 'Thank you, ma'am. I hope so, too!' And ran indoors.

*   *   *

It was to be several months before I saw Patience Swinfen again. The following year, we learned through Mr Jolly that Captain Frederick Swinfen's claim to the Swinfen estate had been referred to the Court of Chancery in London.

'And I don't hold out much hope for her,' Mr Jolly told Mrs C. 'She being only a woman.'

Mrs C., was inclined to agree with him and, indeed, so did the rest of the kitchen staff. Only Ned and I thought otherwise.

'Wouldn't put anythin' past 'er!' said Ned.

'Nor me,' I said. For I had this ridiculous notion that success for Patience Swinfen would also mean success for Cat Marsh in her venture.

*   *   *

The other matter that concerned us during that year of 1855 was the cleaning out of

Stowe and Minster Pools and the establishment of a direct supply of clean water to the mining district of South Staffordshire. What had for a long time been 'only a pipe dream' — so said Mr Jolly, making one of his rare jokes — was now, apparently, to become a reality.

'December,' he told us gloomily, 'that's when it'll all start. And that man McClean's at the bottom of it. I just hope he knows what he's doing.'

However, soon after work had begun on the sinking of a shaft and the diversion of the stream that fed Minster pool while it was cleaned out, something else happened that brought such terrible consequences to all of us, that the whole business went out of our minds.

13

It was on the last day of the old year that it happened — at precisely three o'clock in the afternoon. Looking back, it seemed likely that the Master had known, or at least had had a premonition, of the notice that appeared on the door of Mr Richard Greene's bank in Lichfield at that time, for he had seemed worried and preoccupied throughout the Christmas festivities.

> 'It is with deep concern that I find myself compelled to close the door of this establishment. The circumstances which occasion this necessity are remote, and will be fully explained without delay.
>   Richard Greene'

The 'circumstances', although it was not common knowledge at the time, turned out to be not only 'remote' but bizarre in the extreme and were to do with a Mr William Lawton, Mr Greene's Confidential Clerk, who had apparently 'abstracted' a vast sum of money through neglecting to cut off the corner of worn or dirty bank notes and instead, putting them into his own pocket. The result was that Richard Greene was declared bankrupt; and in his downfall took with him several of his most prominent customers, including Colonel Marshall.

Speechless with shock, we could only stare dumbly at Mr Jolly on that cold January morning when he came to tell us what had happened and then I remembered what Sophie had said about Richard Greene when we had been crouched together on the stairs that first Christmas: 'he is in great cahoots with Papa'.

'It's the end of Ashling as we know it,' said Mr Jolly, his voice breaking with emotion. 'It's the end of *us*!'

Still without a word being spoken, we all suddenly sat down around the table — and continued to stare at him.

'Was *all* their money in the bank?' Mrs C. asked eventually.

'Every penny. The Master trusted Mr Greene, you see. And he wasn't the only one.'

'So — what will happen next?' I asked.

'Ashling will be sold and the money used to pay off the debts.'

'Debts?' quavered Mrs C. 'Wot debts?'

'Apparently Ashling was heavily mortgaged,' said Mr Jolly. 'It takes a lot of money to run a place like this and the Master was generous to a fault. The Mistress didn't know the half of it, just expected things to go on like they always had, so the Master never told her.'

I shuddered, thinking of the condemnation that was surely being heaped upon the Master's head at that moment. 'How is he?' I asked.

Mr Jolly shook his head. 'A broken man.'

'An' the children?' Mrs C. asked.

'At first, I think Miss Sophie saw it as a great adventure. It was only when the Mistress told her Toffee would have to be sold that it really sank in. And Mr Edward's just too stunned to say much. Only the Mistress seems to have found her tongue.'

'She won't want me in the mornin' room, then,' said Mrs C. for she had not yet received her instructions for the day.

'We're all to be in the hall at eleven o'clock,' said Mr Jolly. 'The Master wants to tell us what's happened himself. There's one small consolation,' he added as he got to his feet. 'The Lichfield Savings Bank isn't affected.'

So Nanny and her sister will be all right, I thought, and the countless other small investors in the City; and that included me for I had long since taken Nanny's advice and opened an account there. Not that that presented much consolation in the face of the disaster that had struck at the very heart of Ashling.

★ ★ ★

The Master was very brief. 'As you may have already heard; Mr Greene of the Bank of Palmer and Greene in Lichfield, has been declared bankrupt. Unfortunately, this means that my own affairs are in a similar parlous state and I will no longer be able to sustain the expense of this house. Also — and I cannot tell you how distressed I am at having to tell you this — I will no longer be in a position to offer you employment. Wages will be paid until the end of the month but after that, nothing can be guaranteed. You are at liberty to remain here until the house is sold or to leave immediately, if that is your wish.

From the bottom of my heart, I thank you all for the loyal and conscientious service you have given me and my family over the years. That is all.'

And he just stood there, alone, his head bent, his back — normally straight as a ramrod — visibly sagging, while we filed away. His wife, I presumed, had had no wish either to associate herself with his sentiments or to support him in what was surely his hour of greatest need.

'So wot shall I cook fer luncheon?' was the first thing Mrs C. said when we reached the kitchen.

'I should use whatever you have at your disposal,' said Mr Jolly. 'The tradesmen won't be calling, that's for sure.'

'There's some cold venison in the larder,' I reminded her. 'Perhaps we could make a pie?'

'Yes — us'll do that, Cat,' she said wearily.

Unbidden, I went to make a big pot of tea. 'Good girl,' approved Mr Jolly, 'I'll get something to go in it.' And he left the room to return a moment later with a large bottle of rum.

'Now,' he said, when we were all settled with our cups and I, for one, was choking over the rum but still grateful for the warmth it brought to my stomach, 'what are we all goin' to do? Mrs C.?'

Her eyes brimming with tears, Mrs C. shook her head. 'I dunno, Mr Jolly, an' that's a fact. I'm gettin' too old ter learn the ways of a new mistress.'

'You'd have to go a long way,' said Mr Jolly deliberately, 'to find a worse one than the hell-hound you have now.'

We all stared at him in astonishment. Never before had we heard him speak a single word of criticism of the Mistress.

'There's no point beatin' about the bush,' he said. 'Not now. We all know she's a tyrant. So that's one good thing about the situation — we'll all be shot of her before long.'

'I'll drink to that!' said Ned and the atmosphere around the table lightened perceptibly.

'Now,' Mr Jolly continued, 'we'll all be given good references. The Master will see to that. And I'm sure,' he said kindly to Mrs C. 'that an opportunity for such an excellent cook as yourself, will soon present itself, once it's known you're free. Now, Katie, what about you? What will you do?'

Katie blushed slightly. 'Reckon I'll be gettin' wed sooner than I thought, Mr Jolly.' Katie had been keeping company for some time with one of the ostlers at the George Inn in Lichfield.

'Excellent!' said Mr Jolly. 'And I'm sure that all our good wishes will go with you. Now you, Ada?'

Ada had no such matrimonial prospects. 'Dunno,' she admitted. 'There ain't too many livin'-in jobs round 'ere. An' the last thing I want is ter live at 'ome. I couldn't,' she added gloomily, 'unless I slept in the 'en 'ouse!' For yet another baby had appeared in the tiny cottage already shared by her parents and

Ada's six brothers and sisters. 'An' that goes fer Polly, too,' she added, for Polly had left at sunrise on her day off.

'We'll have to see what we can do, then,' said Mr Jolly, although what he might have in mind, I couldn't imagine. 'And what about you, Cat?' he asked, turning towards me.

'Cat'll be orlright,' said Ned as I hesitated. ''Ow about it, Cat? 'Ire a workshop, why not, an' take us all in ter work fer yer.'

The idea was preposterous and he knew it. But my stomach, whose reaction was always an indication of my emotional state, suddenly gave an enormous lurch and my heartbeat definitely increased its rhythm. Suddenly, I became aware that they were all, Mrs C. included, gazing at me hopefully. Fred, who was sitting next to me, even turned in his seat.

'I — I just don't know. Not yet.' I looked at Mr Jolly as I spoke. 'But Ned's got a point, hasn't he? It would be wonderful if we could all stay together.'

There were murmurs of assent from the others, especially Ada. 'It would, indeed, Cat,' said Mr Jolly, 'although I doubt if I could be associated with any such enterprise, except perhaps in an advisory capacity. I have a sister down in Hastings, widowed now, and I shall probably go to her. But I shall certainly stay here for as long as the Master needs me. So, if you should need any advice, Cat . . . '

Aghast, I looked around at the expectant faces of what had become my surrogate family. Suddenly, they all seemed to be depending upon me — I, who had the flimsiest idea of what I would do next. But at the same time, I knew I couldn't let them down.

'I — I'll think about it,' I promised, 'I really will. Meanwhile,' and I rose to my feet, 'I'll get the venison from the larder, shall I, Mrs C.?'

'Do that, my dear,' she said. 'Wotever yer think.'

* * *

Later that day, I found Sophie sobbing quietly on the front stairs.

'Sophie, darling! Don't take on so!' Without thinking twice, I sat down beside her on the stairs although we were clearly visible from the hall below and the landing above. Within the space of a few hours, the whole atmosphere of the house had changed. It was almost as if the green baize door had ceased to exist, for no longer could any of us be threatened with punishment or dismissal. Had Mrs Marshall suddenly appeared, I

216

would certainly have risen to my feet and stepped aside as politeness dictated, but I wouldn't have flattened myself into the wall and pretended I wasn't there. The worst had already happened and we were all managing as best we could; in Sophie's case, apparently, not very well.

I put my arms around her and hugged her tightly. 'Perhaps it won't be so bad, my love.'

'Oh, Cat, it couldn't be worse! I am to go and live with that dreadful Charlotte! In London! And,' her voice rose hysterically, 'I can't take Toffee. Mama says he must be sold along with everything else. Oh, Cat,' and she clung to me despairingly, 'don't let it happen! *Please* don't let it happen!'

'There, there, my love!' But while I soothed and patted and hugged her close, I was thinking — here it is again, this expectation that I can do something about it. Instinctively, I felt the need to share the burden that Fate seemed to be thrusting upon me. 'Where's Edward?' I asked Sophie. 'And your Mama and Papa?'

'Mama is sulking in her sitting room. Edward has saddled Satan and ridden off somewhere. And Papa has gone out with his gun.'

This time, my stomach shrivelled with a terrible premonition. I leaned back so that I could study Sophie's face more closely but she seemed unaware of the significance of her statement. 'Too cold for rabbits, today,' I observed. 'They'll all be tucked up in their burrows.' But in fact, I had never known the Master go out alone for the express purpose of killing rabbits; that had always been left to Edward and the gamekeepers.

I took my handkerchief from my pocket and wiped Sophie's tear-stained face. 'Why not come down to the kitchen and see what Mrs C.'s got for your tea? She's been baking all afternoon.' That was true, for Mrs C. had determined that nothing should be left on the larder shelves when it came time for us to go. 'I'd rather feed it to them birds!'

As Sophie and I went down the stairs, I remembered how, a short while ago, I had found Rex whining at the front door and how, when I had opened it, he had dashed away into the garden. I had thought nothing of it at the time but now, I wondered — it was not like the Master to leave him behind.

At the door of Mr Jolly's pantry, I stopped and told Sophie to run on to the kitchen. 'I'll soon be with you,' I promised. But, of course, I was not.

★   ★   ★

They brought him home on a hurdle, his body covered with one of Mrs Roberts' sheets, for he had been found in a spinney close to Home Farm. It was Edward who found him, for he had come clattering into the yard as we were all setting out with our lanterns — by then the early winter twilight was creeping up over the fields — and had immediately put the horse into a loose box and joined us.

We scattered in different directions but I was nearest to Edward and had already turned my steps towards him when I'd heard Rex's frenzied barking from the woodland. I found him kneeling beside his father's body, cradling his poor, blood-stained head in his arms. The gun was beside him.

'Oh, Edward!' I sank to my knees beside him, putting one arm around him and the other around the still-barking dog. Unable to speak, we continued to kneel as if we were keeping vigil, but just before we heard footsteps crashing through the undergrowth towards us, Edward raised his head and spoke.

'I should never have left him, Cat. I should have realised what was on his mind.'

'No-one could possibly have known,' I told him. 'It was no-one's fault. And Edward,' I added, 'his life would have been unbearable, had he lived. You must know that.'

I referred, of course, to the existence he would have been forced to endure with his tyrant of a wife, no longer cushioned by the distractions that wealth could provide. But Edward thought I meant otherwise. 'You're right,' he said. 'Leaving Ashling would have broken his heart.'

But leave it he did. His coffin, draped in purple velvet and bearing his regimental sword and insignia, was placed upon a special funeral truck at Alrewas station with his relations and other mourners in carriages behind and taken to Lichfield, and from there to a remote village in Derbyshire where he was laid to rest with his forebears.

'It was a very movin' ceremony,' Mr Jolly told us when he came back from it. 'A detachment from his old regiment went with him to the graveside and a volley was fired over the grave.'

That evening, the door of Mr Jolly's pantry remained firmly closed and it was nearly midnight when Edward and I heard him stumble up the stairs to his bed.

I had seen little of the family, except from a distance, during the days preceding the funeral. The house had been full of people offering their condolences for such a 'dreadful accident', for that was the story the

Mistress had commanded to be circulated. I doubt if many believed it but it did serve to draw a veil of apparent respectability over the whole tragic event and we found ourselves going along with it.

''E fell,' I heard Mrs C. telling the postman. 'Tripped over the root of a tree, seemingly, and the gun went off.'

It was a conclusion arrived at also by the coroner, especially since no suicide note had been found.

'Only a pile of references for each an' every one of us,' said Mr Jolly sadly.

On the day of the funeral, only Mr Jolly and Edward came back to Ashling, for the Mistress and Sophie had gone to stay with friends for a few days. That night, everyone had gone early to bed except for Mrs C. and me and I was just damping down the fire while Mrs C. lit our bedroom candles when Edward came into the kitchen.

'Forgive me for being so late. I wondered,' and he glanced hesitantly at Mrs C., 'if I might speak to Cat for a while.'

'Of course, sir. I'm just goin' up, anyway. Goodnight, Cat. Goodnight, sir.'

At last, the embargo had been lifted! Edward was now the Master, if only for a short while.

When she had gone, he sat down heavily at

the table and I saw how weary he was. There were lines in his face that I swear had not been there a week ago.

'Tea?' I suggested.

He smiled then. 'Would it be a lot of trouble if I were to ask for a cup of cocoa? It was always so — so comforting when I was a child.'

'Pobs,' I said, 'that was what I liked most.'

'Pobs?'

'Bread and milk — and a spoonful of sugar if there was any to spare.'

'I think — if it's all right with you — I'd sooner have cocoa!'

I made two cups of cocoa and filled a plate with gingerbread. He sipped gratefully and then put down his cup, rested his arms on the table and looked at me directly.

'Cat,' he asked 'what am I to do?'

I looked back at him, my heart sinking. Edward, too? Was there no-one to whom *I* could turn for help? Desperately, I longed for my father's presence and for the words of wisdom and comfort he would have spoken. Or would he? Perhaps, he, too, would have been out of his depth in this strange situation. I put out my hand and covered Edward's.

'How long,' I asked, playing for time, 'before you have to leave Ashling?'

He shrugged. 'About three months, the

lawyers say. A valuation has yet to be made but I understand a sum in the region of £4,000 is expected. It will be sold by auction.'

'And will all that money be needed to — to — '

'Pay off our debts? I fear so, Cat.' He laughed bitterly. 'We will be allowed exactly twenty pounds to live on for the rest of our lives, in addition to our clothes. We would be better off if we were artisans of some sort — carpenters, perhaps, or masons — for at least we would then be allowed to keep the tools of our trade. But we have no skills, Cat, other than to live comfortably off the fat of the land. If it were not for my dear old Uncle Perce, we would be completely destitute.'

'Uncle Perce?' I queried.

'He was my father's older brother. He never married and when he died, a few months ago, he left me a small legacy. And this, I am assured, cannot be touched by our creditors. It is only a small amount — two or three hundred pounds — but it should be sufficient to buy a small house for my mother. But there will be nothing left in the way of income. For that, she will depend upon me — and there is nothing that I can think of to do, Cat. Nothing! And where are we to find this small house? For nothing will persuade my mother to continue living anywhere near Lichfield where she is so well known.'

'And Sophie?' I asked, although I knew already of Sophie's fate. 'What will happen to her?'

'That's another thing. She will go to London to live with my mother's cousin.'

'And your mother cannot go, too?'

He shook his head, at the same time giving me a wry grin. 'To be honest, I doubt if they would have her! They plead a lack of income but in truth, I think it is because they could not bear to have her in the same household. And I doubt if *she* could live in another woman's house.'

We were silent for a moment or two and I absentmindedly pushed a crumb of ginger-bread about on the surface of the table. And then, almost as if I had become two separate people, I listened to myself telling Edward about the plans that I had been turning over in my mind during the last few days. So far, there had been one enormous stumbling block — lack of money. But now . . .

'Edward,' I began, 'there is a possible way out of your difficulties — out of all our difficulties.' And hesitantly at first, but growing more confident as I realised that he was listening to me with intense interest, I unfolded my plan.

'There will always be a need for food, Edward. People must eat — but the food they are offered must be matched to their pockets as well as their stomachs. If it can be manufactured cheaply enough, they will buy it. Now — I am a good cook, Edward. And Mrs C. is an even better one. Between us, I think that we could produce good, cheap food that the working classes would buy. But to do this, Edward, we need premises. If you were willing to invest your money in a building where there would not only be living accommodation but also room for a little shop with a kitchen behind, we could be in business, you and I. What do you say?'

But I could see that I was going too quickly for him. I curbed my tongue and waited for him to collect his thoughts.

'You mean,' he said at last, 'like Nanny and her sister have done in Lichfield?'

'Exactly. But not in Lichfield, for we would not wish to compete with them. And your mother . . . '

He shook his head. 'I doubt if my mother would agree to such an enterprise anywhere,' he began doubtfully.

'Edward,' I spoke slowly and deliberately, 'she would have no choice, once you had decided.'

But this state of affairs, he clearly could not

visualise. 'Think about it,' I told him, 'for there is a great deal to consider. And there is no need to reach a decision immediately although, if I am to seek professional advice, I would need to know fairly soon.'

'Professional advice?' He looked up eagerly, obviously wishing to grasp at the straw of a second opinion.

'Oh yes,' I said, 'we would need that. And I think I know where I might find it.'

14

The day after my discussion with Edward — and with his permission — I told the others that he was giving serious consideration to my ideas. The response was immediate.

'Cat,' Mrs C. said earnestly when we were alone in the kitchen, 'I've got a bit saved, yer know. An' I'd be 'appy fer you to 'ave it for wotever you an' Master Edward decides to do.'

Tears came to my eyes. 'Mrs C., I can't tell you how much I appreciate your offer. But you must know more about what is involved before you commit yourself.'

Later on that same day, Ned stopped me in the yard. 'Count me in,' he said without preamble.

'Count you in on what, exactly, Ned?'

'Why — in whatever shenanigans you an' Master Edward are proposin'. An' I don't just mean workin' — I mean investin'!'

'Oh, Ned, thank you!' And I surprised us both by giving him a quick hug. 'But I didn't know you were a man of property.' I spoke teasingly, still unsure about what he meant exactly.

'Yer not the only one with an eye to the future, young Cat, I bin savin' since I were knee-'igh to a grass'opper an' a gaffer give me sixpence for 'oldin' 'is 'oss outside an inn. I got fifty quid saved up now an' yer welcome to it. Well,' he added prudently, 'most of it! May keep a quid or two back fer meself.'

I burst out laughing. 'You're a true business man, Ned. Just the man I could do with. Thank you from the bottom of my heart.'

As I turned away, meaning to go back into the kitchen, Mrs Swinfen came clattering into the yard on Lady and Ned went to help her dismount.

'Hello, the pair of you! I've come to offer my condolences to Mrs Marshall but I've just seen Edward and he tells me she's away with Sophie.'

'You must have some refreshment, ma'am, before you ride home,' I said. 'In the morning room, perhaps?'

'The morning room be blowed! I'll wager the kitchen's a damn sight warmer!'

I smiled at her. 'You'll be very welcome there, ma'am, although we're all at sixes and sevens, as you can imagine.'

I led the way into the kitchen and Mrs C. after a fluster or two, put her in one of the Windsor chairs and I went to make hot chocolate for all of us. Since Mrs C.'s edict that everything must be consumed before the auction, our standard of living had risen dramatically.

'So — what is to become of you all?' she asked without preliminaries.

'You must ask Cat about that, ma'am,' said Mrs C. while I was still wondering what to say. Mrs Swinfen gazed at me expectantly.

'Well,' I began, 'it's what I mentioned to you once before, ma'am. And this seemed the right moment.'

She nodded. 'I remember. And what do you have in mind, exactly?'

'A shop, ma'am, selling pies and cakes and whatever else people want,' I said somewhat lamely, for my plans were still only slowly coming together.

'You will need money for such a project,' she said thoughtfully.

I told her then about Edward's legacy. 'If he were to decide to come in with us, ma'am, it would make a big difference.'

'I can see that,' she said, taking the hot chocolate I had made her and sipping it gratefully. 'I wish that I could help you, too, but as my affairs stand at the moment, I dare not suggest it, for I doubt if my bank manager would sanction either a gift or a loan. It won't always be the case, I hope, but for now I can only offer you the benefit of my advice

— which is not great in these matters, I fear. However, one thing does occur to me. Where would you have such a shop? Lichfield is well served already and I doubt if there would be sufficient trade elsewhere in the area. Unless . . . ' and she pursed her lips thoughtfully.

'Unless, ma'am?' I prompted.

'There is what they're beginning to call the Black Country towards the north of the county where they mine for coal.'

'Cannock Chase, you mean, ma'am?' asked Mr Jolly who had come quietly into the kitchen while she was speaking and who now took the chair opposite hers.

'That's it, Mr Jolly. Beaudesert, the home of the Marquess of Anglesey. You know of it, of course.'

'Of course, ma'am!' It was Mr Jolly's business to know everything there was to know about the gentry and aristocracy of the county. 'I recently attended the funeral of the old Marquess in Lichfield,' he added.

'Well, I've heard that John McClean has sunk another deeper pit in the middle of the Chase. With the Marquess's permission, of course. Chasetown, they call it. There will be coal miners there aplenty, and their families.'

Mr Jolly coughed politely, a sure sign that he was about to disagree. 'Beggin' your pardon, ma'am, but would not such a — a clientele — be of a very rough and unseemly disposition? I remember when they were building the railway line here, back in the forties, the navvies were — well, ma'am, all I can say is that their behaviour left much to be desired.' And he shook his head at the memory.

'But the navvies were mostly immigrants, Mr Jolly,' Mrs Swinfen was quick to point out, 'from other parts of the country and from Ireland. The coal miners will be local people who will have a reputation to consider. And many of them will be married.'

'That's as maybe, ma'am,' said Mr Jolly, clearly not convinced.

'Well, I'm sure it would be worth your while to consider such an area, my dear,' said Mrs Swinfen, turning to me. 'But bearing in mind Mr Jolly's reservations, of course,' she added diplomatically.

Soon afterwards, her chocolate finished, she rose to go, thanking us all for our hospitality and wishing us luck. 'I shall see you at the auction, if not before,' she promised.

When she had gone, Ada and Polly, who had been following the conversation with keen interest, looked at each other and nodded, then Ada turned to me.

'Poll an' me 'ud like to come with yer, Cat, if yer'll 'ave us.'

'Of course I'll have you! I can't think how I'd manage without you both. But are you sure? What about these rough miners that Mr Jolly is so worried about?'

Ada giggled. 'That's wot's decided us, Cat! They sound a lot more promisin' than the lads round 'ere! Beggin' yer pardon, Fred!' she added with a sly glance at him where he lounged by the sinks, using his finger to extract the last trace of chocolate from his cup.

'Take no notice, Fred,' I advised him.

'Oh, I won't. But count me in, too, Cat, if yer will.'

'I will,' I assured him. My workforce, at least, was assured.

★   ★   ★

Two days later, I faced Mr George in the little office which by now had become very familiar to me. Over the years, he had received me there many times as he inspected my work and I think that he truly enjoyed our 'little haggles', as he called them. But this was no 'little haggle'.

His face as impassive as the door of the enormous, wall safe behind him, he listened without comment to what I had to say.

I told him everything; everything, at least, that he did not know already for by then the Master's untimely demise was common knowledge. But he knew nothing of my plans or of Edward's legacy.

'And what do you want of me, exactly?' he asked, once I had sketched a brief outline of what I hoped to achieve.

'More than anything, your advice,' I told him. And I saw an expression of surprise flicker briefly across his face and knew, as I had guessed he would, that he'd expected me to ask directly for money. But I was more subtle than that! Now, I produced what I considered my trump card — the sheets of paper on which Edward, in his beautiful copper-plate and at my direction, had listed our requirements.

Before he wrote them, I had visited several ironmongers in the town and made extensive enquiries about the latest kitchen ranges. The one at Ashling was old and needed to be fed constantly with buckets of coal, also it could be used only for cooking. But now, I had discovered, there was one which not only had numerous new devices — a system whereby the fire could be enlarged for roasting and contracted when it was finished, revolving trivets, several heated drawers and shelves besides the customary spits — but also had at one side and extending along the back of the fire, a large boiler which would produce a constant supply of hot water, fed as it was from a cistern.

Besides the basic requirement of an efficient range, I had listed a variety of utensils which Mrs C. and I considered essential for the production of the good, simple food we wished to offer; saucepans in a variety of sizes and weight, steamers and stew-pans.

'Are you going to live, sleep and have your being in the kitchen?' Mr George enquired caustically when he had studied them. 'There is nothing here about the beds and tables and chairs you would need.'

'Ashling and its contents will be sold by auction,' I told him. 'I would hope that we would be able to bid for what we need and at knock-down prices. Edward — that is, Mr Marshall — already owns several pieces of furniture in his own right. Some of the kitchen equipment would also be worth buying — although not all, by any means,' I added, mindful of a couple of thin-bottomed pans which needed constant scouring.

When Mr George had inspected the lists thoroughly, he leaned back in his chair, placed the tips of his fingers together and considered me long and carefully over the top of them.

'A few questions, if I may, Miss Marsh.' For some time now, he had called me 'Miss Marsh' rather than 'missy' but now he seemed to give it an added importance. 'Exactly why do you wish to undertake such an enterprise? Why not simply come and work in my shop? You would be welcome there, as I've long told you, and your handkerchiefs could still be a profitable side-line.'

'I want, if possible,' I began earnestly, 'to keep us together, those of the staff who wish to join me — and most of them do — not only because I care for them as if they were my own family, but because I think — I *know* — that they are all good workers. Also, I would like to be my own mistress. Not,' I added hastily, 'that you would not be an excellent employer, Mr George.'

He shrugged dismissively. 'That's as maybe! Now — next question. I may be treading on delicate ground here, but ask it I must. I understand that young Mr Marshall is essential to your plans; not only for the purchase of working premises but also for the general support you will need. Now, he is a likeable enough young fellow, I know, and would not object to turning his

235

hand to most things, but what of his mother? What does she say to all this? I know what she can be like for she has been a customer here for many years. Do you have plans for her, too, Miss Marsh? Or is she to live elsewhere?'

'I don't know,' I admitted. 'She doesn't yet know about all this. Mr Marshall is waiting for the right moment to tell her.'

His eyebrows shot heavenward. 'Then he will wait for ever, I'm afraid! There will never be a right moment to inform Mrs Marshall of Ashling Hall that her son is to be associated with — with a glorified soup kitchen.'

I did not care at all for his likening of my Establishment to a soup kitchen. However, I waited a moment for my annoyance to cool, then said brightly, 'Now — that's an idea! I hadn't considered soup. Thank you, Mr George! As to Mrs Marshall, she will just have to make the best of things for I am sure I will have her son's support.' I spoke with more optimism than I felt, for the strength of Edward's independence of his mother had yet to be tested.

'Well,' and here, Mr George gave me one of his rare smiles, 'I have warned you! Now — my final question. Where exactly do you propose setting up your establishment?'

'I understand,' I began knowledgeably and

profoundly grateful for Mrs Swinfen's suggestion, 'that there is a place not far away where coal mining is being developed. Chasetown, is it called?'

He nodded thoughtfully. 'That is right. Near the hamlet of Burntwood. John McClean is the man behind it as he is of so many enterprises.'

'So I understand,' I said, trying to look as if little in the business world escaped me.

'I'll make some enquiries,' Mr George promised. 'Test the coal surface, so to speak!'

'That would be very kind,' I murmured for it was exactly what I had hoped he would say. But there was something else I needed of him. 'If we were to continue with our scheme — and I have no reason for thinking otherwise,' I added hastily, 'the savings of more people than mine will be involved. Mrs Clifford — the cook at Ashling — has told me that she would be willing to invest in it, also the stable lad. He has considerably less than she, but nevertheless, for both of them it is their life savings. This is a great responsibility, Mr George. So I wondered — would you consider being overseer, as it were, of the funds and making sure that it is wisely spent?'

'A trustee, you mean? A very sensible precaution indeed, Miss Marsh.' And he nodded approvingly. 'May I suggest, when we

237

are a little further forward with the enterprise, that we bring in a young lawyer of my acquaintance who is hungry for work and will not charge the earth?'

I stared at him, unable to conceal my delight. 'You said 'we', Mr George! Does that mean I have your support?'

He nodded. 'I have always thought highly of your business acumen, Miss Marsh. Now,' he got to his feet, 'you go home and persuade young Mr Marshall that the sooner he finds the right moment to tell his mother, the better. In the meantime, I will make enquiries among my associates to see if I can strike a satisfactory bargain over the matter of cooking equipment.'

Five minutes later, I was in Nanny Humphries' back kitchen. 'He's agreed!' I told them, for I had called there previously to tell them what was happening.

'The Lord be praised!' said Nanny's sister who was very devout.

'I doubt the Mistress'll see it that way,' said Nanny darkly. 'She's yer next 'urdle, Cat!'

15

Later that day, I returned to Alrewas on the train and made my way home across the fields, feeling both sad and elated. It would be heart-wrenching to leave Ashling and the life I had enjoyed there but the anticipation of at last turning my dreams into reality was intoxicating. In fact, as I entered the yard, the thought of Mrs C.'s cowslip wine was uppermost in my mind. Dare I suggest broaching a bottle that evening to toast our future? Full of such happy thoughts, I entered the kitchen and stopped dead in my tracks.

The door to the passage was open, held thus by Polly and beyond her I could see Mrs C., Ada and Ned with Mr Jolly actually holding open the green baize door to the house. As I began to walk towards her, Polly turned her head and put her finger to her lips; but it wasn't necessary. Even from where I stood in the kitchen, the familiar sound of the Mistress's voice, raised in anger, was clearly audible and filled me with a dreadful foreboding.

'So this is what you get up to in my absence! Have you taken leave of your senses,

Edward? Are you actually proposing that we go into *trade*?'

It was Ada, I discovered afterwards, who was responsible for her premature discovery of our plans, for Edward had assured me he would say nothing unless I was with him, or at least nearby. Unaware that Mrs Marshall knew nothing about it, Ada had dared to try and discuss the future with her.

'Mother,' I heard Edward reply, 'we have no alternative. Otherwise, what are we to live on? Cat has offered to . . . '

'Cat!' And the word was spat out with all the venom of her warped nature. 'I presume you mean Marsh, our servant. Are you really proposing that I live in the same household, share the same table, the same rooms with a servant? You must be mad, Edward. Your father's sudden death has unhinged you.'

'Cat is my friend, Mother. As she would be yours, if you would allow it.'

At this, Polly looked at me and pulled a hideous face and I felt a bubble of hysterical laughter rise in my throat. But it was soon quelled.

'Cat, as you persist in calling her, is no better than she should be. Have you forgotten the circumstances under which she came to us? How she was mixed up in some sordid affair that made it impossible for her to continue living with her family — God-fearing people, that they were.'

And now the expression on Polly's face was one of perplexity, for she knew nothing of the stigma that Mrs Marshall had tried to attach to me; nor, indeed, did anyone except Mrs C., unless she had confided it to Mr Jolly. Even I had forgotten it, for it was years since I had even thought of Sam Bailey and his drunken sot of a father. But Edward, I recalled, had been present when she had hurled her vile accusations at me. Surely, he didn't . . . ?

'Whatever happened to Cat before she came to live with us is her own affair, Mother,' I heard him say and I breathed a sigh of relief. 'It has nothing to do with us.'

'It has everything to do with us! No, Edward, I will not even consider the ridiculous proposition you are making.'

'So, Mother — what are you going to do? I understand that your London cousins are not able to accommodate you.'

There came a slight pause while Mrs Marshall presumably considered a new approach. 'Do I understand that you, my only son, will go against my wishes, flout my authority in favour of a servant girl?'

'If needs must, Mother, that is what I will do.'

At this point, Polly executed a triumphant little jig — so triumphant she let go of the door and only caught it back in the nick of time.

'So, you will allow your mother to — to depend upon charity? To go into the workhouse if necessary?'

The thought of the Mistress taking up residence in the Lichfield Union was altogether too much for Polly. She was now so doubled up with laughter, I had to rush across the kitchen to take the door from her. For it was important that I heard Edward's reply to his mother's blackmail. For I knew that he was a kind, tender-hearted young man who would not willingly hurt another soul, especially his own mother. There came another pause and I guessed he was wrestling with his conscience. When he spoke again, there was a distinct tremor in his voice.

'All I'm asking at this stage, Mother, is that you think about it — give it your full consideration.'

'Nothing will make me change my mind, Edward. Nothing. And if you cared about me, you would never ask me to — to serve penny buns from behind a counter, to become the laughing stock of Lichfield.'

'It wouldn't be in Lichfield, Mother. Cat and I are fully aware of the embarrassment that would cause you. It would be in Chasetown.'

'*Chasetown?*' And now her voice rose to a piercing shriek and Polly covered her ears with her hands. 'Among the *coal miners?* Now I know you must be mad! I will be in my sitting room, Edward, when you have recovered your senses.' And there came the resounding bang of a door.

I gave the kitchen door back to Polly and walked down the passage. Mr Jolly saw me coming and continued to hold open the green baize door until I had walked through it.

★　★　★

I found him sitting in a chair in the morning room with his head in his hands. As I came in, he looked up and reached out a hand to me. 'Oh, Cat, what are we to do?'

I sank on to my knees beside his chair and, ignoring the proffered hand, put both my arms around him pressing his head into my shoulder. And then he began to sob, great retching sobs that shook his whole body and I knew, instinctively, that he cried not only because of his mother but for everything that had happened in the last, dreadful weeks, culminating in the tragic loss of his father.

'There, there!' I soothed him as if it were

Sophie whom I held in my arms and I wondered briefly if Sophie had come home with her mother. As I soothed and patted and murmured what I hoped were words of comfort into Edward's ears, I tried to marshall my thoughts, to decide upon a strategy for the next battle with the Mistress for battles there would be in plenty before the matter was settled. But it was a conflict that I was determined to win; Mr George's acceptance of my plan as a reasonable course of action had bolstered my determination as nothing else could have done.

I let him cry until I deemed he would be utterly exhausted if he did not stop, and then shook him gently. 'Come, Edward, dry your eyes, for we have much to talk about.'

I gazed down into his tear-washed face and for a moment ceased to be Cat, the instigator; Cat, the solver of everyone's problems and became Cat, the woman; Cat who, until now, had put this young man in her arms upon a pedestal, far beyond her reach but about whom she had dreamed impossible dreams. Now, suddenly, they did not seem quite so impossible. But I must not allow myself to travel down that road; at least, not yet. There was too much at stake.

I hoisted Edward upright in his chair, took the opposite one and allowed him a moment or two to mop his eyes and blow his nose. And then I told him about Mr George.

'So you see, Edward,' I finished, 'we have the professional approval that we sought. It's not just — just pie in the sky,' — here, he actually laughed — 'it's a sound, sensible investment that can succeed. I know it can.'

'But how are we going to get round my mother? For there is no way, Cat, that I could allow her to become destitute.'

'I do see that, Edward.' As, of course, I thought grimly, his mother does, too! 'But there must be some way in which she can be made to realise that our plan is the only way forward. How else is she to exist once you have found somewhere for you both to live?'

'If only there were some other more attractive place than Chasetown.'

'I was thinking about that on the way home,' I admitted. 'Mr George said it was near the village of Burntwood. If that were like Alrewas, then surely it would be more congenial for your mother. Perhaps,' I added and sounding more hopeful than I really felt, 'we could afford rooms for her there, once we were truly in business. But most importantly of all, I think she needs someone with whom to discuss the whole matter. Someone other than yourself, Edward. An older person who can show her that it is not such a hare-brained scheme after all — and that there is little alternative.'

'Someone like Mr George?' he suggested.

'Exactly. But not Mr George, of course,' I added with a curl of my lip, 'because he is in *trade*!' And I put a similar inflexion upon the word as his mother had although I think it was lost upon Edward. 'Someone from the professional classes whom she would trust, like — like a solicitor. What about your solicitor, Edward?'

He nodded thoughtfully. 'Old Trumper has served the family for many years.'

I knew 'old Trumper' well from his frequent visits to the house. If it were possible, he would be even more horrified than Mrs Marshall at my ideas.

'Is there no-one young in the firm?' I asked.

'There's *young* Trumper,' Edward conceded. And then, with increasing enthusiasm. 'By Jove, yes! That could be the answer, Cat. I know him well. Rides to hounds whenever the old man lets him off the leash. Loves a good gallop and is a devil at the fences. I could have a word.'

'Edward, that's wonderful! Perhaps you could go to see him tomorrow.'

'Why not? The problem, of course, will be convincing his father.'

'Well, let's cross that bridge when we come to it.' For it was marvellous to see how his depression was lifting, now that there was some positive action to take. 'And another thing, Edward. Does your mother realise that practically the entire staff, with the exception of Mr Jolly, will be coming with us? Or did she think that you and I would be the only participants in our scheme? That we,' and I lowered my eyes modestly at this point, 'and not to put too fine a point upon it, would be living together in the same house with no-one to act as chaperon?'

Considerably startled, he widened his eyes in disbelief. 'Good heavens! Surely not! Could she really think that — that I — that you — that we . . . ?'

I raised my eyes then, as distressed as he. Did the thought really fill him with such repugnance?

'Why,' he continued, 'I would never dream of putting any young lady of my acquaintance into such a compromising situation. Surely she didn't think that of me?'

Greatly relieved that he did not, apparently, find the idea distasteful in itself, I still gazed at him in surprise, for I had not realised how conventional, how straightlaced, he was in such matters. But then, I reminded myself, it would be the natural attitude of a young man of his class even though some, I had heard, were not nearly so moral when it came to their behaviour away from home. I doubted, however, that Edward came into that category. But the thought had reminded me of something else I wanted to talk to him about.

'Edward,' I began hesitantly. 'I could not help overhearing most of the words you exchanged with your mother. This — this matter of the reason she gave for my coming to Ashling in the first place, this — this sordid affair, she mentioned, I would like to explain to you exactly . . . '

But he interrupted me there. 'No, Cat, I do not wish to hear. I meant what I said — that it is your own affair entirely.'

Was it because he truly did not care? Or was it the reaction of a fastidious nature that simply did not want to sully itself with lurid details? Whatever the reason, I did not tell him about Sam Bailey — not then, at least.

★   ★   ★

Next morning, Edward went into Lichfield. 'I'll invite Jack Trumper out to lunch,' he said before he went. 'Get him away from the old man.'

'Good luck!' I wished him then went in

search of Sophie, for Edward had told me she had returned home with her mother but had gone straight to bed with a headache. I found her in the stables, talking to Ned.

'It ain't gonna be so bad,' he was telling her, 'not now Cat's taken over.' And they turned and saw me and Sophie ran to meet me.

'What's this Ned's been telling me?' she asked. 'That you and Edward are going to open a cake shop like Nanny Humphries'? Oh, Cat, can I come, too? I would work so hard — I can, you know, when I put my mind to it. Please, Cat!' And then she threw her arms around my neck.

I kissed her on the cheek, then put her from me. 'I'm sure that you can, sweetheart. But it's not as simple as that. To begin with, it won't be a cake shop, more likely a pie shop and it won't be in Lichfield. It will be in Chasetown, among the miners. Not at all the sort of place for a young lady such as yourself.'

'Now you sound exactly like Mama! Whatever it is, it will be the greatest fun, I'm sure.'

'It won't be fun at all, my love. It will be very hard and sometimes, I'm sure, very dirty and very smelly. Not at all what you are used to.' In fact, although I spoke with such certainty, I had very little idea of what it would be like. Like Burslem, perhaps, with the air thick with smoke, the houses grimy, the streets littered with debris and the countryside some considerable distance away? But it might be none of these things and the sooner I went to see it, the better.

'It's a lovely day,' I told Sophie now, 'why not saddle up Toffee and go for a gallop?'

'While I still have the chance, you mean? All right, Cat, but I am coming with you, you know.'

'Oh, Sophie, you know your Mama would never allow it. Neither,' I dared to say, 'would your Papa if he were still alive.' I had seen little of her since her father had died except for the evening he had been carried home when, risking her mother's disapproval, I had gone to her bedroom and she had cried herself to sleep in my arms.

'But he isn't, is he,' she answered me now and with a quiet, sad acceptance that seemed to show a maturity that I had not expected. 'And Mama,' she added darkly, and a child once more, 'is not the woman she was!' And when I looked at her in surprise, wondering where she could have picked up such a phrase, she admitted, 'I overheard Mrs C. telling Mr Jolly so, only this morning. Anyway,' she added, 'she was talking to herself last night and that's a sure sign of madness, is it not? She was going on and on about some hoar who was no better than she should be. What did she mean, Cat? The only hoar I know is the fruit of a hawthorn.'

I hugged her to me for a moment. 'Some day,' I promised, 'I'll explain it to you. But not yet, you enjoy yourself while you can.' But I shuddered as I watched her skip away. Did her mother really hate me so much?

★　★　★

Two days later, driving out from Lichfield in their brougham, came the Trumpers, father and son.

'I think it might work,' Edward had said after his meeting with Jack. 'He was all for it — thought it a splendid idea.'

'But did he think he'd be able to convince your mother?'

'Well, he'll have to have a word with his Pa, of course. No way to avoid that. But he'd do his best, he said. And another thing he suggested was that I use any influence I might have with the new Marquess of Anglesey to use *his* influence to find Mama reasonable living accommodation, possibly in Burntwood. Pa knew the old Marquess well so it might be worth bearing in mind.'

And might the Marquess be useful for other things, too, I pondered, a ludicrous picture forming in my mind of myself at the tradesman's entrance of Beaudesert Hall with a tray of pies while Edward presented his card at the front. We were going to be an incongruous couple and no mistake — the maidservant and the gentleman — but might not its very incongruity be turned to our advantage? It was something I must think about.

'You did well,' I congratulated Edward. 'Now, we'll just have to be patient and leave the next move to the Trumpers.'

I had resigned myself to a long wait so I was pleasantly surprised when Ada dashed into the kitchen to report their arrival.

'*An*' they're stayin' for lunch, the Mistress asked me to tell yer.'

'Did she indeed!' said Mrs C. grimly although knowing full well that the pot-roast silverside we had prepared could easily be stretched. The cheaper cuts of meat were all that the butcher would supply us with these days.

They stayed until nearly three o'clock and soon afterwards Edward came looking for me. I pulled a shawl over my shoulders and we stepped out into the yard for it was a sunny day in spite of a nip in the air. His jubilant face had already told me that the news was good.

'They were closeted with Mama in the library for a good hour. They seemed to think they'd do better without me but I hung around outside for I fully expected raised voices to tell me all that was happening! But it wasn't so. Mama went on a bit to begin with but then old Trumper took the stage, so to speak — I could hear his voice rumbling away but couldn't make out a word — and Mama actually seemed to listen — and without interrupting! Then there was a lot more chat I couldn't hear and Jack was allowed to say a word or two — and that was it. The next moment they were coming out and I had the devil's own job to disappear in time. And then we had lunch. Not a word, of course, while Mr Jolly and Ada were there. But afterwards over coffee in the drawing room, they came out with it.'

'With what?' I prompted mercilessly as he paused, presumably for breath.

For answer, he seized me about the waist, picked me up and twirled me around. 'It's all agreed, Cat! Provided whatever house we buy is in my name — and that's not important is it? — and that Mama — to use her own words — is suitably housed, I am to go ahead with her approval.'

At this, I kicked him hard, forcing him to put me down. 'Her *approval*?' I shrieked the words in my astonishment.

'That was my reaction at first. I simply could not believe it. But it's true, Cat, it's really true! Are you not overjoyed?'

'Well of course I am, Edward. It's just that — that I cannot take it in — not yet. But I soon will,' I assured him quickly, eager for the happy expression on his face to stay there. 'Let's go inside now and tell the others. And then, of course, we must begin to plan in earnest. Perhaps we can both go to see Mr George and certainly we must go over to Chasetown.' By the time we had reached the kitchen door, I was as excited as he.

But at the end of that eventful day when I climbed wearily into my bed, a feeling of deep unease crept over me. What could possibly have gone on behind the closed doors of the library that morning while Edward had lurked outside? What information could have been given by the Trumpers that had so dramatically changed Mrs Marshall's attitude? Not that it had been apparent in her manner towards me; that had remained unchanged. Indeed, when Edward, at my prompting, had suggested that we explain to her together what we had in mind, she had refused point blank, saying that she had no desire to converse with me and that he was fully aware of her requirements.

In the end, exhaustion made me give up the problem. After all, I comforted myself, there was no doubt that Edward had his legacy and that was sufficient to allow us to go forward. He had already written to Mr George requesting an appointment for us both and afterwards we would go by train to the station at Hammerwich which was, apparently, near Chasetown. That, surely, was enough for now.

16

It was as well that we had so much to occupy our minds for the next day saw the arrival of the auctioneer and his minions. They swarmed all over the house with their measuring tapes and their ladders, entering every room without so much as a 'by your leave,' eyeing the furniture with a gaze that saw only its monetary value and none of its beauty, fingering the silver with grimy hands — greatly to the distress of Ada and Katie who had polished it so assiduously. Nothing was sacred.

And then they moved on to the stables and the conservatories, the tool sheds and workshops; and, of course, the occupants of the stables. We had been careful to arrange for Sophie to spend the day at Home Farm, which was to be sold separately and with the Roberts's as sitting tenants. Crossing the yard while the assessors were still there, I was surprised to see that Toffee's stall was empty and I looked around for Ned. He was standing with his back to the men and, as I caught his eye, he winked broadly.

'Goin' down to the farm are yer then, Cat?'

he called out and I smiled my relief. So that was where Toffee was! And sure enough, he was back in his box soon after the assessors had gone and Sophie with him. Satan had already gone, sold privately to a friend of Edward's.

★ ★ ★

Mr George could not have been more welcoming. Soon after we had arrived, coffee was served and I, at least, was impressed for it had never been given me before. Edward, I think, accepted it as a matter of course.

'So,' said Mr George once we were settled with our cups and a plate of macaroons, 'Mrs Marshall is amenable to the enterprise, I take it?'

'Yes, indeed,' said Edward to whom the question had been put directly. 'I am happy to say that is the case and she will be coming with us.'

'Excellent!' said Mr George and paused for a moment, no doubt to give Edward time to explain how this miracle had come about. But Edward added nothing as, indeed, he could not and Mr George turned to me.

'I have made enquiries, Miss Marsh, among the ironmongers of the town and have obtained what I consider to be a very reasonable estimate for kitchen equipment, provided of course that a large enough order is placed. The cooking range you have in mind is available in various sizes and at various prices, ranging from two pounds to fifteen. I have explained that until you have your premises, you will naturally not know the dimensions you require.'

'Naturally,' I agreed, nodding gravely. 'I am most grateful, Mr George.'

'Which brings me to the next avenue I have explored,' Mr George continued and now bringing Edward back into the discussion. 'Chasetown itself. I had to go in that direction last week on business and took the opportunity to look around and make a few enquiries. I must say that I think it more than justifies your expectations of an outlet for your wares, Miss Marsh. Not only are there the colliery workers themselves, but there are also the bargees working the canals. As you will know,' looking particularly at Edward, 'much of the coal is transported from the pits by canal barge.'

Edward nodded solemnly although I thought it unlikely he possessed any such knowledge. But then, neither did I!

'Most of the rest of it, of course, is carried on the railway, the track for which is being constantly extended. So, besides the miners and the bargees there will also be the navvies. The prospects,' he beamed at us both, 'are good.'

We beamed back although Edward's eyes, I noticed, were becoming a little glazed. I cleared my throat. 'We are most grateful to you, Mr George.'

'*Most* grateful!' Edward echoed.

'It sounds to be a flourishing community,' I confirmed, 'and with money to spare, would you say?'

'I doubt if the men with families will ever admit to having any to spare, Miss Marsh. But there does appear to be many single men among the work force and not all their wages, I trust, will be spent at the ale house.'

I thought of Ada's and Polly's aspirations and hoped so, too.

'Some, I gather,' Mr George continued, 'earn as much as twenty shillings a week.'

I could only stare at him in astonishment. That was wealth indeed.

'Not all, of course,' Mr George cautioned. 'Now, my final piece of news and then I must let you get on your way. I have spoken to James Gallagher, the young solicitor I mentioned on your last visit, Miss Marsh, and he will be happy to act for you in legal matters. He envisages a sort of co-operative in which the investors

259

— such as yourselves, of course, and your friends who have money to invest — will draw from the profits such proportion of money as their investment warrants. For that, of course, he will need their names and, at some point, their signatures. Or their marks, of course, duly witnessed.' I wondered with some embarrassment, if he knew that I would be in that category.

'Of course!' I heard myself say.

'Of course!' Edward echoed dutifully.

Five minutes later we were out in the street. Ten minutes later we were dancing on the banks of Stowe Pool towards which we had gone without prior consultation.

'Chasetown more than justifies your expectations of an outlet for your wares, Miss Marsh,' Edward quoted Mr George at the top of his voice.

'We will draw from the profits such proportion of money as our investment warrants!' I shouted jubilantly.

'Let's go and tell Nanny,' said Edward giving me a final bear hug. 'And then off to Chasetown we will go!'

There could have been few business ventures entered into with such high spirits, I thought as I followed him. Nor with such a complete lack of experience!

Never having seen a coalmine before — not even a picture — I had no idea what to expect. Not, compared with what must lie below ground, that there was a great deal to see. A tall, brick chimney for ventilation, great wheels perched upon giant tripods over the shafts for winching up coal or people, a brick-built engine room housing a pump for the extraction of water from the mine and a huddle of buildings that were either offices or so-called 'hovels' for the men when they were not below.

Horses stood patiently within the shafts of carts into which coal was being loaded, and scattered around the pit-head were heaps of discarded small-coal called 'slag' we were informed by the small boy who had appointed himself our guide.

Beyond the colliery was open countryside, heathland mostly, with clumps of yellow gorse bright against the blue sky and occasional stands of silver birch and scrub oak. At least, I thought, the men will have something to feast their eyes upon when they come up. Or were they more concerned with cleansing their bodies from the coal dust that must surely clog their every pore?

As we stood there, a shift came off duty

and we watched as men stepped out of a sort of cage and stood for a moment or two blinking in the strong sunlight. Many were stripped to the waist, their bodies gleaming with a mixture of sweat and coal dust. At first sight, they seemed a cheery-enough bunch, laughing and joking and some, upon seeing us, touching their foreheads, no doubt thinking that Edward was some sort of official. Certainly, in his long, dark Newmarket and strapped trousers, his tall hat in his hand, he looked the part. I, in my dark blue skirt and jacket, my bonnet with only the narrowest of white frilling around its brim, must have been more difficult to place. As we stood there, a man came out of one of the buildings and approached us. Our small guide sidled away.

'Can I help you, sir, madam?'

Edward rose to the occasion immediately. 'No, thank you, my man. I was speaking to Mr McClean the other day and he told me that if I happened to be passing this way, I was to be sure to stop and — er — inspect the mine.'

The man looked horrified. 'You mean you want to go down the mine, sir? To take the lady . . . ?'

'Indeed, no! I think, for the moment, we have seen enough, don't you agree, my dear?'

And he smiled down at me.

Choking with laughter, I could only nod my head. 'But thank you for your trouble,' said Edward graciously and there came a quick sleight of hand between his pocket and the man's palm.

We turned and walked briskly away towards the town. Once out of earshot of the man, I gave full rein to my laughter.

'Oh, Edward,' I shook my head in mock reproof, 'he is not your man! He is, I hope, your future customer. One thing's certain, though,' I added, 'we must find you suitable working clothes.'

★　★　★

Clearly, Chasetown was still in its infancy but maturing rapidly. The main street, from which terraces of miners' cottages ran, was still unpaved and now, after the previous day's rain was very muddy underfoot. But there were grocers and ironmongers and a draper and even a gentlemen's outfitters displaying mostly men's working garb. Everywhere, there was the sound of builders hard at work as more dwellings were erected.

Not all the houses were small; there were several larger ones which, our small friend, suddenly back at our side, said belonged to the 'butties'.

'Butties?' I queried.

'Them in charge,' he explained. 'When I'm ten, I shall 'ave a butty. An' a doggy.'

'Are you pulling our legs?' Edward asked. 'What's your name?'

Spluttering with indignation, he brought us to a halt by the simple method of standing in front of us. 'No I ain't!' he said crossly. 'Me name's Scabber an' me Da' works 'ere so I knows.' Arms crossed, legs straddled, he then delivered a lecture to the manner born.

'Fust, there's 'prentices. That's wot I'll be when I'm ten. Then there's ornary men — like me Da' — then there's doggies — them's the men 'oo work the 'ardest. An' then there's butties. They march about makin' sure yer not slackin'. Me Da' says they 'ad whips once, but not no more.'

'Where do you live?' I dared to interrupt his flow.

'Burntwood. But when I'm ten, I shall live 'ere wiv a butty.' He turned and indicated the house in front of which we were standing, larger than its neighbours. 'Like I said, that there's a butty's. Ole 'Arper 'as that un. But me — I'll live wiv Ole Perks. Me an' four uvvers. Us'll sleep togevver in Ole Perks's attic. Proper lark, it'll be. An' us'll all eat togevver in Mrs Perks's kitchen. Me Ma says she can't wait ter get shot o' me but she won't say no ter me wage!'

'And how much will that be?' I asked, fascinated.

''Alf a crown, if I'm lucky. 'Alf a bleedin' crown — think o' that!' he boasted, a smile wreathing his grimy face. 'Mrs Perks'll tek a shillin', mind. An' me Ma anuvver, so that'll only leave sixpence fer meself. But that's better'n a kick up the arse, ain't it?'

'It certainly is! Now,' I glanced up at Edward for confirmation, 'how would you like sixpence now for showing us around? What we really want to find is somewhere to live. Somewhere about that size,' and I indicated Mr Harper's house behind us.

Scabber rocked back on his heels while he considered my request. Then he gave a crow of triumph and set off down the street in a series of magnificent cartwheels. 'Ole Renshaw's,' he shouted as he went. 'Tha's the 'ouse fer you. Died last week. Fell off a skip an' broke 'is bleedin' 'ead. I'll tek yer there now.'

'Oh, no!' I said quickly. 'We couldn't possibly intrude. Mr Renshaw's widow . . . '

'S'orlright,' Scabber assured us, righting himself. 'Gawn to 'er sister's at 'Ammerwich. Ain't comin' back no more.'

'It won't hurt us to take a look,' said Edward.

'Won't 'urt a bleedin' bit,' enthused Scabber. 'C'mon!' And he cartwheeled away with us meekly following.

* * *

It stood back from the road by a good six feet, square and solid with bay windows either side a plain wooden door. Three windows were spaced neatly above and dormers occupied similar positions in the steep roof.

Ugly, perhaps, with its uncompromising facade, it still gave an impression of strength and security. I glanced up at Edward and was horrified to see the woebegone expression on his face. But then I saw it through his eyes and knew that he was making an impossible comparison with Ashling. I took his hand. 'Let's look around at the back,' I suggested gently and led him through a wicker gate and down a path at the side of the house. Scabber had vanished once again.

'Oh, Edward!' I drew him to a halt and gazed in wonder at the huge orchard that stretched away before us. Already, the buds of apple and pear, damson and cherry were swelling and greening and here and there,

266

fragile sprays of plum blossom shone on the black branches. Enclosing what was probably a good acre of land were hedges foaming with blackthorn. To one side there was good stabling and a shed or two and a rutted lane that must give access to a road.

I gazed and gazed, my practical eye seeing not only the beauty of the orchard but the countless fruit pies and turnovers, jams and preserves that could emerge from it under Mrs C.'s skilful fingers.

'What do you think?' I asked Edward. 'I know it's not what you're used to but . . . '

'I think it's capital,' he said and I saw that the sadness had gone from his face. At that moment, Scabber reappeared around the side of the house with a somewhat harassed-looking man wearing a large leather apron.

'If this is some joke o' yours, young Scabber,' the man was threatening but then stopped abruptly when he saw us.

'Told yer!' chortled Scabber. 'Them's toffs!'

'Beggin' yer pardon sir, ma'am, but young Scabber's a right one fer a leg pull. Now, I'm Jim Parker, shoe mender, lives next door an' jus' been asked ter 'old the key. Yer'll need ter see the agent if yer interested but I can show yer round if that's yer wish.' And he produced a large bunch of keys from his apron pocket.

'Oh, it is, Mr Parker,' I said. 'It is, indeed, if it's no trouble.'

'No trouble, ma'am. May as well use the back door, now we're 'ere.'

It was as solid and uncompromising inside as it was out. Four large rooms including a kitchen on the ground floor divided by a narrow hallway, four of a similar size on the first floor and three large attics in the roof. ''An two privies outside,' I heard Mr Parker whisper delicately to Edward.

'Quite so!' said Edward, winking at me.

While Edward climbed the narrow staircase to inspect the attics, I went back to the kitchen. Large enough in itself, there was also a good-sized scullery and a wash-house adjoining. Water came from a pump immediately outside the back door and could easily be diverted into the house itself. But at what expense? I mustn't get too excited, I thought, as I heard Edward and Mr Parker returning.

'Mr Parker has given me the name and address of the agent,' Edward told me. He turned to the man and thanked him for his trouble and again there came that quick sleight of hand and I thought, he must get out of that habit or we will be penniless in no time!

'And thank you, too, Scabber,' I reminded him for that young man had now come rushing in from his own inspection of the orchard; with what in mind I had yet to discover.

* * *

By common consent, we walked back to Ashling across the fields.

'Remember the last time?' Edward asked, taking my hand.

I said nothing, only squeezed his in acknowledgement. It would be so easy to pretend we were just an ordinary young couple, to pause by a stile and turn my face up to his and wait expectantly. But I put the thought from me; besides, there was something else I wanted from him.

'Edward,' I began, 'I have a request to make. For reasons unknown — but whatever they are, I am profoundly grateful — your mother has agreed to come with us. May I — would you mind — I have given it a great deal of thought — and I wondered if — I think there should be enough room . . . '

'For pity's sake, Cat,' he interrupted, 'spit it out! You're not usually at such a loss for words.'

I stopped him then and peered up into his face. 'Would you mind if I asked *my* mother and my sister if they would like to join us?'

'Is that all? And I thought you were going to suggest old Jolly joined us!'

'Oh, Edward, would you really not mind?'

'Of course not! It's only fair after all.'

'Oh, Edward, thank you!' And on an impulse, I reached up and pulled his face down to mine, meaning to kiss him upon the cheek in my gratitude. But either my aim was not good or he had other ideas for it was his lips that I touched, at first gentle and undemanding but then suddenly probing and passionate. And then I felt his tongue, heard his breath quicken and mine respond and I drew back. Whatever our bodies were trying to tell us, however much I wanted him and he, me, I knew the time was not right. 'Not yet, Edward! Not yet!'

He laughed shakily. 'Perhaps you're right. Not yet!' And the words seemed to hang between us like a golden promise.

'Thank you,' I said, trying to keep my voice steady, 'for saying that I can ask my mother. She will work her fingers to the bone for us, I know. And Emma, too, of course.'

17

I went home, as I had left, on the carriers' carts.

'It will cost less,' I told Edward, 'for one of us must be thrifty! And when I come back, perhaps you will have heard from the agent,' — for he had written as soon as we had got back to Ashling — 'and Ole Renshaw's will be ours — yours,' I corrected myself swiftly, for I must not assume.

'Ours!' he corrected me with a smile. We were waiting by then, at the end of the lane at the identical spot where the carrier had left me four years ago. I would have liked to remind him of it but then the cart came creaking around the corner and the next moment, he had kissed me briefly upon the forehead and was handing me up.

'God speed,' he wished me, 'and I'll see you in two days.'

'Two days,' I echoed. For one day, perhaps only one hour, would surely be sufficient to persuade Ma and Emma to join us at Chasetown once we were settled.

As we dawdled our way through the countryside, I dozed intermittently for I had been up early, helping Mrs C. There had been no question of asking permission from the Mistress for my absence for we had now all worked through the month's notice the Master had given us and were no longer receiving wages. By rights, I suppose, she could have told us all to leave but I doubt if the thought had ever crossed her mind; she enjoyed her creature comforts too much for that.

It was late evening when I reached Burslem and started up the hill. By now, both Ma and Emma should be home from the potbank. With my face averted, I hurried past the end of the alley where the Baileys had lived — and still did for all I knew. When I reached our house, I was almost breathless — but more from anticipation than from the speed with which I had walked. I was in two minds whether to knock but decided against it for I could not wait to surprise them both. I lifted the latch and walked in — and immediately wondered if I had come to the wrong house.

High up on the mantleshelf, a candle burned and by its feeble light I saw a man and a woman wrapped in each other's arms. My breath caught in my throat. Surely my mother . . . ?

And then the couple moved swiftly apart and the woman spoke. 'Who are you? What do you want?'

I saw then that she was not yet a woman but only a slip of a girl. She was my sister Emma!

'Emma!'

'Cat!'

We stared at each other without further speech and then she turned and reached for the candle but the man was ahead of her. He put the candle stick on the table, then turned and took a lamp from the top of the chest where it had always stood and lit it with a spill from the candle flame. Clearly, he was at home here.

By the light of the lamp, Emma and I continued to stare at each other. She was only a few months older than Sophie but there was a wealth of difference between them. Where Sophie's upbringing had shielded her from anyone except those similarly privileged, Emma had had to grow up fast, just as I had done, learning to adapt to those about her because that was the only way to survive. There could be no comparison between life at Ashling Hall and an existence at the potbank.

'Where's Ma?' I asked at last.

'She's coming. She called in at Old Ma Hopkins's — she's not well.'

'Shouldn't you have the supper on, then?' I asked sharply. 'Instead of — of — ' And I stared hard at the young man.

He moved forward so that I could see him more clearly. 'We weren't doin' no 'arm, Miss.' He was older than Emma, I thought, by several years.

'Of course we weren't!' said Emma crossly. 'And it's none of your business anyway, Cat Marsh. Creeping up on us like that. But maybe I had better get the potatoes on now, Joe.'

'I'll go then, Em. Will I see you later?'

'I doubt it. Not now my sister's condescended to come home.'

'Condescended!' I think I might have laid hands on her then, had Ma not suddenly appeared in the doorway. After one incredulous look her arms flew open.

'Cat! Oh, Cat! By all that's wonderful!' And then we were in each other's arms, laughing and crying at the same time. Some things hadn't changed!

★   ★   ★

'So you see, Cat,' Ma said some hours later. 'I cannot come with you much as I would like to.'

We were sitting together in front of the fire.

274

Emma, still in a huff, still resentful, had gone to bed where I, it went without saying, would not be joining her. I would share Ma's bed tonight.

'Has she known Joe for long?' I asked.

'Ever since she started work but it's only recently he's shown an interest. Oh, he's a nice enough lad, I suppose, but not what I had in mind for Emma.'

'But Ma, she's barely fourteen!'

She smiled at me sadly. 'Almost the same age as you when you went away, Cat. The difference is — you had a head on your shoulders and our Emma, I sometimes think, has nothing more than a dandelion clock on hers. Anyway, I dare not leave her and there is no way she will leave Burslem at the moment without Joe. It may not last but even so, there will be others. But thank you, love, for thinking of us like that.'

'Oh, Ma! I've never stopped thinking of you and wondering how you really were.'

'Oh, I've done well enough.' And indeed, apart from the lines of worry that creased her forehead when she spoke of Emma, she looked well. Her hair was pure white now but her cheeks were plump and her eyes clear. 'I'll go on working at the bank a while longer but when Emma's settled — one way or the other — I'd like nothing more than to join you. Tell me more now, about this Edward.'

So I told her, although deliberately glossing over the way I felt about him but I think she guessed. And then we talked about Pa and how things used to be.

'No news of Rosie and Thomas?' I asked.

She shook her head. 'None. They've never been seen since. Old Seth Bailey drank himself to death a year or two after Lottie died and young Sam took off soon after. No-one knows where he is either — not that anyone cares. But Hannah's fine, lass. She and her little ones.'

'I'll go and see her in the morning,' I promised.

'She'd like that,' said Ma. 'Now, we'd best get to bed. Can I get you anything, Cat, before we go?'

'Yes, please, Ma! A basin of pobs, if you've the milk to spare!'

★   ★   ★

Edward was sitting on the bank, his gun across his knees and Rex beside him guarding a brace of rabbits, when the carrier dropped me off. My heart lifted.

'Cat!' He swung me down and the carrier handed down my bag. 'We've missed you — haven't we, Rex?'

276

I hugged him, patted Rex and turned to thank the carrier. And then, arms around each other's waists, we strolled slowly up the lane.

I told him about Ma and Emma. 'But Ma will come eventually, I'm sure she will. Now — what news of the house?'

'Well I'm afraid it's not as straightforward as we had hoped. Most of the land at Chasetown belongs to the Marquess, and that includes Ole Renshaw's, but the agent says we may lease it for a period of three years. After that, a further leasing might be considered. Subject to your approval, I have agreed to this. It would also mean we would have more money available now when we most need it.'

'It sounds an excellent arrangement,' I said. 'Now, have you a date for the auction yet?'

'The middle of March. So I will take Sophie to London the week before and Mrs Swinfen, bless her, has promised to have Mama. And guess what?' Clearly, he had left the best piece of news until last. I looked at him expectantly. 'Mr George has decided to invest one hundred pounds in our enterprise.'

I smiled to myself. 'I rather thought he might!'

★ ★ ★

It was over. For nearly two weeks we had been subjected, from early morning until late evening, to a constant stream of people, poking and prying, examining down to the last detail and, sometimes, ridiculing.

'Hey, look at this!' I heard one wag call out as he pulled out the Master's hunting jacket from the chest where it had been carefully folded along with his other riding clothes, and draped it about his shoulders. 'Tallyho! Gone Away! An' all that!'

I thanked heaven that Edward was not there to see and, biting my tongue, turned away. Mrs C. had become so upset on the first day of the sale that she had subsequently taken refuge at Home Farm, only returning at nightfall to what was now a travesty of a kitchen.

It was only through Edward's intercession with the new owner that we were all still there. On the first day of the sale, Ashling Hall had become the property of a retired wool merchant from Yorkshire whose wife — we had heard — had nagged him into it.

The furniture from the servants' quarters was among the last lots to be sold on the final day and, again thanks to Edward, the sale of this was held by the obliging auctioneer so early in the morning that no-one else had arrived!

'Good heavens!' he said when informed of this by a disgruntled late arrival who had extracted a large, turnip watch from his waistcoat pocket to make his point. 'I must have mistaken the time!'

There was now no further need for us to stay, for Edward's pieces were already in store in Lichfield. Our purchases were carried out and stacked on the old wagon that Ned had discovered behind a hayrick. Considered unfit for sale by the assessors and therefore discarded, he had been working on it for weeks and it was now not only completely refurbished but also boasted a sort of tarpaulin cover stretched over curved willow wands in the manner of a gipsy's 'bender.' Even when the furniture was in it, there was still room for Mrs C., Ada and Polly. It was pulled by a big, raw-boned piebald called Lofty on whose tail, on the day of the livestock sale, Ned had tied a large red bow. Lofty had been left behind a couple of years back by a travelling circus when he had gone lame on the road and the Master had taken him in. But he had never forgotten his tricks, one of which was to buck or rear on command.

'Careful, gentlemen, 'e kicks!' Ned had

called out when leading Lofty around the yard for the inspection of would-be purchasers and sure enough, obedient to Ned's whisper, Lofty had bucked and reared like a good 'un. Needless to say, no-one had bid and Lofty had, by default, become Ned's property.

I had fully expected Edward to accept the offer I knew Mrs Swinfen had made to accommodate him overnight with his mother, but he had refused.

'We're a team now,' he had maintained. 'This is where I belong from now on.' Although no-one said as much, I knew that we all approved of his action.

And so, just before midday, we rumbled away down the avenue with Ned driving and Edward, Mr Jolly, Fred and me walking beside the wagon. Katie had gone before the sale began and Mr Jolly was accompanying us only as far as the road where he would await the carrier for the first leg of his journey to his sister's.

Just before the bend when the house would be obscured by the trees, Ned stopped the wagon and jumped down to come and stand with us as we gazed back at Ashling; not one of us expected ever to return. From inside the wagon, we could hear the muffled sobs of the others.

The beautiful Georgian house which had been home to me for four happy years and to the others for many more, seemed to smile back at us, its windows winking in the early spring sunshine. I noticed that a window on the first floor had been left open and I hoped that someone would close it before nightfall or the air would 'bloom' the furniture. But then I remembered that there was no furniture, that it was an empty shell awaiting the arrival of the wool merchant and his wife. Tears poured down my cheeks so that the daffodils already blooming beneath the windows of the drawing room became a golden blur. I dared not look at the others but I heard Mr Jolly, who was standing next to me, give a deep sigh. I put out my hand — the one that was not already holding Edward's — and grasped his. Silently, we turned about, Ned jumped up to take the reins and we were on our way; to a future that only I had deliberately chosen but which I was determined should work for us all.

Saying goodbye to Mr Jolly was equally as painful as saying goodbye to Ashling but at least we were not severing our connections with him altogether.

'This will be my address,' he had told Edward on the previous evening, thrusting a piece of paper into his hand. 'Please write and tell me how you are progressing.' And Edward had promised to do so.

There was no way we could leave him standing solitary by the roadside, so we waited with him until the carrier came.

'Goodbye!' we called as the cart drew away with him like a gaunt black crow beside the driver. 'God speed!'

He didn't call back but waved an immaculate handkerchief until he was out of sight.

18

I doubt if Ole Renshaw's had ever had such a turn out before. The kitchen could not be used until the new range had been installed and plumbed. So while we waited, we went to work with brushes and brooms, mops and buckets, whitewash by the gallon and distempers of various shades.

First, we allotted each room its particular purpose. The attics were the sleeping quarters; Ned and Fred in one, Ada and Polly in another and I in the third.

'Are you sure?' I asked Ada and Polly for I had not expected the luxury of a room — and a large one at that — all to myself.

'If yer sure that's wot yer want, you 'ave it,' Ada said. 'I couldn't ever sleep on me own. 'Twouldn't seem right.'

'Nor me neither,' Polly assured me. 'You 'ave it an' welcome, Cat.'

I was delighted. All this space to furnish as I wished!

I had not liked Mrs Marshall's style of furnishing, finding it too dark and heavy for my taste and the sparse simplicity of Ma's rooms had been governed by necessity rather than choice. But my uncle's house at Wolstanton had always appealed to me with its clean, uncluttered lines, its accent upon shape and colour, its qualities of space and, above all, light.

My attic had low sloping ceilings and small dormers but there were two of them, one looking on to the street but the other on to the orchard; and it was from this direction that the sun rose. We could not afford wallpaper, of course, but I persuaded Ned to mix me a bucket of distemper containing a good proportion of white lead so that even when the sun had moved around the side of the house, the walls of my room still reflected what light remained.

My bedstead was of iron but the knobs on it shone like orbs of fire and the patchwork cover I had made at Ashling was a kaleidoscope of soft pink and blue and white.

The paint on the wooden chest of drawers that had also come from Ashling had chipped and worn so I used turpentine to clean it, under Ned's watchful eye, and then applied two coats of white milk-paint. The effect was most pleasing, especially when I filled with spring flowers the cracked lustre jug that I had retrieved from the rubbish dump at Ashling.

But it was my chair of which I was most

proud. It had been given me by Edward who had insisted that I have somewhere comfortable to sit besides my bed. It was a shell chair, its frame made of the finest mahogany with a graceful spoon back that sloped at the sides to make low arm rests and it was covered in a soft moss-green velvet that was a delight to touch as well as to look at. I did not dare tell Edward so but I rarely sat on it and certainly did not put my clothes on it at night; these went on the bottom of my bed and sometimes ended up on the floor!

The floor I scrubbed thoroughly and then treated with oil of turpentine and resin so that the boards shone like amber when the sun struck them.

I still had to acquire some sort of chest in which to hang the rest of my clothes but in the meantime I managed well enough with a couple of sturdy door hooks. I wasn't going to spoil it all with some hasty addition that did not fit in with my scheme.

Most of the first floor of the house had been given over to Edward and his mother. At first, Edward had objected to his being singled out for what seemed like preferential treatment but in the end had seen the wisdom of being near to his mother. She had not only a bedroom but a small sitting room and dining room. 'For there is no way,' said

Polly, 'that I could sit opposite 'er an' swallow me vittles an' not 'ave terrible wind!' A sentiment that we all echoed.

If, when we were sufficiently established to be able to afford it she moved to Burntwood, then we would consider again what to do with the rooms.

''Twould make a nice 'ome fer a young couple startin' out,' I heard Ada remark to Polly with an arch glance in my direction and I felt my cheeks begin to burn.

'That's enough o' that!' said Mrs C.sharply, noticing my embarrassment but I think everyone, she included, had noticed the growing intimacy between Edward and myself.

Because of her legs, Mrs C.'s bedroom was on the ground floor. The realisation that she would no longer have to climb three flights of stairs to her bedroom each night had filled her with joy. 'I shall 'ave a new lease o' life,' she assured me.

The remainder of the downstairs rooms were given over to our trade; besides the kitchen where we would cook and eat, the scullery where some of the food could be prepared, there would be what we called 'the cooling room', a sort of half-way stage for the pies and buns between kitchen and shop. Much advice in this direction had been given us by Nanny Humphries who had promised to visit us at the earliest opportunity.

The shop itself was the large room immediately to the right of the front door and would soon, thanks to Scabber, be graced by a long counter for the display of our wares. The day after we had arrived, he had descended upon us early in the morning, greeting us all like long-lost friends. Ned had sorted him out in a second.

'Nah then, young whipper-snapper, get out from under me feet an' make yerself useful. Know where I can lay me 'ands on some wood? About so big by so big. An' I want it all got above board — in a manner o' speaking'! No nickin'! Understood?'

'Understood, guv!' And Scabber darted away, returning half an hour later to inform us that Mr Johnson, the undertaker, was willing to do business if Ned would care to step around. And Ned did, coming back in no time and carrying, with Scabber's help, several off-cuts of good quality timber.

'Though I didn't like the way he looked at me,' Ned confessed with a grin. 'Proper measured me up, he did!'

Ned, it was abundantly clear, was going to be worth his weight in gold. And so, we had to admit, was Scabber.

'Scabber, where can we buy milk?' No

Home Farm cows now.

'Scabber, where can we get thread?' For the curtains we had brought from Ashling needed alteration.

'Scabber, where's the best place for oats?' For Lofty, munching contentedly enough beneath the trees would soon need a supplement, Ned decreed, or he'd get grass fever.

By midday of that first, busy day, Scabber had certainly earned his share of the cold mutton pie we had brought with us.

''Ow are yer goin' ter tell folk?' he enquired from the back-door step where he was sitting with his portion of pie clutched in a grubby hand.

'Tell folk what, Scabber?' Edward asked. He was sitting beside him for the chairs were still stacked.

'That Ole Renshaw's turned into a pie shop. Folk won't know if yer don't tell 'em.'

That problem had also been occupying my mind. It was unlikely that many of the population could read so some sort of written communication would be useless and I doubted if Chasetown sported a towncrier. On the other hand, why not provide our own 'crier'? It was something we would have to think about when the time came. Meanwhile, I thanked Scabber for his forethought. 'But I think the first thing we should do is to give ourselves a name,' I said. 'We can't go on being Ole Renshaw's for ever.'

'I've been thinkin', too,' said Mrs C. 'Maybe we could 'ave a sort o' tea shop as well as sellin' at the counter, but for dinners more than teas. Put some tables and chairs in the room opposite the shop.'

'But that's supposed to be your bedroom,' I objected.

'I could easily do wi' the smaller one off the kitchen. Anyway, in case we do that, why not call ourselves Cat's Eating 'Ouse? After all, none of us would be 'ere if it wasn't fer you.'

The others agreed with her immediately and so it was decided. 'I'll paint it up over the door soon as we're in business,' Ned promised. 'An' put it on the side o' the wagon.'

★   ★   ★

That first evening, Edward wrote to Sophie. He and I were alone in the kitchen for Ned and Frank, Ada and Polly, had decided to explore the surrounding area and Mrs C. had retired to bed very soon after our simple supper of bread and cheese. Tomorrow, workmen would arrive to install the range which now stood outside the back door, still packed in wood and straw and waiting to be assembled.

'Please give her my love,' I said.

He looked up from where he was sitting at the kitchen table. I had been standing at the sink rinsing our supper plates but now I came and sat opposite him.

'Of course,' he said. 'I've been telling her about all the things we've been doing today and about our plans. I thought it best to write now before we start work in earnest.'

'Don't make it sound too inviting,' I advised, 'or she'll never settle where she is.'

'I just hope Mama has written with news of Rex and Toffee.' For the obliging Mrs Swinfen had taken them in as well as Mrs Marshall. 'Now that Patience Swinfen's case is coming up at the Assizes,' Edward continued, 'she will have enough on her mind without an extra house guest to care for. The sooner we can get Mama over here the better.'

'D'you think she will win the case?' I asked.

He shrugged. 'She certainly has a good man to represent her in Sir Frederick Thesiger but then Captain Swinfen has also in Sir Alexander Cockburn. He's the Attorney General, after all. It should be a most interesting case and I should like to have had the opportunity to attend the Assizes, even if only to support Patience.'

The names he had mentioned meant nothing to me but Edward's obvious interest did. 'Edward, why don't you go to Stafford?' I asked. 'To offer Mrs Swinfen your support — *our* support — after all that she has done for us, it seems the least we can do.'

He was silent for a moment but then he shook his head. 'No — my place is here with you. There isn't much that I can do except to act as Ned's assistant but I shall learn as time goes on.'

'You've been very helpful,' I assured him. And he had been; lifting and carrying, man-handling furniture up the narrow stairs, turning his hand to whatever needed doing. And the others were beginning to accept him as one of them; even Mrs C. had agreed to call him 'Edward', although she couldn't promise that the occasional 'sir' might not slip out.

'Are you truly content?' I asked him now. 'I know that you cannot be really happy after all that has happened in the last few months but are you sure you have no regrets that you've decided to throw in your lot with us? This way of life — Ole Renshaw's, soon to be Cat's Eating House, Chasetown, everything — is so different from what you are used to.'

He smiled at me and reached over to cover my hand where it lay on the table. 'You've left out one very important factor in your list. A girl called Cat! As long as you're there, Cat, keeping an eye on me, telling me what to do, I am content.'

'Dear Edward . . . ' I rose to walk round the table to him, meaning to put my arms around him, perhaps even to press a chaste kiss upon the top of his head and to say that I would always be there for him, but then I heard the front door opening. The others were back.

'We're goin' ter be orlright 'ere,' Ned declared. 'Lots o' fresh air up on the Chase, if yer wants it. Real pretty in the spring, I should think.'

'An' there's a lake. An' a railway,' Fred chipped in.

'An' plenty o'fellers,' said Polly, poking her sister in the ribs and dissolving into giggles.

'Let's hope they've got good appetites,' I said.

'Eh, I'm sure they got them orlright!' said Ada. 'Eh, Poll?'

One way and another, we were settling in well!

19

The range had been installed; our first supplies of flour and yeast, salt and sugar had been delivered from the wholesalers whom Nanny had recommended; a daily delivery of milk, butter, cheese and eggs had been arranged — courtesy of Scabber — from a nearby farm and contact made with a recommended butcher. All that remained to do was to inform the population of Chasetown of their great good fortune in having Cat's Eating House at their disposal. But how?

After much deliberation, we decided that the best method would be to 'cry' the news among the townsfolk.

'Ned's got the loudest voice,' I pointed out.

'But I ain't got Eddie's style. I think 'e should be the one.' By now 'Eddie' came as naturally from Ned's lips as 'sir' had once done, and I think that Edward truly valued the friendship that was being offered with his new title.

In the end, it was decided that Edward, wearing not his now customary working garb of worsted breeches, flannel shirt and waistcoat, but his 'old' attire of narrow trousers, cut-away jacket and tall hat would drive the wagon and Ned would sit beside him with a bell.

They would draw rein in the middle of each thoroughfare to declaim that Cat's Eating House was now open and could provide 'good quality meat pies at three farthings apiece.' That was the cheapest, Mrs C. had worked out, that we could offer them and still make a minute profit. 'An' if they likes 'em, they'll 'ardly notice when we puts 'em up to a penny!'

So, on a bright March morning when daffodils were opening in the orchard grass and Mrs C. had declared herself to be 'master' of the new stove, and with a pile of golden-crusted pies to prove it, Ned and Edward set out. To honour the occasion, a posy of primroses, plucked from the orchard ditches, was tied to Lofty's nose band and wreaths of the same flower encircled Edward's hat and Ned's neck. The effect, to say the least, was arresting. It took Scabber, hopping up and down with excitement, to describe it more accurately as a 'bleedin' circus!'

At half past nine in the morning, we waved them off with Scabber cartwheeling merrily before the wagon and several dogs barking behind, and then rushed to open the shop door in preparation for a horde of customers.

An hour later, the only living creatures that had crossed the threshold were Jim Parker the shoe mender who took a proprietorial interest in us, anyway, and a stray cat. Jim left soon after, clutching a pie donated without charge in return for the help he had given when we were moving in. The cat, knowing when it was on to a good thing, stayed.

Half an hour later, the wagon was back. Mrs C. took one look at its occupants and went to get the cowslip wine. To say that they looked woebegone was to put it mildly.

Edward's hat which had been brushed to a glossy perfection by Ada, was now covered in congealed egg yolk, the primroses a soggy mess around its brim. The shoulders of his jacket were mottled with egg white. 'As if the pigeons 'ad pissed all over 'im!' breathed Polly in my ear.

Ned's jacket showed a smattering of yolk but clearly it was Edward who had born the brunt of the attack. But attack by whom?

Fred went to take the reins and Ned and Edward climbed stiffly down and followed us into the kitchen. Ned spoke first.

'We was doin' orlright ter begin with takin' it in turns ter shout. A coupla women even came out and spoke quite civil to us. An' then a lad about Scabber's age came round a corner followed by 'is mates an' that was it. Where they got the eggs from is anyone's guess but get 'em they did an' poor ole Ed 'ere got the worst of it, like an Aunt Sally at a fair. I laid about 'em wi' the whip as best I could but young Scabber was the 'ero of the day. 'E went for 'em like a young tiger an' in the end, it was Scabber they all turned on. 'E ran off an' they all chased after 'im.'

'So, where's Scabber now?' I asked faintly as I helped Polly to peel Edward's jacket from his shoulders.

Ned shrugged. 'Gawd knows! But I reckon we should go an' look for 'im soon as Eddie's recovered.'

But that proved unnecessary. A minute later, Scabber limped in. His clothes were always ragged and his face always dirty, so it was difficult to tell how much damage had been done to him. But there were several cuts on his face and his knees were bloodied. However, his foes, he assured us, were in much worse condition.

'Soon sorted 'em out,' he boasted as Ada drew hot water from the new boiler to bathe his cuts and Mrs C. thrust a pie upon him.

'So,' Edward summed it up with a rueful grin, 'the expedition wasn't exactly a howling success. We shall have to think of something else.'

And then the shop door bell suddenly pinged and, for a split second, we all just sat and gazed at each other; and then I led the rush.

In the middle of the shop stood what looked like a deputation; one man and two women, and a small boy held there by the ear by one of the women.

'We've come ter say we're sorry,' said the woman. 'At least, 'e's come ter say 'e's sorry.' And she yanked the boy forward, still by the ear and I saw that not only was he sporting the beginnings of a magnificent black eye but that his knees, like Scabber's, were well and truly bloodied. ''E 'ad no business ter throw eggs like that.'

'Specially *my* eggs,' said the man. He wore a long white apron of the sort worn by grocers. 'Rotten they was, an' I'd just put 'em out the back fer the pigs. I wouldn't want yer to think I *sold* 'em like that.'

'So c'mon, our Bert,' ordered the woman who surely must be the boy's mother, 'say yer sorry to the gentleman.'

'Sorry, mister,' said the luckless Bert to Edward, but still managing to scowl at Scabber who was executing a gleeful war dance behind Mrs C.

'Apology accepted,' said Edward gravely. And stepping forward he held out his hand to the lad. 'No hard feelings.'

Clearly stupefied by this courteous action, Bert took the proffered hand. 'Now, shake with Scabber,' said Edward and motioned Scabber forward.

'Not on yer Nellie!' said Scabber. 'I ain't goin' ter shake 'ands wiv 'im, bleedin' little . . .'

'Oh, yes, you are,' said Edward firmly, 'otherwise I shan't teach you how to fight properly. And the same applies to you, Bert. If, that is,' and he bowed politely to Bert's mother who was standing there with her mouth hanging open, 'your mother agrees.'

She managed a nod, at the same time pushing her son forward. 'Do wot the gentleman says, Bertie.'

It was left to Scabber to clarify the offer. 'Yer mean yer can box proper?' he asked Edward. 'Like in the fairs?'

Edward nodded. 'Just like the fairs. Except that I don't take money. I'm an amateur. And I can assure you, madam,' and again he addressed Bert's ma, 'that you have no need to worry. I was properly taught at school.'

But worrying, it was obvious from the besotted expression on her face, was the last thing Bert's ma had on her mind. If Edward had suggested teaching her son to fly, she would have agreed.

'When do us start?' asked Scabber.

'No time like the present,' said Edward, 'if you feel up to it. And if you don't want me for anything, Cat?'

'You do what you like,' I said feebly, still amazed at the way things were going. I turned back to the deputation. 'It was very good of you all to come. Now, won't you come and sit down and sample our wares?'

We ended up round the kitchen table while Edward conducted his pupils out into the orchard, closely followed by Ned and Fred. Bert's ma gazed after them or, more precisely, after Edward.

'Drink, was it?' she asked while I put a plate of pies on the table.

'I — I beg your pardon?' What could she mean?

She nodded after Edward. 'Was drink 'is downfall? A young toff like that drivin' a wagon fer a livin'?'

I suppressed a smile. 'No, not drink. Family circumstances, you might say. And this is his business, Mrs — er — ?'

'Perkins,' she said. 'Amy Perkins. And this 'ere's me neighbour, Mary Smith. An' that's Mr Drew, the grocer.'

Mr Drew, clearly embarrassed to be the

only male left in the company, bobbed his head and said that if we didn't mind he'd take his pie outside to watch the boxing and then he must be going.

Left to ourselves, Mrs C. poured us all cups of tea and we settled down for a good, womanly chat.

'Word o' mouth,' said Amy, 'that's the best way to get known. An' us'll spread the word, won't us, Mary?'

Mary, by now halfway through her second pie, nodded her head vigorously.

'At this price,' Amy continued, 'a lotta women'll be able to afford a pie to put in their man's dinner box. I will, that's for sure.' At this point, she tipped her nose towards the range where Mrs C. had a pan of soup heating for our lunch, and sniffed appreciatively. 'Was yer thinkin' o' sellin' soup, too?'

'Perhaps,' I said raising my eyebrows at Mrs C. who nodded her approval.

'That's wot me man likes most when 'e gets back from the pit, 'specially in the winter.'

'But how would we sell it?' I pondered.

'In a jug, a'course,' said Amy, 'same as yer do milk.'

And of course she was right. Although not in the way we had expected, the morning's activities were proving productive.

Soon afterwards, they rose to go, Amy pausing for one final glance at Edward through the kitchen window.

Scabber and Bert, shirts off, were dancing around each other with fists raised while Edward stood by separating them occasionally and offering such advice as, 'On your toes, lads! Keep up your guard, Scabber! Lead with your left, Bert!' Mr Drew was no longer there but Ned and Fred made an appreciative audience, Ned shouting for Scabber and Fred for Bert.

'Men!' said Amy indulgently.

★   ★   ★

Amy Perkins and Mary Smith stuck to their words. Over the next few days, our trade did improve. But it was a slow business and we found it impossible to estimate the quantities of pies and soup we would need. Some days, Ada, Polly and I would take baskets and hawk the pies from door to door for a ha'penny apiece and tasty though they were, we began to tire of them appearing, night after night, on our own dinner plates.

But no-one grumbled, for we knew that these first days were crucial. No-one drew any wages, of course, but then we hadn't expected to until we were established. And at least, since Edward had started his boxing classes, we could be sure of a safe passage through the streets. By now, Scabber and Bert were firm friends.

Edward proved particularly popular with the housewives, opening the door and bowing as they left.

'Kiss 'em, why doncher?' I heard Polly say saucily.

'Like, this, d'you mean?' he asked and Polly fled, screaming, when he made a grab at her.

In spite of our worries, we were a happy 'family', gathering around the kitchen table most evenings for a game of cards, if the chores for the next day had been done or, as the evenings lengthened, walking up to Chase Water or over to Burntwood Green.

And then, one day when we had been open for about a fortnight, something happened that, while it brought tragedy to the town, served to bring us into the public eye.

We first knew there was something afoot around midday when we heard the blast of a whistle. By then, we were sufficiently accustomed to the daily routine of the town to know that this was unusual. A minute or two later, we noticed people running past the shop in the direction of one of the mines. And then Scabber arrived at the double and told us as best he could between drawing breaths, what had happened.

'Explosion!' he gasped. 'Fire gas! 'Undreds trapped! Follow me!'

And we did; all of us, that is, except Mrs C. It turned out to be the colliery that Edward and I had looked at on our first day in Chasetown and, while Scabber's estimate, as we'd known it must be, was hopelessly exaggerated, ten men and five boys were trapped below by the explosion; he had been right about it being caused by a build-up of fire gas.

A crowd of people, mostly women, were congregated around the shaft, held back by a makeshift barrier of wooden pit props. Many of them were weeping and among these was Amy Perkins, a shawl over her head, and holding a pale-faced Bert by the hand. I made my way to her and put my arm around her.

'Is your . . . ?'

She nodded. 'Yes, my George is down there an' Arthur, Mary's man. She's over there talkin' ter the manager.'

As she finished speaking, Mary came back, fighting tears. ''E says it'll be a coupla 'ours at least afore they can be reached. 'E says they're doin' all they can. There's another lot goin' down now.'

And as we watched, several men stepped

on to the skip at the head of the shaft and were winched below. 'Good luck, lads!' one woman called out and the words were taken up by the crowd; those, that is, who were able to speak through their sobs.

''Ere comes the doctor!' someone said as a pony and trap, driven at speed, came up the rise and a man in a frock coat threw the reins to a bystander and hurried over to speak to the little knot of officials. But after a few minutes he came back, climbed in to the trap and drove away at a more sober pace.

'That settles it,' said Amy. 'Nuthin'll be 'appenin' fer a while, or e'd be stayin',' and she shivered violently in the cold breeze that was blowing off the Chase.

'So will you stay?' I asked although I knew as I asked it, that it was a foolish question. Of course she would stay, as would all the others. She didn't even bother to reply, just wrapped her shawl more closely around her and took a firmer hold of Bert's hand. If only there was something we could do. And then I suddenly realised that there *was* something we could do.

When we had rushed out of the kitchen, we had left Mrs C. stirring a huge pan of broth. I glanced up at Edward who was standing next to me.

'Soup,' I said. 'Why don't we bring up what

we've got and then make some more? It's just what they could do with up here.'

'Good idea!'

We called the others who were standing nearby, told Amy and Mary that we would be back and raced home. Scabber, clearly torn between two exciting events, decided to come with us. 'Back soon, me ole mate,' I heard him tell Bert.

Hurriedly, we explained to Mrs C. what we proposed to do. Before we had even finished speaking, she had sent Ada and Polly to fetch the urn we had brought with us from Ashling and which we had used for summer garden parties and archery contests. Between them, Edward and Frank emptied the pan of broth into it, then carried it out to the wagon where Ned and Scabber were backing Lofty between the shafts.

'Could you make some more quickly?' I asked Mrs C.

She thought for a moment. 'I've got stock simmerin' on the back o'the range now,' she said. 'Meant ter be fer termorrow but if yer can leave me one o' the girls to do some vegetables, I could knock up a fair vegetable consommé. Not as tasty as I'd like, mind.'

I thought of the poor souls huddled around the pit shaft and assured her that it would be like nectar to them. 'We'll take up some pies, too, if you're agreeable. No-one will come in here for them today.'

Polly offered to stay and do the vegetables and Ada and I collected all the basins and cups that we had and, with Ned driving and the rest of us holding the urn and the crockery steady, we set off.

To say that we caused an immediate diversion would not be true. Admittedly, when we drew up, all heads turned but no-one moved. And then Scabber leaped down from the wagon and began to shout as heartily as any street monger.

'Piesansoup! Over 'ere fer yer piesansoup!'

They could not believe at first that we did not want payment. It was the dark-suited officials who came over first and who spread the news.

'We shan't forget this,' said one of them, the manager I think, and there were murmurs of agreement behind him.

But by then we were too busy attending to the needs of the crowd to do more than nod and smile.

'Bless yer, miss!'

'Thank 'ee, sir!'

'Keep us goin', this will!'

They all had some appreciative remark to make.

The urn had been replenished twice over

before the first casualties were brought to the surface. We watched from the now deserted wagon as they came, some on stretchers, some walking with the help of others. Most were taken to one of the hovels where the doctor and his helpers now awaited them.

Two of those on stretchers, one a long, thin shape under the blankets and the other pathetically small, were identified quietly and taken to a separate building. A dreadful hush fell over the waiting throng as the identifications were made and now there came the sound of anguished sobbing as a woman was thrust forward by the others. Only one? Was it the man or the child who had no relative there to weep over him?

Of the remaining four children, three walked out together, apparently unscathed and then the fourth came, limping heavily but calling out to his mother, somewhere in the crowd, that he was all right. There were more sobs but this time, I think, of relief. One of the children was little bigger than Scabber.

My heart went out to Amy and Mary who were still waiting for news of their loved ones but then, as someone shouted, 'That's the lot! All are accounted for!' I saw them move forward towards the last two men who were being helped from the skip and who seemed to be supporting each other. Seconds later,

Amy and Mary were clutching them as if they would never let them go, coal dust and all.

Suddenly, I felt very tired but at the same time buoyed up with a sense of achievement. It had been a privilege to help this close-knit community if only in such a small way.

'Let's go home now,' I said to the others, linking my arms with Ada and Edward and smiling at the others. 'You, too, Scabber, if your mother won't worry.'

''Er won't,' said Scabber confidently. ''Er knows I'm wiv yer!'

* * *

Next day, Amy came with some of the details; she also wanted a jugful of soup for George and Arthur. Apart from severe bruising, they were unharmed and expected to go back to work in a few days. This time, she insisted upon paying for the soup.

'Their butty's a good man,' she explained. ''E won't see us short and the men 'ave 'ad a whip-round. Most of it'll go to Ada Tomkins, mind, 'cos 'er man was the one killed.'

'And what about the child?' I asked. 'Had he no relatives?'

She shook her head. 'Billy Johns were a pauper lad. Sent from the work 'ouse.'

Tears came to my eyes. Poor Billy Johns

with no-one to care whether he lived or died. 'Are there many like him in the mines?' I asked.

Amy nodded. "'Tis cheap labour fer the butties, see. Billy's butty'll just put in fer anuvver pauper.'

As if poor Billy Johns had been just an old pair of shoes, to be replaced immediately by another.

By hand, on the next day, came a letter for Edward sent by the management of the colliery and expressing its appreciation of our 'public-spirited generosity'; and would Edward kindly present himself at the agent's office at his earliest convenience. It was signed by John Robinson McClean himself.

20

Although we had not sought it, publicity from the mine disaster came nevertheless. Not all the miners were married and the single ones often had money to spare after they had paid board to their mothers or their landladies from the pound many of them drew each week. Several of them developed the habit of dropping in each day; morning or afternoon according to their shifts, and staying to eat. We began to cook bacon and eggs for their breakfasts, followed by a slice of home-baked bread and preserves; not yet our own preserves although the sea of blossom, creamy-white and palest pink, in the orchard was a promise of a good yield ahead.

Ada and Polly, I think, were also one of the reasons why they came and I was glad of that. Not only for Ada and Polly's sakes but because it seemed to make us even more part of the community.

Two days after the disaster, Mr George came out to see us and expressed himself well pleased with what he found. It was the first time that he had met the others and he made Mrs C. his slave for life by declaring her cooking to be equal to that of his wife. 'I'll bring her out to sample it,' he promised and greater approval he could not have given.

On the same day, Edward presented himself at the agent's office where he was asked to accept the sum of twenty pounds as 'a token of appreciation'; even more importantly, it was given to him by John McClean in person. Edward came back from the meeting cock-a-hoop.

'He had heard about us, even before the disaster,' he told me. 'I think he had met Patience Swinfen at a dinner party and she had told him. Anyway, he said that he greatly admired our initiative and he has ordered a regular, weekly supply of twenty pies. He will arrange to have them collected each Tuesday morning. He is confident that his cook will not mind their infiltration into his household — those were his words! Personally, I doubt if they will get as far as his household!'

'And perhaps he will spread the word among some of the other big houses,' I suggested.

Edward nodded. 'But he also thinks that we should call on smaller houses near here, like Edjall Hall and Pipe Hall.'

'At the tradesmen's entrance?' I asked, astonished that Mr McClean should make such a suggestion to Edward. Or had Mr

McClean meant … ? I was suddenly reminded of my fantasy of Edward at the front door of a great house with his card and I at the back with my pies. Perhaps it had not been so fantastic after all. 'He meant that *I* should call, did he not?' I challenged Edward.

He reddened slightly. 'He didn't actually say so, Cat. He merely indicated that someone from my — er — staff should call.'

I bit my lip. What else had I expected? And did it matter *who* called as long as it helped our business to prosper? 'So what did you say?' I asked.

'I said that it was an excellent idea and thanked him for it.'

Was he deliberately begging the question? I was afraid to press him further for fear I did not like his reply. So there the matter rested for the time being. And in the end, we both called. But that was Patience Swinfen's doing, not mine.

★　★　★

Edward had read about the result of the Swinfen court case in the local newspaper. Due to a bizarre sequence of events which to us sounded highly suspicious, the court had decided that the estate should pass to Captain Edward Swinfen while Patience received an annuity of £1,000 per annum, charged upon the estate. She was also to be allowed to stay at Swinfen Hall, rent-free, until Michaelmas.

The case, as far as the court was concerned, was now closed; but not as far as Patience was concerned, especially since she had refused point-blank to sign the agreement.

'John McClean told me she intends to fight it,' Edward said. 'But whatever her intentions, Cat, I think we should relieve her of Mama's presence as soon as possible.'

Although I dreaded Mrs Marshall's arrival, I knew he was right. Accordingly, he wrote to Patience asking if she would be kind enough to have his mother driven over to Chasetown. 'There is no way she could endure arriving here in a wagon labelled Cat's Eating House,' he said and laughing at the very thought.

The words 'Why should she not begin as she will have to go on?' trembled on my lips but I bit them back. In any case, perhaps Patience Swinfen would escort her and I would dearly love to know what she thought of our efforts.

I was not disappointed. When the brougham drew up at the door, Patience alighted unaided before the coachman could even reach her.

'Cat, my dear! Edward!' Arms out-stretched, she swept towards us where we stood at the door, alerted by the crack of the coachman's whip as he tried to disperse the group of urchins, Scabber among them, who had followed him up the street. 'How good to see you!'

Edward embraced her briefly then moved on to help his mother who had remained in the brougham and was staring up at the sign — 'Cat's Eating House' as if unable to believe her eyes. I returned Patience's embrace then drew her inside to where the others waited.

There was a chorus of greetings and then she stood back and gazed around her. 'But this is wonderful! I am speechless with admiration.'

But speechless, of course, she was not as we took her on a tour of inspection. Ada and Polly's swains who were sitting, quietly minding their own business, in what we now called, most unimaginatively, the 'eating room' — 'dining room' seeming far too pretentious — rose to their feet, their eyes out on stalks. But she motioned them to sit down again.

'Pray do not let me disturb you, gentle-men!' But it was like asking a pair of serviceable sparrows to ignore a peacock and they remained standing until we had moved her away into the shop itself and then the cooling room. In the kitchen, she went into ecstasies over the new range. 'I must definitely have one at Swinfen Hall!' The orchard, now with a flock of Rhode Island Reds pecking away under the trees, was the crowning glory.

It was on our return journey that we encountered Mrs Marshall and Edward. She had allowed herself to be brought inside — if only, I think, to escape the attentions of Scabber and his friends — and was now standing in the centre of the shop and gazing around her with an expression of the utmost contempt.

'Won't you come in and sit down, Mama?' Edward was suggesting, at the same time trying to usher her through to the eating room from whence Ada and Polly's swains had now fled.

'My dear Mrs Marshall,' Patience Swinfen cried, walking towards her, 'are you not proud of your son's achievements?'

Perhaps she felt that having now dispensed with Patience's hospitality, there was no further need for civility or, more likely I think, she had no words to describe how she felt, but whatever the reason, Mrs Marshall ignored the question and instead commanded Edward to show her to her room. 'For I know that you have no servants to do it for you!'

However, at that moment there came a further commotion out in the street.

'But I lives 'ere!' I heard Scabber's outraged tones. 'Yer can't tell *me* ter bugger off!'

Edward, raising his eyes heavenward, rushed out with me behind him. Scabber, arms akimbo in his favourite attitude, was facing up to the coachman. 'Ask 'im!' he commanded when Edward appeared.

'Lives 'ere, don't I, mister?'

'In a manner of speaking, I suppose you do,' Edward admitted wearily. 'But pipe down now and make yourself useful. Hold the horse while the gentleman comes in for a cup of tea. And if any of your mates so much as lay a finger on the vehicle, I'll leather them to within an inch of their lives. Understood?'

'Understood!' echoed Scabber, taking the reins. And to his friends, 'Bugger off, the lot o' yer!'

I turned away, suppressing an involuntary smile but then saw that Edward was not amused.

'Why don't you take your mother upstairs,' I suggested, 'and I'll send up a cup of tea?'

Followed by the coachman, I went back into the shop and then through into the kitchen where the others had now congregated around the table. The tea was already being mashed.

'Well, I ain't takin' it up,' declared Polly when I mentioned that I'd promised Mrs Marshall a cup. 'She ain't the Mistress no more.'

'We don't 'ave to, do we, Cat?' Ada asked.

'I'll take it,' Ned offered with a wicked grin. 'An' that'll set the cat among the pigeons an' no mistake!'

'*I'll* take it,' said Mrs C., 'the least I can do is offer the 'and o' friendship. Whether she takes it or not, is up to 'er, but at least I've tried.'

In the end, both she and I took it with me holding the tray while she hauled herself up the stairs. Besides the cup for Mrs Marshall and one for Edward, a plate held two slices of cherry cake. ''Er favourite,' Mrs C. had reminded me.

Even so, it was a long way from the paraphernalia of spirit stove and silver teapot behind which she had presided at Ashling, with plates of assorted sandwiches and cakes beside. With some trepidation, I listened from outside on the landing to hear what reception Mrs C. received.

But Mrs Marshall said nothing. It was left to Edward to take the tray.

317

'She's sittin' there like a stone statue,' reported Mrs C. when she came out. 'But the room looks grand, Cat, with Edward's furniture an' the vase o' daffodils yer picked.'

'Never mind,' I consoled her. 'Perhaps she'll come round.'

'When pigs do fly!' observed Mrs C. caustically, going carefully down the stairs.

But we soon forgot about Mrs Marshall in the enjoyment of talking to Mrs Swinfen. When I offered her my condolences upon the result of the court case, she declared herself adamant in her refusal to accept it.

'I shall fight it tooth and nail, Cat. They think just because I am a woman that I'll give in and accept it but they don't know Patience Swinfen. But that's enough of my affairs. Tell me about your doings.'

So we told her everything from the beginning; about the painting and decorating, our abortive attempt to advertise the shop but how, had we not done so, we might not have met Amy Perkins and Mary Smith, and the mine disaster which had led to John McClean's ordering of pies. 'Although from what Edward said,' I told her, 'we have you to thank for that.'

At that moment, Edward came back with the tray and the empty cups, saying that his mother was having a rest and did not wish to be disturbed.

'She'd be lucky!' muttered Polly under her breath.

'Anyway, she ate a slice of cake,' I observed.

'She ate both!' said Edward. 'I was quite put out!'

'Nuthin' wrong with 'er appetite then.' Polly said.

'No,' said Patience Swinfen wryly, 'nothing wrong with her appetite!' But she left it at that and we fell to discussing our plans for the future.

'I'm sure it will be worth your while to call on the larger houses around here. The really big places — Drayton Manor, Shugborough, even my own house — are too far away to be of any use but there's Beaudesert Hall, Edward. That would be worth a visit, surely, especially as you know the Marquess. But that still leaves places like Edjall — both the Hall and the House — and Maple Hayes and Ashenbrook — all in Burntwood. And there's the Vicarage and all the public houses.'

Her eyes shining with excitement, she planned our route. 'Oh, I *wish* I could come with you!' she said. And then, the next second, 'Why *don't* I come with you? Would you mind? I have a reputation to live up to now, you see — the little Welsh parlour maid who dared to challenge the might of the English law courts!' She clapped her hands like a child. 'Oh, *do* let me come!'

* * *

'Is this not the greatest fun?' asked Patience Swinfen, rather as Sophie might have done.

We — Edward, Patience and myself with Ned taking the reins — were in the wagon, clip-clopping through the Staffordshire lanes behind Lofty's massive rump. It was a week after she had declared how much she would like to join us on what she now called our 'selling spree', and during that week, with Scabber's help, we had planned our route.

The hamlet of Woodhouse, Scabber had informed us, was where we would find 'the toffs', so that was where we were now heading. On the way home, we hoped to visit a few establishments in Burntwood Green and also in Burntwood itself. We were now bound for our first port of call; an ancient manor house named Maple Hayes and the seat of the Shawe family.

'I am sure that I have met Mr Shawe only recently,' Patience said. 'At any rate, I shall assure him that I have and trust that he will believe me.' Glancing at her in her modish day dress of crimson velvet, a matching feather nodding in the brim of her bonnet, I felt confident Mr Shawe would believe whatever she said. Not so, however, his parlourmaid.

Patience went, without prior discussion and with Edward and me in attendance, to the front door. She smiled at the maid who answered her imperious knocking and requested to see her master. 'I wish to do business with him.'

But the maid, noticing the wagon drawn up at the front of the house and presumably able to read the printing on its side, was not to be intimidated.

'We do have a tradesmen's entrance, madam,' she pointed out. 'Round to . . . '

'The days when Patience Swinfen of Swinfen Hall used the tradesmen's entrance are long gone, I am pleased to say,' said Patience firmly and extracted a card from her bag. 'So if you will please give your master this . . . '

But the girl had already capitulated and was holding open the door. She left us in the hall and went, presumably, in search of Mr Shawe. I noted that Patience had made no mention of Mrs Shawe if, indeed, there was one. A few moments later, the maid was back. 'The master will see you now, madam.'

He rose from his chair by the fire in a room that was clearly the library. 'Mrs Swinfen? Have I had the pleasure . . . ?'

'Dear Mr Shawe, we met just a few months ago, I cannot remember where exactly but I do remember having a very lively conversation with you.'

Mr Shawe, clearly flattered, smiled amiably. 'I think I *do* remember it, dear lady!'

'You told me that if ever I was in the area, I was to be sure and call. So here I am! And,' she turned and put a hand out to each of us, 'with my two young friends, Catherine Marsh and Edward Marshall, lately removed from Ashling Hall at Alrewas. They are a most enterprising young couple who have recently set up a comestible business in Chasetown under the patronage of no less a personage than Mr John McClean, whom you will know well, of course. A dear man! Catherine, my dear, will you not show Mr Shawe a sample of the many pies, cakes and biscuits that you make?' She motioned me forward and I held out the basket I had been clutching so that Mr Shawe could inspect its contents.

Mrs C. had done us proud. There were pies and patties, buns and biscuits, and an assortment of cakes, all covered with a spotlessly white cloth. They smelled as delicious as they looked and Mr Shawe wrinkled his nose appreciatively.

'Most commendable, my dear Miss Marsh. But it is not my approval you should be seeking but that of my cook's. *She* is the arbiter of my eating habits.'

'Then could I perhaps show our produce to her, sir? If it is no trouble?'

'Certainly, my dear.' And he went to the nearest bell pull. 'And meanwhile perhaps you, my dear Mrs Swinfen and you, Mr Marshall, will take a glass of sherry?'

From then on, everything flowed smoothly; once in the kitchen, I was on home ground. And I was fortunate in that the cook was a pleasant, kindly woman — although she might not have been so accommodating had I appeared, like any other pedlar woman with my basket over my arm at her back door.

Quickly, I explained that we had no wish to appear as a challenge to her culinary skills — which I understood to be quite exceptional — but that I knew from experience that it was useful to have some cold food available, ready for eating.

She nodded vigorously and agreed that that was indeed the case and could she perhaps sample a small piece of pie and perhaps a pasty?

Five minutes later, I was on my way back to the library with an order for two dozen beef pies and three dozen chicken patties to be delivered each Saturday morning.

Ten minutes later, we were driving away, cock-a-hoop with delight. 'Write it in the order book immediately, Cat,' Patience directed, 'in case you forget.'

'I'll do it,' said Edward quickly — too quickly — and from under my lashes I saw Patience's glance of comprehension.

'I can't write, I'm afraid,' I told her, for honesty was always the best policy with Patience Swinfen. 'Nor read. But I have my own method.' And I made my own peculiar entry in the book which both Mrs C. and I would understand.

The same procedure was equally as successful at Pipe Hall and also at Ashenbrook except that there, the master was out and it was left to Edward to charm the mistress; but this was done with a skill that left me open-mouthed with admiration. However, I was able to pull myself together sufficiently to explain our purpose to the cook and she, after considerably more sampling than the cook at Maple Hayes gave me a weekly order of one dozen chicken pies and an assortment of cakes.

'Delivery on a Saturday?' I asked hopefully.

'That will do nicely,' she said.

At Edjall Hall, neither the master nor the

mistress were at home. 'So may we see the cook then, please?' asked Patience sweetly. And so intrigued was the maid by this extraordinary departure from accepted social behaviour that we did indeed see the cook and in the front hall to boot. And she, good woman, made the most of her sudden elevation by sampling everything in the basket! However, she did order the extraordinary amount of five large steak and kidney pies a week.

'She's new, see,' explained the maid as she saw us out, 'an' wants ter impress the Mistress. Yer a god-send!'

At Edjall House, Patience really did know the master and mistress so that the call was on a much more relaxed and friendly footing but strangely, their order was negligible and would not have been worth accepting had we not the other deliveries to make.

'And now the Vicarage at Burntwood?' Edward suggested after we had left Edjall House.

He had a particular reason for wishing to include the Vicarage in our itinerary and it was to do with his mother. For Mrs Marshall had not settled in Chasetown. We had expected problems, of course, but none as difficult as they had proved. She had been there a week but had been out of the house only once, even though the weather had been warm and sunny.

The orchard was now a froth of colour with the pink of apple blossom challenging the pure white of pear, and the quinces a rosy haze against the stable walls. Just to sit there, with the drone of bees like a lullaby was a delight — we regularly drank our 'elevenses' out there — but it was a pleasure that Mrs Marshall seemed happy to forgo in spite of Edward's coaxing. I think perhaps that if there had been another way to reach it other than through the kitchen or down the narrow, and now overgrown path at the side of the house, she might have gone. But the kitchen was somewhere that the late Mistress of Ashling Hall did not demean herself to visit, except perhaps to instruct the cook. And those days were over.

All her meals were taken up to her by Edward, and she insisted that he remain and eat with her. And Edward, dutiful son though he was, did not take kindly to perpetual servitude. Besides, I think he missed the friendly chatter of our meals around the kitchen table.

On the only occasion when she had decided to set foot out of doors, she had insisted that he accompany her and not in his customary working garb, but in the full fig of morning dress and tall hat.

'And you know what happened to me last time I got dolled up like this!' he'd groaned to me. And had insisted that Scabber and Billy should follow at a discreet distance as protection!

I have no idea what the inhabitants of Chasetown thought of the elegantly clad woman lifting her skirts so disdainfully above the dust and mud of the unpaved streets but certainly Edward's temper had not been improved by the excursion, especially since Scabber and Billy had not kept their distance but had sauntered at his heels trying to engage him in conversation.

Rex, who had just been brought over from Swinfen along with Toffee, had also attached himself to the procession and had soon become involved in a fight with a Chasetown bulldog. It had only ended when a woman had rushed out of a house and thrown a bucket of water over them. Unfortunately, not only the dogs but Mrs Marshall had been thoroughly drenched. Consequently, Edward's plan to walk up on to the Chase had had to be abandoned.

We were now seriously considering moving Mrs Marshall to Burntwood and the Vicarage seemed a good starting point for our enquiries; then, if necessary, we would invoke the Marquess's help.

We found the vicar — a robust man somewhere in his early fifties — in his church. Patience, understanding the delicacy of our mission had elected to stay in the wagon with Ned; which was as well, perhaps, because the sherry she had drunk at our various ports of call was now having its effect. We had left her snoring gently against Ned's shoulder.

We had already heard of the benevolence of the Reverend George Poole and of his work among the mining community and were not entirely surprised when he declared that he had already heard of Cat's Eating House. Of more interest to us at the moment was his admission that he had also heard of Mr Marshall's bankruptcy and the circumstances of his death.

'Poor lady,' he observed when Edward told him about his mother's removal to Chasetown. 'She will find her circumstances greatly changed.'

'Yes, indeed,' Edward agreed. 'But we were wondering if life might be easier for her in a more rural community such as Burntwood. There is still a certain brashness about Chasetown.'

The Reverend Poole twinkled amiably. 'Nicely put, sir! And there is another even

328

more important advantage to living in Burntwood.' And he paused expectantly, clearly hoping that Edward would know of it.

'We are blessed with the noble building in which we are now standing,' he said when it became evident that Edward was not going to oblige.

'Indeed, yes!' said Edward hurriedly. 'And my mother is, of course, a regular churchgoer.'

'I have heard,' I added quickly to show that we were not entirely ignorant of such matters, 'that Mr McClean hopes to have a church built in Chasetown.'

The Vicar nodded. 'You are quite right, Miss Marsh. A most godly man.'

'I have also heard,' I added for good measure, 'that in the meantime many people flock here to Christ Church to hear you preach.'

He twinkled even more brightly. 'You flatter me, Miss Marsh! But in truth, our congregation is excellent for such a scattered community. Now about your mother, Mr Marshall. Your purpose, I gather, is to find lodgings for her here?'

'Exactly,' said Edward. 'And we thought that you would be the best person to recommend somewhere suitable.'

'And would you say that a vicarage was suitable?'

Edward's eyes nearly left their sockets. 'Surely you do not mean, sir, that you would be prepared to . . . ?'

'To offer your mother accommodation? But of course. The Vicarage is more than big enough to accommodate an extra person. My wife was only saying so the other day. We have no children, you see.'

'But sir, you do not know my mother. She may not be . . . ' Edward spluttered.

'Might I suggest,' I interrupted before he could say something really damning, 'that Mrs Marshall comes on a temporary footing to begin with? We would not wish to take advantage of your very kind offer.'

'Rest assured, Miss Marsh, that there will be nothing binding on either side. But you may find that we all rub along very well together.'

I said no more although I could not imagine Mrs Marshall rubbing along — well or badly — with anyone.

'We would of course pay for her board,' Edward said swiftly.

The Vicar raised a hand. 'Shall we say that, for the moment, she comes as a guest and that we will reconsider the matter after a couple of weeks?'

'I cannot possibly tell you how grateful I am,' said Edward.

'Pray sir, say no more of it. Now,' and he turned his gaze upon the basket I was carrying, 'my nose tells me that there is something good enough to eat under that cloth, Miss Marsh. A sample of your wares, perhaps?'

We left most of the remaining food with him and, promising to return with Mrs Marshall in a couple of days, made our way back to the wagon; to find Patience awake but disinclined for further action.

'We'll leave the public houses until another day,' Edward decided.

I saw Ned's face fall and my heart went out to him because he had waited most patiently all morning and was probably now hoping for a pint of ale.

'Let's just call in at the Star Inn,' I coaxed Edward. 'It is on our way and we won't stay long, will we Ned?'

'Just long enough to . . . ' and he raised an imaginary pint pot to his lips.

'Why of course,' said Edward. 'I'm sorry, Ned!'

'That's all right, Eddie!' Ned assured him.

And indeed, it proved a most useful call for the Inn, we discovered, was the collecting point for the nails that were manufactured in the area and the landlord was fully occupied in weighing them. It was left to the landlady to serve us and to taste our one remaining pie. We left with a regular weekly order for two dozen.

When we reached home eventually, it was to find the household in a state of uproar. Mrs Marshall had commanded Polly to dispose of the contents of her commode and, of course, she had flatly refused. The news that the Crimean War had ended had passed by almost unnoticed!

'Right!' said Edward grimly. 'That settles it!'

21

To our great relief, Mrs Marshall and the Reverend and Mrs Poole appeared to take to each other; if not exactly like ducks to water, at least with a courteous welcome on their side and a somewhat stiff politeness on hers. And she did have the grace to thank them for allowing her to stay.

'Let's hope she settles there,' said Edward as we drove back in the wagon, 'so that we can get on with our lives.'

I rested my head against his shoulder, glad of this opportunity to be on our own for a little while.

'You're sure you're still happy?' I asked.

For answer, he drew Lofty to a standstill, dropped the reins and took me in his arms.

'Very happy indeed!' he said and kissed me long and thoroughly. It was our first real embrace since leaving Ashling and it left me breathless. 'Oh, Edward!' was all I could say before he kissed me again.

'I love you, Cat, do you know that?'

'And I you, Edward. I think I always have, since the moment I first saw you.'

'For me it was the day Satan threw me and

I realised that you had grown from a child into a woman — a beautiful woman.'

And so, in the way that lovers do, we recalled all manner of incidents, some trivial, some less so.

'Do you remember our first day in Lichfield together?'

'When you went to sleep by Stowe Pool and I kissed you awake.'

'And the day you and Sophie built the snowman and I knocked your mother's hat off?'

'And the night I carried the pail of slops to the back stairs for you without spilling a drop?'

'Even though you were drunk!'

It was only when a farm cart came rumbling up behind us, and the driver demanded passage that we returned to reality. Edward pulled Lofty's head up from the wayside grasses and we trotted home.

There, we found that the atmosphere had undergone a miraculous transformation in our absence. Everyone was either singing or whistling as they worked. It was astonishing how the removal of one woman from our midst had made such a difference.

That evening, no-one seemed to want to leave the supper table, so pleasant was our talk. To their obvious enjoyment, we teased

Ada and Polly about their men friends — Harold Bates and Henry Venables as we now knew them to be called — pulled Fred's leg about Addie, the girl who helped Jim Parker with his shoe-mending business, and, most important of all, discussed Mr Jolly's impending visit. We had just decided that he should be given Mrs Marshall's old room when Rex, who had been lying at Edward's feet, suddenly set up a ferocious barking, then rushed through to the shop door, his tail wagging furiously.

'Heavens, I hope it's not . . . ' Edward got to his feet, seizing a lamp.

'Surely not! She's only been there five minutes!' I answered his unfinished question and followed him through to the shop, the others behind me. Edward unlocked the door and threw it open.

There on the step stood a young girl, her bent head shrouded in a dark shawl.

'Who . . . ?' Edward began, raising the lamp high.

'Sophie!' I all but screamed. 'It's Sophie!' And the next moment she was in my arms and sobbing as if she would never stop.

We carried her into the light and warmth of the kitchen and sat her gently down. Mrs C. seized a cup and filled it with tea from the pot that had just been made. And all the time, her sobbing never ceased. Then Edward knelt by her chair and began to chafe her bare hands and I eased back the shawl from her head to reveal her face, chalk-white in its pallor and streaked with dirt. I think I would have passed her in the street without recognising her.

'Drink this!' said Edward, holding the cup to her lips. And she did so in great, noisy gulps as if she could never get enough of it. And at last she spoke in a voice that was little more than a whisper.

'Oh, Edward, please don't send me back! Please! Please!' And she began to cry again.

Almost as distressed as she, he soothed her as best he could. 'Of course I won't send you back. You're safe now, Sophie. Don't cry, sweetheart!'

'Mama?' Her eyes were like sunken pools in sockets that seemed to have fallen in upon themselves like those of a very old woman.

'She's not here, my love. She's several miles away. Don't worry.'

''Ere you are, me lamb, drink this!' and Mrs C. put a bowl of steaming broth, left over from our supper, on the table in front of her.

Ada eased off her cloak and Ned knelt to remove her shoes — scuffed and down-at-heel, I noticed — while Polly lifted spoonfuls of broth to her lips. Slowly the colour began to seep back into her cheeks and her sobs slowly faded.

'We'll put you to bed as soon as you've finished your broth,' I told her, 'and you can tell us all about it in the morning.'

She clutched at me. 'Don't leave me, Cat. Stay with me. And Edward, too.'

'We will,' I promised.

The soup finished, Edward carried her upstairs to his mother's room where the bed had been freshly made up that afternoon, and Ada, Polly and I undressed her and pulled one of Edward's night shirts over her head.

As we had promised, Edward and I stayed with her until she fell asleep and then Edward made himself comfortable in a chair by her bedside, prepared to spend the night there. But when I came back, soon after midnight and ready to take over the vigil, I found that he had stretched himself out on the bed beside his sister and both were sleeping peacefully. After covering him with a blanket, I crept away to my own bed.

★ ★ ★

Sophie slept almost constantly through the next twentyfour hours, waking only to eat a little and drink a great deal. On the morning of the second day, she sat up in bed, looking almost her old self.

'Do you want to talk, my love?' I asked when I took her up a bowl of porridge, laced with honey and cream.

'Please, Cat. And Edward, too, of course.'

He had been hovering outside the door and came in immediately. 'Are you feeling better now, little sister?'

'Much better. And I must tell you why I acted as I did. But first — will they come after me, my aunt and uncle? Have you told them where I am?'

'They'll know by now,' Edward told her — for he had written immediately — 'and they will also know that I have no intention of allowing you to return to them.'

'But what will Mama say?'

'Leave Mama to me,' said Edward and for the first time since she had come, Sophie smiled.

'She'll be in a great tizzy when she knows!'

'Perhaps not when you have explained why you left.'

And so Sophie told her sad little tale — of an impoverished young girl dependant upon the good will of her rich relations and finding it sadly lacking.

'I ate with Charlotte and I shared her lessons and sometimes I was taken for walks with her, but there it stopped. She rode her pony in Hyde Park but I had no pony. She went to dancing lessons but I did not — not that I minded *that!* She was invited out to tea but I was never allowed to go with her. Not a day passed but I was made to feel unwanted and that I only lived there on sufferance.'

'Oh, Sophie,' Edward said, 'Why did you not tell me all of this?'

'Because my letters were read before they were posted and I was never allowed out on my own. And all the time, I was receiving these lovely letters from you, telling me all about the exciting things that were happening here. And in the end, I could stand no more and I ran away. They were all so busy celebrating the end of the Crimean War, they didn't notice me slipping out through the side door. And I'm sorry, Edward, but I stole some money. It had been left on the hall table for some purpose and I simply took it. Two whole pounds, Edward.'

'You did not steal it, Sophie, you borrowed it under great provocation, and I will return it immediately. Think no more of it.'

'But how did you actually reach here?' I asked gently.

'On the railway,' Sophie said. 'At first it was most exciting and a gentleman in the carriage gave me a bun but then he wanted me to sit on his knee and when I told him that I did not want to because he smelled of beer and tobacco, he grew nasty and I went to sit next to a woman with two children. But then the train stopped at a station and we all had to get out and I did not know what to do next.'

Her voice began to wobble dangerously and I hurriedly spooned more porridge into her.

'And then I caught the wrong train and the ticket collector was very cross and said I must pay more but I said I hadn't any more and that my brother would pay when I reached him. But he said that wasn't good enough and he was going to call the police. So, when we reached the next station, I ran away and this *really* nice man took pity on me and put me on the right train for Lichfield and said, 'Good luck, missy!' when he left me.

'And how did you get from Lichfield?' I asked.

'I walked.'

'Oh, Sophie, why ever didn't you go to Nanny Humphries?' Edward asked.

'I did but when I got there, there was a policeman in the shop and I thought, perhaps he was looking for me and she'd have to give me up and I'd be sent back. I didn't mind walking until I got blisters, and I had to keep hiding in the ditch whenever a coach or a cart came along, in case they were looking for me.

340

They can't *make* me go back, can they, Edward?'

'Of course not,' he assured her, 'although it's possible the London police were looking for you in the beginning.'

'Well, I jolly well hope my uncle and aunt and that horrid Charlotte get into trouble,' said Sophie, beginning to sound more like her old self with every word. 'They were all so busy going on about their precious Jack coming home from the Crimea, they weren't interested in anyone else. I never want to see any of them ever again. And please, Cat, after I've eaten my porridge, may I get up and go and see Toffee?'

★ ★ ★

Naturally I was not with them when Edward drove Sophie to see their mother but I gathered from Edward that Mrs Marshall, while not endorsing her daughter's actions, had no wish to send her back to London.

'Indeed, she has written them a scathing condemnation of their behaviour. I think a rift has occurred that will probably never be healed. And a good thing, too, I say, although I did rather like Jack.'

At first, he had been greatly concerned that Mrs Marshall would consider it her duty to return to Chasetown to be with Sophie. 'But I assured her that we would take the greatest care of her, is that not so, Cat?'

'Of course!' But in fact, we were all now so busy with the shop, the eating room and the now regular weekly deliveries in the countryside, I could not see that we would have much time to devote to Sophie.

But it did not seem to matter for she quickly adapted herself to her new life and was clearly determined not to be a drain upon our resources. She soon proved herself adept at helping Mrs C. and me in the kitchen and the knowledge she gained there would surely be as much use to her, I reasoned, as any expensive finishing school. When she married ... but there my imagination failed me. For whom *could* she marry if she were to remain in Chasetown? Certainly she met men in plenty for she was soon helping in the shop and the eating room, taking great pride in giving the right change and treating the customers with great civility and charm, but the men were not, with all respect, the sort she should marry.

However, it was pointless to worry about such matters at the moment. She was not yet fourteen and all manner of things could happen before she was of marriageable age. But not always pleasant things, I decided one day when she had been with us about six weeks, when I caught one of the unmarried miners, who had dropped in for his breakfast, eyeing her with a gaze that was by no means paternal. I noticed, too, that when she put his plate of food in front of him, his arm came, quite unnecessarily, around her waist and lingered there until she moved away.

I spoke about it to Edward and from then on the eating room was declared out of bounds for Sophie.

'It's Ada's and Polly's task,' I explained, 'and besides, you are so good at serving behind the counter.' And indeed she was, for she was much quicker at adding up than either of them.

But it was not all work for her. Every day she would saddle up Toffee and she and Ned — he mounted on a bony but obliging Lofty — would set off across the Chase, which could be easily reached by a bridleway at the side of the orchard. From these expeditions, she would return with flushed cheeks and sparkling eyes and I truly think she was as happy at Chasetown as she had been at Ashling, although I often wished that there were others of her own age for company.

And then one day she rode home and declared, 'I have found a friend, Cat. Her name is Mattie and she works on the canal barges.'

I glanced at Ned and he nodded. 'We rode up ter the canal that leads from Beaudesert into Chase Water. The old Marquess 'ad it cut ter bring the coal down from the colliery there.'

'How old is Mattie?' I asked.

'Two weeks younger than I,' Sophie told me.

'And have you met her parents?' I had an uncomfortable feeling I sounded just like her mother.

'Oh, yes! They work on the barge, too, loading and unloading the coal. They are not there every day, of course. Sometimes they are at Beaudesert — that's where their cottage is. And they have this lovely horse called Betsy, she walks along the towpath pulling the barge and Mattie walks with her. And she doesn't wear shoes, Cat — Mattie that is, not Betsy, because she *has* to wear shoes, of course — and her legs are all lovely and brown — Mattie's legs, that is, although Betsy's are too, come to think of it — she's a skewbald, you see, and . . . '

'Sophie! For pity's sake, stop! I can't keep up with you. How did you come to meet her?'

'Ned and I were riding along the towpath but coming the other way — we should have been on the other side of the canal. It was our fault entirely so that when Mattie's father pointed this out to us . . . '

I closed my eyes and tried to close my ears. I could just imagine the language he would have used when pointing it out! The choice language of the bargees had become proverbial.

' . . . so Ned and I managed to back into a field while they passed and then Mattie ran back and told me not to worry, it was always happening and there was a bridge a little bit further on where we could cross. And she was such a nice, friendly person I dismounted and Ned held Toffee and I walked a little way with her. And I'm to look out for her tomorrow when they could be back. And if not tomorrow, the next day . . . '

I sat down heavily at the kitchen table on which I had been about to make pastry until Sophie had come dashing in. 'I don't suppose,' I said weakly, 'that Mattie could come to tea one day?' And then I stopped, glancing at Ned for guidance, for the child must be as black as the ace of spades.

'She seemed a nice enough girl, Cat,' he said. 'Very friendly-like.' Well, you would say that, wouldn't you, I thought because *you* were supposed to be looking after her!

But Sophie had seized on my suggestion.

'I'll ask her, shall I? She'd have to ride behind Ned, but you wouldn't mind, would you, Ned?'

In the event, it wasn't necessary. For Mattie wasn't allowed to come to tea. 'Her father says she can't be spared,' Sophie explained. 'But he was very nice about it and said why didn't I come and have a cup with them? So I did and they have this dear little cabin, with furniture stuck to the floor or built into the sides. Mattie's mother says one day she wants to have something called a narrow boat and actually live on the canal all the time. Can you imagine anything more delightful, Cat, than *living* on the water? Waking up each morning to the sound of it slapping on the sides of the barge. Moving about the countryside from one place to another.'

'Did you go on board, too?' I asked Ned.

'Oh, no, Ned held Toffee and Lofty,' Sophie answered before he could extricate his jaws from the bun he was now eating.

I gave up, Edward would have to take Ned's place next morning and find out exactly what was happening.

But Edward didn't prove particularly helpful. 'Mattie seems a nice enough child, Cat. I don't think you need worry. They obviously enjoy each other's company and although you might not think so at first, they have a lot in common. She loves birds and flowers and animals, just like Sophie, and she knows a lot more about them than Sophie does. She's going to show her where there are kingfishers and wild orchids.'

'But doesn't she — er — get very dirty handling the coal?' I asked, voicing one of my main worries.

'Through no fault of her own, of course,' I added hastily.

'Well, no, she is very sensibly clad when she is working, wearing a hood over her head and gloves on her hands and a sort of cape affair over the rest of her. She is a very pretty child as a matter of fact,' he added, 'with a grin that stretches from ear to ear.'

'And her language?' I dared to ask.

'Well, you could cut her accent with a knife, of course!' said Edward cheerfully. 'I had the greatest difficulty understanding what she was saying although Sophie seemed to know. So I really couldn't say what her language is like. The funny thing is, she tried to mimic Sophie and they both ended up shrieking with laughter.'

And what's to stop Sophie mimicking *her*, I thought, but held my peace. If Edward was satisfied, there was little more I could do and Sophie was clearly very happy with her new friend.

'Mind you,' Edward said over his shoulder as he turned to go, 'I'm not saying Mama would approve!'

For once, I thought I might be in agreement with his Mama!

22

I could not believe that time could pass so quickly. Cat's Eating House was now 'on the map' as Patience Swinfen declared on one of her many visits. Not only were many of the mining population now our regular customers but also, on occasion, the 'navvies'. They came either to repair the existing railway lines or to lay new tracks as the Cannock Chase Colliery Company sank yet another shaft which, if it proved profitable would be connected to the South Staffordshire Railway at a place called Anglesey Sidings, half-way between Brownhills and Hammerwich stations.

I doubt if I would have known any of this, had it not been for Fred. For Fred had developed an unexpected interest in anything mechanical, particularly steam engines, and would spend most of his leisure time, when he was not with Addie, watching the navvies at work. So excited was he when he came back one day to report the arrival of a new steam locomotive to pull the string of coal trucks, you would have thought he had made the purchase from his own pocket.

'It's a 0–4–2 saddle tank, an' it's called McClean,' he told us as if he were describing some exotic pet.

'Fancy that!' said Mrs C. obligingly, pausing in her potato mashing.

'It sounds very impressive,' I said. 'I'll try to come and see it with you.'

But of course I never did. There simply wasn't the time. When we had first come to Chasetown, I had had high hopes of taking up Edward's long-ago offer of teaching me to read and write but it had never happened. Now that his mother was at Burntwood, he felt duty bound to call upon her at least twice a week; and not only to call but to sometimes escort her to one of the large houses in the area where they had both been invited for dinner.

It was Patience who was largely responsible for Mrs Marshall's return into society, always sending her coach to collect her when she was invited to Swinfen Hall and soon other landowners in the area, including the Marquess and John McClean began to do the same. Even though she was unable to return their hospitality, the memory of Colonel Marshall still lingered among the gentry and, I think, prompted their hospitality.

It was most acceptable to their hostess that Edward should escort her; not only did his presence mean that dinner tables would be nicely balanced, he was also, in spite of his lack of wealth, still an entertaining young man, able to move with confidence among the highest in the land. And wealth was not everything; if he were to make a good match with a rich man's daughter, it would no longer matter.

There was also, according to Patience, a certain whimsical attraction about his present circumstances. Not only was he admired for his refusal to lie down and accept the cruel hand that Fate had dealt him, there was also a drollness about his present situation that seemed to amuse many.

'And how are the pies selling these days?' he was often asked, so Patience told me, and his reply would be eagerly awaited.

'He usually makes an amusing tale of it,' Patience said, 'but never at the expense of others, I can assure you. And he is always loud in your praises, my dear.'

For this, of course, I was profoundly grateful for I could not have born it if he had made light of our achievements. And often, curiosity would get the better of his enquirers, and a coach would stop outside and a servant be sent inside for 'a dozen pies, if you please.'

At the same time, and against my better

judgement, I found that I sometimes resented the fact that I was never there to make my own contribution to his stories. It was ridiculous to have such feelings for I had always known that it would be impossible for me to mingle with the gentry except on a purely commercial basis.

Patience, bless her, had done her best to make it otherwise, even to the extent of including me in her invitations to Mrs Marshall and Edward, but these I had steadfastly refused. Apart from other considerations — like having nothing suitable to wear — no table could have held both Mrs Marshall and me without some display of acrimony. And while Patience, with her reputation for eccentricity, could perhaps have carried off such a difficult situation, no-one else would ever have followed her example.

Strangely, it was something that Edward and I never discussed. Now that he had declared his love, I felt confident of our future together but what form it would take, I had never allowed myself to imagine. Perhaps I had a vague idea that when we had made sufficient money and were married, family life would be sufficient for both of us. Certainly, I was now so pleased with the way our business was progressing, such thoughts did not concern me for long.

Certainly, Edward seemed happy enough. Sometimes, when he and Patience spoke of events in other parts of the county — a cricket match, perhaps, or a race meeting she had attended — his expression would reflect a certain wistful longing but it never lasted. He seemed just as concerned about the recruitment of the local boys and girls for the fruit picking that had suddenly become an urgent race against time.

Everything seemed to ripen together; luscious red and black currants, fat hairy gooseberries, purple plums and pears that fell from the bough within days of their ripening if we — or the wasps — did not reach them first. The apples were still to come.

In Ole Renshaw's day, we decided, the harvest must have been greatly neglected because the small children of the area descended upon the orchard as if of their right.

'We've only come ter pick, mister,' they asserted, quite indignantly, when Edward enquired what they were about.

'What for, exactly?' he asked. 'To fill your stomachs or to take fruit home to your mothers?'

'Ter sell, more like,' said Scabber who was, of course, at Edward's elbow.

'Yer can talk, Scabber,' said one of the boys, 'Yer was allus one o' the first!'

In the event, they decided it was more profitable to be paid by us than to hawk the fruit in the streets and for a hectic few weeks there was a continual procession of children at the kitchen door to have their baskets weighed and paid for.

We all worked late in to the night, jamming and bottling until the larder shelves groaned under the weight. And then, when we knew we could use no more, we invited everyone in to pick what they could.

Mr Jolly's visit coincided with the picking and he became a familiar sight out there in his shirt sleeves, sometimes picking but more often than not sitting on an old wooden chair, puffing away at the pipe that he now favoured instead of a cigar. On his head was an old straw hat that had once belonged to the Master.

Before he came, I had been a little apprehensive in case he wore the black morning coat and trousers that had been his uniform at Ashling and thereby receive the same treatment as Edward, but I'd had no need to worry. When he stepped down from the train at Hammerwich Station where we had all gone to meet him, Mrs C.included, he wore an informal check jacket and plain brown trousers and sported a tweed deer-stalker on his head. He looked every inch a countryman.

We all fell upon him like bees swarming around a honey pot, hanging on to his arms while we escorted him to the wagon. It was very late that night when we went to our beds, so eager were we to exchange news and reminiscences. Clearly, retirement to the seaside had suited him for his cheeks which used to have the pallor of someone who rarely ventured out of doors, were now sun-kissed and rosy. Even so, it was not difficult to persuade him to stay longer than the fortnight he had originally intended. In fact, he was still with us on Michaelmas Day when Patience had her confrontation with Captain Frederick Swinfen.

As agreed by the court — but not by Patience — that was the day when she was required to leave Swinfen Hall and the Captain to move in. Accompanied by his mother and his lawyer, he duly presented himself there. Needless to say, he was refused admission and had to content himself with walking around the grounds.

'I stood at an upstairs window and watched him like a hawk,' Patience told us a couple of days later, 'all the time keeping him in the sights of my pistol.' She was relating her story in the kitchen and paused at this point so that we could register our alarm at this statement. We didn't fail her.

'You didn't . . . ?' I exclaimed.

'Was it loaded, ma'am?' from Mr Jolly.

'Oh my Gawd!' said Mrs C., her hand flying to her mouth.

The others simply held their breath. Edward was not with us.

'Of course it was loaded, Mr Jolly,' Patience said. 'And what's more, I used it!'

Everyone released their breath in gasps of horror.

'You didn't . . . ?' I began again.

'Kill him? No! I had no intention of serving a prison sentence for the bastard. Besides, it wasn't necessary. Our brave and determined soldier soon gave in and beat a hasty retreat. Resisting an impulse to use his backside as a target, I merely discharged my pistol into the air. However, you should have seen him jump! And I thought his mother would have hysterics. They left Swinfen Hall at a considerably smarter pace than that they arrived at, I can tell you!'

Halfway through her narrative, Edward had come in holding a copy of the Staffordshire Advertiser and now he opened it for her to see. 'Here you are, Patience, read all about yourself! According to them you did discharge your pistol into the rear of the retreating Captain, but happily without effect.'

'As far as I'm concerned,' Patience asserted, seizing the paper, 'it *did* have an effect. They left Swinfen Hall, didn't they, and I doubt if they'll be back in a hurry.'

In the following week's paper there appeared a letter from Patience, mocking the 'gallant Captain' for his reaction to a 'thimbleful of powder' let loose 'in an opposite direction'.

'Well,' said Mr Jolly, 'I really begin to think the lady may win her case.'

But it would be a long battle, I thought. And Edward agreed. 'Why not stay and help us pick the apples,' he suggested when she next appeared and in a somewhat despondent mood. 'It would take your mind off your troubles.'

'There's nothing I'd like better,' Patience declared, 'But I have to see Charles Simpson, my attorney, to plan our campaign. But I'll be back, never fear.'

* * *

Our first apple harvest was prolific. Once again, an army of children descended upon us; but this time Sophie's friend Mattie was among their number. I think that when her parents learned that she would be paid for her services, they decided they could manage without her for a little while. There was now also an older brother at home, recently returned from seeking his fortune in the coalfields of South Wales, which may have influenced their decision.

Edward had been right, I decided when I first saw Mattie — she was a beautiful child. And not really a child so much as a young girl trembling upon the brink of maturity. And that wasn't strictly true either for trembling, except perhaps in mid-winter or with fury if she were thwarted, was not something that Mattie would indulge in. From the topmost curl of her luxuriant chestnut hair down to her bare and dirty toes, she exuded a physical magnetism that demanded the immediate attention of everyone with whom she came into contact.

'A brazen hussy!' declared Mr Jolly without hesitation, before preparing to return to the warmer climes of Hastings. 'And I should count the silver before she leaves!'

'We have none,' I told him, 'as you well know! But I do see what you mean.' For there was a shiftiness about the way her gaze continuously darted hither and thither, missing nothing.

'She's changed since I saw her,' Edward admitted.

Even Ned, whose judgement I greatly respected, was now wary of her. 'It's since that brother of 'ers come 'ome,' he said, 'an' I wouldn't trust 'im as far as I could throw 'im.'

But Sophie, of course, thought 'the sun shines out of 'er arse!' as Ned put it, crudely but succinctly.

'Can I not have my ears pierced like Mattie?' she implored, for she greatly admired the golden hoops that dangled from Mattie's ears.

Or — 'Can I not wear my hair loose like Mattie? I do so hate these silly plaits.'

'All in good time,' I told her. And found myself hoping that it would be a bad winter with the ground too hard for galloping up on to the Chase, or even that the canal would freeze over and the barges be stuck in Beaudesert.

Given my antipathy towards her, it was strange that it was Mattie who was the messenger of tidings that were truly miraculous.

'There's some bloke in shop wants ter see yer,' she informed me, one autumn morning, presenting herself at the back door as usual. 'Wanted ter know if yer name was Marsh, I said 'e'd better ask yer 'isself.'

Greatly intrigued, I hurried into the shop. Could it be my uncle? But surely he would have written that he was coming in one of the occasional letters that he now exchanged with Edward on my behalf?

A tall dark stranger stood there; a presentable, well-set-up young man in a serviceable reefer jacket and drainpipe trousers and with a hard felt hat in his hand. His hair was black and very curly and his eyes were shining brightly, almost as if he were near to tears, although I would not have thought the air outside was *that* cold. He moved towards me.

'Hello, Cat!' he said. 'It's Thomas. Thomas Bailey.'

23

'It was Hannah who was our salvation,' said Thomas, 'although she never knew it. She thought it her duty to tell Mrs Osborne up at Mill House that Rosie and I had left Burslem. And she, in her turn thought it *her* duty to tell her son, Frank Osborne, Rosie's real father. He was in Switzerland at the time. But he came home immediately and started to look for us — a formidable task but he left no stone unturned, alerting the police and having our description circulated among the potbanks and public houses in the area. After a few months, he found us — sleeping rough on our way to Liverpool.'

'Why Liverpool?' I asked.

'We were going to stow away on whatever ship we could crawl into unobserved and going anywhere, we didn't mind.'

By now, we were sitting in my room, he on Edward's chair, I on the bed. When he had picked me up from where I was sprawled across the counter, 'like a stranded fish, gasping for breath!' he told me later, he had called for help and Edward had come rushing in with Polly at his heels.

'She's all right,' I had heard him say, his voice echoing as if coming from a very long way away, 'but I'm afraid I've just given her rather a shock.'

I had fought to stand up then, thrusting out at the arms that were trying to help me. 'It's all right, my love,' I heard Edward say, his voice full of concern. 'I'm here.' And then, to Thomas, 'Who are you, sir, if I may ask?'

And then I began to laugh, foolishly, unable to control myself. 'It's all right,' I told him in my turn. 'This is Thomas. You know — Thomas Bailey.' But of course, I realised, Edward did not know.

But by then, Mrs C. was on the scene and she *did* know. 'It's someone Cat knew when she was a child,' I heard her tell Edward. And to me, 'There, there, lovely! We'll go inter the kitchen an 'ave a nice cup o' tea.'

And that was what we had done and then I had been told that I was to take the rest of the day off while 'yer catch up on yer news!' as Mrs C. put it. To do that would have been impossible in the kitchen and so I had suggested that Thomas and I retire to my room. I wasn't at all sure that Edward approved of the idea but there was little he could do to stop me.

'Just give us a couple of hours together,' I told him, 'and then we'll be down. If, that is,' and I turned to Thomas, 'you can spare the time?'

'Oh yes,' he assured me, a great grin threatening to split his face in two. 'I can spare the time. I'm not due to see Mr McClean until this afternoon.'

That was the second shock of the day for me — that Thomas Bailey whom I had last seen clad in garments little better than rags and with no shoes on his feet had an appointment with the great Mr McClean!

'Go on,' I said now, 'what happened when he found you?'

He shook his head. 'I am still amazed when I think about it. At first, we could not believe our luck — miracles like that simply didn't happen to Rosie and Thomas Bailey. Suddenly we were taken from a situation where stealing it was the only way we were going to eat our next meal to one where we could have whatever we wanted.'

'Both of you?' I queried. 'Not just Rosie?'

'Both of us — at first. Rosie would not be parted from me, anyway, and indeed I think Frank Osborne was truly grateful to me for having cared for her. But it did not last. As strange as it may sound, I think he was jealous of me; of the deep and genuine love we had for each other.'

'I remember,' I said and was astonished

that the memory, after all this time, still had the power to hurt.

'You see,' and Thomas frowned as if having difficulty in finding the right words, 'he was quite besotted with her. He could not do enough to try and make up for the years of neglect.'

'They need not have been neglect,' I pointed out quietly, 'Had it not been for Seth Bailey, your mother would have managed to give you a decent life — *my* mother thought a great deal of her.' And then I realised just what I had said. 'I'm sorry, Thomas,' I said quickly for a spasm of pain had twisted his face, 'I always found it difficult to remember that Seth was your father. Sam, yes, but not you.'

'Thank you. I'm grateful for that.'

'So,' I prompted after a moment or two, 'what happened next?'

'He took us both to London to live, for Rosie insisted that I went with her. And there he employed a tutor for us, teaching us to read and write and a smattering of other things. And an ogre of a woman to teach us how to speak and how to behave. 'If only Cat were here,' I remember Rosie saying on one occasion when the woman had lost her temper with us, 'she'd soon put her to rights.'

'Did she really?' I asked eagerly. 'She didn't

forget me entirely, then?'

He smiled that slow gentle smile that had once tugged at my heart strings. 'Of course not! Neither of us did and spoke of you so often.'

'Go on,' I said, storing his words carefully away in my head to gloat over later.

'Well, we had that time of being taught the ways of Frank's world and at the end of it, Rosie emerged like a butterfly from a chrysalis.' He paused as if remembering. And then he added, almost wistfully, 'She was always beautiful, was she not? Even when her hair was unkempt and her face bruised and she had been crying?'

I nodded. 'Very beautiful.'

'But now she seemed to glow as if, for the first time in her life, she had found true happiness. She was *so* happy, Cat. For she loved looking as she did and having the power over men that she found she now had. At first, it was an innocent power, lacking in guile; she was like a child, prinking and preening in front of the mirror — she could not have enough of herself. But then she began to adopt coquettish airs, to flirt shamelessly with the men she met. For her father had started to take her about with him, as if he had trained her for the purpose of taking the place of the wife he had never had.

But he overdid it. She began to feel suffocated by his attentions and resentful of the way he insisted she do whatever he wanted. I think that the man was a little unbalanced. So, in the end, she ran away.'

'Without you?'

He smiled wryly. 'Oh, yes, she'd outgrown me by then, you see. She ran away with the son of a wealthy American business man.'

'But how old was she?'

'Barely sixteen. And the lad was eighteen. But they must have made a success of it for I read in the social columns of an American newspaper I happened to come across that Mr and Mrs Henry Baker Junior, had attended some function or other. I don't know if Frank ever got in touch with her but I know at the time he was heartbroken.'

'And you?' I asked gently. 'Were you heartbroken, Thomas?'

He got up then and walked to the window where he stood, jingling the small change in his pocket and gazing down upon Edward and his horde of helpers as they laboured in the orchard.

'Yes — and no,' he said at last. 'At first, it was as if I had lost a part of myself. I was bereft, incomplete, but I knew, deep down, that she had grown away from me, that the person I was missing so acutely was the old

Rosie of our childhood and she no longer existed. So,' he shrugged, 'for the first time in my life I was alone but now with the advantages of an education.

Frank, of course, did not want to know me any more, now that Rosie had gone, I was very sorry about that for I owed him a great deal but there was nothing I could do about it. I packed my bags — at least, I had bags to pack this time! — and left. But this time I had a plan.

The railways had always fascinated me and I determined to find work on them if I could. I was fortunate in meeting a man — a surveyor — who was as keen on steam engines as I and he took me on as an apprentice. I still work for him but now it is on more equal a footing and he entrusts me with certain commissions; such as the one I am meeting Mr McClean about later today. I gather he is sinking yet another coal shaft which will need to be connected to the main line. I shall probably be here for a few days.'

'And where are you staying?' I asked.

'Oh, Mr McClean will arrange something.'

'Nonsense,' I said. 'You must stay here with us.'

'You're sure your — Edward will not mind?'

'Of course not! And there is still so much to talk about.'

'You're right, there! I still have no idea by what route you came to Chasetown. All I know,' and he came back to me and put out his hands and drew me up to stand beside him, 'is that I am profoundly grateful that you are here and that I have found you again — at last.'

He kissed me on my forehead and I put my arms around him and burrowed my head into his shoulder and held him as tightly as I could. And then, after we had wiped the tears from our eyes for he was as moved as I, by our embrace, we went downstairs to join the others. But those words — 'at last' — lingered in my mind. For they seemed to imply that Thomas Bailey had had me in his thoughts for a long time — and I was glad of it.

★   ★   ★

'He is like a brother to me,' I insisted.

Edward and I were having our first major confrontation. We had had our disagreements, of course, for no business could have been run without them, but this threatened to become a bitter and acrimonious dispute and I did not like it.

We were at the end of the orchard where I

had gone with a basin to pick blackberries for the blackberry and apple pie Mrs C. wanted to make for supper, once she had discovered it to be one of Thomas's favourite dishes. Edward having listened to our conversation with a steady darkening of his expression, had followed me down there.

'How long is Thomas staying?' he asked without preliminaries.

'Another couple of days, I think. Why? He is no bother, Sophie loves having him to play cards with and Ned and Frank are quite happy to have him on the truckle bed in their room.'

'But I am not so happy thinking of him up there, so near to you.'

I began to grow angry then and to assert that we were as brother and sister to each other. 'There is nothing furtive about our relationship, Edward. There never has been and there never will be.'

'So you admit that you *have* a relationship?'

I put down my basin lest I tip out the fruit in my agitation and turned to face him. 'Edward, don't be so ridiculous! His sister was my dearest friend — my *only* friend — and she was always very close to her brother. They had to be because of Seth . . . '

I stopped abruptly because the last thing I

wanted was to talk to Edward about those days. I knew instinctively that he would find such revelations distasteful and they might only serve to fuel his jealousy.

For the first time since we had come to Chasetown, he was the one who felt excluded and a small part of me felt a certain, childish satisfaction that now the boot was, so to speak, on the other foot. I could not join him on his outings to Beaudesert or Edjall Hall and he could not now join Thomas and me in our reminiscences. For whenever we were together, we could not help a constant stream of 'Do you remember . . . ?' or 'I wonder what happened . . . ' It was as well that Thomas was out for most of the day, going about his work.

Now, Edward and I stood and glared at each other. And then his face seemed to crumple. 'Oh, Cat,' he said miserably, 'the last thing I want is for us to quarrel.' And he looked so woebegone and defenceless, so unlike the Edward I was accustomed to, that I felt my anger fade.

'It's the last thing I want, too.' I told him. 'For truly, Edward, I love you so much. Can you not trust me?'

'Oh, I want to,' he said. 'Believe me, I want to.' And the next moment his arms were around me and he was kissing me like a man parched with thirst who had suddenly found a spring of fresh water. And between his kisses, he murmured, 'I love you, too, Cat. And I want you, my love, more than you can ever imagine,' and he pressed his body hard against mine so that I could hardly breathe.

Suddenly, I was frightened of what might happen next. Forcing myself away sufficiently to look up into his face, I tried to deflate his passion. 'I tell you one thing for what it's worth,' I said, 'you and I should go blackberrying more often. We could be on a desert island down here!'

And then, as if to make a nonsense of my remark, there came the sound of Thomas's voice. 'Cat! Edward! Where are you?'

It wasn't just one call; it came so often with hardly a second in between, giving us no time to reply, I grew suspicious. He must have seen us together and was now allowing us time to separate from our embrace.

At last he 'found' us. 'Ah, there you both are! Forgive me for disturbing you but I have news that I felt I should give you immediately. I must leave tomorrow for my work here has finished earlier than I had expected. I cannot begin to tell you how grateful I am to both of you for putting up with me as you have. However, all good things must come to an end, I fear.'

Stop it! Stop it! I shrieked at him in my brain. Stop using such banal phrases for something that is so precious!

But Edward had moved forward. 'Sad news indeed for Cat, but we understand, of course. Duty calls!' Silently, I picked up my basin and followed them both towards the house.

★　★　★

Thomas must have left very quietly and very early next morning for when I came down at six o'clock to start the day's baking, he had already gone.

There had been no opportunity for us to talk, for me to ask where he was going or if he would come back to Chasetown one day. The others had asked him, of course, at supper, but he had said that it depended entirely upon where he was sent. 'For I am not my own employer — as yet,' seeming to imply that one day he would be. 'There's talk of work in France and Germany. But one day, perhaps, I will come back to Chasetown.' And for a brief second, his eyes had held mine. It was not a great deal to hold on to but it was all I had.

24

Sometime during the weeks that followed Thomas's departure, I almost wished that he had not come. For not only did I miss him dreadfully, I was also greatly unsettled in my mind.

When circumstances had forced us apart for the first time, I had felt a similar deprivation, not only for him but for Rosie, too, but beginning a new life at Ashling, where I had never know them, had forced me to think of other things and other people; the beginning of a new life.

But now Thomas had woven himself into the fabric of that life. At first, I thought it wrong of me to miss him as I did when it was Edward whom I truly loved; but we all missed him.

'He was such *fun*!' said Sophie — 'fun' was still her favourite word.

'An' so easy ter talk to,' said Mrs C. 'A proper gent but wi' no airs an' graces like some I've met. Pulled themselves up by their boot laces — an' there ain't no 'arm in that — then want ter forget where they started from. But Thomas didn't mind talkin' about the potbank. Same as you've never minded, Cat.'

Familiarity, I thought, clutching at the word like a life-line, that's what's so special about my feelings for Thomas. Even now, after months of sharing Edward's life, I still, almost unconsciously, 'looked up' to him; still, on occasion, sought for the right words when I was speaking to him, conscious that he would always be above me in matters of education and social experience. But with Thomas, I had relaxed, used words and phrases from a vocabulary that I had almost forgotten I possessed. Because I missed Thomas so much did not mean that I loved him more than Edward, only differently. He would always be part of my life just as my parents and Emma would be.

Certainly, since Thomas's departure, Edward had been unceasing in his attentions. Soon, I thought, he will talk about our future. Meanwhile, my mind now at rest, I worked harder than ever; we all did. Mr Gallagher, our Lichfield lawyer had come out and inspected the books that Edward kept and had declared that we were now in a position to pay out a small dividend. So, besides receiving a wage and, of course, our board and lodging, we were all given an amount equated to what we had contributed.

Sophie also received a small wage for she now had her own duties in the kitchen and the shop which she did cheerfully. But in another direction she was not so amenable, for Edward was trying to curtail the amount of time she spent with Mattie. Consequently, Ned had received instructions to ride in another direction on their morning outings and only occasionally to seek Mattie out.

''Er brother's still there,' he reported. 'An' I think 'e's stayin' fer a while. South Wales didn't agree with 'im. 'Ad ter work too 'ard, most likely.'

Scabber had also come on to our books. He would soon be ten years old and eligible for work in the mines and I found I was dreading this. I still had vivid memories of the small body we had seen carried away from the pit disaster. Besides, I knew I would miss him.

'Scabber,' I asked him one morning when he presented himself as usual about mid-morning, 'do you really want to go down the mine?'

To my surprise, he seemed to give the matter some consideration. 'Gotta go, ain't I,' he said eventually. 'Ain't nuthin' else I can do.'

'But there is,' I insisted, 'you could go to school for one thing.'

He stopped eating the misshapen pieces of shortbread Mrs C. had kept for him and gazed at me in astonishment. 'School? Me? Yer must be off yer bleedin' rocker, miss, beggin' yer pardon!'

'Why?' I asked. 'There is a Free School in Burntwood, as you must know, with an excellent schoolmaster. A Mr Brindley.'

Scabber grinned. 'Oh, I knows Ole Brindley orlright. An' e' knows me! 'E wouldn't 'ave me, miss, wouldn't touch me wi' a barge pole. I've cheeked 'im too often.'

'Oh, I think he might,' I said, 'if we had a word.'

In fact, Edward had already spoken to Mr Brindley of the possibility and while Scabber would be older than most, he thought that it could be arranged. 'Provided that the boy truly wants to learn.' That, of course, would be the problem; to motivate Scabber.

'You're a bright lad, Scabber,' I now told him. 'If you learned to read and write, you could do great things one day.'

'Like ride an 'oss?'

I stared at him in astonishment. 'Is that what you want to do, more than anything?'

'Oh, yes, miss! I've sat astride the big 'osses — them they call shires. But I ain't never gone up an' down like Miss Sophie an' Ned.'

I grinned to myself. I doubted if Mr

Brindley would teach Scabber to go 'up an' down' but it was a beginning. 'Miss Sophie knows how to read and write,' I said.

'But Ned don't,' he countered quickly. 'An' 'osses don't!'

I abandoned that line of reasoning. 'Tell you what,' I said, 'you go to school in the mornings — that's if your parents agree, of course — and then come here in the afternoons and help Ned. And he'll teach you to go up and down like nobody's business. And we'll pay you half a crown every week like the butty would.'

'Done!' said Scabber, holding out a grimy paw.

'We'll have to see your parents first,' I reminded him as I shook it.

★   ★   ★

But Scabber's father — who called on us next day — raised no objections; although he clearly thought his son to be a little touched in the head.

'And his mother won't mind?' I thought it politic to enquire.

'Not as long as 'e brings 'ome a wage.'

'We'll pay the same as the mine would,' I assured him for I had no doubt we would find Scabber a valuable addition to the work force.

Our country deliveries were now made three times a week as more and more people heard about us and asked us to call. Sometimes Fred accompanied Ned on the deliveries but he couldn't always be spared from maintenance work in the house. Scabber as a stand-in would be invaluable.

The arrangement seemed to work very well. Scabber, now scrubbed to within an inch of his life and clad in 'new' clothes that had either come from the 'old clothes lady', the Chasetown equivalent of the Burslem market stall, or been requested by his father as 'tommy' in his wages — the mining equivalent to the 'truck' I had known in the potbank — would arrive at midday, eager for his riding lesson. This came usually from Sophie who had agreed unreservedly that Toffee could be used for the purpose. A grassy area at the end of the orchard near the blackberry hedge provided a rudimentary 'school' and there Scabber learned to rise to the trot.

'He's good,' Sophie said. 'He has no fear and that's important.' Her own ability as teacher was also commendable and the two, although from such disparate backgrounds, soon became good friends.

'Wouldn't it be nice,' Sophie wheedled, 'if we could have another pony and then we needn't bother Ned — we could go out together.'

'Afraid we can't afford it at the moment, sweetheart,' I told her, quite truthfully although I knew I would never have known a moment's peace if two such high-spirited individuals had been allowed out on their own.

I doubt if Scabber was as dedicated to his lessons with Mr Brindley as he was to those with Sophie but certainly his language improved! Indeed, we were asked — by Scabber at Mr Brindley's insistence — to provide a swear box into which he had to put a farthing every time he swore.

'Blow this for a bleedin' game o'soldiers!' I heard him mutter as he put in a farthing one day. Tactfully, I kept my back turned; he was doing his best! And,

''E's a natural wi' 'osses!' Ned reported.

★ ★ ★

Sadly, Patience Swinfen's affairs were not in such good order as Scabber's. There had been no immediate repercussions after she had seen Captain Swinfen and his mother off the estate, but she knew that if she continued with such actions she could eventually face imprisonment for contempt of court. Meanwhile, the gallant Captain seemed, for the moment to be lying low although there were rumours about him trying to persuade the tenants of the farms on the Swinfen estate to join him in harassing Patience in whatever way presented itself — and she'd heard that some at least were more than willing to be persuaded.

'It's in matters like these,' she told us, 'that you discover who your real friends are.'

'You know you'll always have our support,' I told her.

'I know, my dear, and I'm so grateful.'

'It will be Christmas before long,' I tried to comfort her. 'The season of goodwill to all men.'

'That does *not* include Captain Frederick Swinfen,' she replied grimly.

However, at Cat's Eating House we were determined to celebrate the festival in the true 'Ashling spirit'. The shop would be open for a couple of hours in the morning so that we could serve breakfasts to those who had come to depend upon them — and we now had many such — but after that we would close our doors and enjoy ourselves.

There was much debate about whether to invite Ada's and Polly's swains but in the end we decided against it.

''Cos we ain't sure we wants to go steady yet,' Ada said. And we respected their decision.

However, Scabber would definitely be with us. 'Won't your mother and father want you with them for Christmas dinner?' I asked.

He shook his head. 'More fer everyone else if I ain't there.'

'We'll make up a box o' dainties and such like,' Mrs C. promised him. 'Fer yer ma, mind. No tastin' on the way 'ome.'

'We could always deliver 'em the day before ter make sure,' Ned teased.

'Don't any of yer bleedin' well trust me, then?' yelled Scabber, incensed.

Nobody passed him the swear box. We were all too busy assuring him that of course we trusted him!

★ ★ ★

'Christmas is going to be a difficult time for Edward,' said Mrs C. 'Remembering, I mean. So we must make it really special.'

'At least, it will be different,' I said. 'The first he's spent in the kitchen.'

She and I were making mincemeat tarts a couple of days before Christmas. The kitchen was already festooned with swags of holly and ivy, brought in from the orchard and on the table was a big bowl of Christmas roses that we had found growing in a sheltered corner.

Mrs C. and I were alone and now she looked up from crimping the tarts and asked, 'Wot's goin' ter 'appen between you two, Cat? Yes, I know,' as I looked up from rinsing a bowl at the sink, 'it's none o' my business. But in a way, 'tis. Ever since the day yer marched inter the kitchen at Ashling be'ind Edward, tryin' not ter look scared, I've cared about yer. An' sometimes I worry about yer. Anyone can see Edward an' you cares about each other. An' when that nice young Thomas came, I thought Edward'd kill 'im, so jealous 'e was.'

I looked at her, surprised. 'Was it so obvious?'

She laughed. 'Well, we all noticed it. Ada an' Poll thought it was ever so romantic.'

'Do you,' I hesitated, 'talk about such things often?'

'Only in a nice way, I can tell yer. I dunno wot Ada an' Poll talk about on their own, mind, but in my kitchen, they 'ave ter watch their Ps an' Qs.'

On an impulse, I crossed to her and gave her a quick hug. 'What would you like to happen between Edward and me?'

'Well, Ada an' Poll'd like wedding bells in Burntwood church and them all done up like a dog's dinner.'

'And you?'

'I want wot yer want, Cat.'

'Then I think it's wedding bells for me, too.'

'Only *think*?' asked Mrs C.

'*Know*, then,' I said firmly. 'Because you're right, Mrs C. We do love each other and we're making a success of the business, thanks to all the hard work everyone's putting into it. So — what else but marriage?'

'An 'e thinks the same?'

'Why yes — of course!' I said, conveniently overlooking the fact that we had never actually discussed it in so many words.

'That's orlright, then,' said Mrs C. comfortably. 'I did just wonder when that nice Thomas was 'ere . . . ' she let the words trail away and I made no effort to pursue her train of thought.

★   ★   ★

Christmas was all that we had hoped for. For politeness' sake, Edward had asked his mother if she wished to join us but we had all been greatly relieved when she informed him that she would be eating dinner with the Pooles. Mr and Mrs Brindley, who lived nearby, had also been invited.

In the Ashling tradition, 'The Queen' was

toasted at the beginning of the meal and Absent Friends at the end. Naturally, we all remembered Mr Jolly and I thought of Ma and Emma, no doubt at Wolstanton, and I wondered if Emma's Joe would be with them this year and what my uncle would think of him. I thought, too, of Thomas and wondered where and with whom he might be. It was difficult to think of Rosie in her strange American environment so I thought instead of her in Wolstanton wood, playing hide and seek and more than a little frightened of the rabbits.

And then, to my surprise, Ned sprang to his feet and banged on the table for silence.

'Ladies an' gentlemen . . . '

'Cor!' I heard Scabber mutter. 'Me a gent?'

'I would like you all to raise your glasses,' Ned continued, 'an' drink to two people who certainly ain't absent — they're very much wiv us. And Gawd knows where we'd all be if they weren't. Ladies and gentlemen, I gives yer — Cat an' Eddie!'

'Cat an' Eddie,' everyone echoed, shuffling to their feet and I guessed that they had all known what was coming.

Completely overcome, I could only gaze around the table with tears in my eyes. But Edward, who was sitting next to me, was made of sterner stuff. He rose to his feet.

'Ned — and everyone — thank you on behalf of both of us. But it's really Cat who should have the credit for the success of our enterprise.'

And in front of them all, he bent and kissed me full on the mouth.

There was a moment of stunned silence and then everyone started clapping and cheering — except for Scabber who blew into his cupped hands and produced a whistle that would have put a steam-engine to shame. I had hardly recovered from it when a similar but even louder sound came from the other end of the table and turning, I saw that Sophie was following his example.

But then Fred called out 'Three cheers for Cat and Edward' and Edward drew me to my feet and we stood there with his arm around my waist, grinning like a couple of idiots.

As far as I was concerned, the rest of the day passed in a haze. At some point it was decided that Scabber should spend the night on the truckle bed.

'Won't yer parents worry?' I heard Mrs C. ask.

'Not on yer Nellie,' said Scabber. 'I told 'em I most likely would.' He caught my eye and had the grace to lower his. 'Orlright, ain't it, miss? I ain't sworn all day.'

'That's all right, Scabber,' I told him. I

think I would have agreed to anything that evening. For surely Edward's kiss had been a declaration of our future together.

★ ★ ★

On New Year's Day, the Reverend Poole and his wife invited Edward and Sophie to lunch. It was a generous and thoughtful gesture, typical of the man.

At home, we deliberately told each other anecdotes about the Master as we ate our midday meal. Although there was hardly a dry eye among us, and I know that I, for one, hardly tasted the food I ate, we all felt better for it.

'We must do this every year,' Mrs C. said, 'as long as we're all together.' And we all agreed.

That evening Edward was in a thoughtful mood. 'I think my father would have been pleased with what we've achieved,' he said.

'I'm sure of it,' I said.

We were standing on the back step gazing up at the starry sky, waiting for Rex to come in from his nightly prowl around the orchard.

'I've been thinking, too,' I continued, 'wondering if we might consider extending the premises later this year; if the Marquess was agreeable, of course. We could certainly do with an extra larder, if not two, and somewhere to store vegetables.'

'I'll see what Mr George says next time I'm in Lichfield,' he said. 'Perhaps we could both go, if you can be spared. We haven't had a day out together for ages.'

'Oh, Edward, that would be wonderful!'

25

In January, Sophie, escorted by Edward, attended a party. It was for young people not yet old enough to go to adult functions but who had long since graduated from the nursery. It was held at the home of an erstwhile friend of hers, Angela Freemantle, and was considered by Mrs Marshall who had arranged it, to be a great treat.

As far as Sophie was concerned, it was anything but. 'I never did like Angela Freemantle,' she grumbled to me, 'so why should I go to her beastly party?'

'Because you will probably enjoy it when you get there. And won't it be nice to meet some of your old friends?'

'No, it won't!' she said flatly. 'They're not my friends any more. Ada and Poll and Ned and Scabber and Fred and Mrs C. and you, of course — you're all my friends now. And Mattie,' she added, just when I was congratulating myself that she hadn't mentioned her. 'She's my very best friend.'

I bit my lip and said that as her mother had been good enough to arrange it, the least she could do was to go. And what was she going to wear?

That proved to be another stumbling block because she had long since outgrown her party dresses and no-one had seen the point of making any more. Her usual daily garb now was a serviceable navy skirt and white blouse, both hand-me-downs from my limited wardrobe. For riding, she had a thicker skirt and an old hacking jacket of Edward's that now fitted her perfectly.

In the end, Edward was commissioned to buy four yards of cream taffeta from a draper in Lichfield — he had been summoned, unexpectedly, by Old Trumper — and Polly, who was nimble with her fingers, ran her up a very pretty dress. Not that Sophie thought so. She considered it to be both childish and unfashionable although she did have the grace not to say so in Polly's presence. However, with her hair coaxed back into ringlets and her necklace of seed pearls it was generally agreed that she looked 'real posh' as Scabber put it. We all stood and waved her away in the trap that had been sent to fetch her, with Edward by her side.

Sadly, when they returned several hours later, it was clear that the party had not been a success. Sophie was sulky and Edward cross.

'I just don't belong any more,' Sophie told

me when I went to tuck her in to bed that night, as either Edward or I always did. 'They talk about such silly things like when they're going to put up their hair, or go to finishing school or so-and-so's silly brother. I tried to talk to them about serving in the shop and teaching Scabber to ride — really *useful* things, don't you agree, Cat? — but they just laughed and said how I'd come down in the world since Papa had died and that now I wouldn't be 'coming out' as they called it, nor presented at court. I ask you, who *wants* to be presented at a silly old court?' By now her tears were flowing freely and I sat on the edge of the bed and hugged her.

'Don't worry about it, sweetheart. But didn't you enjoy *any* part of the party? What did Edward think of it?'

'Oh, *he* was all right. He is always good at parties and anyway, he had Miriam to talk to.'

'Miriam?'

'She's Angela's big sister. She was supposed to be looking after us but she spent most of the time talking to Edward. I swear I'm never going to go to any more parties. I needn't, need I?'

But now I was only half listening as I tried to come to terms with Miriam. There would always be girls like her, I told myself firmly, with whom Edward would chatter and flirt but it was me whom he truly loved.

I comforted Sophie as best I could and assured her that we all loved her and wished only for what was best for her. Promising to look in on her again when I went to bed. I turned out her light and went downstairs.

'Problems?' Edward asked when I went back into the kitchen. He was sitting at one end of the table, doing the accounts for the day. Ada and Polly were out with their young men and Mrs C. had gone to bed, having mixed the pastry ready for tomorrow's pies. Ned and Fred were out in the stable, repairing some broken harness.

I went and sat down at the other end of the table. 'I gather Sophie didn't enjoy the party,' I said.

He pushed his ledgers away. 'I'm afraid not.'

'And you?' I asked lightly. 'Did you enjoy it?'

He seemed surprised by the question. 'Well, it wasn't exactly how I would have chosen to pass the afternoon, but it was all right, I suppose.'

So much for Miriam Freemantle!, I thought.

'It was Sophie's outing, after all,' he continued. 'I just wish there was something we could do about Sophie, Cat. I mean if she stays here with us, what will become of her?'

It was more than time that we discussed the question of Sophie's future and I settled myself for a serious discussion. 'With any luck,' I said, 'she'll meet some intelligent, sensible young man, qualified in his work, who will want to marry her and she him.' I was thinking of someone like Thomas who had all these qualities.

But Edward seemed unimpressed by the suggestion. 'But not at Cat's Eating House,' he pointed out, 'selling pies.'

'Well, then, perhaps we should consider moving to larger premises, somewhere where we could entertain more, invite people in for a meal.' I couldn't quite bring myself to say 'hold dinner parties' — but why not? I knew all about organising such a thing even if I'd never given one.

'That's one possibility, I suppose,' he murmured. 'But would that be enough?'

'I think that's all we would be able to afford, Edward, and that not for some time.'

'But meantime,' he pointed out, 'Sophie's behaviour may well deteriorate.'

'Oh, I wouldn't say it was that bad,' I demurred, deliberately shutting my mind to the memory of her whistling through her fingers on Christmas Day. 'At least, she is turning into an excellent little cook. By the way,' I added, as the scullery door opened and Ned and Fred could be heard scraping their boots and thus precluding any further comments about Sophie, 'did you manage to see Mr George when you were in Lichfield the other day?'

'Do you know,' he said as if suddenly realising it, 'I didn't. I was so concerned about the material you'd asked me to buy, it went clean out of my mind.'

'No matter,' I said. 'We'll go another day. The Trumpers are well, I trust?' I added as an afterthought, for Edward hadn't mentioned his visit to them.

'The Trumpers? Oh yes, they're very well. Sent their regards. Sorry I forgot to deliver them.'

'No matter,' I said again and, well-content, went to make our bed-time cocoa. There was no question of prodding Edward into thinking about the future — he was leaping ahead of me.

★   ★   ★

'Where's Sophie?' I asked. We were about to sit down to our midday meal on the day following Angela's party.

Ned looked at me. 'I thought she was 'elpin' yer in the kitchen.'

393

'And I thought she was riding with you.'

'I needed ter put new shoes on Lofty,' he said slowly.

We looked at each other for a moment. And then, 'I'll see if Toffee's in his stable,' Edward said.

He was back within seconds. 'He's not there.' He looked at me. 'What d'you think? The canal?'

I nodded. 'Sure to be.'

He glanced at Ned. 'Lofty all right to ride now? Shoes finished?'

Ned nodded dumbly.

'Right! Come and help me saddle him up, would you?' And to me. 'Don't worry! I'll bring her back safely.'

After he had gone, we made a pretence of eating. 'It's that party wot done it,' Polly suddenly burst out. 'Real unkind they was to 'er from what she said.'

'Prob'ly jus' gone ter see Mattie an' tell 'er all about it,' said Ada comfortingly.

But it was worse. Much worse. When Edward eventually came back with her, both of them were white-faced and silent. Ned and Fred went out to take the horses but before they could reach her, Sophie had dismounted and rushed past them into the house — and didn't stop running until she had reached her own room, pounding up the stairs and slamming the door behind her. But not so fast that I hadn't seen the blood on her mouth.

'Leave her!' said Edward who had now followed her in. 'Just for a moment or two while I tell you what's happened. Cat, can we talk in my room?'

He had never made such a suggestion before, partly I think through propriety, but mostly because we had always wanted to be open with the others, never seeming to have secrets between ourselves.

Once in his room, he motioned me to sit down and took the chair opposite. 'When I reached the barge — they had just finished unloading — it was to find Toffee tethered nearby. I enquired from Mattie's father where Sophie might be but he simply pointed along the tow-path and muttered something about them all having gone for a walk.

All? I repeated

Yes, he said, a couple of the lads went with them.

You can imagine my feelings, Cat. I didn't know whether to run up the tow-path on foot or to ride. In the end, I rode, which was as well because I could see over the hedges.'

He stopped at that point, his face working. 'Edward,' I said swiftly, 'I'm going to fetch you a glass of brandy.' And I got up from my chair.

He motioned me back. 'Thank you but no. The sooner I finish my story, the sooner you can go to Sophie.' I sat down again. 'The devil had Sophie up against a tree,' he continued when he had a grip on himself. 'I think it was Mattie's brother — I don't know where the other two were and I didn't care. He'd pulled her skirt off, Cat, and her jacket and torn her blouse from her shoulders and had begun to tug at her drawers. She was screaming her head off and the blood was running down her chin from where her lips had been bitten.

If only I'd had my whip! As it was, I had to rely on my fists. But I made a good enough job of it, I promise you. The swine won't stand upright for a week or so.'

I was already on my feet. 'Edward, I must go to her at once.'

'Of course, but I had to tell you first. And when you've calmed her, Cat, then we must talk some more.'

But it was several hours before we could talk again. For Edward's apparent conviction that I could calm Sophie was unfounded. True, she let me hold her while she wept but I could not persuade her to talk coherently. All she could do was to scream, again and again.

'I can't tell you, Cat! I can't! It was too horrible!' And then, rocking herself to and fro, 'What is to become of me now? Have I lost my maidenhood? Will other men scorn me for what has happened?'

No amount of assurance that such was not the case and that no-one need know unless she told them herself, seemed to calm her. In the end, we put her to bed and sent for the doctor.

He was a kindly man to whom we felt it safe to recount the full details of what had happened. After he had seen Sophie and given her a sedative, he had a word with Edward in private.

'He wanted me to inform the authorities,' Edward told me afterwards, 'but I have decided against that since it might then become public knowledge and cause Sophie even more distress. Instead, I shall have a word with John McClean and, if necessary, with the Marquess himself.'

★   ★   ★

It was early evening before we faced each other again in Edward's room. Sophie was now sleeping peacefully and should do so until the following morning, the doctor had said.

'Cat,' Edward said now, 'I have something very important to tell you. It arises from my visit to old Trumper the other day.' He leaned forward and took my hand in his, lacing his fingers with mine.

'You remember, nearly a year ago now, when both he and his son came to see Mama and how I was excluded from their discussion?'

I nodded. 'And we couldn't understand why she afterwards changed her mind and said that she would come with us to Chasetown.'

'Well, I now know why she did.' He dropped his eyes, gazing down at our clasped hands and I had a presentiment that I was going to hear something I would not like.

'Bad news?' I asked, trying to keep my voice steady.

'Yes and no, depending upon which way you look at it. It's to do with my Uncle Perce. You remember he bequeathed me the few hundred pounds which enabled us to start the business?'

'Of course I remember.'

'Well, he was a wealthy man and I had thought at the time, grateful though I was, that it was a small amount compared with the rest of his estate. And I had wondered, in a vague sort of way, who had inherited the rest of it. Now, I know. It was me, Cat. Suddenly, I am to be a wealthy man; wealthy, at least, by my present standards.'

I could only stare at him, speechless, unable to grasp the implications of what he was saying. 'But — but why,' I managed to stammer at last, 'why did you not receive it all at the time?'

'Because Uncle Perce was a wise old bird who knew from his own experience that it is too easy to fritter money away in the profligacies of youth. Under the terms of the will, I was to be given only a few hundred pounds at first. If, at the end of a year, I had spent it all in riotous living, then that would be the end of it and some remote fourth cousin in the wilds of Scotland would have inherited the rest. But if I had spent it wisely or even, just put it safely in the bank, then I would be given the remainder. And thanks to you, Cat, the Trumpers consider I have spent it very wisely indeed. To prove it, they are now in the process of inspecting our books.'

'And your mother knew all of this?' I asked.

'Not all of it. Confidentiality prevented them from telling her the terms of the will but they were able to reassure her that if she did as we asked, then it would probably only be for a year.'

'So — what will you do now?' Suddenly,

my voice seemed to be coming from a very long way away and for a moment I thought I might faint.

Edward saw my condition and leaped to his feet. 'I thought it might come as a shock so I took the precaution of providing a restorative!' And he crossed the room to a cupboard and withdrew a bottle of brandy and two glasses. He poured two generous measures and gave me one.

'Drink up, Cat, it will do you good.' And it did, the fiery liquid warming my stomach and giving me the courage to ask again,

'What will you do now, Edward?'

He grimaced. 'It should be so simple, shouldn't it? As you suggested — was it only yesterday? — we could buy a country house near here and live very pleasantly.'

'And your mother?'

'We would have made sure that the house was large enough to house her separately. It could have worked. But now — '

' — we have Sophie to consider,' I finished for him.

'Exactly. I can no longer consider living anywhere near here. I shall make sure the fellow is told just what will happen to him if he attempts such a dastardly action again but even so, it will be of small comfort to Sophie. She cannot continue to live around here, Cat.

It has been a dreadful experience for her, one from which she may never fully recover, but a complete change of circumstances may help. It is not too late for her education to continue from the point where it ceased — it is only a year, after all. It should not be too difficult for her to revert to the habits and accomplishments which she should never have relinquished.'

'But Edward,' I protested, 'she does not like that way of life. She thinks that 'coming out' is a dreadful waste of time and she will hate that endless round of parties and dinners and balls. Oh, I know that living here has not been ideal but at least she has been doing something useful that she has enjoyed. And she has met some interesting people.'

'Including Mattie?' Edward asked grimly. 'And Mattie's brother? No — as I see it, Cat, there is only one way forward. A return to her old way of life but in new surroundings and among people who do not know her. I am quite determined about this.'

There was something about the timbre of his voice that made me look at him more closely. And I saw that the anxious young man who had sought my guidance in an alien world and had accepted my ideas, happily following where I had led, had gone, perhaps for good. In his place was the assured young gentleman of property, confident of his rightful place in the social hierarchy, master of his household. So where did Cat Marsh and her Eating House fit into his life now?

'So what do you have in mind?' I asked boldly, knowing now that he would have already decided.

'A country house, but nearer to London, perhaps in Hertfordshire, where my mother will be able to pick up the threads of her old life, and to make suitable contacts among the local gentry, and from where she will be able to launch Sophie in the London season when the time comes.'

'And you,' I said bitterly, 'will no doubt take up the mantle of the local squire. Perhaps,' and my voice rose shrilly, 'if you ask nicely, you might be able to buy back Satan. And sometimes, when you find life a little tedious because, after all, you will keep meeting the same dull, boring people wherever you go, you may remember us here in Chasetown.'

I had not felt so angry since our set-to in the orchard when Thomas was here. I stood up and glared down at him. But, to my astonishment, I saw that he seemed genuinely puzzled by my outburst.

'But Cat, surely you don't imagine that I would desert you, especially now when fortune is smiling upon us? Please sit down again while I explain what I have in mind.'

Feeling a little foolish, I did so and once again he took my hand. 'You know that I love you. And you love me, is that not so?'

'You know that I do.'

'And eventually, I want to marry you. If, that is, you will have me.'

My hand gave an involuntary leap in his. The simple statement for which I had waited so long was almost shocking in its suddenness. And yet, 'Eventually?' I repeated cautiously.

'You are such a sensible, down-to-earth person, Cat, I am sure you will understand that marriage at the moment, in view of my immediate plans, would not be a sensible step to take. I shall be needed to escort Sophie to the many functions she will have to attend so there is no question but that I shall have to live with her and my mother. And there is no way that I would subject you to the trials of living in the same household as my mother.'

'And I can quite see,' I could not resist pointing out, 'that launching one inexperienced female into society would be enough, without the added complication of a wife whose education in such matters is so sadly lacking.'

'But,' said he, sweeping on almost as if I had not spoken, 'when Sophie *is* safely launched and — and I am sure it would not be long — she is safely married to some suitable young man, *then*, my love, I would be free to live as I wished and to marry you.'

'And do you really think that you would want to after those years of comfortable living, Edward? Because you know as well as I that for someone in your circumstances to marry someone of my background would present enormous problems. It would have done even if you had remained here but I think perhaps we might have overcome them in time; people might have grown to accept me, especially with Patience Swinfen's example to follow, but it would be a hundred times more difficult in the situation you have described. Your mother would see to that.'

'A fig for my mother! Besides, we would not have to remain in England, Cat, if we did not want to. The world would be our oyster and we could live anywhere in it. Travel first, perhaps, while we decided where we wanted to settle.'

The prospect was enticing. And looking at him, at the sparkle of excitement in his eyes, I could see that he truly believed that this Arcadian existence could be achieved.

'It would not be long,' he coaxed. 'Four or five years at most. Would it not be worth waiting for, Cat?' And he seized both my hands, drawing me to my feet. 'Will you not at least think about it?'

'Those four or five years,' I said slowly. 'How do you suggest that I should occupy myself during the period of waiting?'

'By remaining here, of course, and, with the additional money I shall be able to put into it, turn the business into an even more flourishing concern. And I — as befitted a joint shareholder! — would visit at frequent intervals.'

'All right,' I agreed and kissing him lightly on the cheek. 'I promise I will think about it. But may I ask you one more thing? Why did you not tell me all this immediately? Why have you waited until now?'

'Because I had to decide upon the best course of action for all of us, Cat. Surely you see that?'

But what I also saw, although I did not say so, was that our days of true partnership had gone. There would be no more joyful sharing; not, at least, as we had known it.

26

We had what Edward was pleased to call a committee meeting and Mrs C. described more accurately as a 'get-together' around the kitchen table.

We held it in the half hour or so between the ending of breakfasts and the preparation for the midday meal and before Ned went on his first round of the day. Sophie was still asleep and Scabber was at school.

Edward, very much the chairman, controlled the meeting — as much, that is, as anyone can control a gathering where someone has occasionally to go and serve a customer or leap up to take a pan 'off the boil'. However, when he made the preliminary announcement about his change of fortune, there was a full house and for a moment or two there was no question of control.

'Why lad, I'm that pleased fer yer!' said Mrs C.

'Congratulations, Ed!' said Ned, leaving his seat to stride around the table and shake him warmly by the hand.

Ada and Polly contented themselves with

'oohs' and 'aahs' and 'well I never!' and Fred pursed his lips and let out a long whistle of appreciation.

Edward received their expressions of goodwill with his usual courtesy and then announced that there would now be certain changes made.

'A'course!' said Mrs C. giving me a furtive glance from beneath lowered lids.

'The major one,' Edward continued, 'is that I shall be moving south and taking Sophie and my mother with me.'

'Wot? Leavin' Chasetown?' Ned exclaimed.

'No — not altogether, Ned. I shall be coming back at regular intervals to make sure that you are all all right. But I think you will all agree, in view of what has happened to my sister, that my major responsibility is to her.'

I had no idea what Edward had told Ned and Fred about Sophie's dreadful experience but certainly I had left Mrs C., Ada and Polly under no illusions about what had happened. Now, they all nodded solemnly.

'So,' Edward continued. 'I shall have to rely upon you all to keep the flags flying up here. With your agreement, we shall be able to extend our premises, perhaps even to employ more staff. We will talk of that later. But I wanted you all to know what was happening.'

'Thank'ee, Master Edward, I'm sure,' said

Mrs C. and I shot her a swift glance. It wasn't like her to show sarcasm. And then I realised that the change of title had been unconscious; she hadn't even known she was doing it.

The meeting over, everyone got up and went about their business in silence, clearly still dumbfounded at Edward's news. Mrs C. and I found ourselves alone in the kitchen, preparing the Shepherd's Pie that was to be our main course for our customers.

'An' where do yer fit in to all this, Cat?' Mrs C. asked without preliminaries.

Suddenly, it was all too much for me. I bowed my head over the onions I was peeling and cried like a child in great, gasping sobs.

'There, there, my love!' I was dimly aware of Mrs C. sitting beside me, her arms around my shoulders. ''E said 'e'd be back from time to time. It won't be so bad.'

'I know! I know! And he's asked me to marry him!'

'Before 'e goes?' Mrs C. asked eagerly. 'Cat, that's lovely fer yer both. I always 'oped but . . . '

'In five years' time,' I gulped.

'Five years? 'E wants yer ter wait *five* years? Fer pity's sake, why?'

I explained, as precisely as I could exactly what Edward proposed. 'He wants me to think about it and I've promised to do so. But everything's happening at such a rate, I can't keep up with it all. Yesterday, Sophie and today, Edward. What's going to happen tomorrow?'

'I'll tell yer wot's goin' ter 'appen termorrer, an' I'm surprised yer've forgotten it, Cat. It's our first weddin' party.'

She was right. One of the butties who had become a regular customer was being married next day and we had been asked if we would provide a meal for the guests; about twenty in all. It was a great feather in our cap and we had been planning the menu for days. But now all thoughts of it had gone right out of my head.

'So 'tis important that we say wot we've got ter say terday 'cos we wont 'ave time ter draw breath termorrer, let alone discuss yer future. Now, yer love Edward, don't yer?'

I nodded dumbly.

'An' all that 'e says makes sense; 'e's got to look after 'is sister. *But*. . . . ' and she paused as if to give weight to what she was about to say next, 'we both know that five years is a long time; long enough fer people ter change their minds, meet someone else, mebbee. An' I take it 'e ain't given yer no ring? Nor put an announcement in the Advertiser?'

I smiled weakly at the thought. 'Hardly!'

'So there ain't nothin' bindin' either side.

409

So why not tell 'im that if yer both feels the same way about each other in five years' time, then yer'll wed 'im, an' never mind the consequences. That's my advice, any rate. Not that yer likely to take it!'

'You've helped a lot, Mrs C. Honestly. Thank you.'

'Well, get on wi' them onions, then. No need to dry yer eyes, if yer do!'

In fact, she *had* helped but not perhaps in the way she'd intended. She'd mentioned a ring, although not seriously considering it. But why shouldn't Edward give me one as a token of his future intentions?

Patience Swinfen, to whom I poured out my heart on her next visit, was of a similar mind. 'Men!' she stormed. 'They have it all their own way. Rumour has it Captain Swinfen is about to persuade my tenants to withhold their rents, thus putting me in Queer Street. Fortunately, the shopkeepers of Lichfield are behind me to a man and will give me credit.

I like young Edward, don't get me wrong, and there's nothing I'd like better than to see you two wed, but don't leave it all to chance. You get a ring off him if you can — he can afford it now, after all! And don't be put off by thoughts of his mother. I had a right barney with my ma-in-law — several in fact.

So much so, I persuaded Henry to live on the Continent for several years.'

'Really? That is exactly what Edward proposes we do!'

'There you are then!' said Patience as if that settled it.

★ ★ ★

'Edward,' I said, the day after Patience's visit and when we were once more sitting in his room, 'I have been thinking over what you said. About marrying when Sophie is settled,' I added for at first he had gazed at me askance, clearly not knowing what I was talking about. It was understandable for he had many things on his mind just then, uppermost being the finding of a suitable house near London.

'And?' he asked eagerly, once I had reminded him.

'And I will wait for you,' I told him.

'Oh, Cat! That is good news, indeed!' And he pulled me up into his arms, showering my face with kisses. 'You will not regret your decision, I promise you.'

'There is one small request I would make,' I said diffidently, not wishing to broach the subject now that the moment had come.

'Anything, my love, anything!'

'May I have some token of your love then, to comfort me while we are apart?' It was a pretty speech, carefully rehearsed, but I felt guilty as I remembered Patience's forthright statement. 'You get a ring off him, if you can. He can afford it now, after all!' But Edward did not seem to notice anything remotely contrived.

'Of course,' he enthused. 'What a splendid idea! A locket, perhaps, with coils of our hair intertwined? I would gladly scalp myself if necessary!'

'A locket would be very nice. But I was thinking more of a ring. After all, a ring is a symbol of everlasting love, is it not? I would not wear it on my finger, of course, except when I was alone. But I could have it on a chain around my neck.'

'Cat, of course! As soon as I have a moment, I shall go into Lichfield and choose one.'

'Should I not go with you?' I could not resist asking. 'So that you may get the right size.'

For a moment, he hesitated and I saw a flicker of uncertainty in his eyes. But then. 'Of course, my love. You must come with me.'

But I knew that I would not. He had shown willingness and that was enough. There was no point in inflicting unnecessary embarrassment upon him.

★ ★ ★

I had a long talk with Sophie once she was well enough and had been told of Edward's decision. It was a fine sunny day and I took her for a walk up on the Chase, although not in the direction of the canal. Rex came with us, ecstatic in his pursuit of the rabbits which abounded there.

'Hertfordshire will be very dull for him after all this,' I commented.

'He won't be the only one to find it dull,' said Sophie.

'Perhaps it won't be so bad,' I tried to console her. 'After all, there must be other girls with similar interests to yours.'

'I doubt it,' she said, clearly determined to look on the black side. 'But I know that I cannot stay here now.'

Although no one would have chosen such a rapid and horrific way of growing up — I still had nightmares when I considered how much worse it would have been had Edward arrived just a few minutes later — there was no doubt that the experience had caused Sophie to shed many of her childlike attitudes to life.

'But I shall miss you so much, Cat.'

'And I, you. But it will not be for ever. Edward will be coming back to see us and perhaps you will be able to come too.'

413

'I doubt it,' she said sadly. 'Once I am in Mama's clutches, she won't let go.'

'But one day,' I pointed out, 'she will *have* to let you go. When you come of age, Sophie, you will be able to do exactly what you want.'

'And there'll be no holding me then!' she said, her eyes alight at the thought.

'And if there is one thing that I've learned about you, it is that you have a mind of your own. No-one is ever going to make you do something you don't want to do.'

'Oh, Cat,' she stopped walking and rounded on me, 'how can you say that after what has just happened to me? I was powerless, Cat, *powerless*! I kicked and shoved and pushed and even bit but I could do nothing. It was so humiliating. I felt so — so debased.'

I remembered then, the terror I had felt whenever Sam Bailey had come near me or even glanced in my direction. At least, he had never seized me as Sophie had been seized.

'Then do something about it,' I heard myself tell her.

'Like what?'

'Ask Edward to teach you to box for a start.' I had never considered such a possibility until that moment but now it seemed an eminently sensible suggestion.

Sophie looked at me, her eyes shining.

'Cat, what a splendid idea. Do you really think that he would?'

'I don't see why not. If we put it to him in the right way, he'll think it was *his* idea in the first place.' Would I have made such a cynical assertion a few weeks ago, I wondered, before the relationship between Edward and I had changed so dramatically? And I knew that I would not.

But Sophie laughed, thinking it a great joke. 'We'd better not tell Mama, though,' she said.

I fear there will be many things you will not have told your Mama before you're finished, I thought, but did not say so. Instead, 'Be kind to her, Sophie,' I said. 'I'm sure she has your best interests at heart. Now, tell me, what other pursuits can you follow that you will enjoy and that will improve your general physique? Riding, of course. And what about fencing? I've heard that this is excellent for your posture. And archery.'

'Anything but croquet!' she said. 'If only I could do something useful with my life, Cat.'

'Well, Florence Nightingale certainly has,' I pointed out, 'in the Crimea. Edward was telling me about it only the other day.'

'The Lady with the Lamp? That's an idea.'

'Well, think about it,' I advised. 'She is a high-born lady, you know, but with a mind of her own. You're not old enough to become one of her nurses yet, but you will be one day.'

'I was certainly better than Mama at changing Edward's dressing when he tore his arm on some barbed wire once.'

'Good! There's hope for you there, then. And one more thing I would like to say to you, Sophie, before we turn back for home; remember that you don't have to marry anyone you don't want to, and don't let anyone ever try to persuade you otherwise. Wait until you truly love someone.'

'You and Edward love each other, don't you?' she asked.

'Very much! And one day, perhaps . . . '

'Oh, Cat I do hope so! And then you and I will truly be sisters.'

On which pleasing thought, we called Rex to heel and turned towards home.

★ ★ ★

A few days later, Edward went down to London to inspect several properties he had been told about, and returned jubilant.

'I have found exactly what I had in mind,' he told me that evening. 'It is about a hundred years old and in the Elizabethan style with oriel windows and clusters of tall

416

chimneys that give it a most elegant appearance although it is not large — not nearly as large as Ashling. The brick has mellowed over the years and there is a narrow, stone terrace in front with steps leading down into a small rose garden.'

I forced myself to show an interest. 'And good stabling, of course?'

'Excellent stabling and several greenhouses.'

'And when will you be taking your mother and Sophie to see it?'

'As soon as I have signed the contract. There are certain preliminaries of course, but old Trumper does not envisage any difficulties there.'

'You don't want their approval *before* you buy?' I asked.

He smiled. 'I'm not seeking trouble! There are sure to be a hundred questions Mama would ask. Is it draughty? Do the stairs creak? What is the average rainfall? Are the vicar's sermons boring? Are the tradesmen amenable to bullying? You know Mama! I'm not risking it. And Sophie won't mind what it's like.'

I smiled to myself. The new Edward certainly had a mind of his own.

'Now,' he continued, 'have you given any more thought to what you would like done here? The Marquess, by the way, is quite agreeable to our extending in whichever direction we wish, provided he has sight of the plans first.'

'Well, we have all discussed the matter at some length and, besides adding extra larders and store rooms at the rear, we wondered about extending the eating room. The wedding reception we catered for the other day was a great success and I think we shall have further requests as a result, but we could have used more space. They wanted to dance after they had eaten — they'd brought their own fiddlers — and there was not really enough room. Not that that stopped them!'

'That sounds a good idea. I called in to see Mr George after I had seen old Trumper about the house and he has given me the name of a good architect who could draw up the plans.'

'Splendid!' I said, subduing an impulse to ask if Mr George had also been able to recommend a good jeweller!

'I didn't have time,' Edward continued as if reading my mind, 'to visit a jeweller — anyway, you were not with me. But I have not forgotten your ring, Cat.'

I smiled sweetly.

★ ★ ★

As Edward had anticipated, it was not long before he was able to sign his contract and then his mother virtually took over for it was a woman's place, she had declared, to furnish a house. I thought of the dark and heavy furniture of Ashling and was not sorry I would not be living there.

Although Mrs Marshall had now assumed command, Edward was still greatly preoccupied with the house — it was called, rather unimaginatively, The Beeches, because of the avenue of copper beech that led up from the road. Measurements had to be taken, decorators hired and supervised and handymen found for the repairs that needed to be done. At Chasetown, we saw even less of him so that the hours when he was there became infinitely precious to me. When we were in the same room, my eyes would wander towards him as I tried to impress upon my memory every detail of his face and presence; the way he would stand when deep in conversation, hands on hips, head tilted in concentration or thrown back in laughter; the way a smile would begin in his eyes before it reached his lips and, above all, the way his gaze would soften when it met mine.

We got easily into the habit of sitting together in his room each evening when he

419

was there; talking over the events of the day and our plans for the morrow. But we did not always talk. Sometimes, Edward would come to sit beside me and we would kiss; long, searching kisses that grew ever more passionate. Sometimes his hands would move from my face down to my throat and then to my breasts and I would feel my nipples harden under his fingers and yearn to feel his hands on my bare flesh. Once, indeed, his fingers began to fumble at the buttons of my blouse and I held my breath, wondering if I dare put up my own hands to help him. But the next moment, he had leapt up and walked to the other side of the room.

'I'm sorry! What liberty will I take next? This is madness, Cat!'

It was on the tip of my tongue to say that if it were, then I was a little mad, too. And would it matter, since we truly loved each other if . . . But then he spoke again.

'I could not bear it afterwards if we were to make love before our marriage vows. I have always thought that a woman's maidenhood is the most precious gift she can give to a man. That is why I was so angry at what happened — or nearly happened — to Sophie. No man worth his salt would have looked at her if it had.'

I felt a reprehensible urge to point out that

unless he attempted a similar action himself, no man would know of her violation until it was too late, but quickly decided against it, for Edward would have found the remark offensive to say the least. Instead, I lowered my gaze and murmured that of course he was right; and tried not to think of the next few years. Perhaps it was as well that we would not be seeing much of each other.

27

It was early June when Edward finally left us. He had assured us that he would soon be back but in the meantime he had arranged that someone in Mr Gallagher's office would come out each week to keep our books in order and to deal with any correspondence. It had irked me considerably that this was necessary and I had determined, come what may, that I would enlist the services of Mr Brindley, Scabber's schoolmaster, and pay for private tuition in reading and writing, if he was agreeable. We were now in a position for me to afford such a luxury and even to hire extra staff if necessary to cover my absence. And, apart from dealing with the administrative side of the business, I should also be able to write to Edward and he to me.

On the afternoon of the day before Edward was due to leave for The Beeches with his mother and Sophie, I was on duty in the shop. He should really have left us on the previous day but there had been a last-minute delay due to an ill-fitting window frame discovered by the agent when he was making his final inspection. Since it was in the room chosen to be Mrs Marshall's bedroom and since he knew by then of her extreme antipathy to draughts, he had had no alternative but to call back the workmen. Later, I was to reflect how such a minor upset as an ill-fitting window frame could change the course of my life.

Given the unexpected gift of an extra day together, Edward and I had decided we would walk on the Chase for an hour or two once the shop was closed. To this end, he had come into the shop just before closing time so that he could help me with tidying it up once the door had closed at six o'clock. There were barely thirty seconds to go when I decided there would be no more customers and asked Edward to lock the door. At that precise moment it was suddenly flung open.

Stifling my annoyance, I enquired politely what I might get for the workman who now approached the counter. He was not a regular customer and I assumed him to be one of the navvies working on some new branch line — perhaps even the one Thomas had surveyed — for he wore the bright red neckerchief favoured by so many of them.

He did not answer at once and I repeated my question, perhaps with a trace of impatience in my voice for he must know the time as well as I.

'Still Miss 'Igh an' Mighty, then?' he asked with a sneer.

My eyes widened in disbelief. There was only one person who had ever called me that. 'Sam Bailey!' I said.

'The same! Come fer one o' yer famous pies. Cat's Eating 'Ouse, me mates tole me, that's the place ter go fer yer grub. An' wot's this Cat look like then, I asked 'em. An' they tole me. Bit of orlright, they said. Get 'er into bed on a winter's night an' yer won't need no blankets. 'Ot stuff they said. So then I knowed it must be my ole friend Cat Marsh they was talkin' about.'

By this time, Edward had crossed to the counter. 'How dare you speak to a lady like that? Who d'you think you are?'

'Oh, like that, is it? Fancy 'er yerself do yer? Well let me tell yer, matey,' and he thrust his face into Edward's so that Edward instinctively drew back, 'yer a bit late on the scene. How long is it now, Cat? Four years? Five? Since I first laid yer? Remember 'ow it was, Cat? Last thing at night or early in the mornin'. Nobody about, up against the wall o' the dippin' shed. So,' and he leered at Edward who was now staring at him as if mesmerised, 'if yer likes 'em broken in, then Cat's yer girl. But if yer likes 'em fresh an' tender — an' I've a feelin' yer might — then best look elsewhere.'

It was then that I found my tongue. 'Don't believe a word of it, Edward. Never in a million years would I have allowed this man near me.'

'So why did yer Ma pack yer off so sudden, then?' Sam demanded. 'If it weren't to nip it in the bud afore yer got in the family way?'

'Edward, it's not true,' I began, turning towards him, but then the words died on my lips for, to my horror, I saw both revulsion and doubt in his gaze and knew, even if I were to assure him over and over again that Sam Bailey's words were not true, he would never totally disbelieve them. From now on, in his eyes, I would be tainted. Perhaps the very fact that I had even known the likes of Sam Bailey was enough to damn me in his eyes. Why, oh why had I not insisted that he listened to me when I had tried to tell him the reason I had come to Ashling? With a dreadful certainty, I knew that never again would he touch or kiss me if it could be avoided. Now, he turned to Sam.

'Go!' he rapped out between clenched teeth. 'Or by God, you'll rue the day you set foot in here.'

'Keep yer 'air on,' said Sam. 'I'm goin'.' And, with a lascivious wink in my direction, he turned and left the shop, leaving my world in pieces.

★ ★ ★

'It wouldn't 'ave worked,' said Mrs C. a couple of days later. By then, she knew why Edward had made his farewells in such a reserved and tight-lipped fashion, leaving Sophie to hug us all and tell us how much she would miss us and that she would soon be back to see us. She knew, too, why Edward and I had come into the kitchen on the day of Sam Bailey's visit in silence, carrying the unsold goods through to the larder, hanging the key on its customary hook, putting the day's takings into the safe that Mr George had insisted we have, and then gone our separate ways; I to my room, Edward to whistle up Rex for a solitary walk. There had been no suggestion that I go with them. Once the door had been locked behind Sam, Edward had said, without looking at me,

'I must — must be on my own for a while, Cat.'

'Of course!' I'd said quickly although my whole body had yearned for the warmth of his arms around me and my spirit for the reassurance that, no matter what, he still

426

loved me. But I was reaching for the moon and I knew it.

Later that night, when everyone else had gone to bed, I told Mrs C. exactly what had happened. Her face wrinkled in sympathy but she said little, allowing me to finish and then holding me while I sobbed my heart out on her ample bosom.

'It'll all work out fer the best in the end, you'll see,' were the only words of comfort she'd spoken that night and I, of course, had not believed them.

Now, on the evening of the next day she had taken the unprecedented action of inviting me into her room after supper — the others were playing a noisy game of crib around the kitchen table — sitting me down in an easy chair and going to make us tea on the spirit stove she kept there.

'Why wouldn't it have worked?' I asked once we were settled.

'It might 'ave if it weren't fer the money. But 'e changed then, Cat, yer know e' did. 'E was the Master once again an' we was the staff. An' that included you. An' yer wouldn't have liked that after a bit, Cat. You've come a long way in the last year — we all 'ave — an' you'd never knuckle down again to doin' what other folks tell yer. Even Edward. You've bin the one in charge this last year, tellin' 'im wot to do, watchin' over 'im, motherin' 'im almost, but 'e wouldn't let yer do it now, even if yer were wed.'

'But I miss him so!' I burst out.

'A 'course yer do. But it'll pass, Cat. An' there'll be other men, mark my words.'

'There won't!'

'There will,' said Mrs C. firmly. 'A pretty young thing like you. Once it gets about Edward's gone, they'll come flockin'. That nice young Thomas for one, I'll bet.'

Thomas! He had not been in my mind during the last few weeks. Now, the thought of the comfort of his presence, his dear familiarity, the reassurance of his friendship, was overwhelming. Once again, the tears threatened.

'He wouldn't hear about Edward going,' I told Mrs C. 'How could he?'

'These things get about,' said Mrs C. comfortably. ''Appen 'e'll come this way on business again.'

'Happen pigs might fly!' I quoted one of her favourite expressions. 'But thanks for listening to me, Mrs C.'

'That's wot I'm 'ere fer, ain't it?'

'That and making a hundred million pies a day!' I teased. 'I must leave you to your sleep.' And I kissed her soft, plump cheek, thanked her for her hospitality and went up to bed myself.

★ ★ ★

It was Patience Swinfen who put her finger squarely on the main reason for my dejection when she drove over a few days later, having heard of Edward's departure but not of Sam Bailey's visit.

'Didn't he even ask you for your side of the story?' she asked when I had told her about it, for she had seen immediately that something was wrong.

I shook my head. 'We were never alone together after we had closed the shop on that day. There was no opportunity.'

'He could have made the opportunity, could he not?' she said scathingly. 'Really, to think the worst of you like that is beyond my comprehension.'

'Thanks to his mother,' I said, 'he knew that I had come to Ashling under some sort of a cloud. I suppose Sam Bailey's visit simply confirmed it.'

'You're well rid of him,' she declared in her forthright fashion. 'You deserve a man, my dear, not a milk-sop!'

'Oh, Patience, you're such a comfort!'

'That isn't what Captain Frederick Swinfen would call me! D'you know what the bastard's done now? Sent his bloody friends to shoot over *my* estate, which he insists upon

429

calling *his*. Didn't come off, mind you. John Rock, my gamekeeper, had 'em arrested as common poachers and I had 'em brought up for trial before the Lichfield magistrates. And Farmer Bacon, the traitor who was in cahoots with them.'

'Oh, Patience, what a lovely story!' I was already feeling greatly cheered by her company.

★   ★   ★

Patience and Mrs C. were not the only ones who tried to cheer me during those dark days. Ada, Polly and Frank were all most considerate, taking it in turns to do my shop duties in case Sam should come back (they knew only that he was an unwelcome visitor from my previous life). However, it was Ned who demonstrated the most sensitivity and kindness.

'Remember 'ow yer asked me 'ow to saddle up an 'oss when we was at Ashling?' he asked me one sunny morning when I took his ten o'clock cup of tea out to the stable where he was grooming Lofty, preparatory to setting out on his morning round.

'Of course,' I said, 'and you kindly showed me.'

'Well, 'ow about yer learnin' ter ride one?'

he asked, 'now that yer've got a bit more time on yer 'ands? Give yer something else to think about,' he added.

I gazed up at Lofty's bony frame. 'On Lofty d'you mean?'

'Well to begin with, anyway, jus' ter make sure yer don't mind sittin' up there, miles above the ground. Then maybe the business could run to another 'oss. Lofty's not gettin' any younger an' besides, 'e'd like the company now Toffee's gone south wi' Sophie.'

'And you'd teach me?'

''Oo else?' he asked. 'Scabber's doin' orlright, ain't 'e?'

Scabber certainly was, his 'ups and downs' now mastered to perfection.

'What about startin' termorrer evenin', then?' he asked and I agreed.

Some form of physical exercise was just what I needed on these long, light evenings when my traitorous thoughts remembered the delights of the previous summer when we had been so happy.

'Up! Down! Up! Down!' Scabber would shout as he joined Ned and Lofty and me at the bottom of the orchard making me giggle so much, I had to grip Lofty's mane to prevent myself falling off; something I often did anyway.

431

Unfortunately, my riding lessons meant that I had to sacrifice the other lessons I had contemplated for there wasn't time to learn to read and write as well. In the winter, I told myself, that's when I'll start. Meanwhile, it was left to Scabber to achieve academic distinction.

'Miss! Miss! I've writ me name!' he shouted one day, arriving at work waving a piece of lined paper.

'An' I can read it back!'

'Well done, Scabber! Let me see!'

Across the paper was a wavery line of capitals, poorly formed but who was I to criticise? He had achieved more than I. 'Read it, Scabber!'

'Albert Edward Jones,' he read solemnly.

'Albert Edward,' I repeated. 'What a lovely name! Why don't we call you that, instead of Scabber?'

'Oh no, miss! Me mates'd rib me somethin' terrible.'

'But why were you called Scabber in the first place?'

'When I were a little lad, I were always fallin' down so me knees was always scabby. An' I used to pick 'em, see, so they . . . '

'Thank you, Scabber! I've got the idea! Anyway, I think you're very clever. Go and show your paper to Mrs C. and she might give you a reward.'

But Scabber still lingered — we were out in the orchard where I had gone to pull a lettuce from the cleared piece of ground that Fred was slowly turning into a vegetable patch. 'Please, miss, do I still 'ave ter go to school now I can writ me name?'

'Just for a bit longer,' I coaxed. 'Just until you can do joined up writing and count up to a hundred. You're doing so well, it would be a pity to stop half way.'

'An' then can I come an' live 'ere an' sleep wi' Ned all the time?'

'What would your parents say?'

'They'd be pleased as punch, miss. Me Ma says there's another little bleeder on the way an' . . . ' He stopped, clapping his hand to his mouth. 'Sorry, miss!'

'Never mind, Scabber!' He had, after all, only been quoting his mother! 'And we'll see about you coming to live,' I promised, 'in a little while.'

'Oh, thankee, miss!' And he cartwheeled away between the trees, his precious piece of paper clutched between his teeth.

★   ★   ★

In July, work began on the extensions and while this meant that the eating room had to

433

be closed until we were finished, we were able to carry on business as usual in the shop. And our regular customers whom we knew well enough and who had come to depend upon us, were allowed to eat in the kitchen. These, of course, included Harold Bates and Henry Venables the swains of Ada and Polly.

'Ada and Polly will be leaving us before long,' I commented to Mrs C. as we stood side by side at the stove one morning; she making onion gravy for the best-end-of neck we were serving that day and I, custard to go with the apple pie that would follow.

'It'll be a while yet but I think they're both serious,' she said.

'So we ought to think about taking on more staff. And we shall definitely need someone else when the new eating room is finished.'

'Well, we got that weddin' next month,' Mrs C. reminded me. 'Why not 'ire young Jane Clarke from across the road for the day? I've 'eard she's lookin' fer work. She seems a nice enough young thing, always dresses neat an' tidy an' speaks quiet, a bit like you.'

'If you'd heard me shouting at Little Cat the other day when she knocked over the eggs, you wouldn't have said that!' Little Cat was the cat who had adopted us on the day of the opening but had been driven out to the stable by Rex when he'd arrived. Now that Rex had gone with Edward, she'd come back to the house but still had some of the manners of a stable cat. However, she was learning fast.

'But I think that's a good idea, Mrs C.,' I continued. 'We can see how Jane takes to the work without committing ourselves. But she *is* a nice young girl. I wonder if Ned would find her so. It worries me sometimes that he's the only one who hasn't paired off with anyone. Especially now that Fred seems to be keeping regular company with his Addie. When he's not gawping at steam engines, that is!'

Mrs C. gave me a shrewd glance. 'Ned won't wed while yer single an' unattached, Cat.'

I stared at her in astonishment. 'What do you mean?'

She smiled. 'The lad's been sweet on yer since the Ashling days.'

I took the custard off the heat and turned to look at her. 'You can't be serious! He was always pulling my leg and playing tricks on me. Just like a brother.'

'You ain't seen the way 'e looks at yer sometimes. But e's a sensible lad an' I think 'e knows 'e ain't got much chance. But 'e certainly won't look at anyone if they don't take after you.'

'Well, the sooner we get Jane on the payroll the better then,' I said. 'Mr George will be here next week and we can ask him what he thinks.'

Mr George — sometimes bringing his wife — came out to see us regularly now for Edward had not been back and had given no indication of when he might come.

'And we must also ask the others what they think,' I reminded Mrs C. 'especially Ned since he's a shareholder. We can see how he reacts.'

But when we did raise the matter at supper the next time we were all together, Ned followed our announcement with one of his own.

'By the way,' he said when everyone, including himself, had agreed that we should hire Jane Clarke, 'I saw Thomas today.'

28

'He's not coming,' I told Mrs C. for the umpteenth time. 'He'd have been here by now if he were.'

''Appen John McClean's keeping 'im busy,' said Mrs C. also for the umpteenth time.

It was the day after Ned's sudden announcement at supper that he had seen Thomas in Chasetown. He'd mentioned it quite casually and at first, the words hardly registered with me. And then I'd laid down my knife and fork. 'Thomas Bailey d'you mean?'

He nodded and continued to inspect a forkful of spinach before putting it into his mouth. 'Your veggies comin' on a fair treat, Fred,' he said after a moment or two of mastication.

'Thank'ee kind sir!' said Fred, pulling an imaginary forelock.

I could have screamed but fortunately caught Mrs C.'s eye, 'Where was that then?' she asked Ned. 'Did 'e speak to yer?'

Ned shook his head. ''E were sittin' beside Mr McClean in his brougham up near Number Two pit. Didn't see me, they was too

437

busy gassin' but I'm sure it was 'im.'

''Appen 'e'll call ter see us termorrer,' said Mrs C. smiling at me.

But he hadn't called. Each time the shop bell had pinged I had stopped whatever I was doing and cocked my head to listen but it was never him.

Now, as Mrs C. and I put away the dishes after our evening meal, I faced the fact that he would not be coming, not tomorrow nor any day.

'But why not?' Mrs C. asked when I told her of my conviction.

I shrugged. 'Perhaps he thinks Edward is still here and doesn't think he would be welcome. Perhaps,' and my voice shook slightly, 'he doesn't want to come. Perhaps he has a lady friend in London to whom he wishes to return as quickly as possible.' And then I bent and picked up Little Cat who had been weaving herself around my ankles, and buried my face in her fur so that Mrs C. would not see my misery.

'D'you mind if I go up now?' I asked. 'I feel like an early night.'

'You do that, love,' she said, her voice soft with concern. 'And sleep.'

But sleep was the last thing I wanted. I stood at my open window gazing out at the fading streaks of amber light above the

438

velvety dark of the trees, breathing in the scent of the rose that I had planted beside the kitchen door last summer and now almost reached my window and thought of Thomas. I knew now that the pain of Edward's desertion was as nothing compared with the despair into which I was now plunged. True, Edward had touched my heart but Thomas, I now realised, had pierced it to its very core.

Somewhere in the orchard, an owl called and was answered by another up on the Chase and the mournful cries echoed my misery.

* * *

The following day it rained as if it would never stop but at least it gave me an excuse for my lack of cheerfulness.

'What a day!' I groaned along with everyone else. 'Will it never stop?' It had already been decided that Jane Clarke should be invited to join us for an evening meal that day so that we could all get to know each other. However, as far as Mrs C. and I were concerned the real motive was for her and Ned to become better acquainted. It was particularly frustrating therefore, that he was late in for the meal.

'Sorry!' he panted arriving over half an

hour after the time we had told him, and dripping wet into the bargain.

'I'm afraid we 'ad to start, lad,' said Mrs C., getting to her feet and crossing to the stove to remove Ned's plate from the top of a saucepan of boiling water, 'but roast chicken waits fer no man! I 'ope it was nothin' important that kept yer.'

'Thought I'd got us a new customer,' he told her and going to take the plate from her, 'but when I got there, it was nothin' but a wild goose chase.'

'Well, never mind,' she said. 'At least yer tried. Now come an' sit next ter Jane, but take yer jacket off first. There's nothin' like the smell o' wet worsted to put a girl off a lad, eh, Jane?'

But Jane declared it to be an improvement upon the coal dust which was what her father and brothers always smelled of, and smiled kindly upon him. And I did my best to feel happy that, so far, our plan seemed to be working.

Next morning, I woke once again to the sound of rain against my window pane. I was due in the shop at eight o'clock and first the morning's supplies had to be carried through so there was no time to linger. Work, I told myself firmly, as I knotted my apron strings around my waist, was what I needed. A quick

440

cup of tea in the kitchen and then work.

Two minutes after I had opened up, I was astonished to see our wagon draw up outside with Ned up on the box. Why was he out so early? As I watched, a man stepped down on to the pavement and turned to take the big travelling bag that Ned was handing down to him. Mesmerised, I continued to watch as he moved to the shop door and came in.

'Hello, dearest Cat!' said Thomas. And then he put down his bag opened his arms and came towards me and I, without a moment of hesitation, went into them.

'Oh, Thomas,' I said, lifting my face to his. 'I thought you would never come!'

★ ★ ★

'It was Ned,' Thomas told me an hour or so later. We had taken advantage of a temporary break in the weather — angry purple clouds were still banking up in the west — for me to show Thomas our vegetable patch. That, at least, was our excuse. But although we were standing right beside it, neither of us had shown it the least attention, which, considering the neat rows of feathery carrots, the fat, round lettuces and the canes strung with runner beans, was a great pity; however, the last did at least provide an effective screen from the house.

'Ned, in cahoots with Mrs C.,' Thomas continued. 'Apparently, she asked him to discover where I was staying and then to call at my lodgings and ask me directly why I had not come to see you. This he did yesterday evening but I was in Lichfield eating dinner with John McClean at the George and my landlady told him that I would be catching an early train back to London in the morning. Ned only just caught me in time.'

'Oh, Thomas, thank heaven that he did!'

'Amen to that!' and he bent and kissed me, a very thorough kiss that had us clinging to each other as if we stood upon a precipice and to separate by even a hair's breadth would have tumbled us into the abyss.

'Were you really going without seeing me?' I whispered at last when the blood had ceased to pound in my temples and speech, if taken slowly, was just possible.

He nodded. 'John McClean had told me of Edward's inheritance and I had assumed that you would marry almost immediately. It had never occurred to me that he would have left you as he did.' His voice was rough with anger.

'It was not quite like that,' I told him. 'He did indeed propose marriage but in five years'

442

time after Sophie had been launched into society.'

Thomas put back his head and stared down at me in amazement. 'You mean the fellow had the gall to ask you to wait five years?' And when I nodded and murmured something about his obligation to Sophie, he grew even more angry. 'He had no business to ask you to wait, Cat, to expect both the penny and the bun. And I cannot believe that young Sophie as I remember her would have wanted it so, had she realised the sacrifice he was asking you to make.'

'Probably not,' I agreed. 'But it never came to that, thanks to your brother.'

'Sam? Sam has been here?'

'Yes, indeed. And left with my reputation in shreds. He told Edward the most terrible lies about me and him. How we — had — had — ' I could not bear to put it into words.

'And Edward believed them?'

I could only nod for the recollection still had the power to upset me greatly.

'Oh, Cat, my precious Cat!' And he folded me in his arms. 'Both of them should be horse-whipped. On the other hand,' and he paused, kissing my hair in an abstracted fashion, 'perhaps my slob of a brother has inadvertently done me a good turn.' He

443

suddenly took his arms away and went down on one knee in the wet grass. 'Would you, Cat Marsh, consider taking me, Thomas Bailey, for better for worse, in sickness and in health, to love, honour and — ' and he gazed up at me with a whimsical grin, ' — at least pretend to obey?'

'I will,' I answered, grinning back as the first raindrop fell on my nose. And as we turned, arms around each other, a rainbow arched above the house and Little Cat came running to meet us.

★ ★ ★

We were married in late September when the leaves of the silver birches up on the Chase were like new pennies and the oak trees the colour of copper.

I wore a gown of amber velvet, run up by Patience Swinfen's dressmaker and a tiny bonnet ruched to match designed by her milliner. I held a posy of golden orchids; as much, that is, as such an extravagant flower can be confined to a posy. I would have preferred a more homely bunch of the tawny chrysanthemums from Fred's vegetable patch that I had persuaded him to plant there, but the orchids had been sent over that morning from John McClean's glasshouses so I felt duty bound to carry them. The remainder of the enormous sheath was gracing the big table in the eating room where an array of pies and cakes, jellies and trifles, cold meats and savouries awaited our return from the ceremony.

With Mr George in attendance, I arrived at Christ Church, Burntwood in the wagon and driven by Ned. Thomas had offered me a hired coach complete with coachman but I had wanted our old wagon. Admittedly, it had been brushed and scrubbed to within an inch of its life as had Ned, himself, resplendent in a dark suit brightened by a cravat of scarlet silk. The same colour was echoed in the ribbons and bows that festooned Lofty's harness.

At the threshold of the church, the Reverend Poole welcomed us with a distinct twinkle in his eye and a murmured 'No pies today, I see!' before walking ahead of us up the aisle to where Thomas waited with his friend, William Appleby. Heads turned and there was a blur of smiling faces but my eyes were upon Thomas who was gazing back at me, his eyes limpid with love. And then the Reverend Poole, solemn now but with a kindly smile upon his face, began to intone the familiar words of the marriage service. Almost before I realised it, I had become Mrs

445

Thomas Bailey and was emerging into the autumn sunshine on my husband's arm. And there were Scabber and Billy clutching bags of rice.

'Shut yer eyes, miss!' shouted Scabber before nearly blinding me with a stinging handful.

★ ★ ★

Two hours later, I gazed around at my loved ones and breathed a sigh of pure happiness. On one side of me sat Thomas and on the other, Ma and Emma; they had arrived on the previous day, brought by my uncle and aunt and cousin Annie, who were sitting at a separate table.

Emma, sulking at first because the invitation had not included her Joe, had soon relented and was now casting sly glances in the direction of William Appleby.

'Is she still just as friendly with Joe?' I had asked Ma on the previous evening.

'Yes, and to tell you the truth, Cat, the sooner she's wed the better. Bringing up a family might settle her.'

Also seated at our table were Mrs C., Mr Jolly — his holiday extended so that he might be here — and Ned. Ada and Polly and Fred were seated separately with Harold and

Henry and Addie and looking across at them, I thought it likely that they might all soon follow in my footsteps. Jane Clarke had been placed next to Ned which seemed to be to both their liking.

Mr and Mrs George shared a table with Nanny Humphries and her sister and Mr Gallagher and his new young wife. And beyond them again, I could see dear Hannah and Will Hoskins and their four children and Hannah's Aunt Mary and old George, the lodge-keeper, now retired. Thomas had paid for their journey and lodgings overnight in Lichfield.

'Because,' he explained to me, 'after you, they were the first people to show real kindness towards Rosie and me and I have never forgotten it.'

One friend who was absent was Patience Swinfen but sadly, she was away staying with friends on a visit that had been arranged for so long, she could not cancel it. Another was Rosie.

Thomas's efforts to trace her in America had so far been without success but he was still trying. Their absence was the only touch of sadness in that wonderful day; that and the fact that Sophie was not with us. Her presence without Edward's was not possible and Thomas had flatly refused to invite him.

— 'Lest I do the fellow an injury!'

Very soon now, the doors would be thrown open to all our customers who cared to come and wish us well and no doubt the merriment would go on well into the small hours but by then, Thomas and I would not be there to see it. We would be in Armitage where Mr George and his wife had very kindly lent their house to us for our honeymoon. 'We will make do very happily in the rooms over the shop,' they assured us.

After the honeymoon we would be coming back to Chasetown where we would be occupying the rooms originally intended for Edward and his mother. Much of Thomas's work was now in the north of England and Chasetown would make an ideal base for him. As far as I was concerned, it would be work as usual, except that now I would control the majority of the shares of the business. For Thomas, through his solicitors, had made an offer for Edward's holding which had been accepted without reservation.

I turned my head and looked up at him to find him gazing down at me, and I saw my longing mirrored in his eyes. He took my hand in his. 'Not long now, my love!'

Epilogue

It is three years now since the birth of William Thomas and much has happened. Two years after his arrival into the world, he was joined in the nursery by Thirza Isabel and I rarely find the time now, to drive into Chasetown. But when I do, I am always assured of a welcome.

Ned is the major-domo now with Jane, his wife, proving a worthy successor to Mrs C. She, I am happy to say now lives with us in Lichfield, and provides great company when Thomas is away on business.

Fred is no longer there, his passion for steam engines having overtaken his feelings for Addie. With Thomas's help, he found work in the north of the county where he operates a gigantic steam hammer and is as happy as the day is long. Addie is now courting a 'butty' and, I think, considers herself well shot of him.

Ada and Polly, now Mrs Bates and Mrs Venables respectively, still work at the Eating House but go home each evening.

And Scabber? Well, he has been renamed for a start. Only his close friends are now allowed to call Albert Edward Jones, Stable Manager, by his old name. Physically, he has changed beyond all recognition; the skinny little lad who cartwheeled merrily around the streets of Chasetown is now a broad-shouldered youngster with biceps that a professional boxer might envy. Cat's Eating House now boasts two delivery carts and a trap, and three horses — Lofty now spending most of his time in a field leased from the Marquess at Burntwood — and Scabber is in charge of them. To help him he has a young lad called Horace whom he rules with a rod of iron.

'No foul language 'ere, if yer please, young 'Orace,' I heard him say the other day. 'That swear box ain't 'ere as an ornament, yer know!'

However, when I asked him recently if he would stand as god-parent to the child that I am now carrying, he so far forgot himself as to mutter, 'Bloody 'ell, miss! Are yer sure?' Fortunately, Horace was well out of earshot.

Another god-parent standing with him will be Patience Swinfen. Life has treated Patience very kindly of late for her affairs have gone well since another Charles — Charles Rann Kennedy — came into her life. He, like Charles Simpson, is a legal gentleman, a Barrister at Law and, when

450

Patience met him, living with his wife and four children in Leamington. From the beginning, his interest in her case had been profound, as it must have been for many of his profession. However, he had determined to take it a step further and arrange, through a cousin who lived near Swinfen Hall, to meet Patience socially.

She took to him immediately and with her customary impetuosity invited him and his family to stay at the Hall. He and his four children accepted but not his wife, from which you may draw your own conclusions.

Soon after Thomas and I were married, her case had come before the Court of Common Pleas, and Patience herself attended and heard Charles Kennedy's impassioned defence at first hand. Not only she, but the judges, were impressed and a re-trial was ordered, to take place in the following year at the Stafford Assizes. Both Charles Simpson and Charles Kennedy were jubilant and both — to the secret amusement of Thomas and myself — expressed their delight in poetic verses.

'How fortunate,' Thomas observed wickedly, 'that they are both called Charles! At least, she won't upset either by calling him by the name of the other!'

The outcome of the re-trial was a decision

in favour of Patience, a verdict received with wild enthusiasm, not only by those immediately concerned but by what seemed to be the entire population of Lichfield where the bells of St Mary's Church were rung to celebrate her victory. When she returned to Lichfield next day, to the Trent Valley Railway Station, a huge crowd — Thomas and I among them — awaited her and a military band escorted her carriage through the streets. She was the heroine of the hour.

It was a great pity that the matter was not allowed to rest there; as far as Patience was concerned it would have been but Charles Kennedy's ambition had been fired by his success. Nothing would now suffice but that he challenge Sir Frederick Thesiger — now Lord Chelmsford — who had represented Patience originally and allowed the agreement to go through without her signature.

In spite of Patience's reluctance, she eventually allowed Charles to persuade her and brought an action for damages against him, albeit he was now no less a personage than the Lord Chancellor of England. It was hardly surprising that the legal profession closed ranks and that the judge's directions to the jury showed bias in favour of officialdom; their verdict found in favour of the Lord Chancellor.

From then on, Charles Kennedy's fortunes declined, although Patience remained a loyal friend. However, I think that even the remaining ties may soon be broken as we have just heard that she has met 'a most charming man' at the home of a mutual friend in Scotland.

'He is a widower,' she wrote, 'with two delightful daughters, aged eight and nine and two rumbustious lads of seven and four. And I think — nay, I am *sure!* — that he will soon propose marriage.'

As much as Patience will ever settle down, I think she will now do so. And I am glad for her.

Settling down, however, is the last thing on Sophie's mind. After I had married Thomas, I had heard nothing of her which, while it distressed me greatly, did not surprise me for once Edward's shares had been transferred, I heard nothing of him either. I thought it likely that Sophie did not even know of my marriage and certainly would not know that I could now read and write. It was when I read in the newspaper of her engagement to a Dr Michael Fortescue that I decided to write to her myself. Nothing would be lost and much could be gained.

And much was gained! Three days after I had posted the letter, she arrived on our doorstep. I cannot adequately describe the joy we both felt at our reunion. Suffice it to say that our tears prevented coherent speech for at least ten minutes and that when we were at last managing to string a few words together, Mrs C. arrived upon the scene and set us off again.

'You were so right, Cat,' Sophie told me when we were drinking tea — in the kitchen, of course — Mrs C. having tactfully withdrawn to her own room. 'Not all the girls I met were brainless ninnies nor the young men nincompoops! My friend, Sarah, is studying to be a nurse, just as you once suggested I might do, and Louise is already teaching poor children their letters.'

'And the young men?' I probed.

She blushed a delightful shade of rose pink, exactly matching the gown she was wearing. 'I met Michael at Sarah's house. *Her* mama is actually in favour of her becoming a nurse, can you believe? Oh, he is such a lovely man, Cat! I cannot wait for you to meet him! He is so kind and gentle and does not mind my hoydenish ways.'

'And where does he practise?'

'Oh, in the East End, of course,' she said, as if it were a nonsense to even consider he might work elsewhere. 'But he is very clever, Cat. What he does not know about the functioning of the liver is not worth knowing. I think it likely he may soon be offered an appointment at one of the London teaching hospitals.'

'And your mama?' I dared to ask. 'Where does she fit in to all this?'

Sophie grinned wickedly. 'Fortunately for me, Sarah's mother happens to come from a very well-connected family. *Her* father is a Lord and owns the whole of Yorkshire. Well,' as my eyebrows shot up into my hair, 'quite enough of it to impress dear Mama! She lives in hopes that Micheal will end up in Harley Street. But that is as likely as Edward driving a steam locomotive!'

'How is Edward?' I asked. 'Does he approve of the marriage?'

'I think so. But in truth, Cat, he is so busy pursuing his own courtship, he has hardly noticed.' She stopped abruptly, looking at me with the direct gaze I knew so well. 'It does not upset you to talk of him, Cat?'

'Not in the least. I could not be happier with my darling Thomas. Indeed, I would like to think that Edward is equally as happy.'

She wrinkled her nose at that. 'Well, if anyone can be happy living with an over-stuffed pincushion, then I suppose Edward will be very happy with Lucy Proctor. And indeed, I do not dislike her,

Cat. You cannot dislike anyone who is so well-meaning, although her complacency can drive me mad on occasion. But she will suit Edward admirably and no doubt supply him with a set of smaller pincushions as the years roll by.'

We both giggled and I asked Sophie to convey my best wishes to him if she found the right moment.

'I will, I promise. Sometimes, I try to talk to him about Chasetown but he refuses point blank. It's as if he wants to pretend it never happened.'

'And you?' I asked. 'How do you feel about it?'

For answer, she got up and came round the table to hug me. 'I am so grateful for it, Cat. I learned so much there, about life and people. Even the dreadful thing that happened at the end, I can now learn from and understand how others might feel.'

'And Michael?' I asked. 'Does he know about it?'

'Oh, yes! Indeed, he has been of the greatest help in showing me how to come to terms with it. And,' she pulled back and gave me a playful punch on the shoulder, 'he is giving me lessons in the art of self defence. After all, Edward would not teach me to box — he said it was unladylike, in the extreme.

But Michael is different. He's shown me how to maim a man for life.'

'Heavens!' I said weakly. 'I must tell Thomas to watch out!'

★   ★   ★

When my mother — Emma now safely married — came to live with us a year ago, I had thought my cup of happiness full to overflowing but then a few months afterwards, Thomas came home with the most startling news.

We had not long returned from a visit to Mr Jolly and his sister in Hastings, when he came bursting into the nursery just as I had finished putting the children to bed.

'You will never guess what has happened, my love!' he cried and then, as I put my finger to my lips, continued in a whisper, 'I have found Rosie!'

'Thomas!' I shouted and then clapped my hand to my mouth.

'Where is she?' I asked once we were out in the landing, fully expecting him to say London, where he had gone on the previous day.

But for answer, he pointed down the stairwell and the next moment I was flying down the staircase, my feet hardly touching the treads.

She was standing in the drawing room, an arresting figure dressed in the height of fashion in a scarlet, 'Garibaldi' shirt, braided in black and with a matching bolero. Her skirt was also black but banded in scarlet at the hem and I was immediately conscious of my own simple day dress of white cotton splashed with yellow rosebuds. Her hair was dressed in a chignon held high at the back of her head with long ringlets falling from it.

'Cat!' She came towards me, her arms outstretched and I was engulfed in a cloud of cologne. 'It is so good to see you!'

Her voice had a distinct American twang with not a trace of the accent of her childhood. It was like meeting a stranger but one in whom I sought desperately for signs of the girl I had once known. But there were none.

I drew back, murmuring the customary phrases of welcome I would have used to any guest. And then Thomas had joined us and was explaining that Rosie had come to England to see her father who had not been well and, hearing through a mutual friend of Thomas's prowess in engineering circles, had sought him out.

'And your husband?' I asked. 'Is he with you?'

There was a trace of bitterness in her voice

when she answered. 'No, he could not get away. Real estate is big business in America right now and Henry wants to set up offices in Chicago and maybe Boston.'

You could not say that the evening was not a success for the meal — as always — was excellent and Mrs C., once we had dished it up, sat with us as she always did and asked so many questions about America, the conversation was both lively and informative. But it lacked the intimacy I craved. Was Thomas right? Had little Rosie Bailey, beloved companion of my girlhood, been choked to death by this confident, sometimes brash, American woman?

We finished our meal and Mrs C. made coffee while I cleared the table and Thomas took Rosie through to the sitting room. The bed in the spare bedroom was always made up and he had already taken her bags there. No mention had been made of the length of her stay and I had almost begun to hope that it would not be for too long, when my mother came in.

She had spent the evening at our neighbour's house, the home of an elderly widow with whom she had struck up a friendship, and she came into the room unheralded, dropping her cloak on to a chair as she came towards us. And then, seeing that we had a visitor, she stopped and drew back.

'I'm sorry, Cat, I didn't see you had . . .'
And then, as Rosie turned towards her,
smiling in recognition, her hand flew to her
mouth. 'Dear God! If it's not Maggie Bailey
come back from the dead!'

For a moment, I thought she might faint
and both Thomas and I rushed towards her.
But Rosie was ahead of us but not, I think,
providing support as much as taking it, for
Ma's arms went around her and they stood,
locked together and — why, exactly I did not
know — with Rosie sobbing her heart out on
my mother's shoulder.

'It was because she looked the same,' Rosie
tried to explain later when I was sitting on her
bed. 'You were different, Cat, an adult when I
had known you only as a child. But your
mother . . . Well, her hair is white, I grant
you, and there is perhaps the extra line or two
on her cheeks — but otherwise, she is just as
I remembered her. Except that, until then I
hadn't wanted to remember. I had wanted to
put all that behind me — or thought I did.
Suddenly, it all came back, whether I liked it
or not, and I was crying for that little girl and
for Thomas, too. But most of all for the
woman I had called mother and the one I had
never known.'

We both cried a little then but now there

was a blessed relief in our tears for the barrier between us that Rosie had erected, the carapace under which she had thought herself protected, had gone and —

'I can accept it now,' she told me. 'I *want* to accept it.'

'Does your husband know about your childhood?' I asked.

'No — I've never wanted to tell him.'

'And now?'

'I shall tell him everything,' she said firmly.

'And will he understand?'

'I think so. The Americans are good like that, Cat. So many of them have risen from humble beginnings and they're proud of it.'

The other question I wanted to put to her, I kept until next day when she was pushing Thirza's pram through Lichfield's streets and I was holding William's hand as we made our way towards Nanny Humphries' shop and his daily assignation with a gingerbread man.

'Do you want children, Rosie?' It was a very direct question but one I felt I could now ask for the old intimacy was back between us.

'I do now. And I cannot wait to get home and tell Henry so. He has always wanted them. But I have always fobbed him off with some excuse or other, one of them being that I did not wish to lose my figure. Can you believe such a conceit? When I look at you, Cat, how beautiful you are even though you carry all before you and cannot have seen your toes for many a day, I am ashamed. And when I see the love in Thomas's eyes when he looks at you, I cannot wait to see that same look in Henry's. I think perhaps he will not be away from home so often in future.'

'I am sure he will not!' I said.

* * *

And so, my dear children — and perhaps grandchildren — I bid you farewell and thank you if you have had the patience to read my story through to its end. At least, you will now know something of your parents' lives; they have not always been the fuddy-duddies that you, no doubt, consider them to be!

Author's Note

All the major characters in this book are fictitious with the exception of Patience Swinfen. She was very much alive and I can only hope that the liberties I have taken with her are not out of character. From the picture of her I have formed from reading CATHEDRAL CITY, A LOOK AT VICTORIAN LICHFIELD by HOWARD CLAYTON, I think probably not.

We do hope that you have enjoyed reading this large print book.

Did you know that all of our titles are available for purchase?

We publish a wide range of high quality large print books including:
Romances, Mysteries, Classics
General Fiction
Non Fiction and Westerns

Special interest titles available in large print are:
The Little Oxford Dictionary
Music Book
Song Book
Hymn Book
Service Book

Also available from us courtesy of Oxford University Press:
Young Readers' Dictionary
(large print edition)
Young Readers' Thesaurus
(large print edition)

For further information or a free brochure, please contact us at:
Ulverscroft Large Print Books Ltd.,
The Green, Bradgate Road, Anstey,
Leicester, LE7 7FU, England.
Tel: (00 44) 0116 236 4325
Fax: (00 44) 0116 234 0205

APL		CCS	
Cen		Ear	
Mob		Cou	
ALL		Jub	
WIL		CHE	
Aid		Bel	
Fin		Fol	
Can		STO	
TIL		HCL	